EVERY WHICH WAY
BUT DEAD

By Kim Harrison

DEAD WITCH WALKING
THE GOOD, THE BAD, AND THE UNDEAD
A FISTFUL OF CHARMS

EVERY WHICH WAY BUT DEAD

KIM HARRISON

HARPER
Voyager

Harper*Voyager*
An Imprint of HarperCollins*Publishers*
77–85 Fulham Palace Road,
Hammersmith, London W6 8JB

www.harpercollins.co.uk

Published by Voyager 2006
1

A catalogue record for this book
is available from the British Library

ISBN-13 978 0 00 723612 1
ISBN-10 0 00 723612 3

Printed and bound in Great Britain by
Clays Limited, St Ives plc

To the guy who gave me my first pair of handcuffs.
Thanks for being there.

Acknowledgements

I'd like to thank the people closest to me for their understanding while I muddled through all this. But most importantly, I'd like to thank my agent, Richard Curtis – who saw the possibilities, and my editor – Diana Gill – who guided those possibilities and brought them to life.

EVERY WHICH WAY
BUT DEAD

One

I took a deep breath to settle myself, jerking the cuff of my gloves up to cover the bare patch of skin at my wrist. My fingers were numb through the fleece as I moved my next-to-largest spell pot to sit beside a small chipped tombstone, being careful to not let the transfer media spill. It was cold, and my breath steamed in the light of the cheap white candle I had bought on sale last week.

Spilling a bit of wax, I stuck the taper to the top of the grave marker. My stomach knotted as I fixed my attention on the growing haze at the horizon, scarcely discernable from the surrounding city lights. The moon would be up soon, being just past full and waning. Not a good time to be summoning demons, but it would be coming anyway if I didn't call it. I'd rather meet Algaliarept on my own terms—before midnight.

I grimaced, glancing at the brightly lit church behind me where Ivy and I lived. Ivy was running errands, not even aware I had made a deal with a demon, much less that it was time to pay for its services. I suppose I could be doing this inside where it was warm, in my beautiful kitchen with my spelling supplies and all the modern comforts, but calling demons in the middle of a graveyard had a perverse rightness to it, even with the snow and cold.

And I wanted to meet it here so Ivy wouldn't have to spend tomorrow cleaning blood off the ceiling.

Whether it would be demon blood or my own was a question I hoped I wouldn't have to answer. I wouldn't allow myself to be pulled into the ever-after to be Algaliarept's familiar. I couldn't. I had cut it once and made it bleed. If it could bleed, it could die. *God, help me survive this. Help me find a way to make something good here.*

The fabric of my coat rasped as I clutched my arms about myself and used my boot to awkwardly scrape a circle of six inches of crusty snow off the clay-red cement slab where I had seen a large circle etched out. The room-sized rectangular block of stone was a substantial marker as to where God's grace stopped and chaos took over. The previous clergy had laid it down over the adulterated spot of once hallowed ground, either to be sure no one else was put to rest there accidentally or to fix the elaborate, half-kneeling, battle-weary angel it encompassed into the ground. The name on the massive tombstone had been chiseled off, leaving only the dates. Whomever it was had died in 1852 at the age of twenty-four. I hoped it wasn't an omen.

Cementing someone into the ground to keep him or her from rising again sometimes worked—and sometimes it didn't—but in any case, the area wasn't sanctified anymore. And since it was surrounded by ground that was still consecrated, it made a good spot to summon a demon. If worse came to worst, I could always duck onto sanctified ground and be safe until the sun rose and Algaliarept was pulled back into the ever-after.

My fingers were shaking as I took from my coat pocket a white silk pouch of salt that I had scraped out of my twenty-five-pound bag. The amount was excessive, but I wanted a solid circle, and some of the salt would be diluted as it melted the snow. I glanced at the sky to estimate where north was, finding a mark on the etched circle right where I thought it should be. That someone had used this circle to summon demons before didn't instill me with any confidence. It wasn't illegal or immoral to summon demons, just really, really stupid.

I made a slow clockwise path from north, my footprints paralleling the outside track of the salt as I laid it down, enclosing the angel monolith along with most of the blasphemed ground. The circle would be a good fifteen feet across, a rather large enclosure which generally took at least three witches to make and hold, but I was good enough to channel that much ley line force alone. Which, now that I thought about it, might be why the demon was so interested in snagging me as its newest familiar.

Tonight I'd find out if my carefully worded verbal contract made three months ago would keep me alive and on the right side of the ley lines. I had agreed to be Algaliarept's familiar voluntarily if it testified against Piscary, the catch being that I got to keep my soul.

The trial had officially ended two hours after sunset tonight, sealing the demon's end of the bargain and making my end enforceable. That the undead vampire who controlled most of Cincinnati's underworld had been sentenced to five centuries for the murders of the city's best ley line witches hardly seemed important now. Especially when I was betting his lawyers would get him out in a measly one.

Right now the question on everyone's mind on both sides of the law was whether Kisten, his former scion, would be able to hold everything together until the undead vampire got out, because Ivy wasn't going to do it, scion or no. If I managed to get through this night alive and with my soul intact, I'd start worrying about me a little less and my roommate a little more, but first I had to settle up with the demon.

Shoulders so tight they hurt, I took the milky green tapers from my coat pocket and placed them on the circle to represent the points of a pentagram I wouldn't be drawing. I lit them from the white candle I used to make the transfer media. The tiny flames flickered, and I watched for a moment to be sure they weren't going to go out before I stuck the white candle back on the broken grave marker outside the circle.

The hushed sound of a car pulled my attention to the high walls dividing the graveyard from our neighbors. Steadying myself to tap the nearby ley line, I tugged my knit cap down, stomped the snow from the hem of my jeans, and made one last check that I had everything. But there was nothing left to procrastinate with.

Another slow breath, and I touched my will to the tiny ley line running through the church's graveyard. My breath hissed in through my nose and I stiffened, almost falling as my equilibrium shifted. The ley line seemed to have picked up the winter chill, slicing through me with an unusual cold-ness. Putting out a gloved hand, I steadied myself against the candlelit tombstone while the incoming energy continued to build.

Once the strengths equilibrated, the extra incoming force would flow back to the line. Until then I had to grit my teeth and bear it as tingling sensations backwashed at the theoret-ical extremities in my mind that mirrored my real fingers and toes. Each time it was worse. Each time it was faster. Each time it was more of an assault.

Though it seemed like forever, the force balanced in a heartbeat. My hands started to sweat and an uncomfortable sensation of being both hot and cold took me, like being in a fever. I took off my gloves and jammed them into a deep pocket. The charms on my bracelet jingled, clear in the winter-silenced air. They wouldn't help me. Not even the cross.

I wanted to set my circle quickly. Somehow Algaliarept knew when I tapped a line, and I had to summon it before it showed up on its own and robbed me of the thread of power I might claim as its summoner. The copper spell pot with the transfer media was cold when I picked it up and did some-thing no witch ever did and lived to tell of it; I stepped for-ward, putting myself into the same circle I was going to call Algaliarept into.

Standing across from the person-sized monument ce-mented to the ground, I exhaled. The monolith was covered in a black smut from bacteria and city pollution, making it look like a fallen angel. That the figure was bowed weeping over a sword held horizontally in his hands as an offering only added to the creepy feeling. There was a bird's nest wedged into the fold of the wings as they curved around the body, and the face didn't look right. The arms, too, were too long to be human or Inderlander. Even Jenks didn't let his kids play around this one.

"Please let me be right," I whispered to the statue as I mentally moved the white rill of salt from this reality to that of the ever-after. I staggered as most of the energy pooling in my center was yanked out to force the shift. The media in the pot sloshed, and still not having found my balance, I set it down in the snow before it spilled. My eyes went to the green candles. They had turned eerily transparent, having been moved to the ever-after with the salt. The flames, though, existed in both worlds, adding their glow to the night.

The power from the line began to build again, the slow increase as uncomfortable as the first quick influx of tapping a line, but the ribbon of salt had been replaced with an equal amount of ever-after reality arching high to close over my head. Nothing more substantial than air could pass the shifting bands of reality, and because I set the circle, only I could break it—providing I had made it properly to begin with.

"Algaliarept, I summon you," I whispered, my heart pounding. Most people used all sorts of trappings to summon and contain a demon, but seeing as I already had an arrangement with it, simply saying its name and willing its presence would pull it across the lines. Lucky me.

My gut clenched when a small patch of snow melted between the warrior angel and me. The snow steamed, the cloud of reddish vapor billowing up to follow the confines of a body not yet taken shape. I waited, my tension growing. Algaliarept varied its shape, sifting through my mind without me even knowing to choose what scared me the most. Once it had been Ivy. Then Kisten—until I had pinned him in an elevator in a foolish moment of vampire-induced passion. It's hard to be scared of someone after you've French-kissed him. Nick, my boyfriend, always got a slavering dog the size of a pony.

This time, though, the mist was definitely a human shape, and I guessed it was going to show up either as Piscary—the vampire I had just put in prison—or perhaps its more typical vision of a young British gentleman in a green velveteen coat with tails.

"Neither scares you anymore," came a voice from the mist, jerking my head up.

It was my voice. "Aw, crap," I swore, picking up my spell pot and backing away until I almost broke my circle. It was going to show up as me. I hated that. "I'm not afraid of myself!" I shouted, even before it finished coalescing.

"Oh, yes you are."

It had the right sound, but the cadence and accent were wrong. I stared, riveted, as Algaliarept took on my outline, running its hands suggestively down itself, flattening its chest to my lame excuse of womanhood and giving me hips that were probably a little more curvaceous than I deserved. It dressed itself in black leather pants, a red halter top, and high-heeled black sandals that looked ridiculous out in the middle of a snowy graveyard.

Eyelids lightly closed and lips open, it shook its head to make my frizzy shoulder-length red curls take shape out of the lingering haze of ever-after. It gave me more freckles than I could possibly have, and my eyes weren't the red orbs it showed when it opened them, but green. Mine weren't slitted like a goat's either.

"You got the eyes wrong," I said, and I set my spell pot down at the edge of the circle. I gritted my teeth, hating that it heard my voice quaver.

Hip cocked, the demon put out a sandaled foot and snapped its fingers. A pair of black shades materialized in its grip, and it put them on, hiding its unnatural eyes. "Now they're right," it said, and I shuddered at how close it matched my voice.

"You don't look anything like me," I said, not realizing I

had lost so much weight, and deciding I could go back to eating shakes and fries.

Algaliarept smiled. "Perhaps if I put my hair up?" it mocked coyly as it gathered the unruly mass and held it atop my, er, its head. Biting its lips to redden them, it moaned and shifted as if its hands were tied above it, looking like it was into bondage games. Falling back onto the sword the angel held, it posed like a whore.

I hunched deeper into my coat with the fake fur around the collar. From the distant street came the slow sound of a passing car. "Can we get on with this? My feet are getting cold."

It pulled its head up and smiled. "You are *such* the party pooper, Rachel Mariana Morgan," it said in my voice, but now with its customary highbrow British accent. "But a *very* good sport. Not making me drag you into the ever-after shows a *fine* strength of mind. I'm going to enjoy breaking you."

I jerked when a smear of ever-after energy cascaded over it. It was shifting forms again, but my shoulders eased when it turned itself into its usual vision of lace and green velvet. Dark hair styled long and round smoked glasses twisted into existence. Pale skin and a strong-featured face appeared, matching its trim, narrow-waisted figure in elegance. High-heeled boots and an exquisitely tailored coat finished the outfit, turning the demon into a charismatic young business-man of the eighteenth century, possessing wealth and poised for greatness.

My thoughts touched on the horrific crime scene I had contaminated last fall while trying to pin the murders of Cincinnati's best ley line witches on Trent Kalamack. Al had slaughtered them in Piscary's name. Each of them had died in pain for its enjoyment. Al was a sadist, no matter how good the demon looked.

"Yes, let's get on with it," it said as it took a tin of a black dust that smelled like Brimstone and inhaled a pinch deeply. It rubbed its nose and moved to poke at my circle with a boot, making me wince. "Nice and tight. But it's cold. Ceri likes it warm."

Ceri? I wondered as all the snow within the circle melted in a flash of condensation. The scent of wet pavement rose strong, then vanished as the cement dried to a pale red.

"Ceri," Algaliarept said, its voice shocking me in its soft tone, both coaxing and demanding. "Come."

I stared when a woman stepped from behind Algaliarept, seemingly from nowhere. She was thin, her heart-shaped face sallow and her cheekbones showing too strongly. Standing substantially shorter than I, she had a diminutive, almost child-like mien. Her head was down, and her pale translucent hair hung straight to her mid-back. She was dressed in a beautiful gown that dropped to her bare feet. It was exquisite—lush silk dyed in rich purples, greens, and golds—and it fitted her curvaceous form like it had been painted on. Though she was small, she was well-proportioned, if perhaps a shade fragile looking.

"Ceri," Algaliarept said, putting a white-gloved hand to tilt her head up. Her eyes were green, wide, and empty. "What did I tell you about going barefoot?"

A glimmer of annoyance crossed her face, far away and distant behind the numb state she was in. My attention dropped as a matching pair of embroidered slippers materialized about her feet.

"That's better." Algaliarept turned from her, and I was struck by the picture of the perfect couple they made in their finery. She was beautiful in her clothes, but her mind was as empty as she was lovely, insane from the raw magic the demon forced her to hold for it, filtering the ley line power through her mind to keep itself safe. Dread twisted in my gut.

"Don't kill her," I whispered, my mouth dry. "You're done with her. Let her live."

Algaliarept pulled its smoked glasses down to look over them, its red orbs fixing on me. "You like her?" it said. "She is pretty, isn't she? Over a thousand years old, and aged not a moment since the day I took her soul. If I were honest, she's the reason I was invited to most of the parties. She puts out without a fuss. Though, of course, for the first hundred years it was all tears and wailing. Fun in itself, but it does get old. You'll fight me, won't you?"

My jaw clenched. "Give her back her soul, now that you're done with her."

Algaliarept laughed. "Oh, you are a love!" it said, clapping its white-gloved hands once. "But I'm giving that back to her anyway. I've sullied it beyond redemption, leaving mine reasonably pure. And I will kill her before she has the chance to beg forgiveness from her god." Its thick lips split in a nasty grin. "It's all a lie, anyway, you know."

I went cold as the woman slumped into a small spot of purple, green, and gold at its feet, broken. I would die before letting it drag me into the ever-after to become . . . become this. "Bastard," I whispered.

Algaliarept gestured as if to say, "So what?" It turned to Ceri, finding her small hand in the mass of fabric and helping her rise. She was barefoot again. "Ceri," the demon coaxed, then glanced at me. "I should have replaced her forty years ago, but the Turn made everything difficult. She doesn't even hear anymore unless you say her name first." It turned back to the woman. "Ceri, be a love and fetch the transfer media you made this sundown."

My stomach hurt. "I made some," I said, and Ceri blinked, the first sign of comprehension crossing her. Big eyes solemn and blank, she looked at me as if seeing me for the first time. Her attention went to the spell pot at my feet and the milky green candles about us. Panic stirred in the back of her eyes as she stood before the angel monument. I think she had just realized what was going on.

"Marvelous," Algaliarept said. "You're trying to be useful already, but I want Ceri's." It looked at Ceri, her mouth open to show tiny white teeth. "Yes, love. Time for your retirement. Bring me my cauldron and the transfer media."

Tense and shirking, Ceri made a gesture and a child-sized cauldron made of copper thicker than my wrist appeared between us, already filled with amber liquid, the flecks of wild geranium suspended as if it were a gel.

The scent of ozone rose high as it grew warmer, and I unzipped my coat. Algaliarept was humming, clearly in a grand mood. It beckoned me closer, and I took a step, fingering the silver knife tucked in my sleeve. My pulse quickened, and I wondered if my contract would be enough to save me. A knife wasn't going to be much help.

The demon grinned to show me flat, even teeth as it gestured to Ceri. "My mirror," it prompted, and the delicate woman bent to retrieve a scrying mirror that hadn't been there a moment ago. She held it before Algaliarept like a table.

I swallowed, remembering the foul sensation of pushing my aura off of me and into my scrying mirror last fall. The demon took off its gloves, one by one, and placed its ruddy, thick-knuckled hands atop the glass, long fingers spread wide. It shuddered and closed its eyes while its aura precipitated out into the mirror, falling from its hands like ink to swirl and pool in its reflection. "Into the medium, Ceri, love. Hurry now."

She was almost panting as she carried the mirror holding Algaliarept's aura to the cauldron. It wasn't the weight of the glass; it was the weight of what was happening. I imagine she was reliving the night she had stood where I was now, watching her predecessor as I watched her. She must have known what was going to happen, but was so deadened inside that she could only do what was expected. And by her obvious, helpless panic, I knew that something was left in her worth saving.

"Free her," I said, hunched in my ugly coat as my attention flicked from Ceri to the cauldron, and then to Algaliarept. "Free her first."

"Why?" It looked idly at its nails before putting the gloves back on.

"I'll kill you before I let you drag me into the ever-after, and I want her free first."

Algaliarept laughed at that, long and deep. Putting a hand against the angel, the demon bent almost double. A muted thump reverberated up through my feet, and the stone base cracked with the sound of a gunshot. Ceri stared, her pale lips slack and her eyes moving rapidly over me. Things seemed to be starting to work in her, memories and thoughts long suppressed.

"You *will* struggle," Algaliarept said, delighted. "Stupendous. I *so* hoped you would." Its eyes met mine, and it smirked, touching the rim of its glasses. *"Adsimulo calefacio."*

The knife in my sleeve burst into flame. Yelping, I shrugged out of my coat. It hit the edge of my bubble and slid down. The demon eyed me. "Rachel Mariana Morgan. Stop trying my patience. Get over here and recite the damned invocation."

I had no choice. If I didn't, it would call my deal breached, take my soul in forfeit, and drag me into the everafter. My only chance was to play the agreement out. I glanced at Ceri, wishing she would move away from Algaliarept, but she was running her fingers over the dates engraved in the cracked tombstone, her sun-starved complexion now even paler.

"Do you remember the curse?" Algaliarept asked when I came even with the knee-high cauldron.

I snuck a glance in, not surprised to find the demon's aura was black. I nodded, feeling faint as my thoughts went back to having accidentally made Nick my familiar. Was it only three months ago? "I can say it in English," I whispered. *Nick. Oh God. I hadn't said good-bye.* He had been so distant lately that I hadn't found the courage to tell him. I hadn't told anyone.

"Good enough." Its glasses vanished and its damned, goat-slitted eyes fixed on me. My heart raced, but I had made this choice. I would live or die by it.

Deep and resonate, seeming to vibrate my very core, Algaliarept's voice slipped from between its lips. It was Latin, the words familiar, yet not, like a vision of a dream. *"Pars tibi, totum mihi. Vinctus vinculis, prece factis."*

"Some to you," I echoed in English, interpreting the words from memory, "but all to me. Bound by ties made so by plea."

The demon's smile widened, chilling me with its confidence. *"Luna servata, lux sanata. Chaos statutum, pejus minutum."*

I swallowed hard. "Moon made safe, ancient light made sane," I whispered. "Chaos decreed, taken tripped if bane."

Algaliarept's knuckles gripping the vat went white in anticipation. *"Mentem tegens, malum ferens. Semper servus dum duret mundus,"* it said, and Ceri sobbed, a small kitten sound, quickly stifled. "Go on," Algaliarept prompted, excitement making its outline blur. "Say it and put your hands in."

I hesitated, my eyes fixing on Ceri's crumpled form before the gravestone, her gown a small puddle of color. "Absolve me of one of my debts I owe you, first."

"You are a pushy bitch, Rachel Mariana Morgan."

"Do it!" I demanded. "You said you would. Take off one of your marks as agreed."

It leaned over the pot until I could see my reflection, wide-eyed and frightened, in its glasses. "It makes no difference. Finish the curse and be done with it."

"Are you saying you aren't going to hold to our bargain?" I goaded, and it laughed.

"No. Not at all, and if you were hoping to break our arrangement on that, then you're sadly the fool. I'll take off one of my marks, but you still owe me a favor." It licked its lips. "And as my familiar, you belong—to me."

A nauseating mix of dread and relief shook my knees, and I held my breath so I wouldn't get sick. But I had to fulfill my end of the bargain completely before I would see if my beliefs were right and I could slip the demon's snare by a small point called choice.

"Lee of mind," I said, trembling, "bearer of pain. Slave until the worlds are slain."

Algaliarept made a satisfied sound. Jaw gritted, I plunged my hands into the cauldron. Cold struck through me, burning them numb. I yanked my hands out. Horrified, I stared at them, seeing no change in my red-enameled fingertips.

And then Algaliarept's aura seeped farther into me, touching my chi.

My eyes seemed to bulge in agony. I took a huge breath to scream but couldn't let it out. I caught a glimpse of Ceri, her eyes pinched in memory. Across the cauldron, Algaliarept was grinning. Gagging, I struggled to breathe as the air seemed to turn to oil. I fell to my hands and knees, bruising them on the concrete. Hair falling to hide my face, I tried to keep from retching. I couldn't breathe. I couldn't think!

The demon's aura was a wet blanket, dripping with acid, smothering me. It coated me, inside and out, and my strength was surrounded by its power. It squeezed my will to nothing. I heard my heart beat once, then again. I took a shuddering breath, swallowing back the sharp tang of vomit. I was going to live. Its aura alone couldn't kill me. I could do this. I could.

Shaking, I looked up while the shock lessened to something I could deal with. The cauldron was gone, and Ceri was huddled almost behind the huge grave marker beside Algaliarept. I took a breath, unable to taste the air through the demon's aura. I moved, unable to feel the rough concrete scraping my fingertips. Everything was numb. Everything was muted, as if through cotton.

Everything except the power of the nearby ley line. I could feel it humming thirty yards away as if it were a high-tension power line. Panting, I staggered to my feet, shocked to realize I could see it. I could see everything as if I was using my second sight—which I wasn't. My stomach roiled as I saw that my circle, once tinged with a shading of cheerful gold from my aura, was now coated in black.

I turned to the demon, seeing the thick black aura surrounding it and knowing a good portion of it coated mine. Then I looked at Ceri, hardly able to see her features, so strong was Algaliarept's aura on her. She didn't have an aura to combat the demon's, having lost her soul to it. And that was what I had pinned everything on.

If I retained my soul, I still had my aura, smothered as it was under Algaliarept's. And with my soul came free will. Unlike Ceri, I could say no. Slowly I was remembering how.

"Free her," I rasped. "I took your damned aura. Free her now."

"Oh, why not?" the demon chortled, rubbing its gloved hands together. "Killing her will be a banger of a way to get your apprenticeship started. Ceri?"

The slight woman scrambled up, her head high and her heart-shaped face showing panic.

"Ceridwen Merriam Dulciate," Algaliarept said. "I'm giving you your soul back *before* I kill you. You can thank Rachel for that."

I started. Rachel? I had always been Rachel Mariana Morgan before. Apparently as a familiar, I wasn't worth my full name anymore. That ticked me off.

She made a small sound, staggering. I watched with my new vision as Algaliarept's bond fell from her. The barest, faintest glimmer of purest blue rimmed her—her returned soul already trying to bathe her in protection—then vanished under the thousand years of darkness the demon had fostered on her soul while it had been in his keeping. Her mouth worked, but she couldn't speak. Her eyes glazed as she panted, hyperventilating, and I leapt forward to catch her as she fell. Struggling, I dragged her back to my end of the circle.

Algaliarept reached after her. Adrenaline surged. I dropped Ceri. Straightening, I drew on the line. "Rhombus!" I shouted, the word of invocation I had been practicing for three months to set a circle without drawing it first.

With a force that sent me lurching, my new circle exploded into existence, sealing Ceri and me in a second, smaller circle inside the first. My circle had lacked a physical object to focus on, so the excess energy went everywhere instead of back in the ley line where it was supposed to. The demon swore, blown backward until it slammed against the inside of my original circle, still up and running. With a ping that reverberated through me, my first circle broke and Algaliarept hit the ground.

Breathing heavily, I hunched with my hands on my knees. Algaliarept blinked at me from the concrete, then a wicked smile came over it. "We're sharing an aura, love," it said. "Your circle can't stop me anymore." Its grin widened. "Surprise," it sang lightly, standing up and taking the time to meticulously brush its coat of crushed velvet.

Oh, God. If my first circle didn't hold it now, neither would my second. I had thought that might happen. "Ceri?" I whispered. "Get up. We have to move."

Algaliarept's eyes tracked behind me to the hallowed ground that surrounded us. My muscles tensed.

The demon leapt. Shrieking, I jerked Ceri and myself backward. The surge of ever-after flowing into me from breaking the circle was almost unnoticed. My breath was knocked from me as we hit the ground, Ceri on top of me. Still not breathing, I sent my heels scrabbling against the snow and pushed us farther away. The gold-colored trim on Ceri's ball gown was rough under my fingers, and I yanked her to me until I was sure we were both on holy ground.

"Damn you all to hell!" Algaliarept shouted from the edge of the cement, furious.

I got up, shaking. My breath caught, and I stared at the frustrated demon.

"Ceri!" the demon demanded, and the scent of burnt amber rose when it set its foot across the unseen barrier and jerked it back. "Push her at me! Or I'll blacken your soul so badly that your precious god won't let you in no matter how you beg it!"

Ceri moaned, clutching my leg as she huddled, hiding her face, trying to overcome a thousand years of conditioning. My face grew tight from anger. *This would have been me. This still could be me.* "I won't let it hurt you anymore," I said, one hand dropping to touch her shoulder. "If I can stop it from hurting you, I will."

Her grip on me shook, and I thought she seemed like a beaten child.

"You're my familiar!" the demon shouted, spittle flying from it. "Rachel, come here!"

I shook my head, colder than the snow warranted. "No," I said simply. "I'm not going into the ever-after. You can't make me."

Algaliarept choked in disbelief. "You will!" it thundered, and Ceri clutched my leg tighter. "I own you! You're my bloody familiar. I gave you my aura. Your will is mine!"

"No, it isn't," I said, shaking inside. *It was working. God save me, it was working.* My eyes warmed, and I realized I was almost crying from relief. It couldn't take me. I might be its familiar, but it didn't have my soul. I could say no.

"You're my familiar!" it raged, and Ceri and I both cried out as it tried to cross into holy ground and yanked itself back again.

"I'm your familiar!" I yelled back, frightened. "And I say no! I said I'd be your familiar and I am, but I'm not going into the ever-after with you, and you can't make me!"

Algaliarept's goat-slitted eyes narrowed. It stepped back, and I stiffened as its anger chilled. "You agreed to be my familiar," it said softly, smoke curling up from its shiny, buckled boots as they edged the circle of blasphemed ground. "Come here now, or I'll call our agreement breached and your soul will be mine by default."

Double jeopardy. I knew it would come to this. "I've got your stinking aura all over me," I said as Ceri quivered. "I'm your familiar. If you think there's been a breach in contract, then you get someone out here to judge what happened before the sun comes up. And take one of these damned demon marks off me!" I demanded, holding my wrist out.

My arm shook, and Algaliarept made an ugly noise, deep in its throat. The long exhalation set my insides to quiver, and Ceri ventured to peek at the demon. "I can't use you as a familiar if you're on the wrong side of the lines," it said, clearly thinking aloud. "The binding isn't strong enough—"

"That's not my problem," I interrupted, legs shaking.

"No," Algaliarept agreed. It laced its white-gloved hands

behind its back, its gaze dropping to Ceri. The deep fury in its eyes scared the crap out of me. "But I'm making it your problem. You stole my familiar and left me with nothing. You tricked me into letting you slip payment for a service. If I can't drag you in, I'll find a way to use you through the lines. And I will never let you die. Ask her. Ask her of her never-ending hell. It's waiting for you, Rachel. And I'm not a patient demon. You can't hide on holy ground forever."

"Go away," I said, my voice trembling. "I called you here. Now I'm telling you to leave. Take one of these marks off me and leave. Now." I had summoned it, and therefore it was susceptible to the rules of summoning—even if I was its familiar.

It exhaled slowly, and I thought the ground moved. Its eyes went black. Black. Black, black, then blacker still. *Oh, shit.*

"I'll find the way to make a strong enough bond with you through the lines," it intoned. "And I'll pull you through, soul intact. You walk this side of the lines on borrowed time."

"I've been a dead witch walking before," I said. "And my name is Rachel Mariana Morgan. Use it. And take one of these marks off of me or you forfeit everything."

I'm going to get away with it. I outsmarted a demon. The knowledge was heady, but I was too frightened for it to mean much.

Algaliarept gave me a chilling look. Its gaze dropped to Ceri, then it vanished.

I cried out as my wrist flamed, but I welcomed the pain, hunched as I held my demon-marked wrist with my other hand. It hurt—it hurt as if the dogs of hell were chewing on it—but when my blurred vision cleared, there was one scared line crossing the welted circle, not two.

Panting through the last of the pain, I slumped, my entire body collapsing in on itself. I pulled my head up and took a clean breath, trying to unknot my stomach. It couldn't use me if we were on opposite sides of the ley lines. I was still myself, though I was coated with Algaliarept's aura. Slowly my second sight faded and the red smear of the ley line vanished. Algaliarept's aura was getting easier to bear, slipping almost into an unnoticed sensation now that the demon was gone.

Ceri let go of me. Reminded of her, I bent to offer her a hand up. She looked at it in wonder, watching herself as she put a thin pale hand in mine. Still at my feet, she kissed the top of it in a formal gesture of thanks.

"No, don't," I said, turning my hand to grip hers and pull her upright and out of the snow.

Ceri's eyes filled and spilled over as she silently wept for her freedom, the well-dressed, abused woman beautiful in her tearful, silent joy. I put my arm around her, giving her what comfort I could. Ceri hunched over and shook all the harder.

Leaving everything where it was and the candles to go out on their own, I stumbled to the church. My gaze was fixed to the snow, and as Ceri and I made two trails of footprints over the one leading out here, I wondered what on earth I was going to do with her.

Two

We were halfway to the church before I realized Ceri was walking barefoot in the snow. "Ceri," I said, appalled. "Where are your shoes?"

The crying woman made a rough hiccup. Wiping her eyes, she glanced down. A red blur of ever-after swirled about her toes, and a pair of burnt embroidered slippers appeared on her tiny feet. Surprise cascaded over her delicate features, clear in the porch light.

"They're burned," I said as she shook them off. Bits of char stuck to her, looking like black sores. "Maybe Big Al is having a tantrum and burning your things."

Ceri silently nodded, a hint of a smile quirking her blue-ing lips at the insulting nickname I used so I wouldn't say the demon's name before those who didn't already know it.

I pushed us back into motion. "Well, I've got a pair of slippers you can wear. And how about some coffee? I'm frozen through." *Coffee? We just escaped a demon, and I'm offering her coffee?*

She said nothing, her eyes going to the wooden porch that led to the living quarters at the back of the church. Her eyes traveled to the sanctuary behind it and the steeple with its belfry. "Priest?" she whispered, her voice matching the iced-over garden, crystalline and pure.

"No," I said as I tried not to slip on the steps. "I just live here. It's not a real church anymore." Ceri blinked, and I added, "It's kinda hard to explain. Come on in."

I opened the back door, going in first since Ceri dropped her head and wouldn't. The warmth of the living room was like a blessed wave on my cold cheeks. Ceri stopped dead in the threshold when a handful of pixy girls flew shrieking from the mantel above the empty fireplace, fleeing the cold. Two adolescent pixy boys gave Ceri a telling glance before following at a more sedate pace.

"Pixies?" I prompted, remembering she was over a thousand years old. If she wasn't an Inderlander, she wouldn't have ever seen them before, believing they were, ah, fairy tales. "You know about pixies?" I asked, stomping the snow from my boots.

She nodded, closing the door behind her, and I felt better. The adjustment to modern life would be easier if she didn't have to come to grips with witches, Weres, pixies, vampires, and the like being real on top of TVs and cell phones, but as her eyes ranged over Ivy's expensive electronic equipment with only a mild interest, I was willing to bet that things on the other side of the ley lines were as technologically advanced as they were here.

"Jenks!" I shouted to the front of the church where he and his family were living out the duration of the cold months. "Can I see you for a minute?"

There was the tight hum of dragonfly wings faint over the warm air. "Hey, Rache," the small pixy said as he buzzed in. "What's this my kids are saying about an angel?" He jerked to a hovering halt, his eyes wide and his short blond hair swinging as he looked behind me.

Angel, huh? I thought as I turned to Ceri to introduce her. "Oh God, no," I said, pulling her back upright. She had been picking up the snow I had knocked off my boots, holding it in her hand. The sight of her diminutive form dressed in that exquisite gown cleaning my mess was too much. "Please, Ceri," I said, taking the snow from her and dropping it on the carpet. "Don't."

A wash of self-annoyance crossed the small woman's smooth brow. Sighing, she made an apologetic face. I don't think she had even realized what she was doing until I stopped her.

I turned back to Jenks, seeing his wings had taken on a faint red tint as his circulation increased. "What the hell?" he muttered, gaze dropping to her feet. Pixy dust sifted from him in his surprise to make a glittering spot of sun on the gray carpet. He was dressed in his casual gardening clothes of tight-fitting green silk and looked like a miniature Peter Pan minus the hat.

"Jenks," I said as I put a hand on Ceri's shoulder and pulled her forward. "This is Ceri. She's going to be staying with us for a while. Ceri, this is Jenks, my partner."

Jenks zipped forward, then back in agitation. An amazed look came over Ceri, and she glanced from me to him. "Partner?" she said, her attention going to my left hand.

Understanding crashed over me and I warmed. "My business partner," I reiterated, realizing she thought we were married. *How on earth could you marry a pixy? Why on earth would you want to?* "We work together as runners." Taking my hat off, I tossed the red wool to the hearth where it could dry on the stone and fluffed the pressure marks from my hair. I had left my coat outside, but I wasn't going out to get it now.

She bit her lip in confusion. The warmth of the room had turned them red, and color was starting to come back into her cheeks.

In a dry clatter, Jenks flitted close so that my curls shifted in the breeze from his wings. "Not too bright, is she," he pointed out, and when I waved him away in bother, he put his hands on his hips. Hovering before Ceri, he said loudly and slowly as if she were hard of hearing, "We—are— good—guys. We—stop—bad—guys."

"Warriors," Ceri said, not looking at him as her eyes touched on Ivy's leather curtains, plush suede chairs, and sofa. The room was a salute to comfort, all of it from Ivy's pocketbook and not mine.

Jenks laughed, sounding like wind chimes. "Warriors," he said, grinning. "Yeah. We're warriors. I'll be right back. I gotta tell that one to Matalina."

He zipped out of the room at head height, and my shoulders eased. "Sorry about that," I apologized. "I asked Jenks to move his family in for the winter after he admitted he usually lost two children to hibernation sickness every spring. They're driving Ivy and me insane, but I'd rather have no privacy for four months than Jenks starting his spring with tiny coffins."

Ceri nodded. "Ivy," she said softly. "Is she your partner?"

"Yup. Just like Jenks," I said casually to make sure she really understood. Her shifting eyes were cataloging everything, and I slowly moved to the hallway. "Um, Ceri?" I said, hesitating until she started to follow. "Do you want me to call you Ceridwen instead?"

She peeked down the dark corridor to the dimly lit sanctuary, her gaze following the sounds of pixy children. They were supposed to stay in the front of the church, but they got into everything, and their squeals and shrieks had become commonplace. "Ceri, please."

Her personality was thundering back into her faster than I would have believed possible, going from silence to short sentences in a matter of moments. There was a curious mix of modern and old-world charm in her speech that probably came from living with demons so long. She stopped in the threshold of my kitchen, wide-eyed as she took it all in. I didn't think it was culture shock. Most people had a similar reaction when seeing my kitchen.

It was huge, with both a gas and an electric stove so I could cook on one and stir spells on the other. The fridge was stainless steel and large enough to put a cow in. There was one sliding window overlooking the snowy garden and graveyard, and my beta, Mr. Fish, swam happily in a brandy snifter on the sill. Fluorescent lights illuminated shiny chrome and expansive counter space that wouldn't be out of place before the cameras of a cooking show.

A center island counter overhung with a rack of my spelling equipment and drying herbs gathered by Jenks and his family took up much of the space. Ivy's massive antique table took up the rest. Half of it was meticulously arranged as her office, with her computer—faster and more powerful than an industrial-sized package of laxative—color-coded files, maps, and the markers she used to organize her runs. The other half of the table was mine and empty. I wish I could say it was neatness, but when I had a run, I ran it. I didn't analyze it to death.

"Have a seat," I said casually. "How about some coffee?" *Coffee?* I thought as I went to the coffeemaker and threw out the old grounds. What was I going to do with her? It wasn't as if she was a stray kitten. She needed help. Professional help.

Ceri stared at me, her face returning to its numb state. "I . . ." she stammered, looking frightened and small in her gorgeous outfit. I glanced at my jeans and red sweater. I still had on my snow boots, and I felt like a slob.

"Here," I said as I pulled out a chair. "I'll make some tea." *Three steps forward, one back,* I thought when she shunned the chair I offered and took the one before Ivy's computer instead. Tea might be more appropriate, seeing as she was over a thousand years old. *Did they even have coffee in the Dark Ages?*

I was staring at my cupboards, trying to remember if we had a teapot, when Jenks and about fifteen of his kids came rolling in, all talking at once. Their voices were so high-pitched and rapid they made my head hurt. "Jenks," I pleaded, glancing at Ceri. She looked overwhelmed enough as it was. "Please?"

"They aren't going to do anything," he protested belligerently. "Besides, I want them to get a good sniff of her. I can't tell what she is, she stinks of burnt amber so badly. Who is she, anyway, and what was she doing in our garden in her bare feet?"

"Um," I said, suddenly wary. Pixies had excellent noses,

able to tell what species someone was just by smelling them. I had a bad suspicion that I knew what Ceri was, and I *really* didn't want Jenks to figure it out.

Ceri raised her hand as a perch, smiling beatifically at the two pixy girls who promptly landed on it, their green and pink silk dresses moving from the breeze stirred by their dragonfly wings. They were chattering happily the way pixy girls do, seemingly brainless but aware of everything down to the mouse hiding behind the fridge. Clearly Ceri had seen pixies before. That would make her an Inderlander if she was a thousand years old. The Turn, when we all came out of hiding to live openly with humans, had only been forty years ago.

"Hey!" Jenks exclaimed, seeing his kids monopolizing her, and they whirled up and out of the kitchen in a kaleidoscope of color and noise. Immediately he took their place, beckoning his oldest son, Jax, down to perch on the computer screen before her.

"You smell like Trent Kalamack," he said bluntly. "What are you?"

A wash of angst took me and I turned my back on them. *Damn, I was right. She was an elf.* If Jenks knew, he would blab it all over Cincinnati the moment the temperature got above freezing and he could leave the church. Trent didn't want the world to know that elves had survived the Turn, and he would drop Agent Orange on the entire block to shut Jenks up.

Turning, I frantically waved my fingers at Ceri, pantomiming zipping my mouth. Realizing she wouldn't have a clue what that meant, I put my finger to my lips. The woman eyed me in question, then looked at Jenks. "Ceri," she said seriously.

"Yeah, yeah," Jenks said impatiently, hands on his hips. "I know. You Ceri. Me Jenks. But what are you? Are you a witch? Rachel's a witch."

Ceri glanced at me and away. "I'm Ceri."

Jenks's wings blurred to nothing, the shimmer going from

blue to red. "Yeah," he repeated. "But what species? See, I'm a pixy, and Rachel is a witch. You are . . ."

"Ceri," she insisted.

"Ah, Jenks?" I said as the woman's eyes narrowed. The question as to what the Kalamacks were had eluded pixies for the entirety of the family's existence. Figuring that out would give Jenks more prestige in the pixy world than if he took out an entire fairy clan by himself. I could tell he was on the edge of his patience when he flitted up to hover before her.

"Damn it!" Jenks swore, frustrated. "What the hell are you, woman?"

"Jenks!" I shouted in alarm as Ceri's hand flashed out, snagging him. Jax, his son, let out a yelp, leaving a cloud of pixy dust as he darted to the ceiling. Jenks's eldest daughter, Jih peeked around the archway from the hall ceiling, her wings a pink blur.

"Hey! Lego!" Jenks exclaimed. His wings made a furious clatter, but he wasn't going anywhere. Ceri had his pant leg between her thumb and forefinger. Her reflexes were better than even Ivy's if she had enough control to be that precise.

"I'm Ceri," she said, her thin lips tight as Jenks hovered, snared. "And even my demon captor had enough respect that he didn't curse at me, little warrior."

"Yes, ma'am," Jenks said meekly. "Can I go now?"

She raised one pale eyebrow—a skill I envied—then glanced at me for direction. I nodded emphatically, still shocked at how quick it had been. Not smiling, Ceri let him go.

"Guess you aren't as slow as I thought," Jenks said sullenly.

The ruffled pixy brought the scent of store-bought dirt to me as he retreated to my shoulder, and my brow furrowed when I turned my back on her to poke around under the counter for a teapot. I heard the soft familiar clink of pens, recognizing the sound of Ceri tidying Ivy's desk. Her centuries of slavery were showing again. The woman's mix of meek servitude and quick pride had me at a loss for how to treat her.

"Who is she?" Jenks whispered in my ear.

I crouched to reach into the cupboard, pulling out a copper teapot so badly tarnished that it was almost maroon. "She was Big Al's familiar."

"Big Al!" the pixy squeaked, rising up to land upon the tap. "Is that what you were doing out there? Tink's panties, Rachel, you're getting as bad as Nick! You know that's not safe!"

I could tell him now. Now that it was over. Very aware of Ceri listening behind us, I ran the water into the teapot and swirled it around to clean it. "Big Al didn't agree to testify against Piscary out of the goodness of its heart. I had to pay for it."

With a dry rasp of wings, Jenks moved to hover before me. Surprise, shock, and then anger cascaded over his face. "What did you promise him?" he said coldly.

"It's an it, not a him," I said. "And it's done." I couldn't look at him. "I promised to be its familiar if I was allowed to keep my soul."

"Rachel!" A burst of pixy dust lit the sink. "When? When is it coming to get you? We have to find a way out of this. There must be something!" He flew a bright path to my spell books under the center island counter and back. "Is there anything in your books? Call Nick. He'll know!"

Not liking his fluster, I wiped the water off the bottom of the teapot. My boot heels made a dull thumping on the linoleum as I crossed the kitchen. The gas ignited with a whoosh, and my face warmed from embarrassment. "It's too late," I repeated. "I'm its familiar. But the bond isn't strong enough for it to use me if I'm on this side of the ley lines, and as long as I can keep it from pulling me into the ever-after, I'll be okay." I turned from the stove, finding Ceri sitting before Ivy's computer, staring at me with rapt admiration. "I can say no. It's done."

Jenks came to a sputtering halt before me. "Done?" he said, too close to focus on. "Rachel, why? Putting Piscary away isn't worth that!"

"I didn't have a choice!" Frustrated, I crossed my arms before me and leaned against the counter. "Piscary was trying to kill me, and if I survived, I wanted him in jail, not free to come after me again. It's done. The demon can't use me. I tricked it."

"Him," Ceri said softly, and Jenks spun. I had forgotten she was there, she was so quiet. "Al is male. Female demons won't let themselves be pulled across the lines. That's how you can tell. Mostly."

I blinked, taken aback. "Al is male? Why did he keep letting me call him an it?"

She lifted her shoulder in a very modern show of confusion.

My breath came out in a puff and I turned back to Jenks. I started as I found him hovering right before my nose, his wings red. "You're an ass," he said, his tiny, smooth features creased in anger. "You should have told us. What if it had gotten you? What about Ivy and me? Huh? We would have kept looking for you, not knowing what had happened. At least if you had told us, we might have been able to find a way to get you back. Ever think of that, Ms. Morgan? We're a team, and you just stepped all over that!"

My next outburst died. "But there wasn't anything you could have done," I said lamely.

"How do you know?" Jenks snapped.

I sighed, embarrassed that a four-inch man was lecturing me—and had every right to. "Yeah, you're right," I said, slumping. Slowly my arms uncrossed. "I'm just . . . I'm just not used to having anyone I can depend on, Jenks. I'm sorry."

Jenks dropped three feet he was so surprised. "You . . . you agree with me?"

Ceri's head made a smooth turn to the open archway. Her empty expression went even more so. I followed her gaze to the dark hall, not surprised to find it holding Ivy's lithe silhouette, her hip cocked, hand on her thin waist, looking sleek in her body-tight leather.

Suddenly wary, I pulled myself from the counter and

straightened. I hated it when she just appeared like that. I hadn't even felt the air pressure change when she opened the front door. "Hi, Ivy," I said, my voice still carrying its chagrin from Jenks.

Ivy's blank gaze matched Ceri's perfectly as she ran her brown eyes over the small woman sitting in *her* chair. She pushed herself into motion, moving with a living vampire's grace, her boots almost silent. Tucking her long, enviably straight black hair behind an ear, she went to the fridge and pulled out the orange juice. Dressed in her casual leather pants and black tuck-in shirt, she looked like a biker chick gone sophisticate. Her cheeks were red from the cold, and she looked chilled even though she still wore her short leather jacket.

Jenks hovered beside me, our argument forgotten in the more pressing problem of Ivy finding someone unexpected in her kitchen. My last guest she had pinned to the wall and threatened to bleed; Ivy didn't like surprises. That she was drinking orange juice was a good sign. It meant she had succumbed to that damned blood lust of hers, and Jenks and I would only have to deal with a guilt-strewn vampire instead of an irritable, guilt-strewn, and hungry vampire. She was a lot easier to live with now that she was practicing again.

"Ah, Ivy, this is Ceridwen," I offered. "She's staying with us until she finds her feet."

Ivy turned, leaning back against the counter to look predatory and sexy as she took the cap off the jug and drank right from the carton. *Like I'd say anything?* Ivy's gaze ran over Ceri, then flicked to Jenks's obvious agitation, and then to me. "So," she said, her melodious voice reminding me of torn gray silk on snow. "You wiggled out of your agreement with that demon. Good job. Nicely done."

My jaw dropped. "How did you know . . . ?" I stammered as Jenks yelped in surprise.

A faint smile, unusual but honest, pulled the corners of her mouth up. A flash of fang showed, her canines the same size as mine but sharp, like a cat's. She'd have to wait until she was dead to get the extended versions. "You talk in your sleep," she said lightly.

"You knew?" I said, floored. "You never said anything!"

"Nicely done?" Jenks's wings clattered like June bugs. "You think being a demon's familiar is a good thing? What train hit you on the way home?"

Ivy went to get a glass from the cupboard. "If Piscary had been released, Rachel would be dead by sunup," she said as she poured out juice. "So she's a demon's familiar? So what? She said the demon can't use her unless he pulls her into the ever-after. And she's alive. You can't do anything if you're dead." She took a sip of her drink. "Unless you're a vampire."

Jenks made an ugly sound and flew to the corner of the room to sulk. Jih took the opportunity to flit in to hide in the ladle hanging over the center counter, the tips of her wings showing a brilliant red above the copper rim.

Ivy's brown eyes met mine over her glass. Her perfect oval face was almost featureless as she hid her emotions behind the cool facade of indifference she maintained when there was someone in the room beside us two, Jenks included. "I'm glad it worked," she said as she set the glass on the counter. "Are you all right?"

I nodded, seeing her relief in the slight trembling of her long pianist fingers. She would never tell me how worried she had been, and I wondered how long she had stood in the hallway listening and collecting herself. Her eyes blinked several times, and her jaw clenched in an effort to stifle her emotion. "I didn't know it was tonight," she said softly. "I wouldn't have left."

"Thanks," I said, thinking Jenks was right. I had been an ass for not telling them. I just wasn't used to having anyone but my mother care.

Ceri was watching Ivy with a puzzled, rapt attention. "Partner?" she hazarded, and Ivy flicked her attention to the small woman.

"Yeah," Ivy said. "Partner. What's it to you?"

"Ceri, this is Ivy," I said as the small woman got to her feet.

Ivy frowned as she realized the precise order she kept her desk in had been altered.

"She was Big Al's familiar," I warned. "She needs a few days to find her feet is all."

Jenks made an eye-hurting noise with his wings, and Ivy gave me a telling look, her expression shifting to an annoyed wariness when Ceri came to stand before her. The small woman was peering at Ivy in confusion. "You're a vampire," she said, reaching to touch Ivy's crucifix.

Ivy sprang back with a startling quickness, her eyes flashing black.

"Whoa, whoa, whoa!" I said as I stepped between them, ready for anything. "Ivy, take it easy. She's been in the ever-after for a thousand years. She may not have seen a living vampire before. I think she's an Inderlander, but she smells like the ever-after so Jenks can't tell what she is." I hesitated, telling her with my eyes and my last sentence that Ceri was an elf, and therefore a loose cannon as far as magic was concerned.

Ivy's pupils had dilated to almost a full, vampire black. Her stance was domineering and sexually charged, but she had just slaked her blood lust and so was capable of listening. I shot a quick glance at Ceri, glad to see she wisely hadn't moved. "We all okay here?" I asked, my voice demanding they both back down.

Thin lips pressed tight, Ivy turned her back on us. Jenks dropped to my shoulder. "Nicely done," he said. "Got all your bitches in line, I see."

"Jenks!" I hissed, knowing Ivy had heard when her knuckles on her glass turned white. I flicked him off me, and laughing, he rose up and then back down to my shoulder.

Ceri was standing with her arms confidently at her side, watching Ivy grow more and more tense. "Oh-h-h-h-h," Jenks drawled. "Your new friend is gonna do something."

"Uh, Ceri?" I questioned, heart pounding as the petite

woman went to stand beside Ivy at the sink, clearly demanding her attention.

Pale face tight with a repressed anger, Ivy turned. "What," she said flatly.

Ceri inclined her head regally, never taking her green eyes from Ivy's slowly dilating brown ones. "I apologize," she said in her high, clear voice, every syllable carefully pronounced. "I've slighted you." Her attention dropped to Ivy's elaborate crucifix on its silver chain about her neck. "You're a vampire warrior, and yet you can wear the Cross?"

Ceri's hand twitched, and I knew she wanted to touch it. Ivy knew it too. I watched, unable to interfere as Ivy turned to face her. Hip cocked, she gave Ceri a more in-depth once-over, taking in her dried tears, her exquisite ball gown, her bare feet, and her obvious pride and upright carriage. As I held my breath, Ivy took her crucifix off, the chain gathering her hair in front of her as she pulled it from around her neck.

"I'm a living vampire," she said as she put the religious icon in the elf's hand. "I was born with the vampire virus. You know what a virus is, don't you?"

Ceri's fingers traced the lines of the worked silver. "My demon let me read what I wished. A virus is killing my kin." She looked up. "Not the vampire virus. Something else."

Ivy's gaze darted to me, then returned to the small woman standing just a shade too close to her. "The virus changed me as I was forming in my mother's womb, making me some of both. I can walk under the sun and worship without pain," Ivy said. "I'm stronger than you," she added as she subtly put more space between them. "But not as strong as a true undead. And I have a soul." She said the last as if she expected Ceri to deny it.

Ceri's expression became empty. "You're going to lose it."

Ivy's eye twitched. "I know."

I held my breath, listening to the clock tick and the almost subliminal hum of pixy wings. Eyes solemn, the thin woman held the crucifix out to Ivy. "I'm sorry. That's the hell from which Rachel Mariana Morgan saved me."

Ivy looked at the cross in Ceri's hand, no emotion showing. "I'm hoping she can do the same for me."

I cringed. Ivy had pinned her sanity on the belief that there was a witch magic that might purge the vampire virus from her; that all it would take would be the right spell to let her walk away from the blood and violence. But there wasn't. I waited for Ceri to tell Ivy that no one was beyond redemption, but all she did was nod, her wispy hair floating. "I hope she can."

"Me, too." Ivy glanced at the crucifix Ceri was extending to her. "Keep it. It doesn't help anymore."

My lips parted in surprise, and Jenks landed upon my big hoop earrings as Ceri placed it about her neck. The elaborately tooled silver looked right against the rich purple and green of her formal gown. "Ivy—" I started, jerking when Ivy narrowed her eyes at me.

"It doesn't help anymore," she said tightly. "She wants it. I'm giving it to her."

Ceri reached up, clearly finding peace in the icon. "Thank you," she whispered.

Ivy frowned. "Touch my desk again, and I'll snap every one of your fingers."

Ceri took the threat with a light understanding that surprised me. It was obvious she had dealt with vampires before. I wondered where—since vampires couldn't manipulate ley lines and would therefore make lousy familiars.

"How about some tea?" I said, wanting something normal to do. Making tea wasn't normal, but it was close. The pot was steaming, and as I rummaged in a cupboard for a mug good enough for a guest, Jenks snickered, swinging my earring like a tire swing. His kids were flitting into the kitchen in twos and threes—much to Ivy's annoyance—pulled by the novelty of Ceri. They hovered over her, Jih taking the closest stance.

Ivy stood defensively before her computer, and after a moment's hesitation, Ceri sat in the chair farthest from her. She looked lost and alone as she fingered the crucifix about her neck. As I searched the pantry for a tea bag, I wondered how I was going to make this work. Ivy wasn't going to like another roommate. And where would we put her?

The accusing clatter of Ivy's pens was loud as she re-arranged her pencil cup. "Got one," I said in relief as I finally found a tea bag. Jenks left me to bother Ivy, chased off my earring by the steam drifting up as I poured the boiling water into the mug.

"Here, Ceri," I said, waving the pixies away from her and setting it on the table. "Do you want anything with it?"

She looked at the cup as if she'd never seen one before. Eyes widening, she shook her head. I hesitated, wondering what I had done wrong. She looked like she was ready to cry again. "Is it okay?" I asked, and she nodded, her thin hand shaking as she took the mug.

Jenks and Ivy were staring at her. "You sure you don't want sugar or anything?" I asked, but she shook her head. Narrow chin trembling, she brought the cup to her lips.

Brow furrowed, I went to get the coffee grounds out of the fridge. Ivy rose to rinse the carafe. She leaned close to me, running the water to blur her words as she muttered, "What's wrong with her? She's crying over her tea."

I spun. "Ceri!" I exclaimed. "If you want some sugar, it's okay!"

She met my gaze, tears streaming down her pale face. "I haven't had anything to eat for—a thousand years," she choked out.

I felt as if I had been punched in the gut. "Do you want some sugar?"

Still crying, she shook her head.

Ivy was waiting for me when I turned back around. "She can't stay here, Rachel," the vampire said, her brow tight.

"She'll be fine," I whispered, appalled that Ivy was ready to kick her out. "I'll bring my old cot down from the belfry and set it up in the living room. I've got some old T-shirts she can wear until I take her shopping."

Jenks buzzed his wings for my attention. "Then what?" he said from the spigot.

I gestured my frustration. "I don't know. She's much better already. She wasn't talking half an hour ago. Look at her now."

We all turned, finding Ceri sobbing quietly and drinking her tea in small reverent sips as the pixy girls hovered over her. Three were plating her long, fair hair and another was singing to her.

"Okay," I said as we turned back. "Bad example."

Jenks shook his head. "Rache, I really feel bad for her, but Ivy's right. She can't stay here. She needs professional help."

"Really?" I said belligerently, feeling myself warm. "I haven't heard of any group therapy sessions for retired demon familiars, have you?"

"Rachel . . ." Ivy said.

A sudden shout from the pixy children brought Jenks up from the spigot. His eyes went past us to his kids as they descended upon the mouse, who had finally made a dash for the living room and found itself in its own personal hell. "Excuse me," he said, flitting off to rescue it.

"No," I said to Ivy. "I'm not going to dump her in some institution."

"I'm not saying you should." Ivy's pale face had started to color, and the ring of brown about her eyes was shrinking as my body heat rose and my blood grew warm, triggering her instincts. "But she can't stay here. The woman needs normal, and Rachel? We aren't it."

I took a breath to protest, then let it out. Frowning, I glanced at Ceri. She was wiping her eyes, the hand curled about her mug shaking to make rings on the surface of her tea. My eyes went to the pixy children arguing over who was going to get to ride the mouse first. It was little Jessie, and the tiny pixy screamed in delight when the rodent darted out of the kitchen with her on its back. In a blur of gold sparkles, all but Jih followed. Maybe Ivy was right.

"What do you want me to do, Ivy?" I said, calming. "I'd

ask my mom to take her in, but she's a step away from being in an institution herself."

Jenks buzzed back. "What about Keasley?"

Surprised, I looked at Ivy.

"The old guy across the street?" Ivy said warily. "We don't know anything about him."

Jenks landed on the sill beside Mr. Fish and put his hands on his hips. "He's old and on a fixed income. What more is there to know?"

As Ceri collected herself, I sifted the idea through my mind. I liked the old witch whose slow speech hid a sharp wit and high intelligence. He had stitched me up after Algaliarept had torn my neck. He had stitched up my will and confidence, too. The arthritic man was hiding something, and I didn't think his real name was Keasley any more than I believed his story that he had more medical equipment than a small emergency room because he didn't like doctors. But I trusted him.

"He doesn't like the law and he knows how to keep his mouth shut," I said, thinking it was perfect. Eyes pinched, I looked at Ceri talking to Jih in soft tones. Ivy's eyes were doubtful, and peeved, I pushed into motion. "I'm calling him," I added as I motioned to Ceri that I would be right back and went into the living room for the phone.

Three

"Ceri," Jenks said as I flipped the switch and got a pot of coffee going. "If tea makes you cry, you gotta try french fries. Come here, I'll show you how to use the microwave."

Keasley was on his way over. It might take him a while since he was racked by arthritis so badly that even most pain charms wouldn't touch it. I felt bad for pulling him out into the snow, but it would have been even more rude to descend upon his house.

With an intentness I didn't understand, Jenks perched himself on Ceri's shoulder and talked her through the task of microwaving frozen french fries. She bent to watch the little carton spin, my pink slippers on her feet looking overly large and awkward. Pixy girls swirled around her in a whirl of pastel silk and chatter, mostly ignored. The unending noise had driven Ivy into the living room, where she was currently hiding with her earphones on.

My head came up when the air pressure shifted. "'Ello?" came a strong raspy voice from the front of the church. "Rachel? The pixies let me in. Where are you ladies?"

I glanced at Ceri, recognizing her sudden apprehension. "It's Keasley, a neighbor," I said. "He's going to check you over. Make sure you're healthy."

"I'm fine," she said pensively.

Thinking this might be harder than I thought, I padded in my sock feet into the hallway to talk to him before he met Ceri. "Hi, Keasley, we're back here."

His hunched, wizened figure limped down the hallway, eclipsing the light. More pixy children escorted him, wreathing him in circles of sifting pixy dust. Keasley had a brown paper grocery bag in his hand, and he brought the cold scent of snow in with him, mixing pleasantly with a witch's characteristic redwood scent. "Rachel," he said, his brown eyes squinting up at me as he got closer. "How's my favorite redhead?"

"I'm good," I said, giving him a quick hug and thinking that after outwitting Algaliarept, good was an understatement. His overalls were worn and smelling of soap. I thought of him as the neighborhood's wise-old-man and a substitute grandfather figure all in one, and I didn't mind that he had a past he wasn't willing to share. He was a good person; that's all I needed to know.

"Come on in. I have someone I want you to meet," I said, and he slowed with a wary caution. "She needs your help," I said softly.

His thick lips pressed together, and the brown wrinkles of his face deepened. Keasley took a slow breath, his arthritic hands making the grocery bag crackle. He nodded, showing me a thinning spot in his tightly curled, graying hair. Blowing in relief, I led him into the kitchen, holding myself back so I could see his reaction to Ceri.

The old witch rocked to a halt as he stared. But upon seeing the delicate woman standing in pink fuzzy slippers beside the microwave in her elegant ball gown with a folder of steaming fries, I could understand why.

"I don't need a physician," Ceri said.

Jenks rose from her shoulder. "Hi, Keasley. You gonna check Ceri out?"

Keasley nodded, limping as he went to pull out a chair. He gestured for Ceri to sit, then carefully lowered himself into the adjacent seat. Wheezing, he set his bag between his feet, opening it to pull out a blood pressure cuff. "I'm not a doctor," he said. "My name is Keasley."

Not sitting, Ceri looked at me, then him. "I'm Ceri," she said, just above a whisper.

"Well, Ceri, it's nice to meet you." Setting the cuff on the table, he extended his arthritic-swollen hand. Looking unsure, Ceri awkwardly put her hand in his. Keasley shook it, smiling to show his coffee-stained teeth. The old man gestured to the chair, and Ceri arranged herself in it, reluctantly setting her fries down and warily eyeing the cuff.

"Rachel wants me to look you over," he said while he pulled more doctor stuff out.

Ceri glanced at me, sighing as she nodded in surrender.

The coffee had finished, and as Keasley took her temperature, checked her reflexes, her blood pressure, and made her say "Ahhhh," I took a cup into the living room for Ivy. She was sitting sideways in her cushy chair with her earphones on, head on one arm, feet draped over the other. Her eyes were shut, but she reached out without looking, taking the cup the instant I set it down. "Thank you," she mouthed, and still not having seen her eyes, I walked out. Sometimes Ivy gave me the creeps.

"Coffee, Keasley?" I asked as I returned.

The old man peered at the thermometer and turned it off. "Yes, thank you." He smiled at Ceri. "You're fine."

"Thank you, sir," Ceri said. She had been eating her fries while Keasley worked, and she looked glumly at the bottom of the carton.

Immediately Jenks was with her. "More?" he prompted. "Try some ketchup on them."

Suddenly Jenks's zeal to get her to eat french fries became very clear. It wasn't the fries he was interested in, it was the ketchup. "Jenks," I said tiredly as I took Keasley his coffee and leaned against the center island counter. "She's over a thousand years old. Even humans ate tomatoes then." I hesitated. "They did have tomatoes back then, right?"

The hum of Jenks's wings audibly dropped. "Crap," he muttered, then brightened. "Go ahead," he said to Ceri. "You try working the nuker this time without my help."

"Nuker?" she questioned, carefully wiping her hands on a napkin as she stood.

"Yeah. Don't they have microwaves in the ever-after?"

She shook her head, sending the tips of her fair hair floating. "No. I prepared Al's food with ley line magic. This is . . . old."

Keasley jerked, almost spilling his coffee. His eyes tracked Ceri's grace as she went to the freezer and, with Jenks's encouragement, pulled out a box of fries. She meticulously punched the buttons, her lip caught between her teeth. I thought it odd that the woman was over a thousand years old but thought the microwave was primitive.

"The ever-after?" Keasley said softly, and my attention returned to him.

I held my coffee before me with both hands, warming my fingers. "How is she?"

He shifted his shoulders. "She's healthy enough. Maybe a little underweight. Mentally she's been abused. I can't tell what or how. She needs help."

I took a deep breath, looking down into my cup. "I've got a big favor to ask."

Keasley straightened. "No," he said as he put his bag on his lap and started putting things in it. "I don't know who—or even what—she is."

"I stole her from the demon whose work you stitched up last fall," I said, touching my neck. "She was its—I mean, his—familiar. I'll pay for her room and board."

"That isn't it," he protested. Bag in hand, his tired brown eyes went worried. "I don't know anything about her, Rachel. I can't risk taking her in. Don't ask me to do this."

I leaned over the space between us, almost angry. "She has been in the ever-after the last millennium. I don't think she's out to kill you," I accused, and his leathery features shifted to a startled alarm. "All she needs," I said, flustered that I had found one of his fears, "is a normal setting where she can regain her personality. And a witch, a vampire, and a pixy living in a church running down bad guys isn't normal."

Jenks looked at us from Ceri's shoulder as the woman watched her fries warm. The pixy's face was serious; he could hear the conversation as clearly as if he was standing on the table. Ceri asked him a soft question, and he turned away, answering her cheerfully. He had chased all but Jih out of the kitchen, and it was blessedly quiet.

"Please, Keasley?" I whispered.

Jih's ethereal voice rose in song, and Ceri's face lit up. She joined in, her voice clear as the pixy's, managing only three notes before she started to cry. I stared as a cloud of pixies rolled into the kitchen, almost smothering her. From the living room came an irate shout as Ivy complained that the pixies were interfering with the stereo reception again.

Jenks yelled at his kids and all but Jih flitted out. Together they consoled Ceri, Jih soft and soothing, Jenks somewhat awkwardly. Keasley slumped, and I knew he'd do it. "Okay," he said. "I'll try it for a few days, but if it doesn't work, she's coming back."

"Fair enough," I said, feeling a huge weight slip off my chest.

Ceri looked up, her eyes still wet. "You didn't ask me my opinion."

My eyes widened and my face flamed. Her hearing was as good as Ivy's. "Um . . ." I stammered. "I'm sorry, Ceri. It's not that I don't want you to stay here—"

Heart-shaped face solemn, she nodded. "I am a stumbling stone in a fortress of soldiers," she interrupted. "I'd be honored to stay with the retired warrior and ease his hurts."

Retired warrior? I thought, wondering what she saw in Keasley that I didn't. In the corner came a high-pitched argument between Jenks and his eldest daughter. The young pixy was wringing the hem of her pale green dress, her tiny feet showing as she pleaded with him.

"Now wait a moment," Keasley said, curling the top of his

paper bag down. "I can take care of myself. I don't need anyone 'easing my hurts.'"

Ceri smiled. My slippers on her feet made a hush across the linoleum as she came to kneel before him. "Ceri," I protested, right along with Keasley, but the young woman batted our hands away, the suddenly sharp look in her green eyes brooking no interference.

"Get up," Keasley said gruffly as he sat before her. "I know you were a demon's familiar and this might be how he made you act, but—"

"Be still, Keasley," Ceri said, a faint glow of ever-after red blurring her pale hands. "I want to go with you, but only if you let me return your kindness." She smiled up at him, her green eyes losing their focus. "It will give me a feeling of self-worth I truly need."

My breath caught as I felt her tap the ley line out back. "Keasley?" I said, my voice high.

His brown eyes went wide and he froze where he sat as Ceri reached out and placed her hands upon the knees of his work-faded overalls. I watched his face go slack, the wrinkles sliding into themselves to make him look older. He took a deep breath, stiffening.

Kneeling before him, Ceri shivered. Her hands dropped from him. "Ceri," Keasley said, his raspy voice cracking. He touched his knees. "It's gone," he whispered, his tired eyes going watery. "Oh, dear child," he said, standing to help her rise. "I haven't been without pain for so long. Thank you."

Ceri smiled, tears leaking out as she nodded. "Neither have I. This helps."

I turned away, my throat tight. "I have some T-shirts you can wear until I take you shopping," I said. "Just keep my slippers. They'll get you across the street at least."

Keasley took her arm in one hand, his bag in the other. "I'll take her shopping tomorrow," he said as he headed for the hallway. "I haven't felt good enough to go to the mall in three years. It will do me good to get out." He turned to me, his old, wrinkled face transformed. "I'll send the bill to you, though. I can tell everyone she is my sister's niece. From Sweden."

I laughed, finding it was very close to a cry. This was working out better than I had hoped, and I couldn't stop smiling.

Jenks made a sharp noise, and his daughter slowly drooped to land upon the microwave. "All right, I'll ask!" he shouted, and she rose three inches, her face hopeful and her hands clasped before her. "If it's okay with your mother and it's okay with Keasley, it's okay with me," Jenks said, his wings a dismal blue.

Jih rose and fell in obvious nervousness as Jenks hovered before Keasley. "Um, do you have any plants at your house that Jih might tend?" he asked, looking terribly embarrassed. Brushing his blond hair from his eyes, he made a wry face. "She wants to go with Ceri, but I'm not letting her leave unless she can be productive."

My lips parted. I sent my eyes to Ceri, seeing by her held breath that she clearly wanted the company. "I've got a pot of basil," Keasley said reluctantly. "If she wants to stay when the weather breaks, she can work the garden, such as it is."

Jih squealed, pixy dust falling from her in a gold shimmer that turned to white.

"Ask your mother!" Jenks said, looking upset as the excited pixy girl zipped out. He landed on my shoulder, wings drooping. I thought I could smell autumn. Before I could ask Jenks, a shrill tide of pink and green flowed into the kitchen. Appalled, I wondered if there was a pixy in the church that wasn't in that four-foot circle surrounding Ceri.

Keasley's wrinkled face was filled with a stoic acceptance as he unrolled the bag of supplies and Jih dropped inside to make the trip safe from the cold. Above the crinkled top of the bag, the pixies all cried good-bye and waved.

Eyes rolling, Keasley handed the bag to Ceri. "Pixies," I heard him mutter. Taking Ceri's elbow, he nodded to me and headed into the hall, his pace faster and more upright than

I'd ever seen it. "I have a second bedroom," he said. "Do you sleep at night or during the day?"

"Both," she said softly. "Is that all right?"

He grinned to show his coffee-stained teeth. "A napper, eh? Good. I won't feel so old when I drop off."

I felt happy as I watched them head to the sanctuary. This was going to be good in so many ways. "What's the matter, Jenks?" I said as he remained on my shoulder while the rest of his family accompanied Ceri and Keasley to the front of the church.

He sniffed. "I thought Jax would be the first one to leave to start his own garden."

My breath slipped from me in understanding. "I'm sorry, Jenks. She'll be fine."

"I know, I know." His wings shifted into motion, sending the scent of fallen leaves over me. "One less pixy in the church," he said softly. "It's a good thing. But no one told me it was going to hurt."

Four

Squinting over my sunglasses, I leaned against my car and scanned the parking lot. My cherry red convertible looked out of place among the scattering of minivans and salt-rusted, late model cars. At the back, away from potential scratches and dings, was a low-to-the-ground, gray sports car. Probably the zoo's p.r. person, as everyone else was either a part-time worker or a dedicated biologist who didn't care what they drove.

The early hour made it cold despite the sun, and my breath steamed. I tried to relax, but I could feel my gut tightening as my annoyance grew. Nick was supposed to meet me here this morning for a quick run in the zoo. It looked like he was going to be a no-show. Again.

I uncrossed my arms from in front of me and shook my hands to loosen them before I bent at the waist and put my palms against the ice-cold, snow-dusted parking lot. Exhaling into the stretch, I felt my muscles pull. Around me were the soft, familiar sounds of the zoo preparing to open, mixing with the scent of exotic manure. If Nick didn't show in the next five minutes, there wouldn't be enough time for a decent run.

I had bought us both runner passes months ago so we could run anytime from midnight to noon when the park was closed. I had woken up two hours earlier than usual for this. I was trying to make this work; I was trying to find a way to mesh my witch's noon-to-sunup schedule with Nick's human sunrise-to-midnight clock. It had never seemed to be a problem before. Nick used to try. Lately, it had been all up to me.

A harsh scraping pulled me upright. The trash cans were being rolled out, and my pique grew. Where was he? He couldn't have forgotten. Nick never forgot anything.

"Unless he wants to forget," I whispered. Giving myself a mental shake, I swung my right leg up to put my lightweight running shoe atop the hood. "Ow," I breathed as my muscles protested, but I leaned into it. I'd been slacking off on my workouts lately, as Ivy and I didn't spar anymore since she had resumed succumbing to her blood lust. My eye started to twitch, and I closed both of them as I deepened the stretch, grabbing my ankle and pulling.

Nick hadn't forgotten—he was too smart for that—he was avoiding me. I knew why, but it was still depressing. It had been three months, and he was still distant and hesitant. The worst thing was I didn't think he was dumping me. The man called demons into his linen closet, and he was afraid to touch me.

Last fall, I had been trying to bind a fish to me to satisfy some inane ley line class requirement and accidentally made Nick my familiar instead. Stupid, stupid, stupid.

I was an earth witch, my magic coming from growing things and quickened by heat and my blood. I didn't know much about ley line magic—except I didn't like it. I generally only used it to close protective circles when I was stirring a particularly sensitive spell. And to make the Howlers pay what they owed me. And occasionally to fend off my roommate when she lost control of her blood lust. And I had used it to knock Piscary flat on his can so I could beat him into submission with the leg of a chair. It had been this last one that tipped Nick from hot-and-heavy, maybe-this-is-the-one boyfriend, to phone conversations and cold kisses on my cheek.

Starting to feel sorry for myself, I pulled my right leg down and swung the left one up.

Ley line magic was heady in its rush of strength and could drive a witch insane, making it no accident that there were more black ley line witches than black earth witches. Using a familiar made it safer since the power of a ley line was filtered through the simpler minds of animals instead of through plants as earth magic did. For obvious reasons, only animals were used as familiars—at least on this side of the ley lines—and in truth, there were no witch-born spells to bind a human as a familiar. But being both fairly ignorant of ley line magic and rushed, I had used the first spell I found to bind a familiar.

So I had unknowingly made Nick my familiar—which we were trying to undo—but then I made things immeasurably worse by pulling a huge amount of ley line energy through him to subdue Piscary. He had hardly touched me since. But that had been months ago. I hadn't done it again. He had to get over it. It wasn't as if I was practicing ley line magic. Much.

Uneasy, I straightened, blowing out my angst and doing a few side twists to send my ponytail bouncing. After having learned it was possible to set a circle without drawing it first, I had spent three months learning how, knowing it might be my only chance to escape Algaliarept. I had kept my practice to three in the morning, when I knew Nick was asleep—and I always drew directly off the line so it wouldn't go through Nick first—but maybe it was waking him up anyway. He hadn't said anything, but knowing Nick, he wouldn't.

The rattle of the gate opening brought me to a standstill and my shoulders slumped. The zoo was open, a few runners straggling out with red cheeks and exhausted, content expressions, still floating on a runner's high. *Damn it. He could have called.*

Bothered, I unzipped my belt pack and pulled out my cell phone. Leaning against the car and looking down to avoid the eyes of the passing people, I scrolled through my short list. Nick's was second, right after Ivy's number and right before my mom's. My fingers were cold, and I blew on them as the phone rang.

I took a breath when the connection clicked open, holding it when a recorded woman's voice told me the line was no longer in service. *Money?* I thought. Maybe that was why we hadn't been out for three weeks. Concerned, I tried his cell phone.

It was still ringing when the familiar choking rumble of Nick's truck grew loud. Exhaling, I snapped the cover closed. Nick's blue, beat-up Ford truck jostled off the main street and into the parking lot, maneuvering slowly, as the cars leaving were ignoring the lines and cutting across the expanse. I slipped the phone away and stood with my arms over my chest, legs crossed at my ankles.

At least he showed, I thought as I adjusted my sunglasses and tried not to frown. Maybe we could go out for coffee or something. I hadn't seen him in days, and I didn't want to ruin it with a bad temper. Besides, I had been worried sick the last three months about slipping my bargain with Al, and now that I had, I wanted to feel good for a while.

I hadn't told Nick, and the chance to come clean would be another weight off me. I lied to myself that I had kept quiet because I was afraid he would try to take my burden— seeing as he had a chivalrous streak longer and wider than a six-lane highway—but in reality I was afraid he would call me a hypocrite since I was forever on him about the dangers of dealing with demons, and here I was, becoming one's familiar. Nick had an unhealthy lack of fear when it came to demons, thinking that as long as you handled them properly, they were no more dangerous than say . . . a pit viper.

So I stood and fidgeted in the cold as he parked his salt-stained, ugly truck a few slots down from mine. His indistinct shadow moved inside as he shuffled about, finally getting out and slamming the door with an intensity that I knew wasn't directed at me but necessary to get the worn latch to catch.

"Ray-ray," he said as he held his phone up and strode

around the front. His lean height looked good and his pace was quick. A smile was on his face, its once-gauntness muted into a pleasant, rugged severity. "Did you just call?"

I nodded, letting my arms fall to my sides. Obviously he wasn't prepared to run, as he was dressed in faded jeans and boots. A thick fabric coat was unzipped to show a bland, flannel button-down shirt. It was neatly tucked in and his long face was clean-shaven, but he still managed to look mildly unkempt, with his short black hair a shade too long. He had a bookish mien instead of the hint of danger that I usually liked in my men. But maybe I found Nick's danger to be his intelligence.

Nick was the smartest man I knew, his brilliant jumps of logic hidden behind an understated appearance and a deceptively mild temperament. In hindsight, it was probably this rare mix of wicked intellect and harmless human that attracted me to him. Or possibly that he had saved my life by binding Big Al when he tried to rip out my throat.

And despite Nick's preoccupation with old books and new electronics, he wasn't a geek: his shoulders were too broad and his butt was too tight. His long, lean legs could keep up with me when we ran, and there was a surprising amount of strength in his arms, as evidenced by our once frequent, now distressingly absent, mock wrestling, which more often than not had turned into a more, er, intimate activity. It was the memory of our once-closeness that kept the frown off my face when he came around the front of his truck, his brown eyes pinched in apology.

"I didn't forget," he said, his long face looking longer as he tossed his straight bangs out of his way. There was a flash of a demon mark high on his brow, gained the same night I had gotten my first and remaining one. "I got caught up in what I was doing and lost track of time. I'm sorry, Rachel. I know you were looking forward to it, but I haven't even been to bed and I'm dead tired. Do you want to reschedule for tomorrow?"

I kept my reaction to a sigh, trying to stifle my disappointment. "No," I said around a long exhalation. He reached out, his arms going around me in a light hug. I leaned into the expected hesitancy of it, wanting more. The distance had been there so long that it almost felt normal. Pulling back, he shuffled his feet.

"Working hard?" I offered. This was the first time I had seen him in a week, not including the odd phone call, and I didn't just want to walk away.

Nick, too, didn't seem eager to leave. "Yes and no." He squinted into the sun. "I was up sifting through old messages on a chat-room list after finding a mention of that book Al took."

Immediately my attention sharpened. "Did you . . ." I stammered, pulse quickening.

My quick hope squished to nothing as he dropped his gaze and shook his head. "It was some freak wannabe. He doesn't have a copy. It was all made-up nonsense."

I reached out and briefly touched his arm, forgiving him for missing our morning run. "It's okay. We'll find something sooner or later."

"Yeah," he muttered. "But I'd rather it be sooner."

Misery hit me, and I froze. We had been so good together, and now all that was left was this awful distance. Seeing my depression, Nick took my hands, stepping forward to give me a loose embrace. His lips brushed my cheek as he whispered, "I'm sorry, Ray-ray. We'll manage something. I'm trying. I want this to work."

I didn't move, breathing in the smell of musty books and clean aftershave, my hands hesitantly going about him as I looked for comfort—and finally found it.

My breath caught and I held it, refusing to cry. We had been months searching for the counter curse, but Al wrote the book on how to make humans into familiars, and he had a very short print run of one. And it wasn't as if we could advertise in the papers for a ley line professor to help us, as he or she would likely turn me in for dealing in the black arts. And then I'd really be stuck. Or dead. Or worse.

Slowly Nick let go, and I stepped back. At least I knew it wasn't another woman.

"Hey, uh, the zoo is open," I said, my voice giving away my relief that the awkward distance he had been holding himself at finally seemed to be easing. "You want to go in and get a coffee instead? I hear their Monkey Mocha is to come back from the dead for."

"No," he said, but there was true regret in his voice, making me wonder if he had been picking up on my worry about Al all this time, thinking I was upset with him and drawing away. Maybe more of this was my fault than I had guessed. Maybe I could have forged a stronger union between us if I had told him instead of hiding it from him and driving him away.

The magnitude of what I might have done with my silence fell on me, and I felt my face go cold. "Nick, I'm sorry," I breathed.

"It wasn't your fault," he said, his brown eyes full of forgiveness, unaware of my thoughts. "I was the one that told him he could have the book."

"No, you see—"

He took me in a hug, silencing me. A lump formed in my throat, and I couldn't say anything as my forehead dropped to his shoulder. I should have told him. I should have told him right from the first night.

Nick felt the shift in me, and slowly, after a moment's thought, he gave me a tentative kiss on the cheek, but it was a tentativeness born from his long absence, not his usual hesitancy.

"Nick?" I said, hearing the coming tears in my voice.

Immediately he pulled back. "Hey," he said, smiling as his long hand rested on my shoulder. "I've got to go. I've been up since yesterday and I have to get some sleep."

I took a reluctant step back, hoping he couldn't tell how close to tears I was. It had been a long, lonely three months. At last something seemed to be mending. "Okay. You want to come over for dinner tonight?"

And finally, after weeks of quick refusals, he paused. "How about a movie and dinner instead? My treat. A real date . . . thing."

I straightened, feeling myself grow taller. "A date thing," I said, moving awkwardly foot-to-foot like a fool teenager asked to her first dance. "What do you have in mind?"

He smiled softly. "Something with lots of explosions, lots of guns . . ." He didn't touch me, but I saw in his eyes his desire to do so. ". . . tight costumes . . ."

I nodded, smiling, and he checked his watch.

"Tonight," he said, catching my eye as he headed back to his truck. "Seven o'clock?"

"Seven o'clock," I called back, my good feeling growing. He got in, the truck shaking as he slammed the door. The engine rumbled to life, and with a happy wave, he drove away.

"Seven o'clock," I said, watching the taillights flash before he jostled onto the street.

Five

Plastic hangers clattering, I stacked the clothes on the counter beside the cash register. The bored, bottle-dyed blonde with ear-length hair never looked up as her fingers manipulated those nasty metal clips. Gum snapping, she pointed her gun at everything, adding up my purchases for Ceri. She had a phone to her ear, head cocked, and her mouth never stopped as she chatted to her boyfriend about getting her roommate fried on Brimstone last night.

I eyed her in speculation, breathing in the fading aroma of the street drug lingering on her. She was dumber than she looked if she was dabbling in Brimstone, especially now. It had been coming in cut with a little something extra lately, leaving a rash of deaths spanning all the socioeconomic brackets. Maybe it was Trent's idea of a Christmas present.

The girl before me looked underage, so I could either sic Health and Inderland Services on her or haul her ass down to the I.S. lockup. The latter might be fun, but it would put a real crimp in my afternoon of solstice shopping. I still didn't know what to get Ivy. The boots, jeans, socks, underwear, and two sweaters on the counter were for Ceri. She was not going out with Keasley dressed in one of my T-shirts and pink fuzzy slippers.

The girl folded the last sweater, her bloodred manicure garish. Amulets clanked about her neck, but the complexion charm hiding her acne needed to be replaced. She must have been a warlock because a witch wouldn't be caught dead with a bass-ackward charm like that. I glanced at my wooden pinky ring. It might be small, but it was now potent enough to hide my freckles through a minor spell check. *Hack,* I thought, feeling vastly better.

A hum rose from nowhere, and I felt smug that I didn't jump like the register girl when Jenks all but fell onto the counter. He was wearing two black body stockings, one atop the other, and had a red hat and boots on against the chill. It was really too cold for him to be out, but Jih's leaving had depressed him, and he'd never been solstice shopping before. My eyes widened as I took in the doll he had lugged to the counter. It was three times his size.

"Rache!" he exclaimed, puffing as he pushed the black-haired, curvaceous plastic homage to adolescent boys' dreams upright. "Look what I found! It was in the toy department."

"Jenks . . ." I cajoled, hearing the couple behind me snicker.

"It's a Bite-me-Betty doll!" he exclaimed, his wings moving furiously to keep himself upright, his hands on the doll's thighs. "I want it. I want to get it for Ivy. It looks just like her."

Eyeing the shiny plastic leather skirt and red vinyl bustier, I took a breath to protest.

"Look, see?" he said, his voice excited. "You push the lever in her back, and fake blood squirts out. Isn't it great!"

I started when a gelatinous goo jumped from the blank-eyed doll's mouth, arching a good foot before hitting the counter. A red smear dripped down her pointy chin. The register girl eyed it, then hung up on her boyfriend. *He wanted to give this to Ivy?*

Pushing Ceri's jeans out of the way, I sighed. Jenks hit the lever again, watching in rapt attention as red squirted out with a rude sound. The couple behind me laughed, the woman hanging on his arm and whispering in his ear. Warming, I grabbed the doll. "I'll buy it for you if you stop that," I all but hissed.

Eyes bright, Jenks rose up to land on my shoulder, tucking in between my neck and my scarf to stay warm. "She's gonna love it," he said. "You watch."

Pushing it at the girl behind the counter, I glanced behind me at the tittering couple. They were living vamps, well-dressed and unable to go thirty seconds without touching each other. Knowing I was watching, the woman straightened the collar of his leather jacket to show off his lightly scarred neck. The thought of Nick brought a smile to me, the first time in weeks.

As the girl recalculated my total, I dug in my bag for my checkbook. It was nice having money. Real nice.

"Rache," Jenks questioned, "can you put a bag of M&M's in there, too?" His wings sent a cold draft against my neck as he set them vibrating to generate some body heat. It wasn't as if he could wear a coat—not with those wings of his—and anything heavy was too limiting.

I snatched up a bag of overpriced candy whose hand-lettered cardboard sign said the sale would go to help rebuild the fire-damaged city shelters. I already had my total, but she could add it on. And if the vamps behind me had a problem with that, they could curl up and die twice. It was for orphans, for God's sake.

The girl reached for the candy and beeped it, giving me a snotty look. The register chirped to give me the new total, and as they all waited, I flipped to the check register. Freezing, I blinked. It had been balanced with neat tidy numbers. I hadn't bothered to keep a running total as I knew there was tons of money in it, but someone had. Then I brought it closer, staring. "That's it?" I exclaimed. "That's all I have left?"

Jenks cleared his throat. "Surprise," he said weakly. "It was just laying there in your desk, and I thought I'd balance it for you." He hesitated. "Sorry."

"It's almost gone!" I stammered, my face probably as red as my hair. The eyes of the register girl were suddenly wary.

Embarrassed, I finished writing out the check. She took it,

calling her supervisor to run it through their system to make sure it was good. Behind me, the vamp couple started in with a snarky commentary. Ignoring them, I flipped through the check register to see where it went.

Almost two grand for my new desk and bedroom set, four more for insulating the church, and $3,500 for a garage for my new car; I wasn't about to let it sit out in the snow. Then there was the insurance and gas. A big chunk went to Ivy for my back rent. Another chunk went to my night in the emergency room for my broken arm as I hadn't had insurance at the time. A third chunk to *get* insurance. And the rest . . . I swallowed hard. There was money still in there, but I had enjoyed myself down from twenty thousand to high four figures in only three months.

"Um, Rache?" Jenks said. "I was going to ask you later, but I know this accounting guy. You want me to have him set up an IRA for you? I was looking at your finances, and you might need a shelter this year, seeing as you haven't been taking anything out for taxes."

"A tax shelter?" I felt sick. "There's nothing left to put into it." Taking my bags from the girl, I headed for the door. "And what are you doing looking at my finances?"

"I'm living in your desk," he said wryly. "It's kind of all out there?"

I sighed. My desk. My beautiful solid-oak desk with nooks and crannies and a secret cubby at the bottom of the left-hand drawer. My desk that I had used for only three weeks before Jenks and his brood moved into it. My desk, which was now so thickly covered in potted plants that it looked like a prop for a horror movie about killer plants taking over the world. But it was either that or have them set up housekeeping in the kitchen cupboards. No. Not my kitchen. Having them stage daily mock battles among the hanging pots and utensils was bad enough.

Distracted, I tugged my coat closer and squinted at the bright light reflecting off the snow as the sliding doors opened. "Whoa, wait up!" Jenks shrilled in my ear when the blast of cold air hit us. "What the hell do you think you're doing, witch? Do I look like I'm made of fur?"

"Sorry." I made a quick left turn to get out of the draft and opened my shoulder bag for him. Still swearing, he dropped down to hide inside. He hated it, but there was no alternative. A sustained temp lower than forty-five degrees would throw him into a hibernation that would be unsafe to break until spring, but he should be all right in my bag.

A Were dressed in a thick wool coat that went to his boot tops edged from me with an uncomfortable look. When I tried to make eye contact, he pulled his cowboy hat down and turned away. A frown crossed me; I hadn't had a Were client since I made the Howlers pay me for trying to get their mascot back. Maybe I'd made a mistake there.

"Hey, give me those M&M's, okay?" Jenks grumbled up at me, his short blond hair framing delicate features reddened by the cold. "I'm starving here."

I obediently shuffled through the bags and dropped the candy in to him before pulling the ties to my shoulder bag shut. I didn't like bringing him out like this, but I was his partner, not his mom. He enjoyed being the only adult male pixy in Cincinnati not in a stupor. In his eyes, the entire city was probably his garden, as cold and snowy as it was.

I took a moment to dig my zebra-striped car key out from the front pocket. The couple that had been behind me in line passed me on their way out, flirting comfortably and looking like sex in leather. He had bought her a Bite-me-Betty doll, too, and they were laughing. My thoughts went to Nick again, and a warm stir of anticipation took me.

Putting my shades on against the glare, I went out to the sidewalk, keys jingling and bag held tight to me. Even making the trip in my bag, Jenks was going to get cold. I told myself I should make cookies so he could bask in the heat of the cooling oven. It had been ages since I'd made solstice cookies. I was sure I had seen some flour-smeared cookie cutters in a nasty zippy bag at the back of a cupboard somewhere. All I needed was the colored sugar to do it right.

My mood brightened at the sight of my car ankle-deep in crusty slush at the curb. Yeah, it was as expensive as a vampire princess to maintain, but it was mine and I looked really good sitting behind the wheel with the top down and the wind pulling my long hair back. . . . Not springing for the garage hadn't been an option.

It chirped happily at me as I unlocked it and dropped my bags in the unusable backseat. I folded myself into the front, setting Jenks carefully on my lap, where he might stay a little warmer. The heat went on full-bore as soon as I got the engine started. I tunked it into gear and was ready to pull out when a long white car slid up alongside in a slow hush of sound.

Affronted, I glared as it double-parked to block me in. "Hey!" I exclaimed when the driver got out in the middle of the freaking road to open the door for his employer. Ticked, I jammed it into neutral, got out of my car and jerked my bag farther up my shoulder. "Hey! I'm trying to leave here!" I shouted, wanting to bang on the roof of the car.

But my protests choked to nothing when the side door opened and an older man wearing scads of gold necklaces stuck his head out. His frizzed blond hair went out in all directions. Blue eyes glinting in suppressed excitement, he beckoned to me. "Ms. Morgan," he exclaimed softly. "Can I talk to you?"

I took my sunglasses off, staring. "Takata?" I stammered.

The older rocker winced, his face sliding into faint wrinkles as he glanced over the few pedestrians. They had noticed the limo, and with my outburst, the jig, as they say, was up. Eyes pinched in exasperation, Takata stretched out a long skinny hand, jerking me off my feet and into the limo. I gasped, holding my bag so I didn't squish Jenks as I fell into the plush seat across from him. "Go!" the musician cried, and the driver shut the door and jogged to the front.

"My car!" I protested. My door was open and my keys were in the ignition.

"Arron?" Takata said, gesturing to a man in a black T-shirt

tucked into a corner of the expansive vehicle. He slipped past me in a tang of blood that pegged him as a vamp. There was a flush of cold air as he got out, quickly thumping the door shut behind him. I watched through the tinted window as he slipped into my leather seats to look predatory with his shaved head and dark shades. I only hoped I looked half that good. The muffled sound of my engine revved twice, then we jerked into motion as the first of the groupies started patting the windows.

Heart pounding, I spun to look out the back window while we pulled away. My car was edging carefully past the people standing in the road shouting at us to come back. It worked its way into the clear, quickly catching up and running a red light to stay with us.

Stunned at how fast it had been, I turned.

The aging pop star was wearing outlandish orange slacks. He had a matching vest over a soothing earth-toned shirt. Everything was silk, which I thought was his only saving grace. God help him, even his shoes were orange. And socks. I winced. It kind of went with the gold chains and blond hair, which had been teased out until it was so big it could frighten small children. His complexion was whiter than mine, and I dearly wanted to pull out the wood-framed glasses that I had spelled to see through earth charms to know if he had hidden freckles.

"Uh, hi?" I stammered, and the man grinned, showing his impulsive, wickedly intelligent demeanor, and his tendency to find the fun in everything even if the world was falling apart around him. Actually, the innovated artist had done just that, his garage band making the jump to stardom during the Turn, capitalizing on the opportunity to be the first openly Inderland band. He was a Cincy hometown boy who had made good, and he returned the favor by donating the proceeds of his winter solstice concerts to the city's charities. It was particularly important this year, as a series of arson fires had decimated many of the homeless shelters and orphanages.

"Ms. Morgan," the man said, touching the side of his big nose. His attention went over my shoulder and out the back window. "Hope I didn't startle you."

His voice was deep and carefully schooled. Beautiful. I was a sucker for beautiful voices. "Um, no." Setting my shades aside, I unwound my scarf. "How are you doing? Your hair looks . . . great."

He laughed, easing my nervousness. We had met five years ago and had coffee over a conversation centering on the trials of curly hair. That he not only remembered me but also wanted to talk was flattering. "It looks like hell," he said, touching the long frizz that had been in dreadlocks when we last met. "But my p.r. woman says it ups my sales by two percent." He stretched his long legs out to take up almost the entirety of one side of the limo.

I smiled. "You need another charm to tame it?" I said, reaching for my bag.

My breath caught in alarm. "Jenks!" I exclaimed, jerking the bag open.

Jenks came boiling out. "About time you remembered me!" he snarled. "What the Turn is going on? I nearly snapped my wing falling onto your phone. You got M&M's all over your purse, and I'll be dammed before I pick them up. Where in Tink's garden are we?"

I smiled weakly at Takata. "Ah, Takata," I started, "this is—"

Jenks caught sight of him. A burst of pixy dust exploded, lighting the car for an instant and making me jump. "Holy crap!" the pixy exclaimed. "You're Takata! I thought Rachel was pissing on my daisies about knowing you. Sweet mother of Tink! Wait until I tell Matalina! It's really you. Damn, it's really you!"

Takata reached over and adjusted a knob on an elaborate console, and heat poured out of the vents. "Yeah, it's really me. Do you want an autograph?"

"Hell, yes!" the pixy said. "No one will believe me."

I smiled, settling myself farther into the seat, my fluster

vanishing at Jenks's star fawning. Takata tugged a picture of him and his band standing before the Great Wall of China from a dog-eared folder. "Who do I make it out to?" he said, and Jenks froze.

"Uh . . ." he stammered, his hovering wings going still. I shot my hand out to catch him, and his featherlight weight hit my palm. "Um . . ." he stuttered, panicking.

"Make it out to Jenks," I said, and Jenks made a tiny sound of relief.

"Yeah, Jenks," the pixy said, finding the presence of mind to flit over to stand on the photo as Takata signed it with an illegible signature. "My name is Jenks."

Takata handed me the picture to carry home for him. "Pleasure to meet you, Jenks."

"Yeah," Jenks squeaked. "Nice to meet you, too." Making another impossibly high noise to get my eyelids aching, he darted from me to Takata like an insane firefly.

"Park it, Jenks," I breathed, knowing the pixy could hear me even if Takata couldn't.

"My name is Jenks," he said as he lit atop my shoulder, quivering when I carefully put the photo in my bag. His wings couldn't stay still, and the come-and-go draft felt good in the stifling air of the limo.

I returned my gaze to Takata, taken aback at the empty look on his face. "What?" I asked, thinking something was wrong.

Immediately he straightened. "Nothing," he said. "I heard you quit the I.S. to go out on your own." He blew his air out in a long exhalation. "That took guts."

"It was stupid," I admitted, thinking of the death threat my past employer had set on me in retaliation. "Though I wouldn't change a thing."

He smiled, looking satisfied. "You like being on your own?"

"It's hard without a corporation backing you," I said, "but I've got people to catch me if I fall. I trust them over the I.S. any day."

Takata's head bobbed to make his long hair shift. "I'm with you on that." His feet were spread wide against the car's motion, and I was starting to wonder why I was sitting in Takata's limo. Not that I was complaining. We were on the expressway, looping about the city, my convertible trailing three car lengths behind.

"As long as you're here," he said suddenly, "I want your opinion on something."

"Sure," I said, thinking his mind jumped from topic to topic worse than Nick's. I loosened the tie on my coat. It was starting to get warm in there.

"Capital," he said, flipping open the guitar case beside him and pulling a beautiful instrument from the crushed green velvet. My eyes widened. "I'm going to release a new track at the solstice concert." He hesitated. "You did know I was playing at the Coliseum?"

"I've got tickets," I said, my flash of excitement growing. Nick had bought them. I had been worried he was going to cancel on me and I'd end up going to Fountain Square for the solstice as I usually did, putting my name in the lottery to close the ceremonial circle there. The large, inlaid circle had a "permit only" use status except for the solstices and Halloween. But now I had a feeling we would be spending our solstice together.

"Great!" Takata said. "I was hoping you would. Well, I have this piece about a vampire pining after someone he can't have, and I don't know which chorus works the best. Ripley likes the darker one, but Arron says the other fits better."

He sighed, showing an unusual bother. Ripley was his Were drummer, the only band member to have been with Takata for most of his career. It was said she was the reason everyone else only lasted a year or two before striking out on their own.

"I had planned on singing it live the first time on the solstice," Takata said. "But I want to release it to WVMP tonight to give Cincinnati a chance to hear it first." He grinned, to look years younger. "It's more of a high when they sing along."

He glanced at the guitar in his lap and strummed a chord. The vibration filled the car. My shoulders slumped, and Jenks made a choking gurgle. Takata looked up, his eyes wide in question. "You'll tell me which one you like better?" he asked, and I nodded. My own personal concert? Yeah, I could go for that. Jenks made that choking gurgle again.

"Okay. It's called 'Red Ribbons.'" Taking a breath, Takata slumped. Eyes vacant, he modified the chord he had been playing. His thin fingers shifted elegantly, and with his head bent over his music, he sang.

"Hear you sing through the curtain, see you smile through the glass. Wipe your tears in my thoughts, no amends for the past. Didn't know it would consume me, no one said the hurt would last." His voice dropped and took on the tortured sound that had made him famous. "No one told me. No one told me," he finished, almost whispering.

"Ooooh, nice," I said, wondering if he really thought I was capable of making a judgment.

He flashed me a smile, throwing off his stage presence that quickly. "Okay," he said, hunching over his guitar again. "This is the other one." He played a darker chord, sounding almost wrong. A shudder rippled its way up my spine, and I stifled it. Takata's posture shifted, becoming fraught with pain. The vibrating strings seemed to echo through me, and I sank back into the leather seats, the humming of the engine carrying the music right to my core.

"You're mine," he almost breathed, "in some small fashion. You're mine, though you know it not. You're mine, bond born of passion. You're mine, yet wholly you. By way of your will, by way of your will, by way of your will."

His eyes were closed, and I didn't think he remembered I was sitting across from him. "Um . . ." I stammered, and his blue eyes flashed open, looking almost panicked. "I think the first one?" I offered as he regained his composure. The man was more flighty than a drawer full of geckos. "I like the sec-

ond better, but the first fits with the vampire watching what
she can't have." I blinked. "What *he* can't have," I amended,
flushing.

God help me, I must look like a fool. He probably knew I
roomed with a vampire. That she and I weren't sharing
blood probably hadn't made it into his report. The scar on
my neck wasn't from her but from Big Al, and I tugged my
scarf up to hide it.

He looked almost shaky as he put his guitar aside. "The
first?" he questioned, seeming to want to say something
else, and I nodded. "Okay," he said, forcing a smile. "The
first it is."

There was another choked gurgle from Jenks. I wondered
if he would recover enough to make more than that ugly
sound.

Takata snapped the latches on his instrument case, and I
knew the chitchat was over. "Ms. Morgan," he said, the rich
confines of the limo seeming sterile now that it was empty of
his music. "I wish I could say I looked you up for your opinion on which chorus I should release, but I find myself in a
tight spot, and you were recommended to me by a trusted associate. Mr. Felps said he has worked with you before and
that you had the utmost discretion."

"Call me Rachel," I said. The man was twice my age.
Making him call me Ms. Morgan was ridiculous.

"Rachel," he said as Jenks choked again. Takata gave me
an uncertain smile, and I returned it, not sure what was going on. It sounded like he had a run for me. Something that
required the anonymity that the I.S. or the FIB couldn't
provide.

As Jenks gurgled and pinched the rim of my ear, I
straightened, crossed my knees, and pulled my little datebook out of my bag to try to look professional. Ivy had
bought it for me two months ago in one of her attempts to
bring order to my chaotic life. I only carried it to appease
her, but setting up a run for a nationally renowned pop star
might be the time to start using it. "A Mr. Felps recom-

mended me to you?" I said, searching my memory and coming up blank.

Takata's thick expressive eyebrows were high in confusion. "He said he knew you. He seemed quite enamored, actually."

A sound of understanding slipped past me. "Oh, is he a living vamp, by chance? Blond hair. Thinks he's God's gift to the living and the dead?" I asked, hoping I was wrong.

He grinned. "You do know him." He glanced at Jenks, quivering and unable to open his mouth. "I thought he was pissing in my daisies."

My eyes closed as I gathered my strength. Kisten. Why didn't that surprise me? "Yeah, I know him," I muttered as I opened my eyes, not sure if I should be angry or flattered that the living vampire had recommended me to Takata. "I didn't know his last name was Felps."

Disgusted, I gave up on my attempt at being professional. Throwing my datebook back into my bag, I slouched in the corner, my movement less graceful than I hoped, as it was pushed along by the car's motion as we shifted lanes. "So what can I do for you?" I asked.

The older warlock straightened, tugging the soft orange of his slacks straight. I'd never known anyone who could look good in orange, but Takata managed it. "It's about the upcoming concert," he said. "I wanted to see if your firm was available for security."

"Oh." I licked my lips, puzzled. "Sure. That's no problem, but don't you have people for that already?" I asked, remembering the tight security at the concert I'd met him at. Vamps had to cap their teeth, and no one got in with more than a makeup spell. 'Course, once past security, the caps came off and the amulets hidden in shoes were invoked. . . .

He nodded. "Yes, and therein lies the problem."

I waited as he leaned forward, sending the scent of redwood to me. Long musician hands laced, he eyed the floor. "I arranged security with Mr. Felps as usual before I got into town," he said when his attention came back to me. "But a

Mr. Saladan came to see me, claiming he's handling security in Cincinnati and that all monies owed to Piscary should be directed to him instead."

My breath came out in understanding. *Protection. Oh. I got it.* Kisten was acting as Piscary's scion since very few people knew that Ivy had displaced him and now held the coveted title. Kisten continued to handle the undead vampire's affairs while Ivy refused to. *Thank God.*

"You're paying for protection?" I said. "You want me to talk to Kisten and Mr. Saladan to get them to stop blackmailing you?"

Takata tilted his head back, his beautiful, tragic voice ringing out in laugher that was soaked up by the thick carpet and leather seats. "No," he said. "Piscary does a damned-fine job of keeping the Inderlanders in line. My concern is with Mr. Saladan."

Appalled, but not surprised, I tucked my red curls behind my ear, wishing I had done something with them that afternoon. Yeah, I used blackmail, but it was to keep myself alive, not make money. There was a difference. "It's blackmail," I said, disgusted.

He went solemn. "It's a service, and I don't begrudge a dime of it." Seeing my frown, Takata leaned forward to send his gold chains swinging, his blue eyes fixing on mine. "My show has an MPL, just like a traveling circus or fair. I wouldn't keep it one night if it wasn't for arranging protection at every city we play in. It's the cost of doing business."

MPL was short for Mixed Population License. It guaranteed that there was security in place to prevent bloodletting on the premises, a necessity when Inderlanders and humans mixed. If too many vampires gathered and one succumbed to his or her blood lust, the rest were hard-pressed to not follow suit. I was never sure how a slip of paper was enough to keep hunger-driven vampires' mouths to themselves, but establishments worked hard to keep an A rating on their MPLs since humans and living Inderlanders would boycott any place that didn't have one. It was too easy to end up dead or mentally bound to a vampire you didn't even know. And personally, I'd rather be dead than be a vampire's toy, my living with a vampire aside.

"It's blackmail," I said. We had just passed the bridge to cross the Ohio River. I wondered where we were going if it wasn't the Hollows.

Takata's thin shoulders moved. "When I'm touring, I'm at any one place for one night, maybe two. If someone starts trouble, we won't be around long enough to track them down, and every goth out there knows it. Where's the incentive for an excited vamp or Were to behave him- or herself? Piscary puts the word out that anyone causing trouble will answer to him."

I looked up, not liking that it made beautiful, simplistic sense.

"I have an incident-free show," Takata said, smiling, "and Piscary gets seven percent of the ticket sales. Everyone wins. Up to now, I've been very satisfied with Piscary's services. I didn't even mind he upped his cost to pay for his lawyer."

Snorting, I dropped my eyes. "My fault," I said.

"So I hear," the lanky man said dryly. "Mr. Felps was very impressed. But Saladan?" Takata grew concerned, his expressive fingers drumming out a complicated rhythm as his gaze went to the passing buildings. "I can't afford to pay both of them. There would be nothing left to rebuild the city's shelters, and that's the entire point to the concert."

"You want me to make sure nothing happens," I said, and he nodded. My eyes tracked the Jim Beam bottler just off the expressway while I took that in. Saladan was trying to muscle in on Piscary's turf now that the undead master vampire was put away for murder. Murders that I staked to him.

I tilted my head in a vain attempt to see Jenks on my shoulder. "I have to talk to my other partner, but I don't see a problem," I said. "There will be three of us. Me, a living vamp, and a human." I wanted Nick to go, even if he wasn't officially part of our firm.

"Me," Jenks squeaked. "Me too. Me too."

"I didn't want to speak for you, Jenks," I said. "It might be cold."

Takata chuckled. "With all that body heat and under those lights? No way."

"Then it's settled," I said, terribly pleased. "I'm assuming we get special passes?"

"Yes." Takata twisted to reach under the folder that held his band's pictures. "These will get you past Clifford. From there it shouldn't be a problem."

"Super," I said, delighted as I dug in my bag for one of my cards. "Here's my card in case you have to get in touch with me between then and now."

Things were starting to happen fast, and I took the wad of thick cardboard he gave me in return for my black business card. He smiled as he looked at it, and tucked it away in a front shirt pocket. Turning with that same soft look, he tapped a thick knuckle on the glass between the driver and us. I clutched my bag to me when we swerved to the shoulder.

"Thank you, Rachel," he said as the car stopped right there on the freeway. "I'll see you on the twenty-second about noon at the Coliseum so you can go over our security with my staff."

"Sounds good," I stammered as Jenks swore and dove for my bag when the door opened. Cold air blew in, and I squinted in the afternoon glare. Behind us was my car. *He was going to leave me right here?*

"Rachel? I mean it. Thank you." Takata extended his hand. I took, giving it a firm shake. His grip was tight, feeling thin and bony in mine. Professional. "I really appreciate it," he said as he released my hand. "You did good by quitting the I.S. You look great."

I couldn't help but smile. "Thank you," I said, letting the driver help me out of the limo. The vamp driving my car slipped past me and vanished into the darkest corner of the limo as I tightened the tie of my coat and draped my scarf about my neck again. Takata waved his good-bye as the driver shut the door. The small, tidy man nodded to me before turning around. I stood with my feet in the snow as the limo eased into the fast traffic and disappeared.

Bag in hand, I timed the traffic and slipped into my car. The heater was on full, and I breathed the scent of the vamp who had been driving it, pulling it deep into me.

My head hummed with the music Takata had shared with me. I was going to be working security at his solstice concert. It didn't get any better than that.

Six

I had gotten myself turned around and back over the Ohio River and into the Hollows, and still Jenks hadn't said anything. The starstruck pixy had parked himself on his usual spot atop the rearview mirror, watching the encroaching snow clouds turn the bright afternoon dark and depressive. I didn't think it was the cold that had turned his wings blue, as I had the heater cranked. It was embarrassment.

"Jenks?" I questioned, and his wings blurred to nothing.

"Don't say anything," he muttered, barely audible.

"Jenks, it wasn't that bad."

He turned, a look of self-disgust on him. "I forgot my name, Rache."

I couldn't help my smile. "I won't tell anyone."

The pink returned to his wings. "Really?" he asked, and I nodded. It didn't take a genius to realize it was important to the ego-driven pixy to be self-assured and in control. I was sure that's where his bad mouth and short temper came from.

"Don't tell Ivy," I said, "but the first time I met him, I fawned all over him. He could have taken advantage of me; used me like a tissue and thrown me away. He didn't. He made me feel interesting and important, even though I was working peon runs at the I.S. at the time. He's cool, you know? A real person. I bet he didn't think twice about you forgetting your name."

Jenks sighed, his entire body moving as he exhaled. "You missed your turn."

I shook my head, breaking at a red light behind an obnoxious SUV I couldn't see around. The salt-stained bumper sticker read, SOME OF MY BEST FRIENDS ARE HUMANS. YUM, and I smiled. Only in the Hollows. "I want to see if Nick is awake yet, as long as we're out," I explained. My eyes went to Jenks. "You'll be all right for a little longer?"

"Yeah," he said. "I'm okay, but you're making a mistake."

The light changed, and I almost stalled my car. We lurched through the intersection, slipping on the slush when I gunned it. "We talked today at the zoo," I said, feeling warm inside. "I think we're going to be okay. And I want to show him the backstage passes."

His wings made an audible hum. "You sure, Rachel? I mean, that was a big scare when you pulled that ley line through him. Maybe you shouldn't push it. Give him some space."

"I've given him three months," I muttered, not caring that the guy in the car behind me thought I was flirting with him as my eyes were on the rearview mirror. "Any more space and he'd be on the moon. I'm not going to rearrange his furniture, just show him the passes."

Jenks said nothing, his silence making me nervous. My worry shifted to puzzlement when I turned into Nick's parking lot and stopped beside his beat-up blue truck. There was a suitcase in the passenger seat. It hadn't been there this morning.

Lips parted, I glanced at Jenks, and he shrugged, looking unhappy. A cold feeling slipped into me. My thoughts flitted over our conversation at the zoo. We were going to the movies tonight. *And he was packed? He was going somewhere?*

"Get in my bag," I said softly, refusing to believe the worst. This wasn't the first time I had come over to find Nick gone or leaving. He had been in and out of Cincinnati a lot the last three months, me usually being unaware of it until he returned. And now his phone was disconnected and there was a packed bag in his truck? *Had I misread him?* If tonight was supposed to be a dump date, I was going to just die.

"Rachel . . ."

"I'm opening the door," I said as I stiffly put my keys into my bag. "You want to stay here and wait and hope it doesn't get too cold?"

Jenks flitted to hover before me. He looked worried despite his hands being on his hips. "Let me out as soon as we're inside," he demanded.

My throat tightened as I nodded, and he dropped down with a reluctant slowness. I carefully snugged the ties shut on my bag and got out, but a swelling feeling of hurt made me slam the door, and my little red car shook. Glancing into the bed of the truck, I realized it was dry and empty of snow. It seemed likely that Nick hadn't been in Cincinnati the last few days, either. No wonder I hadn't seen him last week.

Thoughts spinning, I paced up the slippery walk to the common door, yanking it open and taking the stairs, to leave successively smaller chunks of snow on the gray carpet. I remembered to let Jenks out at the top of the third-floor landing, and he hovered silently as he took in my anger.

"We were going out tonight," I said as I pulled my gloves off and jammed them in a pocket. "It's been staring at me in the face for weeks, Jenks. The hurried phone calls, the trips out of town without telling me, the lack of any intimate contact for God knows how long."

"Ten weeks," Jenks said, easily keeping up with me.

"Oh, really," I said bitterly, "thank you *so* much for that update."

"Easy, Rache," he said, spilling a trace of pixy dust in his wake from worry. "It might not be what you think."

I'd been dumped before. I wasn't stupid. But it hurt. Damn it, it still hurt.

There was nowhere for Jenks to land in the barren hallway, and he reluctantly lighted on my shoulder. Jaw clenched so hard it hurt, I made a fist to hammer on Nick's door. He had to be home—he didn't go anywhere without his truck—but before I could, the door swung open.

My arm dropped and I stared at Nick, my surprise mirrored on his long face. His coat was unzipped and a homemade hat of soft blue yarn was pulled tight to his ears. He took it off as I watched, shifting it and the keys in his grip to his other hand, which held a slick-looking briefcase at odds with his otherwise ragtag attire. His hair was tousled, and he smoothed it with a deft hand while he regained his composure. There was snow on his boots. *Unlike his truck.*

Keys jingling, he set the briefcase down. He took a breath, then let it slowly out. The guilt in his eyes told me I was right. "Hi, Ray-ray."

"Hi, Nick," I said, hitting the *k* with an excessive force. "I guess our date is off."

Jenks buzzed a greeting, and I hated the apologetic look he gave Nick. Four inches or six-foot-four, they were all in the same club. Nick didn't move to invite me in.

"Was tonight a dump dinner?" I asked abruptly, just wanting to be done with it.

His eyes widened. "No!" he protested, but his gaze flicked to the briefcase.

"Is it someone else, Nick? 'Cause I'm a big girl. I can take it."

"No," he repeated, his voice softer. He shifted, looking frustrated. He reached out, stopping just shy of my shoulder. His hand fell. "No."

I wanted to believe him. I really did. "Then what?" I demanded. *Why didn't he invite me in? Why did we have to do this in the freaking hallway?*

"Ray-ray," he whispered, his brow furrowed. "It's not you."

My eyes closed as I gathered my strength. *How many times had I heard that?*

His foot shoved the expensive briefcase into the hall, and my eyes flew open at the scraping sound. I stepped aside as he came out, shutting the door behind him. "It's not you," he said, his voice suddenly hard. "And it wasn't a dump dinner. I don't want to call it quits between us. But something came up, and frankly it's none of your business."

Surprised, my lips parted. Jenks's words flashed through me. "You're still afraid of me," I said, pissed that he didn't trust me to not pull a line through him again.

"I am not," he offered angrily. Motions stiff, he locked his door from the outside, turning to hold the key up between us. "Here," he said belligerently. "Take my key. I'll be out of town for a while. I was going to give it to you tonight, but since you're here, it will save me the trouble. I've stopped my mail, and the rent is paid up through August."

"August!" I stammered, suddenly afraid.

He glanced at Jenks. "Jenks, can Jax come over and watch my plants for me until I get back? He did a good job last time. It might only be a week, but the heat and electricity are on automatic draw in case it's longer."

"Nick . . ." I protested, my voice sounding small. *How had this turned around so fast?*

"Sure," Jenks said meekly. "You know, I think I'll go wait downstairs."

"No, I'm done." Nick picked up the briefcase. "I'm going to be busy tonight, but I'll swing by later to pick him up before I leave town."

"Nick, wait!" I said. My stomach clenched and I felt light-headed. I should've kept my mouth shut. I should've ignored the packed bag and played the stupid girlfriend. I should've gone to dinner and ordered lobster. My first real boyfriend in five years, and finally when things were starting to get back to normal, here I was, scaring him off. Just like all the others.

Jenks made an embarrassed sound. "Uh, I'll be by the front door," he said, vanishing down the stairwell to leave a trail of glowing pixy dust all the way to the next landing.

Long face tight in unhappiness, Nick pushed the key into my hand. His fingers were cold. "I can't—" He took a breath, meeting and holding my eyes. I waited, frightened at what he was going to say. Suddenly, I didn't want to hear it.

"Rachel, I was going to tell you this over dinner, but . . . I tried. I really did. I just can't do this right now," he said softly. "I'm not leaving you," he rushed to add before I could open my mouth. "I love you, and I want to be with you. Maybe for the rest of my life. I don't know. But every time you tap a line, I feel it, and it's as if I'm back in that FIB cruiser having an epileptic seizure from the line you pulled through me. I can't breathe. I can't think. I can't do anything. When I'm farther away, it's easier. I need to be away for a while. I didn't tell you because I didn't want you to feel bad."

Face cold, I could say nothing. He never told me I had made him seize. God help me, I hadn't known. Jenks had been with him. Why hadn't he told me?

"I have to catch my breath," he whispered, giving my hands a squeeze. "To go a few days without remembering that."

"I'll stop," I said, panicking. "I won't tap a line again. Nick, you don't have to leave!"

"Yes, I do." Dropping my hands, he touched my jawline. His smile was pained. "I want you to pull on a line. I want you to practice. Ley line magic is going to save your life someday, and I want you to become the best damned ley line witch Cincinnati has." He took a breath. "But I have to put some distance between us. Just for a while. And I have some business of out of state. It has nothing to do with you. I'll be back."

But he had said August. "You're not coming back," I said, my throat closing. "You'll come for your books, and then you'll be gone."

"Rachel—"

"No." I turned away. The key was cold in my hand, cutting into my palm. *Breathe,* I reminded myself. "Just go. I'll bring Jax over tomorrow. Just go."

I shut my eyes when he put a hand on my shoulder, but I

wouldn't turn. They flashed open when he leaned closer and the scent of musty books and new electronics filled me. "Thank you, Rachel," he whispered, and there was the lightest touch of lips on mine. "I'm not leaving you. I'll be back."

I held my breath and stared at the ugly gray carpet. *I wouldn't cry, damn it. I wouldn't.*

I heard him hesitate, then the soft thumps of his boots on the stairs. My head started to hurt as the muted rumble of his truck vibrated the window at the end of the hall. I waited until I couldn't hear it anymore before I turned to follow him out, my steps slow and unseeing.

I'd done it again.

Seven

I pulled my car carefully into the tiny garage, turning off the lights and then the engine. Depressed, I stared at the spackled wall two feet in front of the grille. Silence soaked in, broken by the ticking of the engine cooling off. Ivy's bike rested quietly against the side wall, covered in a canvas tarp and stored for the winter. It was going to be dark soon. I knew I should get Jenks inside, but it was hard to find the will to unbuckle my belt and get out of the car.

Jenks dropped to the steering wheel with an attention-getting hum. My hands fell into my lap, shoulders slumping. "Well, at least you know where you stand now," he offered.

My frustration flared, then died, overwhelmed by a wave of apathy. "He said he's coming back," I said glumly, needing to believe the lie until I hardened myself to the truth.

Jenks wrapped his arms about himself, dragonfly wings still. "Rache," he cajoled. "I like Nick, but you're going to get two calls. One where he says he misses you and is feeling better, and the last when he says he's sorry and asks you to give his key to his landlord for him."

I looked at the wall. "Just let me be stupid and believe him for a while, okay?"

The pixy made a sound of wry agreement. He looked positively chilled, his wings almost black as he hunched, shivering. I'd pushed him past his limits by detouring to Nick's. I was definitely going to make cookies tonight. He shouldn't go to sleep cold like that. He might not wake up until spring.

"Ready?" I asked as I opened my bag, and he awkwardly jumped down into it instead of flying. Worried, I debated if I should tuck my bag inside my coat. I settled on putting it in the department store bag and rolling the edges down as far as I could.

Only now did I open the door, being careful not to hit the edge of the garage. Bag in hand, I made my way on the shoveled path to the front door. A sleek black Corvette was parked at the curb, looking out of place and unsafe in the snowy streets. I recognized it as Kisten's, and my face tightened. I'd been seeing too much of him lately for my liking.

The wind bit at my exposed skin, and I glanced up at the steeple, sharp against the graying clouds. Mincing on the ice, I passed Kisten's mobile icon of masculinity and rose up the stone steps to the thick wooden double doors. There was no conventional lock, though there was an oak crossbar inside which I set every sunrise before I went to bed. Bending awkwardly, I scooped out a cup of pelletized de-icer from the open bag sitting beside the door and sprinkled it on the steps before the afternoon's snowmelt had a chance to freeze.

I pushed open the door, my hair drifting in the warm draft that billowed out. Soft jazz came with it, and I slipped inside to latch it softly behind me. I didn't particularly want to see Kisten—no matter how nice he was on the eyes—though I thought I should probably thank him for recommending me to Takata.

It was dark in the small foyer, the glow of dusk slipping in from the sanctuary beyond doing little to light it. The air smelled like coffee and growing things, sort of a mix between a plant nursery and coffeehouse. Nice. Ceri's things went atop the small antique table Ivy had swiped from her folks, and I opened up my bag, peering down to see Jenks looking up.

"Thank God," he muttered as he slowly lifted into the air.

Then he hesitated, head cocked as he listened. "Where is everyone?"

I shrugged out of my coat and hung it up on a peg. "Maybe Ivy yelled at your kids again and they're hiding. Are you complaining?"

He shook his head. He was right, though. It was really quiet. Too quiet. Usually there were head-splitting shrills of pixy children playing tag, an occasional crash from a hanging utensil hitting the kitchen floor, or the snarls of Ivy chasing them out of the living room. The only peace we got were the four hours they slept at noon, and four hours again after midnight.

The warmth of the church was soaking into Jenks, and already his wings were translucent and moving well. I decided to leave Ceri's things where they were until I could get them across the street to her, and after stomping the snow off my boots beside the melting puddles Kisten had left, I followed Jenks out of the dark foyer and into the quiet sanctuary.

My shoulders eased as I took in the subdued lighting coming in through the knee-to-ceiling-high stained-glass windows. Ivy's stately baby grand took up one corner in the front, dusted and cared for but played only when I was out. My plant-strewn, rolltop desk was kitty-corner to it, way up in the front on the ankle-high stage where the altar once sat. The huge image of a cross still shadowed the wall above it, soothing and protective. The pews had been removed long before I moved in, leaving an echoing wooden and glass space redolent of peace, solitude, grace, and security. I was safe here.

Jenks stiffened, sending my instincts flaming.

"Now!" shrilled a piercing voice.

Jenks shot straight up, leaving a cloud of pixy dust hanging where he had been like an octopus inking. Heart pounding, I hit the hardwood floor, rolling.

Sharp patters of impacts hit the planks beside me. Fear kept me spinning until I found a corner. Heady, the strength of the graveyard's ley line surged through me as I tapped it.

"Rachel! It's my kids!" Jenks cried as a hail of tiny snowballs struck me.

Gagging, I choked on the word to invoke my circle, yanking back the cresting power. It crashed into me, and I groaned as twofold the ley line energy suddenly took up the same space. Staggering, I fell to a knee and struggled to breathe until the excess found its way back to the line. Oh God. It felt like I was on fire. I should have just made the circle.

"What in Tink's knickers do you think you're doing!" Jenks yelled, hovering over me as I tried to focus on the floor. "You should know better than to jump a runner like that! She's a professional! You're going to end up dead! And I'm going to let you rot where you fall. We're guests here! Get to the desk. All of you! Jax, I am *really* disappointed."

I took a breath. Damn. That really hurt. *Mental note: never stop a ley line spell midcast.*

"Matalina!" Jenks shouted. "Do you know what our kids are doing?"

I licked my lips. "It's okay," I said, looking up to find absolutely no one in the sanctuary. Even Jenks was gone. "I love my life," I muttered, and I worked myself carefully up from the floor in stages. The flaming tingle in my skin had subsided, and pulse hammering, I let go of the line completely, feeling the remaining energy flow out of my chi to leave me shaking.

With the sound of an angry bee, Jenks flew in from the back rooms. "Rachel," he said as he came to a halt before me. "I'm sorry. They found the snow that Kist brought in on his shoes, and he told them about snowball fights when he was a kid. Oh, look. They got you all wet."

Matalina, Jenks's wife, zipped into the sanctuary in a billow of gray and blue silk. Giving me an apologetic wince, she slipped under the crack in my rolltop desk. My head started to hurt and my eyes watered. Her scolding was so high-pitched that I couldn't hear it.

Tired, I straightened to my full height and tugged my

sweater straight. Small spots of water showed where I'd been hit. If they had been fairy assassins with spells instead of pixies with snowballs, I'd be dead. My heart slowed, and I snatched up my bag from the floor. "It's okay," I said, embarrassed and wanting Jenks to shut up. "No biggie. Kids will be kids."

Jenks hovered in apparent indecision. "Yeah, but they're my kids, and we're guests. They'll be apologizing to you, among a few other things."

Gesturing it was okay, I stumbled down the dark hallway, following the smell of coffee. *At least no one had seen me rolling on the floor evading pixy snowballs,* I thought. But such commotions had become commonplace since the first hard frost and Jenks's family moved in. There was no way I could pretend I wasn't here now, though. Besides, they had probably smelled the flush of fresh air when I opened the door.

I passed the opposing his-and-her bathrooms that had been converted into a conventional bathroom and a combination bathroom/laundry room. The latter was mine. My room was on the right side of the hallway, Ivy's was directly across from it. The kitchen was next, and I made a left turn into it, hoping to grab some coffee and go hide in my room to avoid Kisten entirely.

I had made the mistake of kissing him in an elevator, and he never missed an opportunity to remind me of it. Thinking at the time I wouldn't live to see the sunrise, I had let my guard down and enjoyed myself, all but giving in to the lure of vampiric passion. Even worse? Kisten knew he had tipped me over the edge and that I had been a breath away from saying yes.

Exhausted, I elbowed the light switch and dropped my shoulder bag on the counter. Fluorescent lights flickered on, sending Mr. Fish into a frenzy of motion. Soft jazz and the rise and fall of conversation filtered in from the unseen living room. Kisten's leather coat was draped over Ivy's chair before her computer. There was a half-full pot of coffee, and after a moment's thought, I poured it into my gigantic mug. Trying to be quiet, I started a new batch. I didn't mean to eavesdrop, but Kisten's voice was as smooth and warm as a bubble bath.

"Ivy, love," he pleaded as I got the grounds out of the fridge. "It's only one night. An hour, maybe. In and out."

"No."

Ivy's voice was cold, the warning obvious. Kisten was pushing her past where I would, but they'd grown up together, the children of wealthy parents who expected them to join their families and have little vamp brats to continue Piscary's living-vampire line before they died and became true undead. It wouldn't happen—the marriage, not the dead part. They had already tried the cohabitation route, and while neither would say what happened, their relationship had cooled until all that was left was more of a warped sibling fondness.

"You don't have to do anything," Kisten persuaded, laying his fake British accent on heavy. "Just be there. I'll say everything."

"No."

Someone snapped off the music, and I silently pulled the silverware drawer open for the coffee scoop. Three pixy girls darted out, shrieking. I bit back my yelp, heart pounding as they vanished down the dark hallway. Motions quick from adrenaline, I poked around to find the scoop missing. I finally spotted it in the sink. Kisten must have made the coffee. If it had been Ivy, her asinine need for order would have had it washed, dried, and put away.

"Why not?" Kisten's voice had taken a petulant tone. "He's not asking for much."

Tight and controlled, Ivy's voice was seething. "I don't want that bastard in my head at all. Why would I let him see through my eyes? Feel my thoughts?"

The carafe hung from my fingers as I stood over the sink. I wished I wasn't hearing this.

"But he loves you," Kisten whispered, sounding hurt and jealous. "You're his scion."

"He doesn't love me. He loves me fighting him." It was bitter, and I could almost see her perfect, slightly Oriental features tighten in anger.

"Ivy," Kisten cajoled. "It feels good, intoxicating. The power he shares with you—"

"It's a lie!" she shouted, and I started. "You want the prestige? The power? You want to keep running Piscary's interests? Pretend you're still his scion? I don't care! But I'm not letting him in my head even to cover for you!"

I noisily ran the water into the carafe to remind them I was listening. I didn't want to hear more, and I wished they'd stop.

Kisten's sigh was long and heavy. "It doesn't work that way. If he really wants in, you won't be able to stop him, Ivy love."

"Shut. Up."

The words were so full of bound anger that I stifled a shudder. The carafe overflowed, and I jumped as water hit my hand. Grimacing, I shut the tap off and tipped the excess out.

There was a creak of wood from the living room. My stomach clenched. Someone had just pinned someone else to a chair. "Go ahead," Kisten murmured over the tinkling of the water pouring into the coffeemaker. "Sink those teeth. You know you want to. Just like old times. Piscary feels everything you do, whether you want him to or not. Why do you think you haven't been able to abstain from blood lately? Three years of denial, and now you can't go three days? Give it up, Ivy. He'd love to feel us enjoying ourselves again. And maybe your roommate might finally understand. She almost said yes," he goaded. "Not to you. To me."

I stiffened. That had been directed at me. I wasn't in the room, but I might as well have been.

There was another creak of wood. "Touch her blood and I'll kill you, Kist. I swear it."

I looked around the kitchen for a way to escape but it was too late as Ivy halted in the archway, with a scuff of boots. She hesitated, looking unusually ruffled as she gauged my unease in an instant with her uncanny ability to read body language. It made keeping secrets around her chancy at best. Anger at Kist had pinched her brow, and the aggressive frustration didn't bode well, even if it wasn't aimed at me. Her pale skin glowed a faint pink as she tried to calm herself, bringing the faint whisper of scar tissue on her neck into stark relief. She had tried surgery to minimize Piscary's physical sign of his claim on her, but it showed when she was upset. And she wouldn't accept any of my complexion charms. I had yet to figure that one out.

Seeing me unmoving by the sink, her brown eyes flicked from my steaming mug of coffee to the empty pot. I shrugged and flicked the switch to get it brewing. What could I say?

Ivy pushed herself into motion, setting an empty mug on the counter. She smoothed her severely straight black hair, bringing herself back to at least looking calm and collected. "You're upset," she said, her anger at Kisten making her voice rough. "What's up?"

I pulled my backstage passes out and clipped them to the fridge with a tomato magnet. My thought went to Nick, then to rolling on the floor evading pixy snowballs. And mustn't forget the joy of hearing her threaten Kisten over my blood that she wasn't ever going to taste. *Golly, so much to choose from.* "Nothing," I said softly.

Long and sleek in her blue jeans and shirt, she crossed her arms and leaned against the counter beside the coffeemaker to wait for it to finish. Her thin lips pressed together and she breathed deeply. "You've been crying. What is it?"

Surprise stopped me cold. *She knew I had been crying? Damn.* It had only been three tears. At the stoplight. And I had wiped them away before they even dribbled out. I glanced at the empty hallway, not wanting Kisten to know. "I'll tell you later, okay?"

Ivy followed my gaze to the archway. Puzzlement crinkled the skin about her brown eyes. Then understanding crashed over her; she knew I'd been dumped. She blinked, and I watched her, relieved when the first flicker of blood lust at my new, available status quickly died.

Living vampires didn't need blood to remain sane, as undead vampires did. They still craved it, though, choosing whom they took it from with care, usually following their sexual preferences on the happy chance that sex might be included in the mix. But the taking of blood could range in importance from confirming a deep platonic friendship to the shallowness of a one-night stand. Like most living vamps, Ivy said she didn't equate blood with sex, but I did. The sensations a vampire could pull from me were too close to sexual ecstasy to think otherwise.

After twice being slammed into the wall by ley line energy, Ivy got the message that though I was her friend, I would never, *ever,* say yes to her. It had been easier after she resumed practicing, too, with her slacking her needs somewhere else and coming home satiated, relaxed, and quietly self-loathing for having given in again.

Over the summer she seemed to have turned her energies from trying to convince me that her biting me wasn't sex to ensuring that no other vampire would hit on me. If she couldn't have my blood, then no one could, and she had devoted herself in a disturbing, yet flattering, drive to keep other vampires from taking advantage of my demon scar and luring me into becoming their shadow. Living with her gave me protection from them—protection I wasn't ashamed to accept—and in return I was her unconditional friend. And whereas that might seem one-sided, it wasn't.

Ivy was a high-maintenance friend, jealous of anyone who attracted my attention, though she hid it well. She barely tolerated Nick. Kisten, though, seemed exempt, which made me oh-so-warm and fuzzy inside. And as I took up my coffee, I found myself hoping she would go out tonight and satisfy that damned blood lust of hers so she wouldn't be looking at me like a hungry panther the rest of the week.

Feeling the tension shift from anger to speculation, I looked at the unfinished pot brewing, thinking only of escaping the room. "You want mine?" I said. "I haven't drunk any."

My head turned at Kisten's masculine chuckle. He had appeared without warning in the doorway. "I haven't drunk any either," he said suggestively. "I'd like some if you're offering."

A flush of memory took me, of Kisten and me in that elevator: my fingers playing with the silky strands of his blonddyed hair at the nape of his neck, the day-old stubble he cultivated to give his delicate features a rugged cast harsh against my skin, his lips both soft and aggressive as he tasted the salt on me, the feel of his hands at the small of my back pressing me into him. *Damn.*

I pulled my eyes from him, forcing my hand down from my neck where I had been unconsciously touching my demon scar to feel it tingle, stimulated by the vamp pheromones he was unconsciously putting out. *Double damn.*

Pleased with himself, he sat in Ivy's chair, clearly guessing where my thoughts were. But looking at his well-puttogether body, it was hard to think of anything else.

Kisten was a living vamp, too, his bloodline going back as far as Ivy's. He had once been Piscary's scion, and the glow of sharing blood with the undead vampire showed in him still. Though he often acted the playboy by dressing in biker leather and affecting a bad British accent, he used it to hide his business savvy. He was smart. And fast. And while not as powerful as an undead vampire, he was stronger than his compact build and slim waistline suggested.

Today he was dressed conservatively in a silk shirt tucked into dark slacks, clearly trying to be the professional as he took on more of Piscary's business interests now that the vampire languished in prison. The only hints to Kisten's bad-boy side were the gunmetal gray chain he wore about his neck—twin to the pair Ivy wore about her ankle—and the two diamond studs he had in each ear. At least there were supposed to be two in each ear. Someone had torn one out to leave a nasty tear.

Kisten lounged in Ivy's chair with his immaculate shoes provocatively spread, leaning back as he took in the moods drifting about the room. I found my hand creeping up to my neck again, and I scowled. He was trying to bespell me, get in my head and shift my thoughts and decisions. It wouldn't work. Only the undead could bespell the unwilling, and he couldn't lean on Piscary's strength any longer to give him the increased abilities of an undead vampire.

Ivy pulled the brewed coffee out from under the funnel. "Leave Rachel alone," she said, clearly the dominant of the two. "Nick just dumped her."

My breath caught and I stared at her, aghast. I hadn't wanted him to know!

"Well . . ." Kisten murmured, leaning forward to put his elbows on his knees. "He was no good for you anyway, love."

Bothered, I put the island counter between us. "It's Rachel. Not love."

"Rachel," he said softly, and my heart pounded at the compulsion he put in it. I glanced out the window to the snowy gray garden and the tombstones beyond. What the Turn was I doing standing in my kitchen with two hungry vamps when the sun was going down? Didn't they have somewhere to go? People to bite, that weren't me?

"He didn't dump me," I said as I grabbed the fish food and fed Mr. Fish. I could see Kisten's reflection watching me in the dark window. "He's out of town for a few days. Gave me his key to check on everything and pick up his mail."

"Oh." Kisten glanced sidelong at Ivy. "A long excursion?"

Flustered, I set the fish food down and turned. "He said he was coming back," I protested, my face tightening as I heard the ugly truth behind my words. Why would Nick say he'd be coming back unless it had occurred to him *not* to?

As the two vamps exchanged more silent looks, I pulled a mundane cookbook out from my spell library and set it thumping onto the island counter. I'd promised Jenks the oven tonight. "Don't even try to pick me up on the rebound, Kisten," I warned.

"I wouldn't dream of it." The slow, soft tone of his voice said otherwise.

"'Cause you're not capable of being half the man Nick is," I stupidly said.

"High standards, eh?" Kisten mocked.

Ivy perched herself on the counter by my ten-gallon dissolution vat of saltwater, wrapping her arms about her knees yet still managing to look predatory while she sipped her coffee and watched Kisten play with my emotions.

Kisten glanced at her as if for permission, and I frowned. Then he stood in a sliding sound of fabric, coming to lean on the island counter across from me. His necklace swung, pulling my attention to his neck, marked with soft, almost unseen, scars. "I like action movies," he said, and my breath came fast. I could smell the lingering aroma of leather on him under the dry scent of silk.

"So?" I said belligerently, peeved that Ivy had probably told him about Nick's and my weekend-long stints in front of the Adrenaline channel

"So, I can make you laugh."

I flipped to the most tattered, stain-splattered recipe in the book I'd swiped from my mom, knowing it was for sugar cookies. "So does Bozo the Clown, but I wouldn't date him."

Ivy licked her finger and made a tally mark in the air.

Kisten smiled to show the barest hint of fang, leaning back and clearly feeling the hit. "Let me take you out," he said. "A platonic first date to prove Nick wasn't anything special."

"Oh, please," I simpered, not believing he was stooping this low.

Grinning, Kisten turned himself into a spoiled rich boy.

"If you enjoy yourself, then you admit to me that Nick was nothing special."

I crouched to get the flour. "No," I said when I rose to set it thumping on top of the counter.

A hurt look creased his stubbled face, put-on but still effective. "Why not?"

I glanced behind me at Ivy, silently watching. "You have money," I said. "Anyone can show a girl a good time with enough money."

Ivy made another tally mark. "That's two," she said, and he frowned.

"Nick was a cheap ass, huh," Kisten offered, trying to hide his ire.

"Watch your mouth," I shot back.

"Yes, Ms. Morgan."

The sultry submissiveness in his voice yanked my thoughts back to the elevator. Ivy once told me Kisten got off on playing the submissive. What I had found out was that a submissive vampire was still more aggressive than most people could handle. But I wasn't most people. I was a witch.

I put my eyes on his, seeing that they were a nice steady blue. Unlike Ivy, Kisten freely indulged his blood lust until it wasn't the overriding factor governing his life. "One hundred seventy-five dollars?" he offered, and I bent to get the sugar.

The man thought a cheap date was almost two hundred dollars?

"One hundred?" he said, and I looked at him, reading his genuine surprise.

"Our average date was sixty," I said.

"Damn!" he swore, then hesitated. "I can say damn, can't I?"

"Hell, yes."

From her perch on the counter, Ivy snickered. Kisten's brow pinched in what looked like real worry. "Okay," he said, deep in thought. "A sixty-dollar date."

I gave him a telling look. "I haven't said yes yet."

He inhaled long and slow, tasting my mood on the air. "You haven't said no, either."

"No."

He slumped dramatically, pulling a smile from me despite myself. "I won't bite you," he protested, his blue eyes roguishly innocent.

From under the island counter I pulled out my largest copper spell pot to use as a mixing bowl. It wasn't reliable any longer for spelling, as it had a dent from hitting Ivy's head. The palm-sized paint ball gun I stored in it made a comforting sound against the metal as I took it out to put back under the counter at ankle height. "And I should believe you because . . ."

Kisten's eyes flicked to Ivy. "She'll kill me twice if I do."

I went to get the eggs, milk, and butter out of the fridge, hoping neither of them sensed my pulse quickening. But I knew my temptation didn't stem from the subliminal pheromones they were unconsciously emitting. I missed feeling desired, needed. And Kisten had a Ph.D. in wooing women, even if his motives were one-sided and false. From the looks of it, he indulged in casual blood taking like some men indulged in casual sex. And I didn't want to become one of his shadows that he strung along, caught by the binding saliva in his bite to crave his touch, to feel his teeth sinking into me to fill me with euphoria. *Crap, I was doing it again.*

"Why should I?" I said, feeling myself warm. "I don't even like you."

Kisten leaned over the counter as I returned. The faultless blue of his eyes caught and held mine. It was obvious by his rakish grin that he knew I was weakening. "All the better reason to go out with me," he said. "If I can show you a good time for a lousy sixty bucks, think what someone you like could do. All I need is one promise."

The egg was cold in my hands, and I set it down. "What?" I asked, and Ivy stirred.

His smile widened. "No shirking."

"Beg pardon?"

He opened the tub of butter and dipped his finger into it, licking it slowly clean. "I can't make you feel attractive if you stiffen up every time I touch you."

"I didn't before," I said, my thoughts returning to the elevator. God help me, I had almost done him right there against the wall.

"This is different," he said. "It's a date, and I would give my eyeteeth to know why women expect men to behave differently on a date than any other time."

"Because you do," I said.

He gave a raised-eyebrow look to Ivy. Straightening, he reached across the counter to cup my jaw. I jerked back, brow furrowed.

"Nope," he said as he drew away. "I won't ruin my reputation by taking you out on a sixty-dollar date for nothing. If I can't touch you, it's a no-go."

I stared at him, feeling my heart pound. "Good."

Shocked, Kisten blinked. "Good?" he questioned as Ivy smirked.

"Yeah," I said, pulling the butter to me and scooping out about a half cup with a wooden spoon. "I didn't want to go out with you anyway. You're too full of yourself. Think you can manipulate anyone into doing anything. Your ego-testicle attitude makes me sick."

Ivy laughed as she unfolded herself and jumped lightly to the floor without a sound. "I told you," she said. "Pay up."

Shoulders shifting in a sigh, he twisted to reach his wallet in a back pocket, pulling out a fifty and shoving it into her hand. She raised a thin eyebrow and made another tally mark in the air. An unusual smile was on her as she stretched to drop it into the cookie jar atop the fridge.

"Typical," Kisten said, his eyes dramatically sad. "Try to do something nice for a person, cheer her up, and what do I get? Abused and robbed."

Ivy took three long steps to come up behind him. Curling an arm across his chest, she leaned close and whispered in his torn ear, "Poor baby." They looked good together, her silky sultriness and his confident masculinity.

He didn't react at all as her fingers slipped between the buttons of his shirt. "You would have enjoyed yourself," he said to me.

Feeling as if I'd passed some test, I pushed the butter off the spoon and licked my finger clean. "How would you know?"

"Because you enjoyed yourself just now," he answered. "You forgot all about that shallow, self-centered human who doesn't know a good thing when she bites him on his—" He looked at Ivy. "Where did you say she bit him, Ivy love?"

"His wrist." Ivy straightened and turned her back on me to retrieve her coffee.

"Who doesn't know a good thing when she bites him on his . . . wrist," Kisten finished.

My face was burning. "That's the last time I tell you anything!" I exclaimed to Ivy. And it wasn't as if I had drawn blood. Good God!

"Admit it," Kisten said. "You enjoyed talking with me, pitting your will against mine. It would have been fun," he said as he looked at me through his bangs. "You look like you could use some fun. Cooped up in this church for God knows how long. When was the last time you got dressed up? Felt pretty? Felt desirable?"

I stood very still, feeling my breath move in and out of me, balanced. My thoughts went to Nick leaving to go out of town without telling me, our cuddling and closeness that had ended with a shocking abruptness. It had been so long. I missed his touch making me feel wanted, stirring my passions and bringing me alive. I wanted that feeling back—even if it was a lie. Just for a night, so I wouldn't forget how it felt until I found it again.

"No biting," I said, thinking I was making a mistake.

Ivy jerked her head up, her face expressionless.

Kisten didn't seem surprised. A heady understanding was in his gaze. "No shirking," he said softly, his eyes alive and glinting. I was like glass to him.

"Sixty-dollar maximum," I countered.

Kisten stood, taking his coat from the back of the chair. "I'll pick you up at one A.M., night after tomorrow. Wear something nice."

"No playing on my scar," I said breathlessly, unable to find enough air for some reason. *What in hell was I doing?*

With a predatory grace, he shrugged into his coat. He hesitated, thinking. "Not one breath on it," he agreed. His thoughtful expression shifted to sly anticipation as he stood in the archway to the hall and held out his hand to Ivy.

Motions stiff, Ivy pulled the fifty back out of the cookie jar and gave it to him. He stood and waited, and she took another and slapped it into his hand.

"Thanks, Ivy love," he said. "Now I have enough for my date and a haircut, too." He met my eyes, holding them until I couldn't breathe. "See you later, Rachel."

The sound of his dress shoes seemed loud in the darkening church. I heard him say something to Jenks followed by the faint boom of the front door closing.

Ivy wasn't pleased. "That was a stupid thing to do," she said.

"I know." I wouldn't look at her, mixing the sugar and butter with a rough quickness.

"Then why did you do it?"

I kept stirring. "Maybe because unlike you, I like being touched," I said wearily. "Maybe because I miss Nick. Maybe because he's been gone the last three months and I've been too stupid to notice. Back off, Ivy. I'm not your shadow."

"No," she agreed, less angry than I expected. "I'm your roommate, and Kist is more dangerous than he lets on. I've seen him do this before. He wants to hunt you. Hunt you slow."

I stilled my motions and looked at her. "Slower than you?" I questioned bitterly.

She stared at me. "I'm not hunting you," she said, sounding hurt. "You won't let me."

Letting go of the spoon, I put my hands to either side of the bowl and bowed my head over it. We were the pair. One too afraid to feel anything lest she lose control of her iron-clad hold on her emotions, and the other so hungry to feel anything that she'd risk her free will for one night of fun. How I had kept from being a vampire's flunky this long was a miracle.

"He's waiting for you," I said as I heard Kisten's car revving through the insulated walls of the church. "Go satiate yourself. I don't like it when you don't."

Ivy swung into motion. Not saying a word, she stiffly walked out, boots thumping on the hardwood floor. The sound of the church's door shutting was quiet. Slowly the ticking of the clock above the sink became obvious. Taking a slow breath, I pulled my head up, wondering how in hell I had become her keeper.

Eight

The rhythmic thumps of my running feet jolting up my spine were a pleasant distraction from my thoughts of Nick. It was bright, the sun glittering off the piles of snow to make me squint through my new sunglasses. I had left my old pair in Takata's limo, and the new ones didn't fit as well. This was the second day in a row that I had gotten up at an ungodly ten in the morning to come out and run, and by the Turn, I was going to run this time. Jogging after midnight wasn't as fun—too many weirdos. Besides, I had a date tonight with Kisten.

The thought zinged through me, and my pace increased. Each puffed breath was timed with my steps to make a hypnotic tempo luring me into a runner's high. I picked up the pace even more, reveling in it. An old witch couple was ahead of me doing a fast walk/run as I passed the bear exhibit. They were watching with a hungry interest. The bears, not the witches. I think that's why management let us runners in. We gave the large predators something to watch besides kids in strollers and tired parents.

Actually, our collective group of runners had taken it upon ourselves to adopt the Indochina tiger exhibit with just that in mind. The funds for their upkeep and health care came entirely from our special-pass fees. They ate very well.

"Track!" I exclaimed breathily in time with my steps, and the two witches slid aside, making a spot for me. "Thanks,"

I said as I passed them, catching their heavy redwood scent in the crisp, painfully dry air.

The sound of their companionable conversation quickly retreated. I spared a confused, angry thought for Nick. I didn't need him to run; I could run by myself. He hadn't run with me much lately anyway, not since I got my car and didn't need to bum a ride from him.

Yeah, right, I thought, my jaw clenching. It wasn't the car. It was something else. Something he wouldn't tell me about. Something that "frankly wasn't my business."

"Track!" I heard faintly from someone not far behind.

It was low and controlled. Whoever it was, they were keeping up with me with no trouble. All my warning flags went up. *Let's see if you can run,* I thought, taking a deep breath.

Different muscles eased into play like gears shifting as I pushed into a faster pace, my heart pounding and the cold air slicing in and out of me. I was already going at a good clip, my natural pace somewhere between a long distance run and a sprint. It had made me a favorite in the eight hundred meter in high school and had stood me in good stead when I worked for the I.S. and needed to run down the occasional tag. Now, my calves protested at the increased speed and my lungs began to burn. As I passed the rhinos and cut a left, I vowed to get out here more; I was going soft.

No one was ahead of me. Even the keepers were absent. I listened, hearing his pace increase to match mine. I snuck a quick look back as I made a sharp left.

It was a Were, somewhat short and lanky, sleek in matching gray running pants and long-sleeve shirt. His long black hair was held back with an exercise band, and there was no strain on his placid face as he kept up with me.

Crap. My heart gave an extra hard thump. Even without the cowboy hat and wool duster, I recognized him. *Crap, crap, crap.*

My pace quickened with a surge of adrenaline. It was the same Were. Why was he following me? My thoughts drifted back further than yesterday. I'd seen him before. Lots of be-fores. He was at the watch counter last week when Ivy and I were picking out a new perfume, to overpower my natural scent mixing with hers. He had been putting air into his tires three weeks ago when I was pumping gas and locked myself out of my car. And three months ago I'd seen him leaning against a tree when Trent and I talked at Eden Park.

My jaw clenched. *Maybe it's time we chatted?* I thought as I ran past the cat house.

There was a drop-off ahead by the eagles. I cut a right, leaning back as I went downhill. Mr. Were followed. As I thumped along behind the eagle exhibit, I took stock of what I had. In my belt pack were my keys, my phone, a mild pain amulet already invoked, and my minisplat gun loaded with sleepy time potions. No help there; I wanted to talk to him, not knock him out.

The path opened up into a wide deserted section. No one ran down here because the hill was such a killer to get back up. Perfect. Heart pounding, I went left to take the slope in-stead of heading for the Vine Street entrance. A smile curved over me as his pace faltered. He hadn't expected that. Lean-ing into the hill, I ran up it full tilt, seeming to be in slow mo-tion. The path was narrow and snow-covered. He followed.

Here, I thought as I reached the top. Panting, I snuck a quick look behind me and jerked off the path and into the thick shrubbery. My lungs burned as I held my breath.

He passed me with the sound of feet and heavy breathing, intent on his steps. Reaching the top, he hesitated, looking to see which way I had gone. His dark eyes were pinched and the first signs of physical distress furrowed his brow.

Taking a breath, I leapt.

He heard me, but it was too late. I landed against him as he spun, pinning him against an old oak. His breath whooshed out as his back hit, his eyes going wide and sur-prised. My fingers went chokingly under his chin to hold him there, and my fist hit his solar plexus.

Gasping, he bent forward. I let go, and he fell to sit at the base of the tree, holding his stomach. A thin backpack slid up almost over his head.

"Who in hell are you and why have you been tailing me the last three months!" I shouted, trusting the odd hour and the closed status of the zoo to keep our conversation private.

Head bowed over his chest, the Were put a hand in the air. It was small for a man, and thick, with short powerful-looking fingers. Sweat had turned his spandex shirt a darker gray, and he slowly moved his well-muscled legs into a less awkward position.

I took a step back, my hand on my hip, lungs heaving as I recovered from the climb. Angry, I took off my sunglasses and hung them from my waistband and waited.

"David," he rasped as he looked up at me, immediately dropping his head while he struggled to take another breath. Pain and a hint of embarrassment had laced his brown eyes. Sweat marred his rugged face, thick with a black stubble that matched his long hair. "God bless it," he said to the ground. "Why did you have to hit me? What is it with you redheads, anyway, always having to hit things?"

"Why are you following me?" I shot at him.

Head still bowed, he put up a hand again, telling me to wait. I shifted nervously as he took a clean breath, then another. His hand dropped and he looked up. "My name is David Hue," he said. "I'm an insurance adjuster. Mind if I get up? I'm getting wet."

My mouth dropped open and I took several steps back onto the path as he rose and wiped the snow from his backside. "An insurance adjuster?" I stammered. Surprise washed the remnants of adrenaline from me. I put my arms about myself and wished I had my coat as the air suddenly seemed colder now that I wasn't moving. "I paid my bill," I said, starting to get angry. "I haven't missed one payment. You'd think for six hundred dollars a month—"

"Six hundred a month!" he said, his features shocked. "Oh, honey, we have to talk."

Affronted, I backed up farther. He was in his mid-thirties,

I guessed from the maturity in his jaw and the barest hint of thickening about his middle that his spandex shirt couldn't hide. His narrow shoulders were hard with muscle that his shirt couldn't hide, either. And his legs were fabulous. Some people shouldn't wear spandex. Despite being older than I liked my men, David wasn't one of them.

"Is that what this is about?" I said, both ticked and relieved. "Is this how you get your clients? Stalking them?" I frowned and turned away. "That's pathetic. Even for a Were."

"Wait up," he said, lurching out onto the path after me in a snapping of twigs. "No. Actually, I'm here about the fish."

I jerked to a stop, my feet again in the sun. My thoughts zinged back to the fish I had stolen from Mr. Ray's office last September. *Shit.*

"Um," I stammered, my knees suddenly weak from more than the run. "What fish?" Fingers fumbling, I snapped my sunglasses open. Putting them on, I started walking for the exit.

David felt his middle for damage as he followed me, meeting my fast pace with his own. "See," he said almost to himself. "This is exactly why I've been following you. Now I'll never get a straight answer, I'll never settle the claim."

My stomach hurt, and I forced myself into a faster pace. "It was a mistake," I said, my face warming. "I thought it was the Howlers' fish."

David took off his sweatband, slicked his hair back, and replaced it. "Word is that the fish has been destroyed. I find that extremely unlikely. If you could verify that, I can write my report, send a check to the party Mr. Ray stole the fish from, and you'll never see me again."

I gave him a sidelong glance, my relief that he wasn't going to serve me with a writ or something very real. I had surmised that Mr. Ray had stolen it from someone when no one came after me for it. But this was unexpected. "Someone insured their fish?" I scoffed, not believing it, then realized he was serious. "You're kidding."

The man shook his head. "I've been following you trying to decide if you have it or not."

We had reached the entrance and I stopped, not wanting him to follow me to my car. Not that he didn't already know which one it was. "Why not just ask me, Mr. Insurance Agent?"

Looking bothered, he planted his feet widely with an aggressive stance. He was my height exactly—making him somewhat short for a man—but most Weres weren't big people on the outside. "You really expect me to believe you don't know?"

I gave him a blank look. "Know what?"

Running a hand across his thick bristles, he looked at the sky. "Most people will lie like the devil when they get ahold of a wishing fish. If you have it, just tell me. I don't care. All I want is to get this claim off my desk."

My jaw dropped. "A—A wishing . . ."

He nodded. "A wishing fish, yes." His thick eyebrows rose. "You really didn't know? Do you still have it?"

I sat down on one of the cold benches. "Jenks ate it."

The Were started. "Excuse me?"

I couldn't look up. My thoughts went back to last fall and my gaze drifted past the gate to my shiny red convertible waiting for me in the parking lot. I had wished for a car. Damn, I had wished for a car and gotten it. *Jenks ate a wishing fish?*

His shadow fell over me and I looked up, squinting at David's silhouette, black against the faultless blue of noon. "My partner and his family ate it."

David stared. "You're joking."

Feeling ill, I dropped my gaze. "We didn't know. He cooked it over an open fire and his family ate it."

His small feet moved in a quick motion. Shifting, he pulled a folded piece of paper and a pen from his backpack. As I sat with my elbows on my knees and stared at nothing, David crouched beside me and scribbled, using the smooth concrete bench as a desk. "If you would sign here, Ms. Morgan," he said as he extended the pen to me.

A deep breath sifted through me. I took the pen, then the paper. His handwriting had a stiff preciseness that told me he was meticulous and well-organized. Ivy would love him. Scanning it, I realized it was a legal document, David's handwritten addition stating that I had witnessed the destruction of the fish, unaware of its abilities. Frowning, I scrawled my name and pushed it back.

His eyes were full of an amused disbelief as he took the pen from me and signed it as well. I bit back a snort when he brought out a notarizing kit from his backpack and made it legal. He didn't ask for my identification, but hell, he'd been following me for three months. "You're a notary, too?" I said, and he nodded, returning everything to his backpack and zipping it up.

"It's a necessity in my line of work." Standing, he smiled. "Thank you, Ms. Morgan."

"No sweat." My thoughts were jumbled. I couldn't decide if I was going to tell Jenks or not. My gaze returned to David as I realized he was holding out his card. I took it, wondering.

"Since I've got you here," he said, moving so I wasn't looking into the sun to see him, "if you're interested in getting a better rate on your insurance—"

I sighed and let the card fall. *What a weenie.*

He chuckled, gracefully swooping to pick it up. "I get my health and hospitalization insurance for two fifty a month through my union."

Suddenly, I was interested. "Runners are almost uninsurable."

"True." He pulled a black nylon jacket out of his backpack and put it on. "So are field insurance adjusters. But since there are so few of us compared to the pencil pushers that make up the bulk of the company, we get a good rate. Union dues are one fifty a year. It gets you a discount on your insurance needs, car rentals, and all the steak you can eat at the yearly picnic."

That was too good to believe. "Why?" I asked, taking the card back.

He lifted his shoulder in a shrug. "My partner retired last year. I need someone."

My mouth opened in understanding. *He thought I wanted to be an insurance adjuster? Oh, ple-e-e-e-ease.* "Sorry. I've already got a job," I said, snickering.

David made an exasperated noise. "No. You misunderstand. I don't *want* a partner. I've driven off all the interns they've saddled me with, and everyone else knows better than to try. I've got two months to find someone, or they're going to shave my tail. I like my job, and I'm good at it, but I don't want a partner." He hesitated, his sharp gaze scanning the area behind me with professional intentness. "I work alone. You sign the paper, you belong to the union, you get a discount on your insurance, you never see me but for the yearly picnic, where we act chummy and do the three-legged race. I help you; you help me."

I couldn't stop my eyebrows from rising, and I shifted my attention from him to the card in my grip. Four hundred dollars less a month sounded great. And I'd be willing to bet they could beat what I was paying for my car insurance, too. Tempted, I asked, "What kind of hospitalization do you have?"

His thin lips curled up in a smile to show a hint of small teeth. "Silver Cross."

My head bobbed. It was designed for Weres, but it was flexible enough to work. A broken bone is a broken bone. "So," I drawled, leaning back, "what's the catch?"

His grin widened. "Your salary is deferred to me, as I'm the one doing all the work."

Ahhhh, I thought. He would get two salaries. This was a scam if I ever heard one. Smirking, I handed him his card back. "Thanks, but no thanks."

David made a disappointed sound, backing up with his card. "You can't blame me for trying. It was my old partner's suggestion, actually. I should have known you wouldn't go for it." He hesitated. "Your backup really ate that fish?"

I nodded, going depressed thinking about it. 'Least I got a car out of it first.

"Well . . ." He set the card down beside me, snapping it into the concrete. "Give me a call if you change your mind. The extension on the card will get you past my secretary. When I'm not in the field, I'm in the office from three to midnight. I might consider taking you on as an apprentice for real. My last partner was a witch, and you look like you have some chutzpah."

"Thanks," I said snidely.

"It's not as boring as it looks. And safer than what you're doing now. Maybe after you get beat up a few more times you'll change your mind."

I wondered if this guy was for real. "I don't work for people. I work for myself."

Nodding, he casually touched his head in a loose salute before he turned and walked away. I pulled myself straight as his trim figure slipped past the gate. He got in a gray two-seater across the lot from my little red car and drove off. I cringed, recognizing it and realizing he had watched Nick and me yesterday.

My butt was frozen from sitting on the concrete when I stood. I picked up his card, tearing it in half and going to a trash can, but as I held the ripped pieces over the hole, I hesitated. Slowly, I put them in my pocket.

An insurance adjuster? a small voice in my head mocked. Grimacing, I took the pieces out and dropped them in the can. Work for someone else again? No. Never.

Nine

Peace sat warm in me as I sprinkled the yellow sugar on the iced cookie shaped like the sun. Okay, so it was a circle, but with the sparkling sugar it could be the sun. I was tired of the long nights, and the physical affirmation of the turning seasons had always filled me with a quiet strength. Especially the winter solstice.

I set the finished cookie aside on the paper towel and took another. It was quiet but for music filtering in from the living room. Takata had released "Red Ribbons" to WVMP, and the station was playing it into the ground. I didn't care. The refrain was the one I had told him fitted with the theme of the song, and it pleased me I had played some small part in its creation.

All the pixies were sleeping in my desk for at least two more hours. Ivy probably wouldn't be up stumbling about in search of coffee for even longer. She had come in before sunrise looking calm and relaxed, self-consciously seeking my approval for having slacked her blood lust on some poor sap before falling into bed like a Brimstone addict. I had the church to myself, and I was going to squeeze every drop of solitude out of it that I could.

Swaying to the heavy beat of drums in a way I wouldn't if anyone were watching, I smiled. It was nice to be alone once in a while.

Jenks had made his kids do more than apologize to me,

and I had woken this afternoon to a hot pot of coffee in a sparkling clean kitchen. Everything shone, everything was polished. They had even scoured the accumulated dirt out of the circle I had etched into the linoleum around the center island counter. Not a breath of dust or cobweb marred the walls or ceiling, and as I dipped my knife into the green icing, I vowed to try to keep it this clean all the time.

Yeah, right, I thought as I layered frosting on the wreath. I'd put it off until I was back to the same level of chaos that the pixies had dragged me out of. I'd give it two weeks, tops.

Timing my movements with the beat of the music, I placed three little hot candies to look like berries. A sigh shifted my shoulders, and I set it aside and took up the candle cookie, trying to decide whether to make it purple for aged wisdom or green for change.

I was reaching for the purple when the phone rang from the living room. I froze for an instant, then set the butter tub of frosting down and hustled after it before it could wake the pixies. They were worse than having a baby in the house. Snatching the remote from the couch, I pointed it at the disc player to mute it. "Vampiric Charms," I said as I picked up the phone and hoped I wasn't breathing hard. "This is Rachel."

"How much for an escort on the twenty-third?" a young voice asked, cracking.

"That depends on the situation." I frantically looked for the calendar and a pen. They weren't where I'd left them, and I finally dug through my bag for my datebook. I thought the twenty-third was a Saturday. "Is there a death threat involved or is it general protection?"

"Death threat!" the voice exclaimed. "All I want is a good-looking girl so my friends won't think I'm a dweeb."

My eyes closed as I gathered my strength. *Too late,* I thought, clicking the pen closed. "This is an independent runner service," I said tiredly, "not a bloodhouse. And kid? Do yourself a favor and take the shy girl. She's cooler than you think, and she won't own your soul in the morning."

The phone clicked off, and I frowned. This was the third such call this month. Maybe I should take a look at the yellow pages ad that Ivy bought.

I wiped my hands free of the last sugar and shuffled in the narrow cabinet that the message machine sat on, pulling out the phone book and dropping it on the coffee table. The red message light was blinking, and I tapped it, leafing through the heavy book to Private Investigators. I froze when Nick's voice came rolling out, guilty and awkward, telling me he had stopped by about six this morning and picked up Jax and that he would call me in a few days.

"Coward," I breathed, thinking it was one more crucifix tied to the coffin. He knew no one but the pixies would be up then. I vowed to enjoy myself on my date with Kisten, whether Ivy would have to kill him afterward or not. I jabbed the button to clear his message, then went back to the phone book.

We were one of the last listings, and as I found Vampiric Charms in a friendly font, my eyebrows rose. It was a nice ad, more attractive than the full-page ads around it, with a line drawing of a mysterious-looking woman in a hat and duster ghosted into the background.

" 'Fast. Discreet. No questions asked,' " I said, reading it. " 'Sliding scale. Payment options. Insured. Week, day, and hourly rates.' " Under it all were our three names, address, and phone number. I didn't get it. There was nothing here that would lead anyone to think bloodhouse or even a dating service. Then I saw the tiny print at the bottom saying to see the secondary entries.

I flipped through the thin sheets to the first one listed, finding the same ad. Then I looked closer; not at our ad, but the ones around it. Holy crap, that woman was hardly clothed, having the perky body of an animé cartoon. My eyes flicked to the heading. "Escort Service?" I said, flushing at the steamy, suggestive ads.

My gaze jerked to our advertisement again, the words taking on an entirely new meaning. No questions asked? Week, day, or hourly rates? *Payment options?* Lips pressed together, I shut the book, leaving it out to talk to Ivy about. No wonder we were getting calls.

More than a little irate, I unmuted the stereo and headed back into the kitchen, Steppenwolf's "Magic Carpet Ride" trying its best to lighten my mood.

It was the hint of a draft, the barest scent of wet pavement, that made my step hesitate and the palm streaking out at me past the archway to the kitchen miss my jaw.

"God bless it!" I swore as I dove past it into the kitchen instead of falling back into the cramped hall. Remembering Jenks's kids, I tapped the ley line out back but did nothing else as I fell into a defensive crouch between the sink and the island counter. I almost choked when I saw whom it was standing by the archway.

"Quen?" I stammered, not getting out of my stance as the lightly wrinkled, athletic man stared at me with no expression. The head of Trent's security was dressed entirely in black, his tight-fitting body stocking looking vaguely like a uniform. "What in hell are you doing?" I said. "I ought to call the I.S., you know that? And have them haul your ass out of my kitchen for illegal entry! If Trent wants to see me, he can come down here just like anyone else. I'll tell him he can suck dishwater, but he ought to have the decency to let me do it in person!"

Quen shook his head. "I have a problem, but I don't think you can handle it."

I made an ugly face at him. "Don't test me, Quen," I all but snarled. "You'll fail."

"We'll see."

That was all the warning I got as the man pushed off the wall, headed right for me.

Gasping, I dove past him instead of backward the way I wanted. Quen lived and breathed security. Backing away would only get me caught. Heart pounding, I grabbed my dented copper spell pot with white frosting in it and swung.

Quen caught it, yanking me forward. Adrenaline hurt my

head as I let it go, and he tossed it aside. It made a harsh bong and spun into the hallway.

I snatched the coffeemaker and threw it. The appliance jerked back at its cord, and the carafe fell to shatter on the floor. He dodged, his green eyes peeved when they met mine, as if wondering what in hell I was doing. But if he got a grip on me, I was a goner. I had a cupboard of charms in arm's reach, but no time to invoke even one.

He gathered himself to jump, and remembering how he had evaded Piscary with incredible leaps, I went for my dissolution vat. Teeth gritted in effort, I tipped it over.

Quen cried out in disgust as ten gallons of saltwater cascaded over the floor to mix with the coffee and glass shards. Arms pinwheeling, he slipped.

I levered myself onto the island counter, stepping on frosted cookies and knocking over vials of colored sugar. Crouched to avoid the hanging utensils, I jumped feet first as he rose.

My feet hit him squarely in the chest and we both went down.

Where was everyone? I thought as my hip took the fall and I grunted in pain. I was making enough noise to wake the undead. But as such commotion was more common than silence these days, Ivy and Jenks would probably ignore it and hope it went away.

Slipping, I skittered from Quen. Hands reaching unseeing, I scrabbled for my paint ball gun kept purposely at crawling height. I yanked it out. Nested copper pots rolled noisily.

"Enough!" I shouted, arms stiff as I sat on my butt in saltwater, aiming at him. It was loaded with water-filled splat balls for practice, but he didn't know that. "What do you want?"

Quen hesitated, water making darker smears on his black pants. His eye twitched.

Adrenaline surged. He was going to risk it.

Instinct and practice with Ivy made me squeeze the trigger as he leapt onto the table to land like a cat. I tracked him, squeezing out every last splat ball.

His expression went affronted as he pulled himself to a crouching halt, his attention jerking from me to the six new splatters on his skintight shirt. Crap. I'd missed him once. Jaw clenched, his eyes narrowed in anger. "Water?" he said. "You load your spell gun with water?"

"Ain't you just lucky for that?" I snapped. "What do you want?" He shook his head, and my breath hissed in as I felt a dropping sensation in me. He was tapping the line out back.

Panic jerked me to my feet, and I flung my hair out of my eyes. From his vantage point on the table, Quen straightened to his full height, his hands moving as he whispered Latin.

"Like hell you will!" I shouted, throwing my splat gun at him. He ducked, and I snatched up whatever I could to throw it at him, desperate to keep him from finishing the charm.

Quen dodged the butter tub of frosting. It thunked into the wall to make a green smear. Grabbing the cookie tin, I ran around the counter, swinging it like a board. He dove off the table to avoid it, cursing at me. Cookies and red-hot candies went everywhere.

I followed him, grabbing him about the knees to bring us both down in a sodden splat. He twisted in my grip until his livid green eyes met mine. Hands scrabbling, I shoved saltwater soggy cookies into his mouth so he couldn't verbally invoke a charm.

He spit them at me, his deeply tanned, pockmarked face vehement. "You little canicula—" he managed, and I jammed some more into him.

His teeth closed on my finger, and I shrieked, jerking back. "You bit me!" I shouted, incensed. My fist swung, but he rolled to his feet, crashing into the chairs.

Panting, he stood. He was soaked, covered in water and sparkles of colored sugar. Growling an unheard word, he leapt.

I lurched upright to flee. Pain lanced through my scalp as

he grabbed my hair and spun me around into an embrace, my back to his chest. One arm went chokingly around my neck. The other slipped between my legs, yanking me up onto one foot.

Furious, I elbowed him in the gut with my free arm. "Get your hands . . ." I grunted, hopping backward on one foot, "off my hair!" I reached the wall, and smashed him into it. His breath exploded out as I jabbed his ribs, and his grip around my neck fell away.

I spun to stiff-arm his jaw, but he was gone. I was staring at the yellow wall. Shrieking, I went down, my legs pulled out from under me. His weight landed on me, pinning me to the wet floor with my arms over my head.

"I win," he panted as he straddled me, his green eyes from under his short hair wild.

I struggled to no effect, ticked that it was going to be something as stupid as body mass that decided this. "You forgot something, Quen," I snarled. "I have fifty-seven roommates."

His lightly wrinkled brow furrowed.

Taking a huge breath, I whistled. Quen's eyes widened. Grunting in effort, I jerked my right hand free and slammed the heel of my hand at his nose.

He jerked back out of the way and I pushed him off me, rolling. Still on my hands and knees, I flipped my wet stringy hair out of the way.

Quen had gained his feet, but he wasn't moving. He was standing stock-still, cookie-smeared palms raised above his head in a gesture of acquiescence. Jenks was hovering before him, the sword he kept to fight off encroaching fairies aimed at Quen's right eye. The pixy looked pissed, dust spilling from him to make a steady sunbeam from him to the floor.

"Breathe," Jenks threatened. "Blink. Just give me a reason, you bloody freak of nature."

I stumbled upright as Ivy dove into the room, moving faster than I would have believed possible. Robe loose and flowing, she grabbed Quen by the throat.

The lights flickered and the hanging utensils swung as she slammed him into the wall beside the doorway. "What are you doing here?" she snarled, her knuckles white with pressure. Jenks had moved with Quen, his sword still touching the man's eye.

"Wait!" I exclaimed, worried they might kill him. Not that I'd mind, but then there'd be I.S. personnel in my kitchen, and paperwork. Lots of paperwork. "Slow down," I soothed.

My eyes flicked to Ivy, still holding Quen. There was frosting on my hand, and I wiped it off on my damp jeans as I caught my breath. Saltwater marked me and I had cookie crumbs and sugar in my hair. The kitchen looked like the Pillsbury Doughboy had exploded. I squinted at the purple frosting on the ceiling. *When had that happened?*

"Ms. Morgan," Quen said, then gurgled as Ivy tightened her grip. The music from the living room softened to talk.

I felt my ribs, wincing. Angry, I paced to where he hung in Ivy's hold. "Ms. Morgan?" I shouted, six inches from his reddening face. "Ms. Morgan? I'm Ms. Morgan now? What in hell is wrong with you!" I yelled. "Coming into my house. Ruining my cookies. Do you know how long it's going to take to clean this up?"

He gurgled again, and my anger started to slow. Ivy was staring at him with a shocking intensity. The scent of his fear had tripped her past her limits. She was vamping out at noon. This wasn't good, and I took a step back, suddenly sobered. "Um, Ivy?" I said.

"I'm okay," she said huskily, her eyes saying different. "Want me to bleed him quiet?"

"No!" I exclaimed, and I felt another drop in me. Quen was tapping a line. I took an alarmed breath. Things were spiraling out of control. Someone was going to get hurt. I could set a circle, but it would be around me, not him. "Drop him!" I demanded. "Jenks, you too!" Neither of them moved. "Now!"

Shoving him up the wall, Ivy dropped him and stepped

away. He hit the floor in a slump, his hand at his neck as he coughed violently. Slowly he moved his legs into a normal position. Flipping his very black hair from his eyes, he looked up, sitting cross-legged and barefoot. "Morgan," he said roughly, his hand hiding his throat, "I need your help."

I glanced at Ivy, who was tightening her black silk robe about herself again. *He needed my help? Ri-i-i-i-ight.* "You okay?" I asked Ivy, and she nodded. The ring of brown left to her eyes was too thin for my comfort, but the sun was high, and the tension in the room was easing. Seeing my concern, she pressed her lips together.

"I'm fine," she reiterated. "You want me to call the I.S. now or after I kill him?"

My gaze ran over the kitchen. My cookies were ruined, sitting in soggy clumps. The globs of frosting on the walls were starting to run. Saltwater was venturing out of the kitchen, threatening to reach the living room rug. Letting Ivy kill him was looking really good.

"I want to hear what he has to say," I said as I slid open a drawer and put three dish towels in the threshold as a dike. Jenks's kids were peeking around the corner at us. The angry pixy rubbed his wings together to make a piercing whistle, and they vanished in a trill of sound.

Taking a fourth towel, I wiped the frosting off my elbow and went to stand before Quen. Feet spread wide and my fists on my hips, I waited. It must have been big if he was willing to risk Jenks figuring out he was an elf. My thoughts went to Ceri across the street, and my worry grew. I wasn't going to let Trent know she existed. He would use her some way—some very ugly way.

The elf felt his ribs through his black shirt. "I think you cracked them," he said.

"Did I pass?" I said snidely.

"No. But you're the best I've got."

Ivy made a sound of disbelief, and Jenks dropped down before him, staying carefully out of his reach. "You ass," the four-inch man swore. "We could have killed you three times over."

Quen frowned at him. "We. It was *her* I was interested in. Not *we*. She failed."

"So I guess that means you'll be leaving," I said, knowing I wouldn't be that lucky. I took in his subdued attire and sighed. It was just after noon. Elves slept when the sun was high and in the middle of the night, just like pixies. Quen was here without Trent's knowledge.

Feeling more sure of myself, I pulled out a chair and sat down before Quen could see my legs trembling. "Trent doesn't know you're here," I said, and he nodded solemnly.

"It's my problem, not his," Quen said. "I'm paying you, not him."

I blinked, trying to disguise my unease. Trent didn't know. Interesting. "You have a job for me that he doesn't know about," I said. "What is it?"

Quen's gaze went to Ivy and Jenks.

Peeved, I crossed my legs and shook my head. "We're a team. I'm not asking them to leave so you can tell me of whatever piss-poor problem you've landed yourself in."

The older elf's brow wrinkled. He took an angry breath.

"Look," I said, my finger jabbing out to point at him. "I don't like you. Jenks doesn't like you. And Ivy wants to eat you. Start talking."

He went motionless. It was then I saw his desperation, shimmering behind his eyes like light on water. "I have a problem," he said, fear the thinnest ribbon in his low, controlled voice.

I glanced at Ivy. Her breath had quickened and she stood with her arms wrapped about herself, holding her robe closed. She looked upset, her pale face even more white than usual.

"Mr. Kalamack is going to a social gathering and—"

My lips pursed. "I already turned down one whoring offer today."

Quen's eyes flashed. "Shut up," he said coldly. "Someone

is interfering in Mr. Kalamack's secondary business ventures. The meeting is to try to come to a mutual understanding. I want you to be there to be sure that's all it is."

Mutual understanding? It was an I'm-tougher-than-you-so-get-out-of-my-city party. "Saladan?" I guessed.

Genuine surprise washed over him. "You know him?"

Jenks was flitting over Quen, trying to figure out what he was. The pixy was getting more and more frustrated, his shifts of direction becoming jerky and accented with sharp snaps of his dragonfly wings. "I've heard of him," I said, thinking of Takata. My eyes narrowed. "Why should I care if he assumes Trent's *secondary* business ventures? This is about Brimstone, isn't it?" I said. "Well, you can take a leap of faith and burn in hell. Trent is killing people, not that he hasn't done it before, but now he's killing them for no reason." Outrage pulled me to my feet. "Your boss is moth crap. I ought to bring him in, not protect him. And you," I said, louder, pointing, "are lower than moth crap for doing nothing while he does it!"

Quen flushed, making me feel vastly better about myself. "Are you that stupid?" he said, and I stiffened. "The bad Brimstone isn't from Mr. Kalamack; it's from Saladan. That's what this meeting is about. Mr. Kalamack is trying to get it off the streets, and unless you want Saladan taking over the city, you'd better start trying to keep Mr. Kalamack alive like the rest of us. Are you going to take the run or not? It pays ten thousand."

From Jenks came an eyeball-hurting pulse of ultrasonic surprise.

"Cash up front," Quen added, pulling a narrow wad of bills from somewhere on his person and throwing it at my feet.

I looked at the money. It wasn't enough. A million dollars wouldn't be enough. I shifted my foot, and it slid across the wet floor to Quen. "No."

"Take the money and let him die, Rache," Jenks said from the sun-strewn windowsill.

The black-clad elf smiled. "That's not how Ms. Morgan works." His pockmarked face was confident, and I hated the self-assured look in his green eyes. "If she takes the money, she'll protect Mr. Kalamack down to her last breath. Won't you?"

"No," I said, knowing I would. But I wasn't going to take his lousy ten grand.

"And you will take the money and the job," Quen said, "because if you don't, I'm going to tell the world about your summers at that little camp of his father's. You're the only person who has a ghost's chance in hell to keep him alive."

My face went cold. "Bastard," I whispered, refusing to feel afraid. "Why don't you just leave me alone? Why me? You just smeared me into the floor."

His eyes dropped from mine. "There will be vampires there," he said softly. "Powerful ones. There's the chance—" He took a breath and met my eyes. "I don't know if—"

I shook my head, somewhat reassured. Quen wouldn't tell. Trent would be mildly ticked if I was packed up and shipped off to Antarctica; he still had hopes of luring me to his payroll himself. "If you're afraid of vampires, that's your problem," I said. "I'm not going to let you make it mine. Ivy, get him out of my kitchen."

She didn't move, and I turned, my ire evaporating at the blank look on her face. "He's been bitten," she whispered, the wistful faltering in her voice shocking me. Hunched into herself, she leaned back against the wall, closed her eyes, and took a slow breath to scent him.

My lips parted in understanding. Piscary had bitten him, right before I clubbed the undead vampire into unconsciousness. Quen was an Inderlander, and so couldn't contract the vamp virus and be turned, but he might be mentally bound to the master vampire. I found my hand covering my neck, my face cold.

Big Al had taken the form and abilities of a vampire when he had torn open my neck and tried to kill me. He had filled my veins with the same potent cocktail of neurotransmitters that now ran through Quen. It was a survival trait to help ensure that vamps had a willing blood supply, and it turned pain into pleasure when stimulated by vampire pheromones. If the vamp had enough experience, they could sensitize the response such that they, and only they, could stimulate the bite into feeling good, binding the person to them alone and preventing easy poaching of their private supply.

Algaliarept hadn't bothered to sensitize the neurotransmitters—seeing as he was trying to kill me. I was left with a scar that any vamp could play on. I didn't belong to anyone, and as long as I kept vampire teeth on the right side of my skin, I wouldn't. In the ranking of the vampire world, an unbound bitee was the lowest of the low, a party favor, a pathetic remnant that was so beneath notice that any vampire could take what they wanted. Unclaimed property didn't last long, passed from vamp to vamp, soon drained of their vitality and will, left to rot in a confused loneliness of betrayal when the ugliness of their life started to show on their face. I'd be among their ranks if it wasn't for Ivy's protection.

And Quen had either been bitten and left unclaimed like me, or bitten and claimed by Piscary. As I stared in pity at the man, I decided he had a right to be afraid.

Seeing my understanding, Quen rose smoothly to his feet. Ivy tensed, and I raised my hand to tell her it was all right. "I don't know if the bite has bound me to him or not," Quen said, the evenness of his voice failing to hide the fear in him. "I can't risk Mr. Kalamack relying on me. I might . . . be distracted at a sensitive moment."

Waves of bliss and promises of pleasure coming from that bite might indeed be a large distraction, even in the midst of a fight. Pity pulled me forward. Tracks of sweat marred his lightly wrinkled face. He was as old as my father would be if he were still alive, with the strength of a twenty-year-old and the sturdiness only maturity imparted.

"Has any other vamp made your scar tingle?" I asked him, thinking it was a really personal question, but he had come to me.

Never dropping my gaze, he said, "I've yet to get into a situation where it might."

"Rache?" Jenks called, and there was a clatter of wings as he dropped to hover beside me.

"Then I don't know if Piscary bound you or not," I said, then froze as I realized my scar was tingling, sending hints of deeper feelings to bring me to a wide-eyed alertness. Quen stiffened. Our eyes met, and I knew by his frightened look that he was feeling it too.

"Rache!" Jenks shouted, his wings red as he got in my face and forced me to back up. "Quen isn't the only one with a problem here!"

I followed his frightened gaze behind me to Ivy. "Oh . . . crap," I whispered.

Ivy had pressed herself into a corner, her robe falling open to show her black silk nightgown. Her awareness was lost, black eyes unseeing as her mouth worked. I froze, not knowing what was going on.

"Get him out of here," she whispered, a bead of saliva dropping from her teeth. "Oh, God, Rachel. He's not bound to anyone. Piscary . . . He's in my head." She took a gasping breath. "He wants me to take him. I don't know if I can stop. Get Quen out of here!"

I stared, not knowing what to do.

"Get him out of my head!" she moaned. "Get him out!" Horrified, I watched her slide down the wall to huddle with her hands over her ears. "Get him out!"

Heart pounding, I spun to Quen. My neck was a flaming mass of promise. I could see by his expression that his scar was alight and flaming. God help me, it felt good.

"Get the door," I said to Jenks. Grabbing Quen's arm, I pulled him into the hallway. From behind us came a frightening guttural groan. I broke into a run, dragging Quen behind me. Quen stiffened when we entered the sanctuary, breaking my hold.

"You're leaving!" I shouted, reaching for him. "Now!"

He was hunched and trembling, making the martial arts

master look vulnerable. Lines from his internal struggle showed on his face. His eyes showed his broken spirit. "You will accompany Mr. Kalamack in my place," he said, his voice haggard.

"No, I won't." I reached for his arm.

Flashing alive, he sprang back. "You will accompany Mr. Kalamack in my place," he repeated, his face falling back into despair. "Or I will give in and go back into that kitchen." His face twisted, and I panicked that he might anyway. "He's whispering to me, Morgan. I can hear him through her. . . ."

My mouth went dry. My thoughts spiraled to Kisten. If I let him bind me to him, I could end up like this. "Why me?" I asked. "There's a university of people better at magic than I am."

"Everyone else relies on their magic," he panted, bent almost double. "You use it as a last resort. It gives you . . . the advantage." He gasped. "She's weakening. I can feel it."

"Okay!" I exclaimed. "I'll go, damn it! Just get out of here!"

A sound of agony, soft as a brush of wind, slipped from him. "Help me," he whispered. "I can't make myself move anymore."

Heart pounding, I grabbed his arm and dragged him to the door. Behind us was Ivy's tortured cry of anguish. My stomach twisted. What was I doing, going on a date with Kisten?

A bright stab of snow-reflected light lanced into the church as Jenks and his brood worked the elaborate pulley system we had rigged so they could open the door. Quen balked at the cold blast of air that sent the pixies hiding. "Get out!" I exclaimed in frustration and fear as I pulled him out onto the stoop.

A long Gray Ghost limo idled at the curb. My breath hissed in relief as Jonathan, Trent's number-one lackey, opened the driver's door and emerged. I never thought I'd be happy to see the shockingly tall, distasteful man. They were in this together, working behind Trent's back. This was a badder mistake than usual. I could feel it already.

Quen panted as I helped him lurch down the steps. "Get him out of here," I demanded.

Jonathan yanked open the passenger-side door. "Are you going to do it?" he said, his thin lips pressed tight as he took in my cookie-smeared hair and wet jeans.

"Yes!" I pushed Quen in. He fell onto the leather seat, collapsing like a drunk. "Go!"

The tall elf shut the door and stared at me. "What did you do to him?" he said coldly.

"Nothing! It's Piscary! Get him out of here!"

Apparently satisfied, he strode to the driver's side. With an odd quietness, the car accelerated. I stood on the icy sidewalk and shivered, watching it speed away until it turned a corner and was gone.

Pulse slowing, I wrapped my arms around myself. The winter sun was cold. Slowly I turned to go inside, not knowing what I'd find curled up on my kitchen floor.

Ten

I watched myself in the mirror above my new, solid-ash dresser as I put my hoop earrings in, the ones big enough for Jenks to ride on. The little black dress looked good on me, and the above-the-knee boots that went with it would keep me warm enough. I didn't think Kisten had planned a snowball fight in the park, as corny and cheap as that was. And he had said wear something nice. I stood sideways and checked myself out. This was nice. This was very nice.

Pleased, I sat on my bed and snapped my boots up, leaving the last few inches open so I could walk easier. I didn't want to get excited about going out with Kisten, but the chance to dress up and have a good time had been so infrequent lately that it was hard not to. I told myself that I could be going out with the girls and still feel like this. It wasn't Kisten; it was just going out.

Wanting a second opinion, I went clattering into the hall in search of Ivy. The memory of her fighting Piscary off in her mind was very real. The undead vampire had given up as soon as Quen was gone, but she had been very subdued the rest of the day, refusing to talk about it as she helped me clean the kitchen. She didn't want me going out with Kisten now, and I was inclined to agree with her that it was a stupid idea. But it wasn't as if I couldn't fight Kisten off. He had said he wouldn't bite me, and I wasn't about to let a moment of passion change my mind. Not now. Not ever.

I ran my hand down my sparkling party dress as I entered the living room, hesitating for Ivy's inspection. Curled up on the couch, she looked up from her magazine. I couldn't help but notice she was on the same page as when I had gone in to change thirty minutes ago.

"What do you think?" I said, making a slow circle and feeling tall in my spike-heeled boots.

She sighed, closing her magazine on her finger to mark the page. "I think it's a mistake."

My brow furrowed and I looked down at myself. "Yeah, you're right," I said as my thoughts went to my closet. "I'll put on something else."

I turned to leave, and she threw her magazine across the room to hit the wall before me. "That's not what I meant!" she exclaimed, and I spun, startled.

Ivy's oval face was creased and her thin eyebrows pinched as she sat up in her chair, fidgeting. "Rachel . . ." she cajoled, and I knew where this conversation was going.

"I'm not going to let him bite me," I said, becoming angry. "I'm a big girl. I can take care of myself. And after this afternoon, you can be damned sure his teeth aren't going to get anywhere near me."

Brown eyes worried, she curled her legs up under her to make herself look uncertain. It was a mien I didn't see on her very often. Her eyes closed as she took a breath as if gathering herself. "You look nice," she said, and I could almost feel my blood pressure drop. "Don't let him bite you," she added softly. "I don't want to have to kill Kisten if he binds you to him."

"You got it," I said, trying to lighten her mood as I walked out, knowing she might. It would be the only way to reliably break his hold on me. Time and distance would do it eventually, too, but Ivy wasn't one to take chances. And being bound to him after I had said no to her would be more than she could take. My heels clacked a little slower as I went back to my room to change into something more subdued. This outfit was asking for trouble.

Standing before my open closet, I pushed hangers around hoping something would jump out and say, "Wear me! Wear me!" I'd already been through everything and was starting to think I didn't have anything that wasn't too sexy and yet attractive enough for a night on the town. With all the money I'd spent filling my closet last month, there ought to have been something. My stomach tightened at the thought of my shrinking bank balance, but Quen had left his ten thousand on the kitchen floor. And I *had* agreed to baby-sit Trent . . .

The soft knock at my door startled me, and I spun, my hand to my collarbone.

"Um," Ivy said, her closed-lipped smile telling me she found something funny in having surprised me. "I'm sorry. I know you aren't going to let him bite you." She raised a long hand in a gesture of exasperation. "It's the vamp thing. That's all."

I nodded, understanding. I'd been living with Ivy long enough that her unconscious vampire instincts thought of me as her property even though her conscious mind knew different. It was why I didn't spar with her anymore, wash my clothes with hers, bring up ties of family and blood, or follow her out of the room if she abruptly left in the middle of a conversation for no apparent reason. All pushed her vampire-instinct buttons and would put us right back where we were seven months ago, fumbling about as we figured out how to live with each other.

"Here," Ivy said, coming one step into my room and holding out a fist-sized package wrapped in green foil and a purple bow. "It's an early solstice gift. I thought you might like to use it on your date with Kisten."

"Oh, Ivy!" I exclaimed, taking the elaborate, clearly store-wrapped package. "Thank you. I, ah, haven't wrapped yours yet. . . ." *Wrapped? I hadn't even bought it.*

"That's okay," she said, clearly flustered. "I was going to wait, but I thought you could use it. For your date," she fumbled. Eyes eager, she looked at the box in my hand. "Go on. Open it."

"Okay." I sat on my bed, carefully undoing the fabric and foil ribbon, as I might want to use it next year. The paper was embossed with the Black Kiss logo, and I slowed my fingers, wanting to prolong the suspense. The Black Kiss was an exclusive shop catering to vamps. I didn't even window-shop there. The associates knew by looking that I couldn't afford a hanky.

The paper came away to reveal a small wooden box, and inside that amid a cushion of crushed red velvet was a cutglass perfume bottle. "Ooooh," I breathed. "Thank you." Ivy had been getting me perfume since I'd moved in as we tried to find a scent that covered up her lingering aroma on me and help her curb her vampiric tendencies. It wasn't the romantic gift one might think it was, but kind of a vampire antiaphrodisiac. My dresser was covered in castoffs of varying degrees of effectiveness. Actually, the perfume was more for her than me.

"It's really hard to find," she said, starting to look discomforted. "You have to special order it. My dad told me about it. I hope you like it."

"Mmmm," I said, opening it and dabbing some behind my ear and on my wrists. I breathed deeply, thinking it smelled like a green woods and dash of citrus: clean and crisp, with a hint of darker shadows. Scrumptious. "Oh, this is wonderful," I said, standing to give her a quick impromptu hug.

She held very still, and I busied myself at my dresser, pretending I didn't notice her surprise. "Huh," she said, and I turned, finding a bemused expression on her. "It works."

"What . . ." I said warily, wondering what I had put on.

Her gaze rove before settling on mine. "It blocks a vampire's sense of smell," she said. "At least the more sensitive aromas that run to the unconscious." She gave me a lopsided smile to make her look harmless. "I can't smell you at all."

"Cool," I said, impressed. "I should wear it all the time."

Ivy's expression went subtly guilty. "You could, but I got the last bottle, and I don't know if I could find it again."

I nodded. She meant it was more expensive than a gallon of water on the moon. "Thank you, Ivy," I said earnestly.

"You're welcome." Her smile was genuine. "Happy early solstice." Her attention went to the front of the church. "He's here."

The rumble of an idling car filtered in through my thin stained-glass window. I took a deep breath and glanced at my bedside clock. "Right on time." I turned to her, pleading with my eyes for her to get the door.

"Nope." She grinned to show an unconscious slip of teeth. "You get it."

She turned and left. I looked down at myself, thinking what I had on was grossly inappropriate, and now I had to answer the door in it. "Ivy . . ." I complained as I followed her out. She never slowed, holding her hand up in refusal as she walked into the kitchen.

"Fine," I muttered, boot heels clicking to the front of the church. I flicked on the lights in the sanctuary in passing, the high, dim glow doing little to brighten the gloom. It was after one in the morning, and the pixies were all safe and snug in my desk until about four, when they would wake up. There was no light in the foyer, and I wondered if we ought to do something about that as I pushed open one side of the heavy wooden door.

With the soft sound of shoes grinding on rock salt, Kisten shifted back.

"Hi, Rachel," he said, his eyes taking in my clothes. A faint stiffening of the skin about his eyes told me I had guessed correctly; I wasn't dressed for whatever he had planned. I wished I knew what he had on under the luscious gray wool coat he was wearing. It went all the way to his boot tops and looked classy. He had shaved, too—his usual day-old stubble gone—giving him a polished look I wasn't used to seeing on him.

"This isn't what I'm wearing," I said by way of greeting. "Come on in. I just need a minute to change."

"Sure." Past him at the curb was his black Corvette, the light snow melting as it hit. He edged in past me, and I pulled the door thumping shut behind him.

"Ivy's in the kitchen," I said, starting back to my room, his soft steps following right behind me. "She had a bad afternoon. She won't talk to me, but she might talk to you."

"She called me," he said, the careful cadence of his words telling me he knew about Piscary asserting his dominance over her. "You're going to put on different boots, right?"

I jerked to a stop at the door to my room. "What's wrong with my boots?" I said, thinking they were the only thing that I was going to keep on. Ah . . . the only thing from this outfit, not the only thing total.

He looked at them, his dyed-blond eyebrows high. "They're what, five inches?"

"Yeah."

"It's icy. You're going to slip and break your ass." His blue eyes widened. "I mean your rear end."

A smile crossed my face at the thought that he was trying to clean up his mouth for me. "They make me as tall as you, too," I said smugly.

"I noticed." He hesitated. With a little jiggle, he whisked past me and into my room.

"Hey!" I protested as he went right to my closet. "Get out of my room!"

Ignoring me, he pushed all the way to the back where I put everything I didn't like. "I saw something here the other day," he said, making a small exclamation as he leaned to tug at something. "Here," he said, holding out a pair of drab black boots. "Start with these."

"Those?" I complained as he set them aside and stuck his arms back into my closet. "There's no heel to those at all. And they're four years old and out of style. And what were you doing in my closet?"

"That's a classic boot," Kisten said, affronted. "It never goes out of style. Put them on." He shuffled about again, pulling something out by feel, as he couldn't possibly see anything back there. My face warmed when I saw an old suit I'd forgotten I had. "Oh, this is just ugly," he said, and I snatched it out of his hands.

"It's my old interview suit," I said. "It's supposed to be ugly."

"Throw it away. But keep the pants. You're wearing them tonight."

"I am not!" I protested. "Kisten, I am fully capable of picking out my own clothes!"

Silently he raised his eyebrows, then went right back in to get a black long-sleeve shirt, from my don't-go-there section, that my mother bought for me three years ago. I hadn't the heart to give it away as it was silk, even though it was so long it hung mid-thigh on me. The neckline was too low, and it made my small chest look even flatter.

"This too," he said, and I shook my head.

"No," I said firmly. "It's too long, and it's something my mother would wear."

"Then your mother has better taste than you," he said in good humor. "Wear a camisole under it, and for God's sake, don't tuck it in."

"Kisten, get out of my closet!"

But he reached back in, bowing his head over something small in his hands as he rocked back. I thought it might be that ugly purse with the sequins I wished I had never bought, but I went mortified when he turned with an innocuous looking book. It had no title and was bound with a soft brown leather. The glint in Kisten's eyes told me he knew what it was.

"Give me that," I said, reaching out for it.

A wicked grin on him, Kisten held it up over his head. I could probably still get it, but I'd have to climb him. "Well, well, well . . ." he drawled. "Ms. Morgan. You have shocked and delighted me. Where did you get a copy of Rynn Cormel's guide to dating the undead?"

I pressed my lips together and fumed, stymied. Hip cocked, I could do nothing as he took a distancing step back and flipped through it.

"Have you read it?" he asked, then made a surprised *Mmmm* sound as he paused at a page. "I forgot about that one. I wonder if I can still do that."

"Yes, I've read it." I extended my hand. "Give it here."

Kisten pulled his attention from the pages, his long masculine hands cradling the book open. His eyes had gone black just a wee bit, and I cursed myself as a thrill of excitement went through me. Damn vamp pheromones.

"Ooooh, it's important to you," Kisten said, glancing out the door when Ivy banged something in the kitchen. "Rachel . . ." he said, his voice softer as he moved a step closer. "You know all my secrets." Without looking, his fingers dog-eared a page. "What drives me crazy. What instinctively tips me over—the—edge . . ."

He said the last word carefully, and I stifled a delicious shudder.

"You know how to . . . manipulate me," he murmured, the book dangling from an inattentive hand. "Do witches have a manual?"

He had somehow gotten within two feet of me, and I didn't remember him moving. The smell of his wool coat was strong, and under that was the heady scent of leather. Flustered, I snatched the book away, and Kisten dropped back a step. "Don't you wish," I muttered. "Ivy gave it to me so I would stop pushing her buttons. That's all it is." I shoved it under my pillow, and his smile widened. Damn it, if he touched me, I was going to slug him.

"That's where it belongs," he said. "Not a closet. Keep it close for quick reference."

"Get out," I said, pointing.

Long coat drifting about his shoe tops, he moved to the door, his every motion holding a confident seductive grace. "Put your hair up," he said as he sauntered through the archway. A grin came over him, showing me his teeth. "I like your neck. Page twelve, third paragraph down." He licked his lips, hiding the flash of fang even as I saw it.

"Out!" I shouted, taking two steps and slamming the door.

Fuming, I turned to what he had laid out on my bed, glad I'd made it that afternoon. A faint tingling at my neck drew my hand up, and I pressed my palm into it, willing it away. I stared at my pillow, then hesitantly pulled the book out. Rynn Cormel had written it? Cripes, the man had single-handedly run the country during the Turn, and he had enough time to write a vampire sex manual, too?

The scent of lilac rose as I opened it at the dog-eared page. I was prepared for anything, having been through the book twice and finding myself more appalled than turned on, but it was only about the use of necklaces to send messages to your lover. Apparently the more you covered your neck, the more you were inviting him or her to rip it open. The gothic metallic lace that was so popular lately was like walking around in a teddy. Going completely bare at the neck was almost as bad—a delicious claim of vampiric virginity and a complete and utter turn-on.

"Huh," I muttered, closing the book and dropping it on my new bedside table. Maybe a reread was in order. My gaze went to the outfit Kisten had chosen for me. It looked frumpy, but I'd try it on, and when Ivy told him I looked like I was forty, he could wait another ten minutes while I changed back.

Motions quick, I took off my boots and tossed them thumping aside. I had forgotten that the gray slacks were lined with silk, and they made a pleasant sensation slipping over my legs. I chose a black halter top—without Kisten's help—and put the long shirt on over it. It didn't do a thing to show off my curves, and I turned to my mirror, frowning.

I froze at my reflection, shocked. "Damn," I whispered. I had looked good before in my black dress and boots. But in this? In this I looked . . . sophisticated. Remembering page twelve, I fumbled for my longest gold chain and looped it over my head. "Double damn," I breathed, shifting to see myself from a different angle.

My curves were gone, hidden behind the simple straight lines, but the subdued statement of the modest slacks, silk shirt, and gold chain screamed confidence and casual wealth. Now my pale skin was softly alabaster instead of sickly white, and my athletic build appeared sleek. It was a new look for me. I didn't know I could do high-class wealthy.

I hesitantly pulled my hair up off my neck and held it atop my head. "Whoa," I breathed, when it turned me from sophisticated to elegant. Looking this good outweighed the embarrassment of letting Kisten know he could dress me better than I could dress myself.

Digging in a drawer, I found and invoked my last amulet to tame the frizz of my hair, then put my hair up, pulling a few strands to drape artfully before my ears. I dabbed on a bit more of my new perfume, checked my makeup, hid my hair-taming amulet behind my shirt, then grabbed a small clasp purse, as my shoulder bag would ruin everything. The lack of my usual charms gave me a moment of pause, but it was a date, not a run. And if I had to fight Kisten off, I'd be using ley line magic anyway.

My flat-heeled boots were subdued as I left my room and followed the soft give-and-take murmurs of Kisten and Ivy into the amber-lit sanctuary. I hesitated at the doorway, looking in.

They had woken the pixies, who were flitting everywhere, concentrating about Ivy's grand piano as they played tag among the wires and stops. There was a faint hum of sound shifting the air, and I realized the vibrations from their wings were making the strings resonate.

Ivy and Kisten stood by the archway to the foyer. She had that same uneasy, defiant look on her that she'd been wearing earlier when she refused to talk to me. Kisten was bent close, clearly concerned, with his hand on her shoulder.

I cleared my throat for their attention, and Kisten's hand fell. Ivy's posture shifted back to her usual equanimity, but I could see her shattered confidence underneath.

"Oh, that's better," Kisten said as he turned, his eyes lighting briefly on my necklace.

He had unbuttoned his coat, and I ran my eyes apprecia-
tively over him as I approached. No wonder he had wanted
to dress me. He looked fabulous: navy Italian pinstripe suit,
shiny shoes, hair slicked back and smelling faintly of
soap . . . and smiling at me with an attractive self-assurance.
His usual chain was a quick flash hidden behind the collar of
his starched white shirt. A tasteful tie was snugged up to his
neck, and a watch fob ran from a vest pocket through a but-
tonhole and then to the other vest pocket. Looking at his
trim waist, broad shoulders, and slender hips, there was
nothing to argue with. Nothing at all.

Ivy blinked as she took me in. "When did you buy that?"
she asked, and I smiled widely.

"Kist picked it out of my closet," I said brightly, and that
would be the only admission of my lack of polish he was going to get.

It was a date, so I went to stand beside Kisten; Nick would
have gotten a kiss, but as Ivy and Jenks were hovering—and
in Jenks's case, literally—a little discretion was in order.
More importantly, he wasn't Nick.

Jenks landed on Ivy's shoulder. "Do I need to say anything?" the pixy asked Kisten, his hands on his hips to look
like a protective father.

"No, sir," Kisten said, entirely serious, and I fought to
keep a smile from me. The picture of a four-inch pixy threatening a six-foot living vampire would have been ridiculous
if Kisten weren't taking him seriously. Jenks's warning was
real and very enforceable. The only thing more unstoppable
than fairy assassins were pixies. They could rule the world if
they wanted.

"Good," Jenks said, apparently satisfied.

I stood by Kisten and rocked back and forth on my flat
heels twice, staring at everyone. No one said a word. This
was really weird. "Ready to go?" I finally prompted.

Jenks snickered and flitted off to corral his kids back into
the desk. Ivy gave Kisten a last look, and walked out of the
sanctuary. Sooner than I would have expected, the TV

blared. I ran my eyes over Kisten, thinking he looked as far away from his biker image as a goat is to a tree.

"Kisten," I said, putting a hand to my necklace. "What does this . . . say?"

He leaned close. "Confidence. Not looking for anything, but naughty behind closed doors."

I stifled a thrill-invoked shudder when he pulled away. *Okay. That . . . works.*

"Let me help you with your coat," he said, and a sound of dismay came from me as I followed him into the foyer. My coat. My ugly, ugly coat with the fake fur around the collar.

"Ouch," Kisten said, his brow furrowed in the dim light seeping in from the sanctuary as he saw it. "Tell you what." He shrugged out of his coat. "You can wear mine. It's unisex."

"Now wait up," I protested, taking a step back before he could put it on me. "I'm smarter than that, fang-boy. I'll end up smelling like you. This is a platonic date, and I'm not going to break rule number one by mixing our scents before I even step out of my church."

He grinned, his white teeth glinting in the dim light. "Got me dead to rights," he admitted. "But what are you going to wear? That?"

A wince pulled my face tight while I looked at my coat. "All right," I agreed, not wanting to ruin my new facade of elegance with fake fur and nylon. And there was my new perfume . . . "But I'm not putting this on to intentionally mix our scents. Understand?"

He nodded, but his smile made me think otherwise, and I let him help me slip into it. My gaze went distant as its heavy weight eased over my shoulders, comforting and warm. Kisten might not be able to smell me, but I could smell Kisten, and his lingering body warmth sank into me. Leather, silk, and the barest hint of a clean-scented after-shave made a mix I was hard-pressed not to sigh into. "Will you be okay?" I asked, seeing he had only his suit jacket.

"The car is already warm." He intercepted my reach for

the door, his hand touching mine atop the handle. "Allow me," he said gallantly. "You're my date. Let me act like it."

Thinking he was being silly, I nevertheless let him open the door and take my arm as he helped me down the steps lightly dusted with snow. The snow had started shortly after sundown, and the ugly gray splotches kicked up by the snowplows were covered in pristine white. The air was crisp and cold, and there was no wind.

I wasn't surprised when he maneuvered to open the car door for me, and I couldn't help but feel special as I arranged myself. Kisten shut the door and hustled around to the front. The leather seats were warm, and there was no cardboard tree hanging from the rearview mirror. I took a quick look at the discs in the console as he got in. They ranged from Korn to Jeff Beck, and he even had one of singing monks. *He* listened to singing monks?

Kisten settled himself. As soon as the car started, he flipped the heater on full. I sank into the seat, relishing the deep rumble of the engine. It was markedly stronger than my little car, vibrating through me like thunder. The leather, too, was of a higher quality, and the mahogany on the dash was real, not fake. I was a witch; I could tell.

I refused to compare Kisten's car to Nick's drafty, ugly truck, but it was hard not to. And I liked being treated special. Not that Nick didn't make me feel special, but this was different. It was fun to get dressed up, even if we ended up eating at Mickey-d's. Which was a very real possibility as Kisten had only sixty dollars to spend.

Glancing at him sitting beside me, I realized I didn't care.

Eleven

"So," I said slowly as I fought to keep myself from reaching for the handle of the door to keep it from swinging open when we went over a railroad track. "Where are we going?"

Kisten gave me a sideways smile, the lights from the car behind us illuminating him. "You'll see."

My eyebrows rose, and I took a breath to press for details when a soft chirping came from his pocket. My playful mood faltered into one of exasperation as he gave me an apologetic look and reached for his phone.

"I hope this isn't going to happen all night," I muttered, putting my elbow on the door handle and staring at the dark. "Just turn around and take me home if it is. Nick never took a call when we were on a date."

"Nick wasn't trying to run half the city, either." Kisten flipped the silver top up. "Yes," he said, his sharp annoyance pulling my elbow from the door and my attention back to him. The muted, tiny sound of pleading filtered out. In the background I could hear thumping music. "You're kidding." Kisten flicked his attention from the road to me and back to the road. His eyes held a mix of hassle and disbelief. "Well get out there and open the floor."

"I tried that!" the tiny voice shouted. "They're animals, Kist. Bloody savages!" The voice subsided into an unrecognizable high-pitched panic.

Kisten sighed as he looked at me. "Okay, okay. We'll stop in. I'll take care of it."

The voice on the other end gushed in relief, but Kisten didn't bother to listen, flipping the phone closed and tucking it away. "Sorry, love," he said in that ridiculous accent. "One quick stop. Five minutes. I promise."

And it had started off so well, too. "Five minutes?" I questioned. "Something's got to go," I threatened, half serious. "Either the phone or that accent."

"Oh!" he said, putting his hand to his chest dramatically. "Wounded to the quick." He looked askance at me, clearly relieved I was taking this as well as I was. "I can't do without my phone. The accent goes . . ." He grinned. ". . . my love."

"Oh, please," I moaned, enjoying the light banter. I had been walking on eggshells around Nick so long, afraid to say anything lest I make things worse. Guess I didn't have to worry about that anymore.

I wasn't surprised when Kisten turned toward the waterfront. I had already surmised the trouble was at Piscary's Pizza. Since losing its Mixed Public License last fall, it had gone to a strictly vamp cliental, and from what I heard, Kisten was actually turning a profit. It was the only reputable establishment in Cincinnati without an MPL to do so. "Savages?" I questioned when we pulled into the parking lot of the two-story restaurant.

"Mike is being histrionic," Kisten said as he parked in a reserved spot. "It's only a bunch of women." He got out of the car and I sat tight, my hands in my lap as his door shut. I would have expected him to leave the car running for me. My head jerked up when he opened my door, and I stared blankly at him.

"Aren't you coming in?" he said, hunched as the cold breeze off the river shifted his bangs. "It's freezing out here."

"Ah, should I?" I stammered, surprised. "You lost your MPL."

Kisten reached for my hand. "I don't think you need to be worried."

The pavement was icy, and I was glad that I was wearing flat boots as I got out of his car. "But you don't have an MPL," I said again. The parking lot was full, and watching vampires bleeding each other couldn't be a pleasant sight. And if I willingly went in there knowing it lacked an MPL, the law wouldn't help me if anything went wrong.

Kisten's coat was long, dragging while he held my arm and escorted me to the canopy covered entrance. "Everyone in there knows you beat Piscary into unconsciousness," he said softly, inches from my ear to make me very aware of his breath on my cheek. "None of them would dare even think to do that. And you could have killed him but you didn't. It takes more guts to let a vampire live than to kill one. No one will mess with you." He opened the door, and light and music spilled out. "Or is it the blood you're worried about?" he questioned as I balked.

I fixed my eyes on his and nodded, not caring if he saw my apprehension.

Expression distant, Kisten gently led me forward. "You won't see any," he said. "Everyone here came to relax, not feed the beast. This is the only place in Cincinnati where vampires can go in a public setting and be themselves without having to live up to some human's, witch's, or Were's idea of what they should be and how they should act. There won't be any blood unless someone cuts a finger opening a beer."

Still unsure, I let him guide me in, stopping just inside the door while he knocked the snow from his dress shoes. The heat of the place struck me first, and I didn't think it was all coming from the fireplace at the far end of the room. It had to be pushing eighty, the warmth carrying the pleasant aroma of incense and dark things. I breathed deeply as I untied Kisten's coat, and it seemed to settle in my brain, relaxing me the way a hot bath and a good meal did.

A stirring of unease ruined the feeling when a living vamp came forward with an unsettling quickness. His shoulders looked as wide as I was tall, and he massed three hundred pounds if he was an ounce. But his eyes were sharp, revealing a quick intelligence, and he moved his muscular bulk with the sexy grace most living vamp's had. "I'm sorry," he said in an iron-pumping-gym accent as he came close. His hand was reaching out—not to touch but clearly indicating that I should leave. "Piscary's lost its MPL. Vamps only."

Kisten slid behind me and helped me slip his coat off. "Hi, Steve. Any trouble tonight?"

"Mr. Felps," the large man exclaimed softly, his speech taking on a well-educated accent to match the intelligence his eyes couldn't hide. "I wasn't expecting you until later. No. No trouble apart from Mike upstairs. We're all quiet down here." Brown eyes apologetic, he glanced at me. "Sorry, ma'am. I didn't know you were with Mr. Felps."

Seeing a golden opportunity to pry, I smiled. "Does Mr. Felps often bring young women not of the vampiric persuasion to his club?" I asked.

"No, ma'am," the man said so naturally that I had to believe him. His words and actions were so innocuous and unvampiric, that I had to sniff twice to make sure he was one. I hadn't realized how much of the vampire identity stemmed from attitude. And as I scanned the lower floor, I decided it was like any upscale restaurant, more mundane than when it had its MPL.

The wait staff was appropriately dressed with most of their scars hidden, and they moved with an efficient quickness that wasn't the least provocative. My gaze roved over the pictures above the bar, faltering when I saw a blurry shot of Ivy in her biker leather, riding her cycle with a rat and a mink perched on the gas tank. *Oh God. Someone had seen us.*

Kisten gave me a wry look upon seeing where my eyes were. "Steve, this is Ms. Morgan," he said as he handed my borrowed coat to the bouncer. "We aren't staying long."

"Yes, sir," the man said, then stopped in his tracks and turned. "Rachel Morgan?"

My smile grew wider. "Pleasure to meet you, Steve," I said.

A rush of fluster ran through me as Steve took my hand and kissed the top of it. "The pleasure is mine, Ms. Morgan." The large vampire hesitated, gratitude passing behind his expressive eyes. "Thank you for not killing Piscary. It would have made Cincinnati hell."

I chuckled. "Aw, it wasn't just me; I had help bringing him in. And don't thank me yet," I said, not sure if he was serious or not. "Piscary and I have an old argument, and I simply haven't decided if it's worth the effort to kill him or not."

Kisten laughed, but it sounded somewhat forced. "All right, all right," he said as he pulled my hand from Steve's. "That's enough. Steve, will you have someone get my long leather coat from downstairs? We're leaving as soon as I open the floor."

"Yes, sir."

I couldn't hide my smile as Kisten moved his grip to my elbow and subtly guided me to the stairway. I decided that though he kept touching me, it wasn't for any ulterior motive—yet—and I could tolerate him moving me around like a Barbie doll. It kinda went with my sophisticated look tonight and made me feel special.

"Good God, Rachel." His whisper in my ear made me shiver. "Don't you think you have enough of a badass attitude already without dumping blood on the floor?"

Steve was already gossiping to the help, and heads were turning to watch Kisten escort me to the second floor. "What?" I said, smiling confidently at anyone who would meet my eyes. I looked good. I felt good. Everyone could tell.

Kisten pulled me close to put his hand at the small of my back. "Do you really think it was a good idea to tell Steve that Piscary lives only because you haven't decided if you want to kill him or not? What kind of an image do you think that gives you?"

I smiled at him. I felt good. Relaxed. Like I had been sipping wine all afternoon. It had to be the vamp pheromones, but my demon scar had yet to even twinge. This was something else. Apparently there was nothing more relaxed and comfortable than a sated vampire, and they apparently liked to share the feeling. How come Ivy never felt like this? "Well, I did say I had help," I admitted, wondering if my words were slurring. "But killing Piscary is gonna move to the top of my wish list if he ever gets out of prison."

Kisten said nothing, peering at me with his brow furrowed, and I wondered if I had said something bad. But he had given me Egyptian embalming fluid that night, thinking it would knock Piscary out. He had said he wanted me to kill him. Maybe he'd changed his mind?

The music coming from the second floor grew louder the higher we rose up the stairway. It was a steady dance beat, and as it thumped into me, I found myself wanting to move to it. I could feel my blood humming, and I swayed as Kisten pulled me to a halt at the top of the stairs.

It was warmer up there, and I fanned myself. The huge plate-glass windows that had once overlooked the Ohio River had been replaced with walls, unlike the openings remaining downstairs. The dining tables had been removed to leave a building-wide, high-ceilinged open space ringed with tall cocktail tables pressed against the walls. There were no chairs. At the far end was a long bar. Again no chairs. Everyone was standing.

Above the bar just below the ceiling was a dark loft where the DJ and light-show panel was. Behind that was what looked like a pool table. A harried-looking tall man was standing in the center of the dance floor with a cordless mike, pleading to the mixed crowd of vampires: living and dead, men and women, all dressed similar to what I had been wearing earlier. It was a vamp dance club, I decided, wanting to cover my ears against the loud catcalls.

The man with the mike caught sight of Kisten, and his long face lifted in relief. "Kisten!" he said, his miked utterance turning heads and causing a cheer from the surrounding women in skimpy party dresses. "Thank God!"

The man beckoned to him, and Kisten took my shoulders.

"Rachel?" he questioned. "Rachel!" he exclaimed, pulling my attention from the pretty spinning lights above the floor. His blue eyes went worried. "Are you okay?"

I nodded, my head bobbing up and down. "Yup, yup, yup," I said, giggling. I felt so warm and relaxed. I liked Kisten's dance club.

Kisten's brow furrowed. He glanced at the overdressed man everyone was laughing at, then back to me. "Rachel, this will only take a moment. Is that okay?"

I was watching the lights again, and he turned my chin to look at him. "Yes," I said, moving my mouth slowly so it would come out right. "I'll wait right here. You go open the floor." Someone bumped me, and I almost fell into him. "I like your club, Kisten. It's fab."

Kisten stood me upright, waiting until I had my balance before letting go. The crowd had started to chant his name, and he raised a hand in acknowledgment. They redoubled their calls, and I put my hands over my ears. The music pounded into me.

Kisten gestured to someone at the bottom of the stairs, and I watched Steve take them two at a time, moving his hulking size like it was nothing. "Is she what I think she is?" Kisten asked the big man as he came close.

"Ye-e-e-e-ah," the big man drawled as they both peered at me. "She's blood-sugared. But she's a witch." Steve's eyes left me and fixed on Kisten. "Isn't she?"

"Yes," Kisten said, almost having to shout over the noise from the people for him to take the mike. "She's been bitten, but she's not bound to anyone. Maybe that's why."

"Vampy, vampy pher . . . uh . . . pher—" I licked my lips, frowning. "Pheromones," I said, my eyes wide. "Mmmm, nice. How come Ivy never feels like this?"

"Because Ivy is a tightass." Kisten frowned. A sigh shifted him, and I reached for his shoulders. He had nice shoulders, all hard with muscle and possibility.

Kisten took my hands from him and held them before me. "Steve, stay with her."

"Sure, boss," the big vampire said, moving to stand beside and slightly behind me.

"Thanks." Kisten peered into my eyes, holding them. "I'm sorry, Rachel," he said. "This isn't your fault. I didn't know this would happen. I'll be right back."

He shifted away, and I reached out after him, blinking at the tumult that rose as he took the center of the room. Kisten stood for a moment, looking sexy in his Italian suit as he gathered his thoughts with his head bowed and waited. He was working the crowd before he even said a word; I couldn't help but be impressed. A closed-lipped, roguish smile quirked his mouth when he pulled his head up, eyeing them from under his blond bangs. "Holy shit," he whispered into the mike, and the crowd cheered. "What the hell are you all doing here?"

"Waiting for you!" a female voice shouted.

Kisten grinned, moving his body suggestively as he nodded in the direction of the voice. "Hey, Mandy. You here tonight? When did they let you out?"

She screamed happily at him, and he smiled. "You are a ba-a-a-a-ad bunch of vixens, you know that? Giving Mickey a hard time. What's wrong with Mickey? He's good to you."

The women cheered, and I covered my ears, almost falling over as my balance shifted. Steve took my elbow.

"Well, I was trying to go out on a date," Kisten said, dropping his head dramatically. "My first one in I don't know how long. You see her, over there by the stair?"

A huge spotlight slammed into me, and I winced, squinting. The heat from it made my skin tingle, and I straightened, almost falling when I waved. Steve caught my arm, and I smiled up at him. I leaned into him, and he shook his head good-naturedly, running a finger along the underside of my jaw before gently standing me upright.

"She's a little out of it tonight," Kisten said. "You are all enjoying yourself *far* too much, and it's rubbing off on her. Who knew witch runners needed to party like us?"

The noise redoubled, and the pace of the lights quickened,

racing over the floor and up the walls and ceilings. My breath came faster as the beat of the music grew.

"But you know what they say," Kisten said over the rhythm. "The bigger they are—"

"The better it is," someone yelled.

"The more they need to party!" Kisten shouted over the laughs. "So take it easy on her, okay? She just wants to relax and have some fun. No pretenses. No games. I say any witch with enough balls to bring down Piscary and let him live has long enough fangs to party with. Are you all A-positive with that?"

The second floor exploded into sound, pressing me into Steve. My eyes warmed as my emotions swung from one extreme to the other. They liked me. How cool was that?

"Then let's get this party started!" Kisten yelled, spinning to the DJ nest behind him. "Mickey, give me the one I want."

The women screamed their approval, and I watched in slack-jawed surprise when the floor was suddenly covered in women, their eyes wild and their motions sharp. Short revealing dresses, high heels, and extravagant makeup was the rule, though there were a few older vampires dressed as classy as me. The living barely outnumbered the undead.

Music rolled from the speakers in the ceiling, loud and insistent. A heavy beat, a tinny snare drum, a corny synthesizer, and a raspy voice. It was Rob Zombie's "Living Dead Girl," and as I stared in disbelief, the varying motions of the clean-limbed and scantily clad female vamps shifted to the rhythmic, simultaneous movements of a choreographed dance.

They were line dancing. Oh—my—God. The vampires were line dancing.

Like a school of fish, they swayed and moved together, feet thumping with the strength to shake the dust from the ceiling. Not a one made a mistake or misstep. I blinked as Kisten did a Michael Jackson to move to the front, looking indescribably alluring in his confidence and suave movements, following it up with a Staying Alive. The women behind him followed him exactly after the first gesture. I couldn't tell if they had practiced or if their quicker reactions allowed them such a seamless improvisation. Blinking, I decided it didn't matter.

Lost in the power and intensity, Kisten all but glowed, riding the combined agreement of the vampires behind him. Numb from an overload of pheromones, music, and lights, I felt myself go hazy. Every motion had a liquid grace, every gesture was precise and unhurried.

The noise beat at me, and as I watched them party with a wild abandonment, I realized that it stemmed from the chance to be as they wanted to be without fear of anyone reminding them that they were vampires and therefore *had* to be dark and depressed and carry a mysterious danger. And I felt privileged to be respected enough to see them as they wished they could be.

Swaying, I leaned into Steve while the base line beat my mind into a blessed numbness. My eyelids refused to stay open. A thunder of noise shook through me, then subsided to mutate into a faster beat of different music. Someone touched my arm, and my eyes opened.

"Rachel?"

It was Kisten, and I smiled, giddy. "You dance good," I said. "Dance with me?"

He shook his head, glancing at the vampire who was holding me upright. "Help me get her outside. This is fucking weird."

"Bad, bad mouth," I slurred, my eyes closing again. "Watch your mouth."

A giggle escaped me, and it turned into a delighted shriek when someone picked me up to carry me cradled in his arms. I shivered as the noise lessened, and my head thumped into someone's chest. It was warm, and I snuggled closer. The thundering beat softened to casual conversation and the clatter of china. A heavy blanket covered me, and I made a sound of protest when someone opened a door and cold air hit me.

The music and laughter behind me subsided into an icy silence broken by twin steps crunching on grainy snow and the chiming of a car. "Do you want me to call someone?" I heard a man ask as an uncomfortably cold draft made me shiver.

"No. I think all she needs is some air. If she isn't right by the time we get there, I'll call Ivy."

"Well, take it easy, boss," the first voice said.

I felt a drop, and then the cold of a leather seat pressed against my cheek. Sighing, I snuggled deeper under the blanket that smelled of Kisten and leather. My fingers were humming, and I could hear my heartbeat and feel my blood moving. Even the thump of the door closing did nothing to stir me. The sudden roar of the engine was soothing, and as the car's motion pushed me into oblivion, I could have sworn I heard monks singing.

Twelve

The familiar rumble of driving over railroad tracks woke me, and my hand shot out to grab the handle before the door could jiggle open. My eyelids flashed apart when my knuckles smacked into the unfamiliar door. Oh yeah. I wasn't in Nick's truck; I was in Kisten's Corvette.

I froze, slumped and staring at the door with Kisten's leather coat draped over me like a blanket. Kisten took a slow breath, and the volume of the music dropped. He knew I was awake. My face warmed, and I wished I could pretend I was still passed out.

Depressed, I sat up and put Kisten's long coat on the best I could in the tight confines of the car. I wouldn't look at him, gazing out the window to try to place where in the Hollows we were. The streets were busy, and the clock on the dash said it was nearing two. I had passed out like a drunk in front of a fair slice of Cincinnati's upper-middle-class vampires, high on their pheromones. They must have thought I was a weak-willed, skinny witch who couldn't hold her own.

Kisten shifted in his seat as he eased to a halt at a light. "Welcome back," he said softly.

Lips pressed tight, I subtly felt my neck to make sure everything was the way I'd left it. "How long was I out?" I asked. *This is going to do wonders for my reputation.*

Kisten moved the gearshift out and back into first. "You didn't pass out. You fell asleep." The light changed and he inched up on the car in front of us to bully it into moving. "Passing out implies a lack of restraint. Falling asleep is what you do when you're tired." He glanced at me as we went through the intersection. "Everyone gets tired."

"No one falls asleep in a dance club," I said. "I passed out." My mind sifted through the memories, clear as holy water instead of mercifully blurred, and my face flamed. Sugared, he had called it. I had been blood-sugared. I wanted to go home. I wanted to go home, crawl into the priest hole the pixies had found in the belfry stairway, and just die.

Kisten was silent, the tensing of his body while he drove telling me he was going to say something as soon as he double-checked it against his patronizing meter. "I'm sorry," he said, surprising me, but the admission of guilt fed my anger instead of pacifying it. "I was an ass for taking you into Piscary's before finding out if witches could get blood-sugared. It never occurred to me." His jaw clenched. "And it's not as bad as you think."

"Yeah, right," I muttered, hand searching under the seat until I found my clasp purse. "I bet it's halfway across the city by now. 'Hey, anybody want to go over to Morgan's tonight and watch her get sugared? All it takes is enough of us having fun and down she goes! Whoo hoo!'"

Kisten's attention was riveted on the road. "It wasn't like that. And there were over two hundred vamps in there, a good portion undead."

"And that's supposed to make me feel better?"

Motions stiff, he pulled his phone from a pocket, punched a button, and handed it to me.

"Yeah?" I questioned into the phone, almost snarling. "Who is this?"

"Rachel? God, are you okay? I swear I'll kill him for taking you into Piscary's. He said you got sugared. Did he bite you?"

"Ivy!" I stammered, then glared at Kisten. "You told Ivy? Thanks a hell of a lot. Want to call my mom next?"

"Like Ivy wouldn't find out?" he said. "I wanted her to hear it from me. And I was worried about you," he added, stopping my next outburst.

"Did he bite you!" Ivy said, jerking my attention from his last words. "Did he?"

I turned back to the phone. "No," I said, feeling my neck. *Though I don't know why. I was such an idiot.*

"Come home," she said, and my anger shifted to rebellion. "If someone bit you, I could tell. Come home so I can smell you."

A sound of disgust came from me. "I'm not coming home so you can smell me! Everyone there was really nice about it. And it felt good to let go for five stinking minutes." I scowled at Kisten, seeing why he had given me Ivy to talk to. The manipulative bastard smiled. How could I stay angry with him when I was defending him?

"You got blood-sugared in five minutes?" Ivy sounded horrified.

"Yeah," I said dryly. "Maybe you ought to try it. Go sit and soak up the pheromones at Piscary's. They might not let you in, though. You might kill everyone else's buzz."

Her breath caught, and I immediately wished I could take it back. *Shit.* "Ivy . . . I'm sorry," I said quickly. "I shouldn't have said that."

"Let me talk to Kisten," came her soft voice.

I licked my lips, feeling like dirt. "Sure."

Fingers cold, I handed the phone to him. His unreadable eyes met mine for a flash. He listened for a moment, muttered something I didn't catch, then ended the call. I watched him for any hint of his mood as he tucked the little silver phone away behind his wool coat.

"Blood-sugared?" I questioned, thinking I ought to know what happened. "You want to tell me what that is exactly?"

His hands shifted on the wheel and he took a more relaxed position. The come-and-go flashes from the streetlights made eerie shadows on him. "It's a mild depressant," he said, "that vampires kick out when they're sated and relaxed.

Sort of like an afterglow? It came as a surprise the first time a few of the newest undead got sugared shortly after Piscary's went to an all-vamp clientele. It did them a world of good, so I took out the tables upstairs and put in a light show and DJ. Made it into a dance club. Everyone got sugared after that."

He hesitated as we made a sharp turn into an enormous parking lot down by the riverfront. Piles of snow rose six feet up at the edges. "It's a natural high," he said as he downshifted and drove slowly to the small cluster of cars parked by a large brightly lit boat at the dock. "Legal, too. Everyone likes it, and they've started self-policing themselves, kicking out anyone who comes in looking for a quick bleed and protecting the ones who come in hurting and fall asleep like you did. It's making a difference, too. Go ask that FIB captain of yours. Violent crimes being perpetrated by single young vamps have dropped."

"No kidding," I said, thinking it sounded like an informal vampire support group. *Maybe Ivy should go. Nah. She'd ruin it for everyone else.*

"You wouldn't have been so receptive if you hadn't needed it so much," he said, parking at the outskirts.

"Oh, so it *is* my fault," I said dryly.

"Don't," he said, his words harsh as he yanked the parking brake up. "I let you yell at me once already tonight. Don't try to flip this back on me. The more you need it, the harder it hits you is all. That's why no one thought anything less of you—and maybe they think a little more."

Taken aback, I made an apologetic face. "Sorry." I kinda liked that he was too smart to be manipulated by wicked female logic. It made things more interesting. Slowly he relaxed, turning off the heater and the softly playing disc.

"You were hurting inside," he said as he took the singing monk CD out and put it in its case. "From Nick. I've watched you hurt since you drew on that line through him and he got scared. And they got a kick out of seeing you unwind." He smiled with a distant look. "It made them feel good that the big bad witch who beat up Piscary trusted them. Trust is a feeling we don't get very often, Rachel. Living vampires lust after it almost as much as blood. That's why Ivy is ready to kill anyone who threatens your friendship with her."

I said nothing, staring as it started to make sense.

"You didn't know that, did you?" he added, and I shook my head, uncomfortable with digging into the whys of my relationship with Ivy. The car was getting cold, and I shivered.

"And showing your vulnerability probably upped your reputation, too," he said. "That you didn't feel threatened by them and let it happen."

I looked at the boat sitting before us, decorated with blinking holiday lights. "I didn't have a choice."

He reached out and adjusted the collar of his coat about my shoulders. "Yes, you did."

Kisten's hand fell from me, and I gave him a weak smile. I wasn't convinced, but at least I didn't feel like so much of a fool. My mind went over the events, the slow slide from a relaxed state into sleep, and the attitudes of those around me. There hadn't been any laugher at my expense. I had felt comforted, cared for. Understood. And there hadn't been a flicker of blood lust coming from any of them. I hadn't known vampires could be like that.

"Line dancing, Kisten?" I said, feeling my lips quirk into a wry smile.

A nervous laugh came from him and he bowed his head. "Hey, ah, could you not tell anyone about that?" he asked, the rims of his ears reddening. "What happens at Piscary's stays at Piscary's. It's an unwritten rule."

Being stupid, I reached out and ran a finger over the arch of his blood-reddened ear. He beamed, shifting to take my hand and brush his lips against my fingers. "Unless you want to get yourself banned from there as well," he said.

A shiver went through me at his breath on my fingers, and I pulled my hand away. His speculative look went right to my core, pulling my stomach into knots of anticipation.

"You looked good out there," I said, not caring if it was a mistake. "Do you have a karaoke night?"

"Mmmm," he murmured, shifting in his seat to fall into his bad-boy slump against the door. "Karaoke. There's an idea. Tuesdays are slow. We never get enough people to get a good buzz going. That might be just the thing."

I turned my attention to the boat to hide my smile. The image of Ivy on stage singing "Round Midnight" flitted through me and was gone. Kisten's attention followed mine to the boat. It was one of those remade riverboats, two stories tall and almost entirely enclosed. "I'll take you home if you want," he said.

Shaking my head, I tightened the tie on his coat, and the scent of leather puffed up. "No, I want to see how you pay for a dinner cruise on an iced-over river with only sixty dollars."

"This isn't dinner. This is the entertainment." He went to toss his hair artfully aside, then stopped mid-movement.

The lights in my head started to go on. "It's a gambling boat," I said. "That's not fair. Piscary owns all the gambling boats. You won't have to pay for a thing."

"It's not Piscary's boat." Kisten got out of the car and came around to my side. Looking good in his wool coat, he opened my door and waited for me to get out.

"Oh," I said, more lights turning on. "We're here checking out the competition?"

"Something like that." He bent to look at me. "Coming? Or are we going to leave?"

If he wasn't going to get his chips for free, it would be legal under our arrangement. And I'd never gambled before. It might be fun. Accepting his hand, I let him help me out of the car.

His pace was rapid as we hustled to the railed gangplank. A man in a parka and gloves waited at the foot of the ramp, and as Kisten talked with him, I glanced at the boat's waterline. Rows of bubbles kept the riverboat from becoming iced in. It was probably more expensive than taking the boat out for the winter, but city regulations stipulated you could only gamble on the river. And even though the boat was tied to the dock, it *was* on the water.

After speaking into a radio, the big man let us pass. Kisten put a hand on the small of my back and pushed me forward. "Thanks for letting me borrow your coat," I said as my boots clattered up and we found ourselves on the covered walkway. Tonight's snow made a white icing, and I brushed it off the railing to make slushy clumps in the open water.

"My pleasure," he said, pointing to a half wood, half glass door. There was an etched intertwined pair of capital S's on it, and I shuddered when a shimmer of ley line force passed through me when Kisten opened the door and we crossed the threshold. It was probably the casino's antitampering charm, and it gave me the willies, like I was breathing air coated in oil.

Another big man in a tux—a witch, by the familiar scent of redwood—was there to greet us, and he took both Kisten's and my coat. Kisten signed the guest book, putting me down as "guest." Peeved, I wrote my name below his with big loopy flourishes, taking up three entire lines. The pen made my fingers tingle, and I looked at the metal barrel before I set it down. All my warning flags went up, and while Kisten bought a single chip with most of our date allowance, I made a precise line through both my and Kisten's name to prevent our signatures from possibly being used as a focusing object for a ley line charm.

"And you did that because . . ." Kisten questioned as he took my arm.

"Trust me." I smiled at the stone-faced witch in a tux handling the guest book. There were subtler ways to prevent such thefts of focusing objects, but I didn't know them. And that I had just insulted the host didn't bother me at all. Like I would ever be back there again?

Kisten had my arm so I was free to nod, as if I was important to anyone who looked up from his or her gaming. I was glad Kisten had dressed me; I'd have looked like a whore here in what I had picked out. The oak and teak paneling was comforting, and the rich green carpet felt scrumptious on my feet, clear through my boots. The few windows were draped with deep burgundy and black fabric, pulled aside to show the lights of Cincinnati. It was warm with the scent of people and excitement. The clatter of chips and bursts of sound quickened my pulse.

The low ceiling could have been claustrophobic, but it wasn't. There were two tables of blackjack, a craps table, a wheel, and an entire bank of one-armed bandits. In the corner was a small bar. Most of the staff was of the witch or warlock persuasion, if my gut instinct was right. I wondered where the poker table was. Upstairs, perhaps? I didn't know how to play anything else. Well, I could play blackjack, but that was for sissies.

"How about some blackjack?" Kisten said as he subtly guided me that way.

"Sure," I said, smiling.

"Do you want a drink?"

I glanced at the surrounding people. Mixed drinks were the rule, except for the one guy with a beer. He was drinking it out of the bottle, and it ruined his entire look, tux aside. "Dead Man's Float?" I asked as Kisten helped me up onto a stool. "Double shot of ice cream?"

The hovering waitress nodded, and after getting Kisten's order, the older witch left. "Kisten?" My gaze rose, drawn by an enormous disk of gray metal hanging from the ceiling. Ribbons of a shiny metal radiated from it like a sunburst, running to the edges of the ceiling. It could have been a decoration, but I'd be willing to bet the metal continued behind the wood paneling and even under the floor. "Kisten, what is that?" I whispered as I nudged him.

His gaze flicked to the disk. "Probably their security system." His eyes met mine and he smiled. "Freckles," he said. "Even without your spells, you're the most beautiful woman here."

I blushed at his compliment—sure now that the enormous disk was more than art deco—but when he turned back to the dealer, I frantically looked at the mirror wall by the stairway. My shoulders slumped as I saw me in my sophisticated outfit with freckles and my hair starting to frizz. The entire boat was a no-spell zone—at least for us earth witches using amulets—and I suspected that big purple disk had something in there to hinder ley line witches, too.

Just having the boat on the water was some protection against ley line tampering since you couldn't tap a line over the water unless you went the roundabout way through a familiar. In all likelihood, the boat's security system dampened already invoked ley line spells and would detect anyone tapping a line through a familiar to invoke a new one. I had once had a smaller version on my long-gone I.S. issue cuffs.

While Kisten made nice with the dealer over his paltry fifty-dollar chip, I sat back and studied the people. There were about thirty, all well-dressed and most older than Kisten and I. A frown crossed me as I realized Kisten was the only vamp here: witches, Weres, and a few red-eyed humans up past their bedtime, but no vampires.

That struck me as wrong, so while Kisten doubled his money with a few hands, I unfocused my attention, wanting to see the room with my second sight. I didn't like using my second sight, especially at night when I could see an overlay of the ever-after, but I'd rather suffer a bad case of the heebie-jeebies than not know what was happening. I spared a thought wondering if Algaliarept would know what I was doing, than decided there was no way he could unless I tapped a line. Which I wouldn't.

Settling myself, I closed my eyes so my little used second sight wouldn't have to compete with my more mundane vision, and with a mental shove, I opened my mind's eye. Immediately the wisps of my hair that had worked themselves free moved in the wind that always blew in the ever-after. The memory of the ship dissolved to nothing, and the broken landscape of the demon city took its place.

A soft sound of disgust slipped from me, and I reminded

myself just why I never did this so close to the center of Cincinnati; the demon city was broken and ugly. The waning crescent moon was probably up now, and there was a definite red glow to the bottoms of the clouds, seeming to light the stark cascade of broken buildings and vegetation-stained rubble with a haze that covered everything and made me feel slimy somehow. It was said the demons lived belowground, and seeing what they had done to their city—built on the same ley lines as Cincinnati—I didn't wonder why. I'd seen the ever-after once during the day. It wasn't much better.

I wasn't in the ever-after, just viewing it, but I still felt uncomfortable, especially when I realized the reason everything looked clearer than usual was because I was coated in Algaliarept's black aura. Reminded of my slipped bargain, I opened my eyes, praying that Algaliarept wouldn't find a way to use me through the lines as he had threatened.

The gambling boat was just the way I left it, the noises that had been keeping me mentally connected to reality taking on meaning again. I was using both my visions, and before my second sight could become overwhelmed and lost, I hurriedly looked around.

My gaze was immediately drawn to the metal disk in the ceiling, and my mouth twisted in distaste. It pulsated with a thick purple smear, coating everything. I would have bet that this was what I had felt when I crossed the threshold.

It was everyone's aura that interested me most, though. I couldn't see mine, even when I looked in the mirror. Nick had once told me it was yellow and gold—not that anyone could see it under Al's now. Kisten's was a healthy, warm, orangy red shot through with slices of yellow concentrating about his head, and a smile quirked my lips. He used his head to make decisions, not his heart; I wasn't surprised. There was no black in it, though almost everyone else's in the room was streaked with darkness, I realized as I scanned the floor.

I stifled a twitch when I found a young man in the corner watching me. He was in a tux, but it had a comfortable look on him, not the stiff, uptight demeanor of the doorman or the professional dullness of the dealers. And the full glass by his hand said patron, not wait staff. His aura was so dark, it was hard to tell if it was a deep blue or deep green. A hint of demon black ran through it, and I felt a wash of embarrassment that if he was looking at me with his second sight—which I was sure he was—he could see me coated in Algaliarept's black slime.

Leaning back with his chin on his inward-curled fingertips, he fixed his gaze on mine from across the room, evaluating. He was deeply tanned—a neat trick in midwinter—and combined with the faint highlights in his straight black hair, I guessed he was from out of state and somewhere warm. Of average build and average looks, he didn't strike me as particularly attractive, but his confident assurance warranted a second look. He appeared wealthy, too, but who didn't in a tux?

My eyes slid from him to the guy swilling beer, and I decided tux-trash could be done after all. And with that thought making me smile, I turned back to surfer boy.

He was still watching me, and upon seeing my smile, he matched it, tilting his head in speculation and inviting conversation. I took a breath to shake my head, then stopped. Why in hell not? I was fooling myself that Nick was coming back. And my date with Kisten was a one-night-only offer.

Wondering if his trace of black was from a demon mark, I narrowed my concentration to try to see past his unusually dark aura. As I did, the purple glow coming from the ceiling disk brightened to take on the first tinges of yellow.

The man started, his attention jerking to the ceiling. Shock marred his clean-shaven face. An abrupt call went through the room from about three different places, and at my forgotten elbow, Kisten swore as the dealer said this hand had been tampered with and that all play was suspended until he could break a new deck.

I lost my second sight completely then, as the witch manning the guest book pointed me out to a second man, clearly security by his serious lack of any emotional expression.

"Oh crap," I swore, turning my back on the room and picking up my Dead Man's Float.

"What?" Kisten said irately while he stacked his winnings according to color.

I winced, meeting his eyes over the rim of my glass. "I think I made a boo-boo."

Thirteen

"What did you do, Rachel?" Kisten said flatly, stiffening as he looked over my shoulder.

"Nothing!" I exclaimed. The dealer gave me a tired look and broke the seal on a fresh deck of cards, and I didn't turn when I felt a presence loom heavy behind me.

"Is there a problem?" Kisten said. His attention was fixed a good three feet above my head. Slowly I turned, finding a really, really big man in a really, really big tux.

"It's the lady I need to talk with," his voice rumbled.

"I didn't do anything," I said quickly. "I was just looking over, um, the security. . . ." I finished weakly. "Just as a professional interest. Here. Here's one of my cards. I'm in security myself." I fumbled in my clasp purse for one, handing it to him. "Really, I wasn't going to tamper with anything. I didn't tap a line. Honest."

Honest? How lame was that? My black business card looked small in his thick hands, and he glanced at it once, quickly reading it. He made eye contact with a woman at the foot of the stairs. She shrugged, mouthing, "She didn't tap a line," and he turned to me. "Thank you, Ms. Morgan," the man said, and my shoulders eased. "Please don't assert your aura over the house spells." He didn't smile at all. "Any more interference and we will ask you to leave."

"Sure, no problem," I said, starting to breathe again.

He walked away, and play resumed around us. Kisten's

eyes were full of annoyance. "Can't I take you anywhere?" he said dryly, putting his chips into a little bucket and handing them to me. "Here. I have to use the little boys' room."

I stared blankly as he gave me a warning look before he ambled off, leaving me alone in a casino with a bucket of chips and no idea what to do with them. I turned to the blackjack dealer, and he arched his eyebrows. "Guess I'll play something else," I said as I slipped from the stool, and he nodded.

Clutch purse tucked under my arm, I glanced over the room with my chips in one hand and my drink in the other. Surfer boy was gone, and I stifled a sigh of disappointment. Head down, I looked at the chips, seeing they were engraved with the same intertwined S's. Not even knowing the monetary value of what I had, I drifted to the excitement of the craps table.

I smiled at two men who slid apart to make a spot for me, setting my drink and chips on the lower rim of the table while I tried to figure out why some people were happy at the five that was rolled and some were upset. One of the witches who'd made room for me was standing too close, and I wondered when he would inflict his pickup line on me. Sure enough, after the next roll he gave me a sloppy grin and said, "Here I am. What are your last two wishes?"

My hand trembled and I forced it to remain unmoving. "Please," I said. "Just stop."

"Oh, nice manners, babe," he said loudly, trying to embarrass me, but I could embarrass myself a hell of a lot easier than he could.

The chatter of the game seemed to vanish as I focused on him. I was ready to let him have it, my self-respect wounded to the quick, when surfer boy appeared. "Sir," he said calmly, "that was the worst line I've ever heard, not only insulting but showing a severe lack of forethought. You're obviously bothering the young woman. You should leave before she does permanent damage to you."

It was protective, yet implied I could take care of myself, not an easy thing to accomplish in one paragraph, much less one sentence. I was impressed.

One-line-wonder took a breath, paused, and with his eyes rising over my shoulder, he changed his mind. Muttering, he took his drink and his buddy on the other side of me and left.

My shoulders eased and I found myself sighing as I turned to surfer boy. "Thank you," I said, taking a closer look at him. His eyes were brown and his lips were thin, and when he smiled, the expression encompassed both of them, full and honest. There was some Asian heritage in his not-too-distant past, giving him straight black hair and a small nose and mouth.

He ducked his head, seemingly embarrassed. "No thanks needed. I had to do something to redeem all men for that line." His strong-jawed face took on a false sincerity. "What're your other two wishes?" he asked, chuckling.

I laughed, ending it by looking at the craps table as I thought of my big teeth.

"My name is Lee," he said, stepping into the silence before it became awkward.

"Rachel," I said, relieved when he extended his hand. He smelled like sand and redwood, and he slipped his thin fingers into my grip to meet my pressure with an equal force. Our hands yanked apart and my eyes jerked to his when a slip of ley line energy equalized between us.

"Sorry," he said as he tucked his hand behind his back. "One of us must be low."

"It's probably me," I said, refusing to wipe my hand. "I don't keep line energy in my familiar."

Lee's eyebrows rose. "Really? I couldn't help but notice you looking at the security."

Now I was really embarrassed, and I took a sip of my drink and turned to lean with my elbows on the upper railing about the table. "That was an accident," I said as the amber dice rolled past. "I didn't mean to trip the alarms. I was just trying to get a closer look at—um—you," I finished, certainly as red at my hair. *Oh God, I was screwing this up royally.*

But Lee seemed amused, his teeth white in his suntanned face. "Me too."

His accent was nice. West Coast, perhaps? I couldn't help but like his easy demeanor, but when he took a sip of his white wine, my gaze fixed to his wrist peeping from behind his cuff and my heart seemed to stop. It was scarred. It was scarred exactly like mine. "You have a demon sca—" His eyes jerked to mine, and my words cut off. "Sorry."

Lee's attention flicked to the nearby patrons. None seemed to have heard. "It's okay," he said softly, his brown eyes pinched. "I got it by accident."

I put my back against the railing, understanding now why my demon-tainted aura hadn't scared him off. "Don't we all?" I said, surprised when he shook his head. My thoughts went to Nick, and I bit my lower lip.

"How did you get yours?" he asked, and it was my turn to be nervous.

"I was dying. He saved me. I owe him for safe passage through the lines." I didn't think it necessary to tell Lee that I was the demon's familiar. "How about you?"

"Curiosity." Eyes squinting, he frowned at a past memory.

Curious myself, I gave him another once-over. I wouldn't say Al's real name and break the contract we had come to when I had bought a summoning name from him, but I wanted to know if it was the same demon. "Hey, uh, does yours wear crushed green velvet?" I asked.

Lee jerked. His brown eyes went wide under his sharply cut bangs, and then a smile born of shared trouble came over him. "Yes. He talks in a British accent—"

"And has a thing for frosting and french fries?" I interrupted.

Lee ducked his head and chuckled. "Yes, when he isn't morphing into my father."

"How about that?" I said, feeling an odd kinship. "It's the same one."

Tugging his sleeve down to cover the mark, Lee rested his side against the craps table. "You seem to have a knack for ley lines," he said. "Are you taking instruction from him?"

"No," I said forcefully. "I'm an earth witch." I twiddled my finger with my ring amulet and touched the cord of the one around my neck that was supposed to defrizz my hair.

His attention went from the scar on my wrist to the ceiling. "But you . . ." he drawled.

I shook my head and sipped my drink, my back to the game. "I told you it was an accident. I'm not a ley line witch. I took a class is all. Well, half of one. The instructor died before the class was finished."

He blinked in disbelief. "Dr. Anders?" he blurted. "You had a class with Dr. Anders?"

"You knew her?" I pulled myself straighter.

"I've heard of her." He leaned close. "She was the best ley line witch east of the Mississippi. I came out here to take classes from her. She was supposed to be the best."

"She was," I said, depressed. She was going to help get Nick unbound as my familiar. Now, not only was the spell book gone, but she was dead and all her knowledge with her. I jerked upright as I realized I had been wool gathering. "So, you're a student?" I asked.

Lee rested his elbows on the rail, watching the dice skitter and roll behind me. "Road scholar," he said shortly. "I got my degree years ago from Berkeley."

"Oh, I'd love to see the coast some time," I said, playing with my necklace and wondering how much of this conversation had turned into exaggeration. "Doesn't the salt make everything difficult?"

He shrugged. "Not so much for ley line witches. I feel bad for earth witches, locked into a path that has no power."

My mouth dropped open. No power? Hardly. Earth magic's strength stemmed from ley lines as much as ley line witches' spells. That it was filtered through plants made it more forgiving, and perhaps slower, but no less powerful. There wasn't a ley line charm written that could physically change a person's form. Now that was power. Chalking it up to ignorance, I let it slide lest I drive him away before I got a chance to know just how big of a jerk he was, first.

"Look at me," he said, clearly recognizing that he had stuck his foot so far down his throat that his toes might wiggle out of his ass. "Here I am bothering you, when you probably want to play some before your boyfriend gets back."

"He's not my boyfriend," I said, not as excited as I could be for the subtle inquiry as to my attached status. "I told him he couldn't take me out on a decent date for sixty dollars, and he accepted the challenge."

Lee ran his eyes over the casino. "How's it going?"

I sipped my drink, wishing the ice cream hadn't melted. Behind me there was a loud cheer as something good happened. "Well, so far I've gotten sugared and passed out in a vamp dance club, insulted my roommate, and tripped the security system of a casino boat." I lifted a shoulder in a half shrug. "Not bad, I guess."

"It's early yet." Lee's gaze followed the rolling dice behind me. "Can I buy you a drink? I've heard the house wine is good. Merlot, I think it is."

I wondered where this was going. "No thanks. Red wine . . . doesn't sit well with me."

He chuckled. "I'm not particularly fond of it either. It gives me migraines."

"Me too," I exclaimed softly, truly surprised.

Lee tossed his bangs from his eyes. "Now, if I had said that, you would have accused me of dropping you a line." I smiled, feeling shy all of a sudden, and he turned to the cheering at the table. "You don't gamble, do you?" he said.

I glanced behind me and then back to him. "It shows, huh?"

He put a hand on my shoulder and turned me around.

"They've rolled three fours in a row, and you haven't noticed," he said softly, almost in my ear.

I did nothing to either discourage or encourage him, the sudden pounding of my heart not telling me what to do. "Oh, is that unusual?" I said, trying to keep my voice light.

"Here," he said, motioning to the craps man. "New roller," he called loudly.

"Oh, wait," I protested. "I don't even know how to bet."

Not to be deterred, Lee took my little chip bucket and guided me to the head of the table. "You roll, I'll bet for you." He hesitated, brown eyes innocent. "Is that . . . okay?"

"Sure," I said, grinning. What did I care? Kisten had given me the chips. That he wasn't there to spend them with me wasn't my problem. Teaching me how to throw craps was what he was supposed to be doing, not some guy in a tux. Where was he, anyway?

I glanced over the assembled faces around the table as I took the dice. They felt slippery—like bone in my hand—and I shook them.

"Wait . . ." Lee reached out and took my hand in his. "You have to kiss them first. But only once," he said, his voice serious though his eyes glinted. "If they think they'll get loved all the time, they won't put out."

"Right," I said, his hands falling when I pulled the dice to my lips but refused to touch them. I mean, really. Yuck. People shuffled their chips around, and heart faster than the game warranted, I threw the dice. I eyed Lee, not the dice, as they skittered and danced.

Lee watched in rapt attention, and I thought that though he wasn't pretty like Kisten, he was far more likely to be on a magazine cover than Nick. Just an average guy, and a witch with a degree. My mother would love me to bring this one home. Something had to be wrong with him. *Besides his demon mark?* I thought dryly. God, save me from myself.

The watching people had various reactions to the eight I rolled. "Not good?" I asked Lee.

His shoulders rose and fell as he took the dice the craps man pushed to him. "It's okay," he said. "But you have to roll an eight again before a seven comes up to win."

"Oh," I said, pretending I understood. Mystified, I threw the dice. This time they came up nine. "Keep going?" I said, and he nodded.

"I'll place some one-roll bets for you," he said, then paused. "If that's okay?"

Everyone was waiting, so I said, "Sure, that will be great."

Lee nodded. His brow furrowed for a moment, then he set a pile of red chips on a square. Someone snickered, leaning to whisper "Innocent slaughter" in their neighbor's ear.

The dice were warm in my hand, and I sent them rolling. They bounced off the wall, coming to halt. It was an eleven, and everyone at the table groaned. Lee, though, was smiling. "You won," he said, putting a hand on my shoulder. "See?" He pointed. "Odds are fifteen-to-one of rolling an eleven. I figured you'd be a zebra."

My eyes widened as the predominate color of my pile of chips went from red to blue as the craps man piled a stack on them. "Beg pardon?"

Lee set the dice in my hand. "When you hear hoofbeats, look for horses. That would be the common rolls in this case. I knew you'd roll something odd. A zebra."

I grinned, rather liking the idea, and the dice flew from me almost before he moved my chips to another square. My pulse quickened, and as Lee explained the details of odds and betting, I rolled again, and again, and again, the table becoming louder and more excited. It wasn't long before I caught on. The risk, the question of what would happen and the breathless wait until the dice settled, was akin to being on a run, only better because here it was little plastic chips on the line, not my life. Lee switched his tutorial to other ways to wager, and when I dared to make a suggestion, he beamed, gesturing that the table was mine.

Delighted, I took over the betting, letting it ride where it was while Lee put a hand on my shoulder and whispered the odds of throwing this and that. He smelled like sand. I could feel his excitement through the thin material of my silk shirt, and the warmth of his fingers seemed to linger on my shoulder when he shifted to put the dice in my hand.

I looked up when the table cheered my latest roll, surprised that almost everyone was clustered about us and that we had somehow become the center of attention. "Looks like you have it." Lee smiled as he took a step back.

Immediately my face went slack. "You're leaving?" I asked as the red-cheeked guy drinking beer pressed the dice into my hand and urged me to throw them.

"I need to go," he said. "But I couldn't resist meeting you." Leaning close, he said, "I enjoyed teaching you craps. You're a very special woman, Rachel."

"Lee?" Confused, I set the dice down and the people around the table groaned.

Lee slid the dice into his hand and put them in mine. "You're hot. Don't stop."

"Do you want my phone number?" I asked. *Oh God, I sounded desperate.*

But Lee smiled, his teeth hidden. "You're Rachel Morgan, the I.S. runner who quit to work with last living Tamwood vamp. You're in the phone book—in four places, no less."

My face flamed, but I managed to stop myself before I told everyone I wasn't a hooker.

"Till next time," Lee said, raising his hand and inclining his head before he walked away.

Setting the dice down, I backed from the table so I could watch him vanish up the stairway at the back of the boat, looking good in his tux and purple sash. It matched his aura, I decided. A new shooter took my place, and the noise returned.

My good mood soured, I retreated to a table by a cold window. One of the wait staff brought me my three buckets of chips. Another set a fresh Dead Man's Float on a linen napkin. A third lit the red candle and asked me if I needed anything. I shook my head, and he eased away. "What's wrong with this picture?" I whispered as I rubbed my fingers into my forehead. Here I was dressed up like a young rich widow, sitting alone in a casino with three buckets of chips. Lee had known who I was and never let on? Where in hell was Kisten?

The excitement at the craps table nosedived, and people started pulling away in twos and threes. I counted to a hundred, then two hundred. Angry, I stood, ready to cash in my chips and find Kisten. Little boys' room, my ass. He was probably upstairs playing poker—without me.

Chip buckets in hand, I jerked to a stop. Kisten was coming down the stairs, movements sharp and quick with a living vampire's speed. "Where have you been?" I demanded when he came even with me. His face was tight and I could see a line of sweat on him.

"We're leaving," he said shortly. "Let's go."

"Hold up." I jerked out of the grip he had on my elbow. "Where've you been? You left me all alone. Some guy had to teach me how to throw craps. See what I won?"

Kisten glanced down at my buckets, clearly not impressed. "The tables are fixed," he said, shocking me. "They were entertaining you while I talked to the boss."

I felt as if I'd been punched in the gut. I jerked back when he went for my elbow again. "Stop trying to drag me around," I said, not caring that people were watching. "And what do you mean, you were talking to the boss?"

He gave me an exasperated look, the first hints of stubble showing on his chin. "Can we do this outside?" he said, obviously in a hurry.

I glanced at the big men coming down the stairway. This was a gambling boat. It wasn't Piscary's. Kisten was handling the undead vampire's affairs. He was here leaning on the new guy in town, and he had brought me in case there was trouble. My chest tightened in anger as it all started to come together, but discretion was the wiser part of valor.

"Fine," I said. My boots made muted thumps in time with my pulse as I headed for the door. I dropped my buckets of chips on the counter and smiled grimly at the chip lady. "I want my winnings donated to the city fund for rebuilding the burned orphanages," I said tightly.

"Yes, ma'am," the woman said politely, weighing them out.

Kisten took a chip from the pile. "We're going to cash this one out."

I plucked it from his fingers, mad at him for having used me like this. This was where he wanted Ivy to go with him. And I had fallen for it. Whistling, I tossed the chip to the craps dealer. He caught it, inclining his head in thanks.

"That was a hundred-dollar chip!" Kisten protested.

"Really?" Ticked, I took another, throwing it after the first. "I don't want to be a cheap ass," I muttered. The woman handed me a receipt for $8,750, donated to the city's fund. I stared at it for a moment, then tucked it in my clutch purse.

"Rachel," Kisten protested, his face going red behind his blond hair.

"We're keeping nothing." Ignoring Kisten's coat that the doorman was holding for me, I blew out the door with its double S's. One for Saladan, perhaps? *God, I was a fool.*

"Rachel . . ." Anger made Kisten's voice hard as he leaned out the door after me. "Come back here and tell her to cash one of them out."

"You gave me the first ones, and I won the rest!" I shouted from the foot of the ramp, my arms wrapped around me in the falling snow. "I'm donating all of them. And I'm pissed at you, you bloodsucking coward!"

The man at the foot of the ramp snickered, steeling his face into impassivity when I glared at him. Kisten hesitated, then closed the door and came down after me, my borrowed coat over his arm. I stomped to his car, waiting for him to unlock the door for me or tell me to call a cab.

Still putting on his coat, Kisten stopped beside me. "Why are you mad at me?" he said flatly, his blue eyes starting to go black in the dim light.

"That is Saladan's boat, isn't it?" I said furiously, pointing. "I may be slow, but I eventually catch on. Piscary runs the gambling in Cincinnati. You came out here looking for Piscary's cut. And Saladan turned you down, didn't he? He's moving in on Piscary's turf, and you brought me as backup knowing I would fight for your ass if things got out of control."

Incensed, I ignored his teeth and his strength and put my face inches from his. "Don't you *ever* trick me into backing you up again. You could have gotten me killed with your little games. I don't get a second chance, Kisten. Dead is dead for me!"

My voice echoed off the nearby buildings. I thought of the ears listening from the boat, and my face burned. But I was angry, damn it, and this was going to be settled before I got back in Kisten's car. "You dress me up to make me feel special," I said, my throat tight and my anger high. "Treat me as if taking me out was something you wanted to do for me even if it was only in the hope of sinking your teeth in, and then I find out it's not even that but *business*? I wasn't even your first choice. You wanted Ivy to come with you, not me! I was your *alternate plan*. How cheap do you think that makes me feel?"

He opened his mouth, then shut it.

"I can understand you using me as a second-choice date because you're a man and therefore a jerk!" I exclaimed. "But you knowingly brought me out here into a potentially dangerous situation without my spells, without my charms. You said it was a date, so I left everything at home. Hell, Kisten, if you wanted backup, I would have!

"Besides," I added, my anger starting to slow since he seemed to actually be listening instead of spending the time formulating excuses. "It would have been fun knowing what was going on. I could have pumped people for information, stuff like that."

He stared at me, surprise mirrored in his eyes. "Really?"

"Yeah, really. You think I became a runner for their dental

plan? It would've made for more fun than having some guy teach me craps. That was your job, by the way."

Kisten stood next to me, a dusting of snow starting to accumulate on his leather coat draped over his arm. His face was long and unhappy in the dim light from a streetlamp. He took a breath, and my eyes narrowed. It escaped him in a quick sound of defeat. I could feel my blood racing, and my body was both hot and cold from my anger and the cutting wind off the river. I liked even less that Kisten could probably read my feelings better than I could.

His eyes with their growing rim of blue flicked past me to the boat. As I watched, they flashed to black, chilling me. "You're right," he said shortly, his voice tight. "Get in the car."

My anger flamed back. *Son of a bitch* . . . "Don't patronize me," I said tightly.

He reached out, and I jerked away before he could touch me. Black eyes looking soulless in the dim light, he turned his reach for me into opening my door. "I'm not," he said, his motions edging into that eerie vamp quickness. "There are three men coming off the boat. I can smell gunpowder. You were right, I was wrong. Get in the damn car."

Fourteen

Fear flashed through me, and sensing it, Kisten took a breath as if I had slapped him. I froze, reading in his rising hunger that I had more to worry about than the feet booming down the gangplank. Heart pounding, I got in the car. Kisten handed me my coat and his keys. My door thumped shut, and while he crossed in front of his car, I jammed the key into the ignition. Kisten got in, and the sudden rumble came simultaneously with him shutting his door.

The three men had shifted direction, their pace quickening as they headed for an early model BMW. "They'll never catch us in that," Kisten scoffed. Wipers going to push off the snow, he put the car in gear, and I braced against the dash when he punched it. We skidded, fishtailing into the street and running a late yellow light. I didn't look behind us.

Kisten slowed as the traffic increased, and pulse hammering, I wiggled into his coat and put on my seat belt. He flicked the heater on high, but it only blew cold air. I felt naked without my charms. Damn it, I should have brought something, but it was supposed to have been a date!

"I'm sorry," Kisten said as he cut a sudden left. "You were right."

"You *idiot*!" I shouted, my voice harsh in the close confines of the car. "Don't you *ever* make my decisions for me, Kisten. Those men had guns, and I had nothing!" Fading adrenaline made my words louder than I had intended, and I glanced at him, suddenly sobered as I remembered the black of his eyes when my fear had hit him. He might look safe, dressed in his Italian suit and his hair slicked back—but he wasn't. He could shift between one heartbeat and the next. *God, what was I doing here?*

"I said I was sorry," Kisten said again, not looking from the road as the lit buildings, hazy with snow, passed. There was more than a hint of bother in his tone, and I decided to stop shouting at him even if I was still pissed and shaking. Besides, he wasn't cowering, begging for forgiveness, and his confident admission of having made a mistake was nice for a change.

"Don't worry about it," I said sourly, not yet ready to forgive him, but not wanting to talk about it anymore, either.

"Shit," he said, his jaw clenching as he watched the rearview mirror instead of the road in front of him. "They're still following us."

I twitched, managing to not turn and look, satisfying myself with what I could see in the side mirror. Kisten took a sudden right and my lips parted in disbelief. The road ahead of us was empty, a dark tunnel of nothing compared to the lights and the security of commerce behind us. "What are you doing?" I asked, hearing a tinge of fear in my voice.

His eyes were still on the road behind us when the dark Cadillac jerked out in front of us, blocking the road as it spun sideways.

"Kisten!" I shouted, bracing my arms against the dash. A tiny shriek escaped me as he swore and jerked the wheel. My head smacked the window and I bit back a cry of pain. Breath held, I felt the wheels lose contact with the pavement and we slipped on the ice. Still swearing, Kisten reacted with his vamp reflexes, the car fighting him. The little Corvette gave a final little hiccup of motion as it found the curb and we swayed to a shaken halt.

"Stay in the car." He reached for the door. Four men in dark suits were getting out of the Cadillac ahead of us. Three were in the BMW behind us. All witches, probably, and here I was, with only a couple of vanity charms. *This was going to look really good in the obituaries.*

"Kisten, wait!" I said.

Hand on the door, he turned. My chest clenched at the blackness in his eyes. *Oh God, he had vamped out.*

"It will be okay," he said, his voice a black-earth, rich rumble that went to my core and gripped my heart.

"How do you know?" I whispered.

A blond-dyed eyebrow shifted up so slightly, I wasn't sure it even moved. "Because if they kill me, then I'd be dead and I'll hunt them down. They want to—talk. Stay in the car."

He got out and shut the door. The car was still running, the thrum of the engine tightening my muscles one by one. Falling snow hit the windshield to melt, and I turned off the wipers. "Stay in the car," I muttered, fidgeting. I glanced behind me, seeing the three guys from the BMW moving closer. Kisten was lit to a stark severity as he crossed in front of his lights, approaching the four men with his palms forward with a casualness that I knew was false. "Like hell I'm going to stay in the car," I said, reaching for the handle and lurching into the cold.

Kisten turned. "I told you to stay in the car," he said, and I pushed down my fear at the starkness in his expression. He had already divorced himself from what was going to happen.

"Yeah, you did," I shot back, forcing my arms down. It was cold and I shivered.

He hesitated, clearly torn. The approaching men spread out. We were surrounded. Their faces were shadowed but confident. All they needed was a bat or crowbar to thump against their hand to make it complete. But they were witches. Their strength was in their magic.

My breath came slow, and I rocked forward on my flat boots. Feeling the stir of adrenaline, I moved into the car's headlights and put my back to Kisten's.

The black hunger in his eyes seemed to pause. "Rachel,

please wait in the car," he said his voice making my skin crawl. "This won't take long, and I don't want you to get cold."

He didn't want me to get cold? I thought, watching the three guys from the BMW behind us settle in to make a living fence. "There are seven witches here," I said softly. "It only takes three to make a net, and one to hold it once it's in place."

"True, but it only takes me three seconds to drop a man."

The men in my sight faltered. There was a reason the I.S. didn't send witches to bring in a vampire. Seven against one might do it, but not without someone getting really hurt.

I risked a glance over my shoulder to see that the four guys from the Cadillac were looking at the man in the long coat who had gotten out from the BMW. *Top guy*, I thought, thinking he was too confident as he adjusted his long coat and jerked his head to the men around us. The two in front of Kisten started forward and three dropped back. Their lips were moving and their hands were gesturing. The hair on the back of my neck pricked at the sudden rise of power.

At least three ley line witches, I guessed, then went cold as one of the advancing men pulled out a gun. Crap. Kisten could come back from the dead, but I couldn't.

"Kisten . . ." I warned, my voice rising and my eyes fixed on the gun.

Kisten moved, and I jumped. One moment he was next to me, and the next he was among the men. There was a pop of a gun. Gasping, I ducked, blinding myself in the Corvette's headlights. Crouched, I saw one guy was down, but not the one with the gun.

Encircling us, almost lost in the glare, the ley line witches muttered and gestured, their net tightening when they took a step in. My skin tingled as the lacework fell over us.

Moving too fast to readily follow, Kisten grabbed the wrist of the man with the gun. The snap of bone was clear in the cold, dry air. My stomach lurched as the man screamed and fell to his knees. Kisten followed it up with a powerful blow to his head. Someone was shouting. The gun fell, and Kisten caught it before it hit the snow.

With a flick of his wrist, Kisten sent the gun arching to me. It glinted in the headlights as I lurched forward to catch it. The heavy metal landed in my grip. It was hot, surprising me. There was another pop of a gun, and I jerked. The gun fell to the snow.

"Get that weapon!" the man in the long coat at the outskirts shouted.

I peeked over the hood of Kisten's Corvette, seeing he had a gun, too. My eyes widened as I saw the black shadow of a man coming at me. There was a ball of orange ever-after in his hand. My breath hissed as he smiled and threw it at me.

I hit the pavement, the snow-covered ice making a hard landing. The ever-after exploded into a shower of sulfur-smelling sparkles as it struck Kisten's car and ricocheted away. Cold slush seeped against me, the shock clearing my head.

From the ground, I put my palms against the cold pavement and levered myself up. My clothes . . . My clothes! My silk-lined pants were covered in filthy gray snow. "Look what you made me do!" I shouted, furious as I shook the cold slop from me.

"You son of a bitch!" Kisten cried, and I spun to see three witches down in a messy circle about him. The one that had thrown the ever-after made a pained motion, and Kisten savagely kicked him. *How had he gotten there so fast?* "You burned my paint job, you mother!"

As I watched, Kisten's mien shifted in a breathless instant. Eyes black, he lunged at the closest gesturing ley line witch. The man's eyes widened, but he had no time for more.

Kisten's fist rammed into his face, rocking his head back. There was an ugly sounding crunch, and the witch crumpled. Arms slack, he arched backward through the air, landing to skid into the headlights of the Cadillac.

Spinning before the first had stopped moving, Kisten landed before the next, turning in a tight circle. His dress shoes smacked into the back of the startled witch's knees. The man cried out as his legs buckled. The sound cut off with a frightening suddenness when Kisten stiff-armed his throat. My stomach clenched at the gurgle and crackle of cartilage.

The third witch backpedaled into a run. *Mistake. Terrible, terrible mistake.*

Kisten paced the ten feet between them in half a heartbeat. Grabbing the fleeing witch, he spun him in a circle, never letting go of his arm. The pop of his arm dislocating hit me like a slap. I put a hand to my stomach, sickened. It had taken a moment's thought, and nothing more.

Kisten stopped before the last witch standing, an aggressive eight feet back. I shuddered, remembering Ivy looking at me like that. He had a pistol, but I didn't think it was going to help him.

"You going to shoot me?" Kisten snarled.

The man smiled. I felt him tap a line. My breath came quick to shout a warning.

Kisten jerked forward, catching the man about the throat. The man's eyes bulged in fear as he struggled for air. The pistol dropped, his hand hanging useless. Kisten's shoulders tensed, his aggression shining from him. I couldn't see his eyes. I didn't want to. But the man he held could, and he was terrified.

"Kisten!" I shouted, too afraid to interfere. *Oh God. Please no. I don't want to see this.*

Kisten hesitated, and I wondered if he could hear my heart pounding. Slowly, as if fighting himself, Kisten pulled the man closer. The witch was gasping, struggling to breathe. Headlights glinted on the spit frothing at the corner of his mouth, and his face was red.

"Tell Saladan I'll be seeing him," Kisten almost growled.

I jerked when Kisten's arm thrust out and the witch went flying. He landed against a defunct light post, and the shock reverberated up the pole to make the light flicker on. I was afraid to move as Kisten turned. Seeing me standing in the falling snow lit by the car's headlights, he paused. Eyes that awful black, he brushed a spot of dampness from his coat.

Poised and tense, I tore my gaze from him to follow his attention when he glanced over the carnage, brightly lit from the three pair of headlights and the one streetlamp. Men sprawled everywhere. The one with the dislocated shoulder had vomited and was trying to get to a car. From down the street a dog barked and a curtain fluttered against a lit window.

I put a hand to my stomach, nauseous. I had frozen. Oh God, I had frozen, unable to do anything. I had let myself get stupid because my death threats were gone. But because of what I did, I would always be a target.

Kisten strode into motion, the ring of blue around his black pupils a thin rim. "I told you to stay in the car," he said, and I stiffened as he took my elbow and led me to his Corvette.

Numb, I didn't resist. He wasn't angry with me, and I didn't want to make him any more aware of my pounding heart and lingering fear. But a tingle of warning brought me stiff. Jerking out of Kisten's grip, I turned, eyes wide and searching.

From the under the streetlamp the broken man slitted his eyes, his face ugly in pain. "You lose, bitch," he said, then mouthed a savage word in Latin.

"Look out!" I cried, pushing Kisten away from me.

He fell back, catching his balance with his vampire grace. I went sprawling when my boots slipped. A raw scream shocked through me. Heart pounding, I scrambled up, my eyes going first to Kisten. He was all right. It was the witch.

My hand went to my mouth, horrified as his ever-after–smeared body writhed on the snow-covered sidewalk. Fear slithered through me as the kicked-up snow took on a tinge of red. He was bleeding through his pores. "God save him," I whispered.

He shrieked, then shrieked again, the harsh sound striking a primal chord in me. Kisten strode to him quickly. I couldn't stop him; the witch was bleeding, screaming in pain and fear. He was pushing every button Kisten had. I turned away, a trembling hand resting on the rumbling warm hood of the Corvette. I was going to get sick. I knew it.

My head jerked up as the man's terror and pain ended in a sodden crack. Kisten stood from his crouch, a horrible, angry look on him. The dog barked again, filling the icy night with the sound of alarm. A pair of dice rolled from the man's slack hand, and Kisten picked them up.

I couldn't think anymore. Kisten was suddenly next to me, his hand on my elbow hustling me to the car. I let him move me, glad he hadn't succumbed to his vampiric instincts, and wondering why he hadn't. If anything, his vampire aura was completely washed away, his eyes normal and his reactions only mildly fast.

"He's not dead," he said, handing me the dice. "None of them are dead. I didn't kill anyone, Rachel."

I wondered why he cared what I thought. Taking the pieces of plastic, I gripped them until my fingers ached. "Get the gun," I whispered. "My fingerprints are on it."

Not acknowledging he heard me, he tucked my coat in out of the door and shut it.

The sharp tang of blood drew my attention down, and I forced my hand open. The dice were sticky. My gut twisted, and I held a winter-cold fist to my mouth. They were the pair I had used in the casino. The entire room had seen me kiss them; he tried to use them as a focal object. But I hadn't made a link to them and so the black charm swung back to its maker instead.

I stared out the window trying not to hyperventilate. That was supposed to be me there, limbs contorted and sprawled in a smear of blood-melted snow. I had been a wild card in Saladan's game, and he had been prepared to take me out to tip the balance back to his men. And I had done nothing, too frozen by my lack of charms and shock to even make a circle.

There was a flash of brighter light as Kisten stepped in front of the car's headlights, bending to come up with the weapon. His eyes met mine—tired and weary—until a soft movement behind him brought him spinning around. Someone was trying to leave.

I made a small moan as Kisten took incredibly long, fast steps and had him, jerking him upright, feet dangling. A whimper came from the man, going right to my core as he pleaded for his life. I told myself that to pity him was foolish, that they had planned worse for me and Kisten. But all Kisten did was talk to him, faces touching as the vampire whispered into his ear.

In a splurge of motion, Kisten threw him onto the hood of the Cadillac, wiping the weapon off on the hem of the witch's coat. Finished, he dropped the gun and turned away.

Kisten's back was hunched when he stomped back to the car, making him a bad mix of anger and worry. I said nothing as he got in and turned the wipers on. Still silent, he jerked the gearshift back and forth, maneuvering the car to get out of the box the two cars had made.

I held onto the door handle and said nothing as our momentum shifted, stalled, and shifted again. Finally there was only clear road ahead of us, and Kisten floored it. My eyes widened as the wheels spun and we started to drift on the ice to the left, but then the tires caught and we lurched forward. We left the way we had come, in a sliding sound of racing engine.

I kept silent as Kisten drove, his motions quick and sudden. The lights abruptly brightened around us, falling onto his face, lined with stress. My stomach was tense and my back hurt. He knew I was trying to figure out how to react.

Watching him had been both exhilarating and scary as all hell. Living with Ivy had taught me vamps were as changeable as a serial killer, fun and captivating one moment, aggressive and dangerous the next. I knew it, but seeing it had been a shocking reminder.

Swallowing hard, I looked at my posture, seeing I was wound up tighter than a chipmunk on speed. Immediately I forced my clasped hands apart and my shoulders down. I stared at the bloody dice in my hand and Kisten muttered, "I wouldn't do that to you, Rachel. I wouldn't."

The rhythm of the wipers was slow and steady. *Maybe I should've stayed in the car.*

"There're hand wipes in the console."

His voice carried the softness of an apology. Dropping my eyes before he could meet them, I flipped open the console and found some tissues. My fingers were shaking as I wrapped the dice up and, after a moment of hesitation, dropped them into my clutch purse.

Digging deeper, I found the wipes. Unhappy, I handed Kisten the first, then cleaned my hands with the second. Kisten easily drove the snowy, busy streets and meticulously cleaned his cuticles at the same time. When finished, he held out his hand for my used wipe, and I gave it to him. There was a little trash bag hanging behind my seat, and he effortlessly reached back and threw them both away. His hands were as steady as a surgeon's, and I curled my fingers under my palms to hide their trembling.

Kisten resettled himself, and I could almost see him force the tension from him as he exhaled. We were halfway across the Hollows, the lights of Cincinnati sharp before us.

"Snap, crackle, pop," he said lightly.

Bewildered, I looked at him. "I beg your pardon?" I said, glad my voice was even. Yeah, I had watched him down a coven of black art witches with the effortless grace of a predator, but if he wanted to discuss breakfast cereals now, I'd go along with it.

He smiled with his lips closed, a hint of an apology, or perhaps guilt, in the back of his blue eyes. "Snap, crackle, pop," he said. "Bringing them down sounded like a bowl of cereal."

My eyebrows rose and a wry smile came over me. With a small movement, I stretched my feet to the floor vent. If I didn't laugh, I was going to cry. And I didn't want to cry.

"I haven't done too well tonight, have I?" he said, his eyes back on the road.

I didn't say anything, not sure what I felt.

"Rachel," he said softly. "I'm sorry you had to see that."

"I don't want to talk about it," I said, recalling the man's terrified, agony-laced screams. I had known Kisten did ugly things because of who he was and who he worked for, but seeing it left me both repelled and fascinated. I was a runner; violence was part of my existence. I couldn't blindly label what happened as bad without casting my own profession into darkness.

Though his eyes had been black and his instincts wound tight, he had acted quickly and decisively, with a grace and succinct movement that I envied. Even more, throughout it all, I had felt Kisten's attention lightly on me, always aware of where I was and who was threatening me.

I had frozen, and he had kept me safe.

Kisten accelerated smoothly into the intersection before us when the light turned green. He sighed, clearly unaware of my thoughts as he took the turn to head to the church. The glowing clock on the dash read three-thirty. Going out didn't sound like fun anymore, but I was still shaking, and if he didn't feed me, I was going to end up eating cheese crackers and leftover rice for dinner. Yuck. "Mickey-d's?" I prompted. *It was just a date, for God's sake. One platonic . . . date.*

Kisten's head jerked up. Lips parted in wonder, he almost rammed the car ahead of us, slamming on the brakes at the last moment. Used to the way Ivy drove, I simply braced myself and rocked forward and back.

"You still want to have dinner?" he asked while the guy before us shouted unheard insults through his rearview mirror.

I shrugged. I was coated in dirty snow slime, my hair was falling down about my ears, my nerves were shot—if I didn't get something in my stomach, I was going to get snippy. Or sick. Or worse.

Kisten settled back, a thoughtful expression smoothing his pinched features. A wisp of his usual, cocky self glimmered in his slumping posture. "Fast food is all I can afford—now," he grumbled lightly, but I could see he was relieved I wasn't demanding he take me home. "I was planning on using some of those winnings to take you up to Carew Tower for a sunrise dinner."

"The orphans need the money more than I need an overpriced dinner at the top of Cincinnati," I said. Kisten laughed at that, the sound making it easy to stifle my last thread of lingering caution. He kept me alive when I had frozen. It wasn't going to happen again. Ever.

"Hey, uh, is there any way you might see to not tell Ivy about . . . that?" he asked.

I smiled at the unease in his voice. "It'll cost you, fang-boy."

A small noise escaped him and he turned, his eyes wide in mock concern. "I'm in the position to offer you a supersized shake for your silence," he intoned, and I stifled a shiver at the play menace he had put in it. Yeah, color me stupid. But I was alive, and he had kept me safe.

"Make it chocolate," I said, "and you've got yourself a deal."

Kisten's smile widened, and he gripped the wheel with more surety.

I settled back into the heated leather cushions, stifling the small, oh-so-small, thought of concern. *What. Like I was going to tell Ivy anyway?*

Fifteen

The crunch of ice and salt was loud as Kisten escorted me to my door. His car was parked at the curb in a puddle of light, diffuse from the falling snow. I rose up the steps, wondering what would happen in the next five minutes. It was a platonic date, but it was a date. That he might kiss me had me nervous.

I turned as I reached the door, smiling. Kisten stood beside me in his long wool coat and shiny shoes, looking good with his hair falling over his eyes. The sifting snow was beautiful, and it was gathering on his shoulders. The ugliness of the night's trouble drifted in and out of my thoughts. "I had a good time," I said, wanting to forget it. "Mickey-d's was fun."

Kisten's head drooped and a small chuckle escaped him. "I've never pretended to be health inspectors to get a free meal before. How did you know what to do?"

I winced. "I, uh, flipped burgers during high school until I dropped a charm into the fry vat." His eyebrows rose and I added, "I got fired. I don't know what the big deal was. Nobody got hurt, and the woman looked better with straight hair."

He laughed, turning it into a cough. "You dropped a potion in the fry vat?"

"It was an accident. The manager had to pay for a day at a

spa, and I got pushed off the broomstick. All she needed was a salt bath to break the spell, but she was going to sue."

"I can't imagine why . . ." Kisten rocked to his toes and down, his hands behind his back as he looked up through the snow at the steeple. "I'm glad you had a good time. I did, too." He took a step back, and I went still. "I'll stop by sometime tomorrow night to pick up my coat."

"Hey, um, Kisten?" I said, not knowing why. "Do you . . . want a cup of coffee?"

He came to a graceful halt with one foot on the next step down. Turning back, he smiled, his pleased expression reaching all the way to his eyes. "Only if you let me make it."

"Deal." My pulse was just a shade faster as I opened the door and preceded him in. The sound of slow jazz met us, drifting up from the living room. Ivy was home, and I hoped she had already been out and back from her twice-weekly fix. A soulfully sung "Lilac Wine" made a soft mood, accentuated by the darkness of the sanctuary.

I shuffled off Kisten's coat, the sound of the silk lining a soft hush as it slid from me. The sanctuary was dim and silent, the pixies snug in my desk though they ought to have been up by now. Wanting to preserve the mood, I slipped off my boots while Kisten hung his coat beside the one he had let me borrow.

"Come on back," I whispered, not wanting to wake the pixies. Kisten's smile was soft as he followed me into the kitchen. We were quiet, but I knew Ivy had heard us when she turned the music down a shade. Tossing my clutch purse to my side of the table, I felt like someone else as I padded in my stocking feet to the fridge for the coffee. I caught sight of my reflection in the window. If you ignored the snow stains and falling hair, I didn't look too bad.

"I'll get the coffee," I said, searching the fridge as the sound of tinkling water intruded on the jazz. Grounds in hand, I turned to find him looking relaxed and comfortable in his pin-striped suit as he stood at the sink and cleaned the new coffee carafe. His mind was entirely on his task, seemingly unaware that I was in the same room while he threw out the old grounds and pulled a filter from the cupboard with a smooth, unthinking motion.

After an entire four hours with him without one flirting comment or sexual/blood innuendo, I felt comfortable. I hadn't known he could be like this: normal. I watched him move, seeing him with his thoughts on nothing. I liked what I saw, and I wondered what it would be like to be this way all the time.

As if feeling my eyes on him, Kisten turned. "What?" he asked, smiling.

"Nothing." I glanced at the black hallway. "I want to check on Ivy."

Kisten's lips parted to show a glimpse of teeth as his smile widened. "Okay."

Not sure why that seemed to please him, I gave him a last, high-eyebrow look and headed into the candlelit living room. Ivy was sprawled across her cushy suede chair, her head on one arm, her legs draped over the other. Her brown eyes flicked to mine as I entered, taking in the smooth, elegant lines of my clothes all the way to my feet in their nylons.

"You've got snow all over you," she said, her expression and position unchanging.

"I, uh, slipped," I lied, and she accepted that, taking my nervousness as embarrassment. "Why are the pixies still asleep?"

She snorted—sitting up to put her feet on the floor—and I sat on the matching couch across from her with the coffee table between us. "Jenks kept them up after you left so they wouldn't be awake when you got home."

A thankful smile came over me. "Remind me to make him some honey cakes," I said, leaning back and crossing my legs.

Ivy slumped into her chair, mirroring my posture. "So . . . how was your date?"

My eyes met hers. Very aware of Kisten listening from the kitchen, I shrugged. Ivy often acted like a cloying ex-boyfriend, which was really, really weird. But now that I knew it stemmed from her need to keep my trust, it was a bit easier to understand, though still odd.

She took a slow breath, and I knew she was scenting the air to make sure no one had bitten me at Piscary's. Her shoulders eased, and I rolled my eyes in exasperation.

"Hey, um," I started. "I'm really sorry about what I said earlier. About Piscary's?" Her eyes jerked to mine and I quickly added, "You want to go sometime? Together, I mean? I think if I stay downstairs, I won't pass out." My eyes pinched, not knowing why I was doing this except if she didn't find a way to relax soon, she was going to snap. I didn't want to be around for that. And I'd feel better if I was there to keep an eye on her. I had a feeling she would pass out quicker than I had.

Ivy shifted in the chair, moving back where she was when I came in. "Sure," she said, her voice not giving me a clue to her thoughts as she looked at the ceiling and closed her eyes. "We haven't had a girls' night out in a while."

"Great."

I settled back into the cushions to wait for Kisten. From the stereo, a soft-spoken voice dripping sex whispered as the songs changed. The scent of brewing coffee became obvious. A smile came over me as Takata's newest single came on. They were playing it even on the jazz stations. Ivy opened her eyes. "Backstage passes," she said, smiling.

"Al-l-l-l-l-l the way backstage," I countered. She had already agreed to work the concert with me, and I was eager to introduce her to Takata. But then I thought of Nick. No chance he'd be going now. Maybe I could ask Kisten to help us. And since he was posing as Piscary's scion, he would be doubly effective as a deterrent. Kinda like a cop car parked in the median. I looked at the black archway, wondering if he'd say yes if I asked, and if I wanted him there.

"Listen." Ivy held up a finger. "This is my favorite part.

That low thrum goes all the way to my gut. Hear the pain in her voice? This has got to be Takata's best CD yet."

Her voice? I thought. Takata was the only one singing.

"You're mine, in some small fashion," Ivy whispered, her eyes closed, the inner pain showing on her brow making me uneasy. "You're mine, though you know it not. You're mine, bond born of passion . . ."

My eyes widened. She wasn't singing what Takata was. Her words were interlaced with his, an eerie backdrop that set my skin to crawl. That was the chorus he wasn't going to release.

"You're mine, yet wholly you," she breathed. "By the way of your will—"

"Ivy!" I exclaimed, and her eyes flashed open. "Where did you hear that?"

She looked blankly at me as Takata continued, singing of bargains made in ignorance.

"That's the alternate chorus!" I said, sitting up to the edge of the couch. "He wasn't going to release that."

"Alternate chorus?" she said as Kisten came in, setting the tray with three cups of coffee on the table beside the thick red candles and pointedly sitting next to me.

"The lyrics!" I pointed to the stereo. "You were singing them. He wasn't going to release those. He told me. He was going to release the other ones."

Ivy stared at me as if I had gone insane, but Kisten groaned, hunching to put his elbows on his knees and his head in his hands. "It's the vamp track," he said, his voice flat. "Damn. I thought something was missing."

Bewildered, I reached for my coffee. Ivy sat up and did the same. "Vamp track?" I said.

Kisten's head came up. His expression was resigned as he brushed his blond bangs back. "Takata puts a track in his music that only the undead can hear," he said, and I froze, my mug halfway to my lips. "Ivy can hear it because she's Piscary's scion."

Ivy's face went white. "You can't hear her?" she asked. "Right there," she said, looking at the stereo as the refrain came back on. "You can't hear her singing between Takata?"

I shook my head, feeling uneasy. "All I can hear is him."

"The drum?" she asked. "Can you hear that?"

Kisten nodded, leaning back with his coffee and looking sullen. "Yes, but you're hearing a hell of a lot more than we are." He set his cup down. "Damn it," he swore. "Now I'll have to wait until I'm dead and hope to find an old copy laying around." He sighed in disappointment. "Is it good, Ivy? Her voice is the eeriest thing I've ever heard. She's in every CD, but she's never listed in the credits." He slumped. "I don't know why she doesn't burn her own album."

"You can't hear her?" Ivy said, her words a sharp staccato. She set the cup down hard enough to spill, and I stared, surprised.

Kisten made a wry face and shook his head. "Congratulations," he said bitterly. "Welcome to the club. Wish I was still in it."

My pulse quickened as Ivy's eyes flashed into anger. "No!" she said, standing.

Kisten glanced up, his eyes wide, only now realizing Ivy wasn't pleased.

Ivy shook her head, wire-tight. "No," she said adamantly. "I don't want it!"

Understanding pulled me straight. That she could hear it meant that Piscary's grip on her was tightening. I looked at Kisten and his expression went worried. "Ivy, wait," he soothed as her usually placid face went ugly with anger.

"Nothing is mine anymore!" she exclaimed, her eyes flashing to black. "It was beautiful, and now it's ugly because of him. He's taking everything, Kist!" she shouted. "Everything!"

Kisten stood, and I froze as he went around the table and reached for her. "Ivy . . ."

"This is going to stop," she said, knocking his hand aside with a quick jerk before he could touch her. "Right now."

My jaw dropped as she strode from the room with a vampire quickness. The candles flickered, then steadied. "Ivy?" I set my coffee down and stood, but the room was empty. Kisten had darted out after her. I was alone. "Where are you going. . . ." I whispered.

I heard the muffled rumble of Ivy's sedan start, borrowed from her mother for the winter. In an instant she was gone. I went into the hall, the soft thump of Kisten shutting the door and his steps on the hardwood floor clear in the silence.

"Where's she going?" I asked him as he came even with me at the top of the hallway.

He put a hand on my shoulder in a silent suggestion that I go back into the living room. In my stocking feet I felt the difference in our height keenly. "To talk to Piscary."

"Piscary!" Alarm brought me to a standstill. I pulled out of his light grip and stopped in the hall. "She can't talk to him alone!"

But Kisten gave me a mirthless smile. "She'll be fine. It's high time she talk to him. As soon as she does, he'll back off. That's why he's been bothering her. This is a good thing."

Not convinced, I returned to the living room. I was very conscious of him behind me, silent, close enough to touch. We were alone, if you didn't count the fifty-six pixies in my desk. "She'll be all right," he said under his breath as he followed me, shoes silent on the gray carpet.

I wanted him to leave. I was emotionally whipped, and I wanted him to leave. Feeling his eyes on me, I blew out the candles. In the new darkness, I gathered the coffee cups onto the tray in the hopes that he would take the hint. But as my gaze rose to the hallway, a thought stopped me cold. "Do you think Piscary can make her bite me? He almost made her bite Quen."

Kisten shifted into motion, his fingers brushing mine as he took the tray from me in the smoke-scented air. "No," he said, clearly waiting for me to go into the kitchen before him.

"Why not?" I padded into the brightly lit room.

Squinting at the new glare, Kisten slid the tray beside the sink and dumped the coffee to make brown puddles in the white porcelain sink. "Piscary was able to exert such an influence on her this afternoon because he caught her off guard. That, and she didn't have any set behavior to fight it. She's been battling her instincts to bite you since you were partners in the I.S. Saying no has gotten easy. Piscary can't make her bite you unless she gives in first, and she won't give in. She respects you too much."

I opened the dishwasher, and Kisten stacked the cups in the top rack. "Are you sure?" I asked softly, wanting to believe.

"Yes." His knowing smile made him a bad boy in an expensive suit again. "Ivy takes pride in denying herself. She values her independence more than I do, which is why she fights him. It'd be easier if she'd give it up. He'd stop forcing his dominance then. It's not degrading to let Piscary see through your eyes, channel your emotions and desires. I found it uplifting."

"Uplifting." I leaned against the counter in disbelief. "Piscary exerting his will over her and making her do things she doesn't want to is 'uplifting'?"

"Not when you put it like that." He opened the cupboard under the sink and pulled out the dish detergent. I briefly wondered how he knew it was there. "But Piscary is being a pain in the ass only because she's resisting him. He likes her fighting him."

I took the bottle from him and filled the little cup in the door of the dishwasher.

"I keep telling her that being Piscary's scion doesn't make her less, but more," he said. "She doesn't lose any of herself, and gains so much. Like the vampire track, and having almost the full strength of an undead without any of the drawbacks."

"Like a soul to tell you it's wrong to view people as walking snack bars," I said tartly, snapping the door shut.

A sigh slipped from him, the fine fabric of his suit bunching at his shoulders when he took the bottle of soap from me and set in on the counter. "It's not like that," he said. "Sheep are treated like sheep, users are used, and those who deserve more receive everything."

Arms crossed over my chest, I said, "And who are you to make that decision?"

"Rachel." He sounded weary as he cupped my elbows in his hands. "They make the decision themselves."

"I don't believe that." But I didn't pull away, and I didn't push his hands off me. "And even if they do, you take advantage of it."

Kisten's eyes went distant, falling from mine as he gently pulled my arms into a less aggressive posture. "Most people," he said, "are desperate to be needed. And if they don't feel good about themselves or think they're undeserving of love, some will fasten upon the worst possible way to satisfy that need to punish themselves. They're the addicts, the shadows both claimed and unclaimed, passed like the fawning sheep they make themselves into as they search for a glimmer of worth, knowing it's false even as they beg for it. Yes, it is ugly. And yes, we take advantage of those who let us. But which is worse, taking from someone who wants you to, knowing in your soul that you're a monster, or taking from an unwilling person and proving it?"

My heart pounded. I wanted to argue with him, but everything he had said, I agreed with.

"And then there are those who relish the power they have over us." Kisten's lips thinned from a past anger, and he dropped his hands from me. "The clever ones who know that our need to be accepted and trusted runs so deep it can be crippling. Those who play upon that, knowing we will do almost anything for that invitation to take the blood we desperately crave. The ones who exalt in the hidden domination a lover can exert, feeling it elevates them to an almost godlike status. Those are the ones who want to be us, thinking it will make them powerful. And we use them, too, casting them aside with less regret than the sheep unless we grow to hate them, upon which we make them one of us in cruel restitution."

He cupped my jaw with his hand. It was warm, and I didn't pull away. "And then there are the rare ones who know love, who understand it. Who freely give of themselves, demanding only a return of that love, that trust." His faultless blue eyes never blinked, and I held my breath. "It can be beautiful, Rachel, when there is trust and love. No one is bound. No one loses his or her will. No one becomes less. Both become more than they can be alone. But it is so rare, so beautiful when it happens."

I shivered, wondering if he was lying to me.

The soft touch of his hand down my jaw as he pulled away sent my blood humming. But he didn't notice, his attention on the coming dawn visible out the window. "I feel bad for Ivy," he whispered. "She doesn't want to accept her need for belonging, even as it charts her every move. She wants that perfect love but thinks she isn't deserving of it."

"She doesn't love Piscary," I whispered. "You said there was no beauty without trust and love."

Kisten's eyes met mine. "I wasn't talking about Piscary."

His attention went to the clock above the sink, and when he took a backward step, I knew he was leaving. "It's getting late," he said, his distant voice telling me he was already mentally somewhere else. Then his eyes cleared and he was back. "I enjoyed our date," he said as he drew away. "But next time, there isn't going to be a limit on what I can spend."

"You're assuming there's going to be a next time?" I said, trying to lighten the mood.

He met my smile with his own, the new bristles on his face catching the light. "Maybe."

Kisten started for the front door, and I automatically followed to see him out. In my stockings, my feet were as soundless as his on the hardwood floor. The sanctuary was quiet, not a peep from my desk. Still not having said anything, Kisten shrugged into his wool coat.

"Thank you," I said as I handed him the long leather coat that he had let me borrow.

His teeth were a glimmer in the dark foyer. "My pleasure."

"For the night out, not the coat," I said, feeling my nylons go wet from the snowmelt. "Well, thanks for letting me use your coat, too," I stammered.

He leaned closer. "Again, my pleasure," he said, the faint light a glimmer in his eyes. I stared, trying to tell if his eyes were black from desire or shadow. "I *am* going to kiss you," he said, his voice dusky, and my muscles tensed. "No shirking."

"No biting," I said, deadly serious. Anticipation bubbled up inside me. But it was from me, not my demon scar, and accepting that was both a relief and a fear—I couldn't pretend it was the scar. Not his time.

His hands enfolded my lower jaw, both rough and warm. I inhaled as he drew closer, his eyes closing. The scent of leather and silk was strong, the hint of something deeper, primal, tugging at my instincts making me not know what to feel. Eyes open, I watched him lean in, my heart pounding with the anticipation of his lips on mine.

His thumbs shifted, following the curve of my jaw. My lips parted. But the angle was wrong for a full kiss, and my shoulders eased when I realized he was going to kiss the corner of my mouth.

Relaxing, I leaned forward to meet him, flashing into a near panic when his fingertips moved farther back, burying themselves in my hair. Adrenaline pounded through me in a cold wash as I realized he wasn't headed for my mouth at all.

He was going to kiss my neck! I thought, freezing.

But he stopped just shy, exhaling when his lips found the soft hollow between my ear and jaw. Relief mixed with fear, making me incapable of anything. The remnants of the adrenaline scouring through me made my pulse thunder. His lips were gentle, but his hands about my face were firm with restrained need.

A cool warmth took the place of his lips when he pulled away, yet he held himself poised for a moment, then another. My heart beat wildly, and I knew he could feel it almost as if it were his own. His breath came in a slow exhalation that I mirrored.

In the sound of rustling wool, Kisten stepped back. His eyes found mine, and I realized my hands had risen and were about his waist. They fell from him reluctantly, and I swallowed hard, shocked. Though he hadn't touched my lips or neck, it had been one of the most exhilarating kisses I'd ever experienced. The thrill of not knowing what he was going to do had put me in a tizzy that a full-mouthed kiss never could have.

"That's the damnedest thing," he said softly, a puzzled arch to his eyebrow.

"What?" I questioned breathily, still not having shaken off the feeling.

He shook his head. "I can't smell you at all. It's kind of a turn-on."

I blinked, unable to say a word.

"'Night, Rachel." A new smile hovered about him as he shifted another step back.

"Good night," I whispered.

He turned and opened the door. The chill air shocked me out of my daze. My demon scar hadn't made a single twinge, dormant. *That,* I thought, *was frightening. That he could do this to me without even playing upon my scar. What in hell was wrong with me?*

Kisten gave me a final smile from the landing, the snowy night a beautiful backdrop. Turning, he walked down the icy steps, his footsteps crunching on the salt.

Bewildered, I shut the door behind him, wondering what had happened. Still feeling unreal, I dropped the locking bar, then reopened it upon remembering Ivy was out.

Arms clasped about myself, I headed for my bedroom. My thoughts were full of what Kisten had told me about how people dictated their own fate when letting a vampire bind them. That people paid for the ecstasy of vampire passion with different levels of dependency ranging from food to equal. *What if he was lying?* I thought. *Lying to trick me into letting him bind me to him?* But then a more frightening thought pulled my feet to a halt and made my face go cold.

What if he was telling the truth?

Sixteen

Boots thumping in the hallway, I followed Ivy to the front door. Her tall frame moved with a preoccupied grace, predatorial as always in her tasteful leather pants. She might get away solstice shopping in leather, but I had opted for jeans and a red sweater. Even so, we both looked good. Shopping with Ivy was fun. She always treated for cookies, and dodging the offers for dates took on a delicious sense of danger, as she attracted *all* sorts of people.

"I've got to be back by eleven," she said as we entered the sanctuary and she swung her long hair back. "I've got a run tonight. Someone's underage daughter was lured into a bloodhouse, and I'm going in to get her out."

"You want some help?" I asked, buttoning my coat and hitching my bag higher up my shoulder while I walked.

Pixies were clustered at the stained-glass windows, hovering at the lighter colors and squealing at something outside. A harsh smile came over Ivy. "No. It won't take much."

The hard anticipation on her pale oval face worried me. She had come back from visiting Piscary in a very bad mood. Clearly it hadn't gone well, and I had a feeling she was going to take her frustration out on whoever had abducted that girl. Ivy was rough with vampires who preyed on the underage. Someone was going to spend their holiday in traction.

The phone rang, and Ivy and I froze, looking at each

other. "I'll get it," I said. "But if it's not a run, I'll let the machine pick it up."

She nodded, heading out the door with her purse. "I'll warm up the car."

Taking a quick breath, I jogged to the back of the church. On the third ring the machine engaged. The outgoing message spewed its spiel, and my face tightened. Nick had recorded it for me—I thought it posh for it to appear that we employed a male secretary. Though now, seeing as we were listed with professionals of another sort, it probably only added to the confusion.

My frown deepened when the outgoing message cut off and Nick's voice continued. "Hey, Rachel?" he said hesitantly. "Are you there? Pick up if you are. I . . . I was hoping you'd be home. It's what, about six there?"

I forced my hand to pick up the phone. *He was in a different time zone?* "Hi, Nick."

"Rachel." The relief was thick in his voice, in stark contrast to my flat tone. "Good. I'm glad I caught you."

Caught me. Yeah. "How are you doing?" I asked, trying to keep the sarcasm from my voice. I was still stinging, hurt and confused.

He took a slow breath. I could hear water in the background and a hiss of something cooking. The soft clink of glasses and the murmur of conversation intruded. "I'm doing okay," he said. "I'm doing good. I slept really well last night."

"That's great." *Why in hell didn't you tell my ley line practice I was waking you up? You could have been sleeping well here, too.*

"How are you doing?" he asked.

My jaw hurt, and I forced my teeth apart. *I'm confused. I'm hurt. I don't know what you want. I don't know what I want.* "Fine," I said, thinking of Kisten. At least I knew what he wanted. "I'm fine." My throat hurt. "Want me to get your mail, or will you be home soon?"

"I've got a neighbor picking it up. But thanks."

You didn't answer my question. "Okay. Do you know if you'll be back by the solstice, or should I give your ticket to . . . someone else?" I hadn't meant to hesitate. It just happened. It was obvious Nick had heard it, too, given his silence. A seagull cried in the background. He was on a beach? He was at a bar on a beach and I was dodging black charms in cold slush?

"Why don't you do that," he said finally, and I felt as if someone punched me in the gut. "I don't know how long I'm going to be here."

"Sure," I whispered.

"I miss you, Rachel," he said, and I closed my eyes.

Please don't say it, I thought. *Please.*

"But I'm feeling much better. I'll be home soon."

It was exactly what Jenks had told me he would say, and my throat closed up. "I miss you, too," I said, feeling betrayed and lost all over again. He said nothing, and after three heartbeats, I stepped into the breach. "Well, Ivy and I are going shopping. She's in the car."

"Oh." He sounded relieved, the bastard. "I won't keep you. Um, I'll talk to you later."

Liar. "All right. 'Bye."

"I love you, Rachel," he whispered, but I hung up as if I hadn't heard. I didn't know if I could answer him anymore. Miserable, I pulled my hand from the receiver. My red nail polish looked bright against the black plastic. My fingers were trembling and my head hurt.

"Then why did you leave instead of telling me what's wrong?" I asked the empty room.

I exhaled with a measured slowness to try to wash the tension from me. I was going shopping with Ivy. I wouldn't ruin it by brooding about Nick. He was gone. He wasn't coming back. He felt better when he was a time zone away from me; why would he come back?

Hitching my bag higher up my shoulder, I headed for the

front. The pixies were still clustered at the windows in small knots. Jenks was somewhere else, for which I was grateful. He'd only tell me "I told you so" if he had heard my conversation with Nick.

"Jenks! You have command of the ship!" I shouted as I opened the front door, and a smile, faint but real, crossed me when a piercing whistle emanated from my desk.

Ivy was in the car already, and my eyes were drawn across the street to Keasley's house, pulled by the sound of kids and a dog barking. My steps slowed. Ceri was in his yard, wearing the jeans I had dropped off earlier and an old coat of Ivy's. Bright red mittens and a matching hat made a vivid splash against the snow as she and about six kids ranging from ten to eighteen rolled snowballs around. A mountain was taking shape in the corner of Keasley's small lot. Next door were four more kids doing the same. It looked like there was going to be a snowball fight before too much longer.

I waved to Ceri, then Keasley—who was standing on his porch watching with an intent hunch that told me he'd like to be down there, too. Both of them waved back, and I felt warm. I'd done something good.

I lifted the door latch of Ivy's borrowed Mercedes, slipping in to find it still blowing cold air from the vents. It took forever for the big four-door sedan to warm up. I knew Ivy didn't like driving it, but her mother wouldn't lend her anything else and a cycle in slush was asking for stitches. "Who was it?" Ivy asked as I angled the vent off me and buckled myself in. Ivy drove as if she couldn't be killed, which I thought was a little ironic.

"Nobody."

She gave me a telling look. "Nick?"

Lips pressed together, I set my bag on my lap. "Like I said, nobody."

Not looking behind her, Ivy pulled away from the curb. "Rachel, I'm sorry."

The sincerity in her gray silk voice pulled my head up. "I thought you hated Nick."

"I do," she said, not at all apologetic. "I think he's manipulative and withholds information that might get you hurt. But you liked him. Maybe . . ." She hesitated, her jaw tightening and relaxing. "Maybe he's coming back. He does . . . love you." She made an ugly sound. "Oh God, you made me say it."

I laughed. "Nick isn't that bad," I said, and she turned to me. My eyes flicked to the truck we were about to rear-end at a stoplight, and I braced myself against the dash.

"I said he loved you. I didn't say he trusted you," she said, her eyes on me as she braked smoothly to a halt ending with our grille six inches from his bumper.

My stomach clenched. "You don't think he trusts me?"

"Rachel," she cajoled, inching forward as the light changed but the truck didn't move. "He leaves town without telling you? Then doesn't tell you when he's coming back? I don't think some*one* has come between you, I think some-*thing* has. You scared the hell out of him, and he's not enough of a man to admit it, deal with it, and get over it."

I said nothing, glad when we started moving again. I hadn't just scared him, I had made him seize. It must have been awful. No wonder he left. Great, now I'd feel guilty all day.

Ivy jerked the wheel and shifted lanes. A horn blew, and she eyed the driver in the rearview mirror. Slowly the car put space between us, pushed back by the force of her gaze. "Do you mind if we stop at my folks' house for a minute? It's on the way."

"Sure." I stifled a gasp when she cut a right in front of the truck we'd just passed. "Ivy, you may have lightning reflexes, but the guy driving that truck just had kittens."

She snorted, dropping back two whole feet off the bumper of the car now ahead of us.

Ivy made an obvious effort to drive normally through the busier areas of the Hollows, and slowly I relaxed my death grip on my bag. It was the first time we'd been together and away from Jenks in about a week, and neither one of us knew what to get him for the solstice. Ivy was tending to the heated doghouse she had seen in a catalog; anything to get him and his brood out of the church. I'd settle for a lockbox we could cover with a rug and pretend was an end table.

As Ivy drove, slowly the yards grew larger and the trees taller. The houses began moving back from the street until only their roofs showed from behind stands of evergreens. We were just inside the city limits, right next to the river. It really wasn't on the way to the mall, but the interstate wasn't far, and with that, the city was wide-open.

Ivy pulled unhesitatingly into a gated drive. Twin tracks made a black trail on the dusting of snow that had fallen since it had been plowed. I leaned to look out the window, never having seen her parents' house. The car slowed to a halt before an old, romantic-looking three-story home painted white with hunter green shutters. A little red two-seater was parked out front, dry and free of snow.

"You grew up here?" I asked as I got out. The two names on the mailbox gave me pause until I remembered vampires maintained their names after marriage to keep living blood-lines intact. Ivy was a Tamwood, her sister was a Randal.

Ivy slammed her door and dropped her keys into her black purse. "Yeah." She looked to holiday lights making a taste-ful, subdued display. It was getting dusky. The sun was only about an hour from setting, and I was hoping we would be gone before then. I didn't particularly want to meet her mom.

"Come on in," she said, her boots thumping on the brushed steps, and I followed her onto the covered porch. She opened the door, shouting, "Hi! I'm home!"

A smile curved over me as I hesitated just outside to stomp the snow off. I liked hearing her voice so relaxed. Coming inside, I shut the door and breathed deeply. Cloves and cinnamon—someone had been baking.

The large entryway was all varnished wood and subtle shades of cream and white. It was as stark and elegant as our living room was warm and casual. A runner of cedar bough made graceful loops up the railing of the nearby stairway. It was warm, and I unbuttoned my coat and stuffed my gloves in the pockets.

"That's Erica's car outside. She's probably in the kitchen," Ivy said, dropping her purse on the small table beside the door. It was polished so highly that it looked like black plastic.

Taking her coat off, she draped it over an arm and headed for a large archway to the left, coming to a halt at a thumping of feet on the steps. Ivy looked up, her placid face shifting. It took me a moment to realize she was happy. My gaze followed her to a young woman slumping downstairs.

She looked to be about seventeen, dressed in a skimpy goth short skirt to show her midriff, with black fingernails and lipstick. Silver chains and bangles swung everywhere as she hopped down the stairs, bringing that dog-eared page to mind. Her black hair was cut short and styled into wild spikes. Maturity hadn't yet finished filling her out, but I could tell already that she was going to look exactly like her big sister apart from being six inches shorter: lean, sleek, predatory, and with just enough oriental cast to make her exotic. Nice to know it ran in the family. Of course, right now she looked like a teenage vamp out of control.

"Hi, Erica," Ivy said, reversing her steps and waiting for her at the foot of the stairs.

"My God, Ivy," Erica said, her high voice heavy on the valley girl accent. "You *have* to talk to Daddy. He's being total Big Brother. Like, *I* don't know the difference between good Brimstone and bad Brimstone? Listening to him, you'd think I was still two, crawling around in diapers trying to bite the dog. God! He was in the kitchen," she continued, her mouth going as she eyed me up and down, "making Mom her organically grown, earth-friendly, politically correct *stinking* cup of tea, when I can't go out one night with my friends. It's so *unfair*! Are you staying? She'll be up rattling the windows soon."

"No." Ivy drew back. "I'm here to talk to Dad. He's in the kitchen?"

"Basement," Erica said. Mouth finally stopping, she sent her gaze over me again as I stood in a bemused wonder at how fast she talked. "Who's your friend?" she asked.

A faint smile curled up the corners of Ivy's mouth. "Erica, this is Rachel."

"Oh!" the young woman exclaimed, her brown eyes that were almost hidden behind her black mascara going wide. She stepped forward and grabbed my hand, pumping it up and down enthusiastically with her bangles jingling. "I shoulda known! Hey, I saw you at Piscary's," she said, giving me a whack on the shoulder that sent me forward a step. "Man, you were sugared up good. Riding the short bus. Walking with the ghost. I didn't recognize you." Her eyes traveled over my jeans and winter coat. "You had a date with Kisten? Did he bite you?"

I blinked, and Ivy laughed nervously. "Hardly. Rachel doesn't let anyone bite her." She took a step to her sister, giving her a hug. I felt good when the young woman returned it with a careless attention, apparently not knowing or caring how rarely Ivy touched anyone. The two pulled apart, and Ivy's features stilled. She took a breath, nostrils widening.

Erica grinned like the cat who ate the canary. "Guess who I picked up at the airport?"

Ivy straightened. "Skimmer's here."

It was almost a whisper, and Erica all but danced back a step. "Came in on a morning flight," she said, as proud as if she had landed the plane herself.

My eyes widened. Ivy was wire-tight. Breath catching, she spun to an archway at the sound of a door closing. A feminine voice echoed, "Erica? Is that my cab?"

"Skimmer!" Ivy took a step to the archway, then rocked back. She looked at me, more alive than I'd seen her in a long time. A small scuff at the archway pulled her attention from me. Emotion cascaded over her, and the happiness settled in to stay, telling me that Skimmer was one of the few people Ivy felt comfortable to be herself around.

So there were two of us, I thought, turning to follow her gaze to a young woman standing in the threshold. I felt my brows rise in speculation as I took in what had to be Skimmer. She was dressed in faded jeans and a crisp, white button-down shirt to make a nice mix of casual sophistication. Understated black boots brought her height to about mine. Slim and well-proportioned, the blond woman stood with a confident grace typical of living vampires.

She had a single silver chain about her neck, and her blond hair was pulled back in a simple ponytail to accentuate a bone structure that models could spend a small fortune on plastic surgery to find. I stared at her eyes, wondering if they were really that blue or if they just seemed that way because of her incredibly long eyelashes. Her nose was small and turned up at the end to give her smile a look of shy confidence.

"What are you doing here?" Ivy said, her face alight as she went to greet her. The two women gave each other a long hug. My lips parted and I froze at the lingering kiss before they parted. *Okay* . . .

Ivy slipped me a glance, but she was smiling when she turned back to Skimmer, smiling, still smiling, with her hands on the woman's elbows. "I can't believe you're here!" she said.

Skimmer glanced at me once before focusing on Ivy. She looked like she had enough confidence and smarts to break horses, teach aboriginal children, and dine out at a five-star restaurant all in one day. *And she and Ivy had kissed? Not just a peck, but a real . . . kiss?*

"I'm out here on business," she said. "Long-term business," she added, her pleasant voice thick with a pleased emotion. "A year, I'm guessing."

"A year! Why didn't you call me? I would have picked you up!"

The woman took a step back, and Ivy's hold on her fell

away. "I wanted to surprise you," she said, her smile rising to encompass her blue eyes. "Besides, I wasn't sure of your situation. It's been so long," she finished softly.

Her eyes fell on me, and I warmed in my new understanding. *Aw, crap on toast. How long had I been living with Ivy? How could I have not known? Was I blind or just stupid?*

"Damn," Ivy swore, still obviously excited. "It's good to see you. What are you out here for? Do you need a place to stay?"

My pulse quickened and I tried to keep my worry from showing. Two of them together in the church? Not good. Even more disturbing was that Skimmer seemed to relax at her offer, losing interest in me and focusing entirely on Ivy.

Erica stood beside me, grinning mischievously. "Skimmer came out to work for Piscary," she said, clearly eager to tell what she thought was good news, but my face went cold. "It's all arranged. She looks to him now." Twirling her necklaces, the young vampire beamed. "Just like I always thought she should."

Ivy took a breath and held it. Wonder crossed her, and she reached out to touch Skimmer's shoulder as if not believing she was really there. "You look to Piscary?" she breathed, and I wondered what the significance was. "Who or what did he give for you?"

Skimmer shrugged, lifting one narrow shoulder and letting it fall. "Nothing yet. I've been trying the last six years to wiggle into his camarilla, and if I work this right, it will be permanent." She dropped her head briefly, her eyes alight and eager when they rose. "I'm staying at Piscary's place meantime," she said, "but thanks for the offer to bunk with you."

Piscary's, I thought, my worry strengthening. That was where Kisten was living. This was getting better and better. Ivy, too, seemed to have to think about that. "You left your place with Natalie to run Piscary's restaurant?" she asked, and Skimmer laughed. It was comfortable and pleasant, and the volumes that were left unsaid made me uneasy.

"No. Kist can have that job," she said lightly. "I'm here to get Piscary out of prison. My permanent inclusion into Piscary's camarilla is contingent upon it. If I win my case, I stay. If I lose, I go back home."

I froze. *Oh my God. She was Piscary's lawyer.*

Skimmer hesitated at Ivy's lack of response. Ivy turned to me, a panicked look on her face. I watched the wall come down, sealing everything away. Her happiness, her joy, her excitement at reuniting with an old friend; it was all gone. Something slipped between us, and I felt my chest tighten. Erica's bangles clanked as the young vampire clearly realized something was wrong but not understanding. Hell, I didn't think I understood.

Suddenly wary, Skimmer glanced from me to Ivy. "So, who's your friend?" she asked into the awkward silence.

Ivy licked her lips and turned to face me more fully. I shifted forward, not knowing how to react. "Rachel," Ivy said, "I'd like you to meet Skimmer. We roomed together for our last two years of high school out on the West Coast. Skimmer, this is Rachel, my partner."

I took a breath, trying to decide how I should handle this. My hand went out to shake hers, but Skimmer walked past it, taking me into an expansive hug.

I tried not to stiffen, determined to go with the flow until I had a chance to talk to Ivy about just what we were going to do about this. Piscary couldn't get out of prison; I'd never sleep again. My arms went about her in a loose generic hug, and I froze when the woman put her lips under my ear and breathed, "Pleasure to meet you."

Adrenaline jolted through me as my demon scar flashed into waves of heat. Shocked, I shoved her away, collapsing to a defensive posture. The living vampire fell back, surprise making her long lashes and blue eyes look enormous. She caught her balance a good five feet away. Erica gasped, and Ivy was a black blur coming between us.

"Skimmer!" Ivy shouted, her voice almost panicked as she stood with her back to me.

My heart pounded and sweat broke out. The flaming promise on my neck hurt, it was so strong, and I put a hand to it, feeling betrayed and shocked.

"She's my business partner!" Ivy exclaimed. "Not my blood partner!"

The slim woman stared at us, flashing into a red-faced embarrassment. "Oh God," she stammered, hunching into a slightly submissive posture. "I'm sorry." She put a hand to her mouth. "I am really, really sorry." She looked at Ivy, who was slowly relaxing. "Ivy, I thought you'd taken a shadow. She smells like you. I was just being polite." Skimmer's gaze darted to me as I tried to slow my heartbeat. "You asked me to stay with you. I thought—God, I'm sorry. I thought she was your shadow. I didn't know she was your . . . friend."

"It's all right," I lied, forcing myself upright. I didn't like the way she had said "friend." It implied more than what we were. But I currently wasn't up to trying to explain to Ivy's old roommate that we weren't sharing blood or a bed. Ivy wasn't much help, standing with a deer-in-the-headlights look. And I had this weird feeling I was still missing something. *God, how did I get to this place?*

Erica was standing by the foot of the stairs, her eyes wide and her mouth open. Skimmer looked distressed as she tried to cover her error, smoothing her hands on her pants and touching her hair. She took a deep breath. Still flushed, she stiffly extended her hand in an obvious show of intent and stepped forward. "I'm sorry," she said as she halted before me. "My name is Dorothy Claymor. You can call me that if you want to. I probably deserve it."

I managed to dredge up a stilted smile. "Rachel Morgan," I said, shaking her hand.

The woman froze, and I pulled away. She looked at Ivy, the pieces falling into place.

"The one who put Piscary in prison," I added, just to be sure she knew where I stood.

A sick smile came over Ivy. Dropping back a step, Skimmer's gaze went between us. Confusion made her cheeks bright red. This was a mess. This was a sticky, stinking mess of crap, and the levels were steadily rising.

Skimmer swallowed hard. "It's a pleasure to meet you." Hesitating, she added, "Boy, this is awkward."

I felt my shoulders ease at her admission. She was going to do what she had to do, and I was going to do what I had to do. And Ivy? Ivy was going to go insane.

Erica moved forward, the jingling of her jewelry sounding loud. "Hey, ah, does anyone want a cookie or something?"

Oh yeah. A cookie. That would make everything better. Dunked in a shot of tequila, maybe? Or better yet, just the bottle? Yeah, that ought to do it.

Skimmer forced a smile. Her crisp mien was wearing thin, but she was holding up well considering she had left her home and master to rekindle a relationship with her high school girlfriend who was rooming with the woman who had put her new boss behind bars. *Join us next time for* Days of the Undead *when Rachel learns her long lost brother is really a crown prince from outer space.* My life was so screwed up.

Skimmer glanced at her watch—I couldn't help but notice it had diamonds on it in place of numbers. "I've got to go. I'm meeting with—someone in about an hour."

She was going to meet someone in about an hour. Just after the sun went down. Why didn't she just say Piscary?

"You need a ride?" Ivy said, sounding almost wistful, if she would ever let that particular emotion come from her.

Skimmer looked from Ivy to me and back to Ivy, hurt and disappointment flickering in the back of her eyes. "No," she said softly. "I've got a cab coming." She swallowed, trying to scrape herself back together. "Actually, I think that's it now."

I didn't hear anything, but I didn't have a living vampire's hearing.

Skimmer shifted awkwardly forward. "It was nice meeting you," she said to me, then turned to Ivy. "I'll talk to you later, sweets," she said, eyes closed as she gave her a long hug.

Ivy was still in a shocked quandary, and she returned it looking numb.

"Skimmer," I said as they broke apart and the shaken, subdued woman took a thin jacket from the hall closet and put it on. "This isn't what you think."

She stopped with her hand on the doorknob, looking at Ivy for a long moment with deep regret. "It's not what I think that matters," she said as she opened the door. "It's what Ivy wants."

I opened my mouth to protest, but she left, latching the door softly behind her.

Seventeen

Skimmer's departure left an awkward silence. As the cab accelerated down the drive, I looked at Ivy standing in the sterile white entryway with its elegant decorations that utterly lacked any warmth. Guilt was thick on her. I knew it was from the reminder that she still harbored the belief that someday I'd be her scion—apparently with a little extra something on the side. It was a position that I think Skimmer had moved out here hopefully to fill.

Not sure what I was feeling, I faced her. "Why did you let her think we were lovers?" I said, shaking inside. "God, Ivy. We aren't even sharing blood, and she thinks we're lovers."

Ivy's face closed, the barest tightening of her jaw giving away her emotion. "She doesn't think that at all." She strode out of the room. "Do you want some juice?" she called back.

"No," I said softly as I followed her deeper into the house. I knew if I pressed the issue right now, she would likely become more closed. This conversation wasn't over, but having it in front of Erica wasn't a good idea. My head hurt. Maybe I could get her to talk about it over coffee and cheesecake while we were shopping. Maybe I should move to Timbuktu, or the Tennessee mountains, or somewhere else where there weren't any vampires. (Don't ask. It's weird, even for Inderlanders—which is saying a lot.)

Erica was tight on my heels, her mindless chatter an obvious attempt to cover up the issues that Skimmer had raised.

Her bright voice filled the sterile house with life as she trailed after us through large dim rooms full of hardwood furniture and cold drafts. I made a mental note to never get Erica and Jenks in the same room. No wonder Ivy didn't have a problem with Jenks. Her sister was cut from the same cloth.

Ivy's boots were slow on the polished floor when we left a dark blue formal dining room and entered a brightly lit, spacious kitchen. I blinked. Ivy met my startled gaze and shrugged. I knew that Ivy had remodeled the church's kitchen before I had moved in, and as I looked around, I realized she had patterned it after the one she grew up with.

The room was nearly as spacious, that same center island counter taking up the middle. Cast-iron pots and metal utensils hung over it instead of my ceramic spoons and copper spell vats, but it made the same comfortable spot to lean against. There was a heavy antique table—twin to ours—against the near wall, right where I'd expect it. Even the cupboards were the same style, and the counters had an identical color. The floor, though, was tile instead of linoleum.

Past the sink where I had a single window overlooking the graveyard, there was a bank of windows that showed a long snowfield running down to the gray ribbon of the Ohio River. Ivy's parents owned a lot of property. You could graze cattle down there.

A kettle steamed on the stove, and as Ivy moved it off the burner, I dropped my bag on the table where my chair would be if I was home. "This is nice," I said wryly.

Ivy gave me a cautious look, clearly glad I had shelved the pending discussion about Skimmer. "It was cheaper to do both kitchens at once," she said, and I nodded. It was warm, and I took my coat off, draping it on the back of the chair.

Stretching to show the small of her back, Erica stood on one foot to reach a glass jar half full of what looked like sugar cookies. Leaning against the counter, she ate one, offering Ivy another but none to me. I had a feeling they weren't sugar cookies but those awful cardboard-tasting disks that Ivy had kept shoving down my throat last spring when I was recovering from a massive blood loss. Sort of a vampire pick-me-up that helped support their—ah—lifestyle.

A muffled thumping grew louder, and I turned to what I had thought was a pantry door. It creaked opened to show a staircase leading down. A tall gaunt man was coming up and out of the shadows. "Hi, Dad," Ivy said, and I straightened, smiling at the softness in her voice.

"Ivy . . ." The man beamed as he set a tray with two tiny empty cups down on the table. His voice was gravely, matching his skin: rough and pebbly. I recognized the texture as scars left from the Turn. It had affected some more than others, and witches, pixies, and fairies not at all. "Skimmer's here," he said gently.

"I saw her," Ivy said, and he hesitated at the lack of anything more.

He looked tired, his brown eyes content as he gave Ivy a quick hug. Gently waving black hair framed his serious face softly lined with what looked like worry rather than age. It was obvious that this was where Ivy got her height. The living vampire was tall, with a refinement that turned his gaunt frame pleasing rather than unattractive. He was wearing jeans and a casual shirt. Small, almost unseen lines scarred his neck, and his arms showing past his rolled-up sleeves had the same marks on the underside. It must be hard being married to an undead.

"I'm glad you came home," the man said, his eyes flicking briefly to me and the cross on my charm bracelet before settling back on his daughter with an obvious warmth. "Your mother will be up in a bit. She wants to talk to you. Skimmer put her in a rare mood."

"No." Ivy dropped back out of his touch. "I wanted to ask you something, is all."

He nodded once, his thin lips falling into a resigned disappointment. I felt a slight tingle from my demon scar as he poured the steaming water into a second teapot. The clanking of the porcelain was loud. Arms crossed before me, I leaned to rest against the table to distance myself. I hoped the tingle was a lingering sensation from Skimmer and didn't stem from Ivy's dad. I didn't think it was him. He looked too calm to be fighting a need to slack his hunger.

"Dad," Ivy said, seeing my unease. "This is Rachel. Rachel, this is my dad."

As if aware my scar was tingling, Ivy's dad stayed at the other end of the kitchen, taking the cookies from Erica and putting them back into the cookie jar. The girl huffed, then grimaced at her dad's raised eyebrow. "It's a pleasure to meet you," he said, his attention returning to me.

"Hello, Mr. Randal," I said, not liking the way he was eyeing Ivy and me standing beside each other. I suddenly felt as if I was on a date, meeting the parents, and I flushed. I didn't like his knowing smile. Apparently neither did Ivy.

"Stop it, Dad." Ivy pulled out a chair and sat. "Rachel is my roommate, not my live-in."

"You'd better make sure Skimmer knows that." His narrow chest moved as he breathed deeply to take in the emotions on the air. "She came out here for you. Left everything. Think hard before you walk away from that. She has good breeding behind her. An unbroken millennium line is hard to find."

Tension slammed back into me and I felt myself stiffen.

"Oh God," Erica moaned, her hand back in the cookie jar. "Don't start, Daddy. We just had an ugly in the hallway."

Smiling to show teeth, he reached across to take the cookie from her and ate a bite. "Don't you have to be to work soon?" he said when he swallowed.

The young vampire jiggled. "Daddy, I want to go to the concert. All my friends are."

My eyebrows rose. Ivy shook her head with the smallest of movements, a private answer to my question as to whether we should tell him we were going and that we'd keep an eye on her.

"No," her father said, brushing the crumbs from himself as he finished his cookie.

"But, Daddy . . ."

Opening the jar, he took out three more. "You don't have enough control—"

Erica puffed, slumping against the counter. "My control is fine," she said sulkily.

He straightened, the first hints of steel tightening his face. "Erica, your hormones are jumping up and down right now. One night you have control in a stressful situation, the next you lose it while you're watching TV. You aren't wearing your caps like you're supposed to, and I don't want you to accidentally bind someone to you."

"Daddy!" she cried, flushing a dull, embarrassed red.

Getting two glasses from the cupboard, Ivy snickered. My uneasiness faded slightly.

"I know . . ." her father said, his head bowed and a hand raised. "A lot of your friends have shadows, and it looks like fun having someone trailing behind you, seeking your attention and always there. You're the center of their world, and they see only you. But Erica, bonded shadows are a lot of work. They aren't pets you can give to a friend when you tire of them. They need reassurance and attention. You're too young to have that kind of responsibility."

"Daddy, stop!" Erica said, clearly mortified. I sat as Ivy got a carton of orange juice from the fridge. I wondered how much of this was for Erica and how much of it was his way of trying to scare me off from his eldest daughter. It was working. Not that I needed any encouragement.

The living vampire's face went stern. "You're being careless," he said, his gravely voice harsh. "Taking risks that might put you in a place you don't want to be yet. Don't think I don't know you take your caps off as soon as you leave this house. You aren't going to that concert."

"That's not fair!" she shouted, spiked hair bobbing. "I'm pulling all A's *and* working part-time. It's *just* a *concert!* There won't even be any Brimstone there!"

He shook his head as she huffed. "Until that bad Brimstone is off the streets, you will be home before sunrise, young lady. I'm not going down to the city tombs to identify and bring a member of my house home. I've done that once, and I'm not ready to do it again."

"Daddy!"

Ivy handed her father a glass of juice, then sat down with her drink in the chair adjacent to mine. Crossing her legs at the knees, she said, "I'm going to the concert."

Erica gasped, her jewelry tinkling as she jumped. "Daddy!" she cried. "Ivy's going. I won't take any Brimstone and I won't bite anyone. I promise! Oh God! Please let me go!"

Eyebrows high, Ivy's dad looked at Ivy. She shrugged, and Erica held her breath. "If it's all right with your mother, it's all right with me," he finally said.

"Thank you, Daddy!" Erica squealed. She flung herself at him, almost knocking her taller father down. In a clatter of boots, she yanked the door to the stairwell open and thumped downstairs. The door arched closed, and Erica's shouts grew muffled.

The man sighed, his thin shoulders moving. "Just how long were you going to let her beg before you told me you were going?" he asked wryly.

Her eyes on her juice, Ivy smiled. "Long enough that she will listen to me when I tell her to wear her caps or I'll change my mind."

A chuckle rose. "You learn well, young grasshopper," he said, affecting a strong accent.

There was a thumping on the stairs and Erica burst out, eyes black in excitement, chains swinging. "She said yes! Gotta go! Love you, Daddy! Thanks, Ivy!" She made a pair of bunny ears with her fingers, crooking them as she said, "Kiss, kiss!" and darted out of the room.

"Do you have your caps?" her father shouted after her.

"Yes!" she called back, her voice faint.

"Take some of those necklaces off, young lady!" he added, but the door slammed. The quiet was a relief, and I met Ivy's smile with bemused wonder. Erica could really fill a room.

Ivy's father put his glass down. His face seemed to take on more wrinkles, and I could see the strain his body was enduring to supply the blood his undead wife needed to stay sane.

I watched Ivy shift her fingers on her glass to spin it where it sat. Slowly her smile faded. "Has she been to see Piscary?" she asked softly, the sudden worry in her voice drawing my attention. This was why Ivy had come to talk to her dad, and as I thought of Erica's carefree, wild innocence in Piscary's manipulative embrace, I worried, too.

Ivy's dad, though, didn't seem to have a problem with it, taking a slow sip of juice before answering, "Yes. She visits him every two weeks. As is respectful." My brow pinched at the implied question, and I wasn't surprised when he followed up with, "Have you?"

Ivy stilled the fingers encircling her glass. Uncomfortable, I looked for a way to excuse myself and go hide in the car. Ivy glanced at me, then her father. He leaned back, waiting. From outside came the rumble of Erica's car, fading to leave the hum of the clock on the oven the only sound. Ivy took a breath. "Dad, I made a mistake."

I felt Ivy's dad's eyes land on me, even though I was staring out the window trying to divorce myself from the conversation. "We should talk about this when your mother is available," he said, and I took a quick breath.

"You know," I said as I got up, "I think I'll go wait in the car."

"I don't want to talk about it with Mom, I want to talk about it with you," Ivy said crossly. "And there's no reason Rachel can't hear this."

The hidden request in Ivy's voice stopped me short. I sank back down, ignoring the obvious disapproval from her dad. This wasn't going to be fun. Maybe she wanted my opinion of the conversation to balance out her own. I could do that for her.

"I made a mistake," Ivy said softly. "I don't want to be Piscary's scion."

"Ivy . . ." There was a tired weariness in that one word. "It's time to start taking on your responsibilities. Your mother was his scion before she died. The benefits—"

"I don't want them!" Ivy said, and I watched her eyes closely, wondering if the ring of brown about her pupil was shrinking. "Maybe if he wasn't in my head all the time," she added, moving her juice away. "But I can't take it anymore. He just keeps pushing."

"He wouldn't if you would go see him."

Ivy sat straighter, eyes on the table. "I did go see him. I told him that I wasn't going to be his scion and to get out of my head. He laughed at me. He said I had made a choice and now I had to live and die by it."

"You did make a choice."

"And now I'm making another one," she shot back, her eyes lowered submissively but her voice determined. "I'm not going to do it. I don't want to run Cincinnati's underground, and I won't." She took a deep breath, her eyes rising to his. "I can't tell if I like something anymore because *I* like it or because Piscary likes it. Dad, will you talk to him for me?"

My eyes widened at her pleading tone. The only time I had heard it before was when she thought she was dead and was begging me to keep her safe. My jaw clenched as I remembered. God, that had been awful. When I looked up at his continued silence, I was startled to find Ivy's dad watching me. His lips were pressed tight and his gaze was angry, as if this was my fault.

"You're his scion," he said, his eyes accusingly on mine. "Stop shirking your duties."

Ivy's nostrils flared. I really didn't want to be here, but if I moved, I would only draw attention to myself. "I made a mistake," she said angrily. "And I'm willing to pay the cost to get out of it, but he's going to start hurting people to make me do what he wants. That's not fair."

He made a scoffing laugh and rose. "Did you expect anything different? He's going to use everything and everyone he can to manipulate you. He's a master vampire." Putting his hands on the table, he leaned toward Ivy. "It's what they do."

Cold, I sent my gaze down to the river below. It didn't matter if Piscary was in jail or not. All he had to do was say the word, and his minions would not only bring Ivy in line but get me out of his hair as well. Expensive, but effective.

But Ivy pulled her head up, shaking it in reassurance before turning her damp eyes to her father. "Dad, he said he's going to start calling on Erica."

The man's face went ashen to make the small fever scars stand out starkly. Relief that Piscary wasn't targeting me flashed through me, then guilt that I could feel such a thing. "I'll talk to him," he whispered, the worry in his voice for his innocent, so-alive daughter clear.

I felt sick. In their conversation were the dark, ugly shadows of the hidden pacts older children made to each other to protect a younger, innocent sibling from an abusive parent. The feeling solidified when her dad repeated softly, "I'll talk to him."

"Thank you."

All of us seemed to draw away in an uncomfortable silence. It was time to go. Ivy stood first, quickly followed by me. I grabbed my coat from the back of the chair and shrugged into it. Ivy's dad rose slowly, seeming twice as tired as when we came in. "Ivy," he said as he came close. "I'm proud of you. I don't agree with what you're doing, but I'm proud of you."

"Thanks, Dad." Smiling a close-lipped smile in relief, she gave him a hug. "We gotta go. I've got a run tonight."

"Darvan's girl?" he asked, and she nodded, the hint of guilt and fear on her still. "Good. You keep doing what you're doing. I'll talk to Piscary and see what I can work out."

"Thanks."

He turned to me. "It was a pleasure meeting you, Rachel."

"Same here, Mr. Randal." I was glad the vampire talk seemed to be over. We could all pretend to be normal again; hide the ugliness under the five-thousand-dollar rug.

"Wait, Ivy. Here." The man reached into his back pocket and pulled out a worn wallet, turning himself from a vampire into just another dad.

"Dad," Ivy protested. "I've got my own money."

He smiled with half his mouth. "Think of it as a thank-you for watching Erica at the concert. Have lunch on me."

I said nothing as he shoved a hundred dollar bill into Ivy's hand, pulling her forward into a one-armed hug. "I'll call you tomorrow morning," he said softly.

Ivy's shoulders lost their usual upright posture. "I'll come by. I don't want to talk over the phone." She shot me a forced, close-lipped smile. "Ready to go?"

I nodded, giving Ivy's dad a head bob as I followed her out into the dining room and to the front door. Knowing how good vamp hearing was, I kept my mouth shut until the elegantly carved door thumped shut behind us and our feet were again on the snow. It had grown dusky, and the snowdrifts seemed to glow in the light reflected off the sky.

Erica's car was gone. Key's jingling, Ivy hesitated. "Hold up," she said, boots squeaking in the snow as she went to where the red car had been parked. "I think she ditched her caps."

I stood by my open door and waited while Ivy came to a standstill beside the wheel marks. Eyes closed, she flung her hand as if throwing something, and then strode to the other side of the drive. As I watched in a mystified silence, she searched the snow. Bending at the waist twice, she picked something up. She came back and got into the car without comment.

I followed her in and fastened my belt, wishing it were darker so I didn't have to watch her drive. At my questioning silence, Ivy held out her hand and dropped two bits of hollow plastic into my grip. The car started, and I aimed the vents at me, hoping the engine was still warm. "Caps?" I asked, looking at them small and white in my palm as Ivy pulled away. *How on earth did she find these in the snow?*

"Guaranteed to keep from breaking skin," Ivy said, her thin lips pressing together. "And with that, she can't accidentally bind anyone to her. She's supposed to wear them until Dad says so. And at this rate, she's going to be thirty before that happens. I know where she works. Mind if we drop them off?"

I shook my head, extending them back to her. Ivy checked both ways at the end of the drive before pulling out in front of a blue station wagon, wheels spinning in the slush. "I've got an empty caps case in my purse. Would you put them in there for me?"

"Sure." I didn't like digging around in her purse, but if I didn't, she'd do it while driving, and my stomach was in enough knots already. I felt odd as I put Ivy's purse on my lap and opened it up. It was disgustingly tidy. Not a single used tissue or lint-covered candy.

"Mine is the one with the colored glass on it," Ivy said, watching the road with half her attention. "I should have a plastic one in there, somewhere. The disinfectant is probably still good. Dad would kill her if he knew she threw them in the snow. They cost as much as her summer camp last year in the Andes."

"Oh." My three summers spent at Kalamack's Make-A-Wish camp for dying children suddenly looked pale. Shifting past a small container that looked like an elaborately decorated pillbox was a thumb-sized white vial. I unscrewed the top to find it full of a bluish liquid.

"That's the one," Ivy said, and I dropped them in. They floated, and when I went to stick my pinky in to sink them, she added, "Just put the top on and give it a shake. They'll sink."

I did just that, dropping the vial into her purse and setting it beside her.

"Thanks," Ivy said. "The time I 'lost' mine, he grounded me for a month."

I gave her a weak smile, thinking it was kind of like losing your glasses or retainer . . . or maybe your diaphragm. *Oh God. Did I really want to know all this?*

"You still wear caps?" I said, curiosity getting the better of me. She didn't seem to be embarrassed about it. Maybe I should just go with it.

Ivy shook her head, signaling an instant before she crossed two lanes of traffic to get to the expressway's on-ramp. "No," she said as I clutched the door handle. "Not since I was seventeen. But I keep them in case—" She cut her words off. "Just in case."

Just in case what? I wondered, then decided I didn't want to know. "Uh, Ivy?" I questioned as I tried not to figure out where she was going to force herself into traffic. I held my breath while we merged and, from behind us, horns blew. "What the heck does bunny ears and 'kiss, kiss' mean?"

She stared at me, and I made a peace sign and crooked my fingers twice in quick succession. An odd smile quirked the corners of her mouth. "Those aren't bunny ears," she said. "Those are fangs."

I thought about that, then flushed. "Oh."

Ivy chuckled. I eyed her for a moment, then deciding there would be no better time, I took a slow breath. "Um, about Skimmer . . ."

Her good mood vanished. She shot me a look, then put her eyes back on the road. "We were roommates." A faint flush came over her, telling me it was more than that. "We were *very* close roommates," she added carefully, as if I hadn't already figured it out. Ivy hit the brakes hard to avoid a black BMW that wanted to pen her in behind a minivan. Accelerating quickly, she darted around to the right, leaving him behind.

"She came out here because of you," I said, feeling my blood quicken. "Why didn't you tell her we aren't like that?"

Her grip on the wheel tightened. "Because . . ." She took a soft breath and tucked her hair behind her ear. It was a nervous tic that I didn't see very often. "Because I didn't want to," she said as she settled in behind a red Trans-Am doing fifteen over the posted limit.

Eyes worried, she looked at me, ignoring the green minivan that both the Trans-Am and we were roaring up on. "I'm not going to apologize, Rachel. The night you decide taking and giving blood isn't sex, I'm going to be there. I'll take what I can until you do."

Horribly uncomfortable, I shifted in my seat. "Ivy . . ."

"Don't," she said lightly as she yanked the car to the right, hitting the gas to dart ahead of both of them. "I know how you feel about it. I can't change your mind. You're going to have to figure it out for yourself. Skimmer being here doesn't change anything." She slipped in front of the van, giving me a soft smile that convinced me even more that blood was sex. "And then you'll spend the rest of your life kicking yourself for waiting so long to take that chance."

Eighteen

The commercial cut in, the volume jarring me as I sat on the couch. Sighing, I pulled my knees to my chin and hugged my legs. It was early, just after two in the morning, and I was trying to find the gumption to go make something to eat. Ivy was still on her run, and even with the awkward conversation in the car, I was hoping she'd be home early enough so we could go out. Warming up a potpie and eating alone had all the appeal of pulling the skin off my shins.

Grabbing the remote, I muted the TV. This was depressing. I was sitting on the couch on a Friday night watching *Die Hard*, alone. Nick should have been there with me. I missed him. I think I missed him. I missed something. Maybe I just missed being held. Was I that shallow?

Tossing the remote down, I realized a voice was coming from the front of the church. I sat up; it was a man's voice. Alarmed, I tapped the line out back. Between one breath and the next, my center filled. With the force of the line running through me, I gathered myself to rise, only to sink down when Jenks flew into the room at head height. The soft hum of his wings told me in an instant that whatever was up front wasn't going to kill me *or* put money in my pocket.

Eyes wide, he landed on the lampshade. The dust sifting from him floated upward with the rising heat of the bulb. He was usually tucked in my desk asleep at this hour, which was why I was having my pity party now so I could sulk without interference. "Hey, Jenks," I said as I let go of the line and the unfocused magic left me. "Who's here?"

His face became worried. "Rachel, we might have a problem."

I eyed him sourly. I was sitting alone watching *Die Hard*. That was a problem, not whatever had come waltzing in our door. "Who is it?" I said flatly. "I already ran off the Jehovah Witnesses. You would think living in a church, they might get the idea, but no-o-o-o."

Jenks frowned. "Some Were in a cowboy hat. He wants me to sign a paper saying I ate that fish we stole for the Howlers."

"David?" I jerked out of the chair and headed for the sanctuary.

Jenks's wings were a harsh buzz as he flew beside me. "Who's David?"

"An insurance adjustor." My brow furrowed. "I met him yesterday."

Sure enough, David was sanding in the middle of the empty room, looking uncomfortable in his long coat and hat pulled down over his eyes. Pixy children were watching from under the crack of the rolltop desk, their pretty faces all lined up in a row. He was on a cell phone, and upon seeing me, he muttered a few words, closed the cover, and tucked it away.

"Hello, Rachel," he said, cringing as his voice echoed. His eyes ran over my casual jeans and red sweater, and then went to the ceiling as he shifted from foot to foot. It was obvious he wasn't comfortable in the church, like most Weres, but it was psychological not biological.

"I'm sorry to bother you," he said as he took off his hat and crushed it in a tight grip. "But hearsay won't stand up in this case. I need your partner to verify he ate that wishing fish."

"Holy crap! It was a wishing fish!" There was a chorus of shrill cries from the desk. Jenks made a harsh sound, and the faces lining the crack scattered back into the shadows.

David took a trifolded paper from a pocket of his duster and unfolded it atop Ivy's piano. "If you could sign here?" he said, then straightened, his eyes suspicious. "You *did* eat it?"

Jenks looked scared, his wings a blue so dark they were almost purple. "Yeah. We ate it. Are we going to be all right?"

I tried to hide my smile, but David grinned, his teeth looking white in the dim light of the sanctuary. "I think you'll be fine, Mr. Jenks," he said, clicking open a pen and holding it out.

My eyebrows rose. David hesitated, looking from the pen to the pixy. The pen was the larger of the two. "Ummm," he said, shifting on his feet.

"I've got it." Jenks zipped to the desk, returning with a pencil lead. I watched him carefully write his name, the ultrasonic chatter from the desk making my eyes hurt. Jenks rose, pixy dust sifting from him. "Hey, uh, we aren't in any trouble, are we?"

The pungent scent of ink assailed me, and David looked up from notarizing it. "Not from our end of things. Thank you, Mr. Jenks." He looked at me. "Rachel."

A soft rattling of the windows from an air-pressure shift brought both our heads up. Someone had opened the back door to the church. "Rachel?" came a high voice, and I blinked.

It was my mom? Bewildered, I looked at David. "Ah, it's my mom. Maybe you ought to go. Unless you want her to bully you into taking me on a date."

David's face went startled as he tucked the paper away. "No. I'm done. Thanks. I probably should have called first, but it *is* normal business hours."

My face warmed. I had just added ten thousand to my bank account, courtesy of Quen and his "little problem." I could sit on my butt and sulk for one night if I wanted. And I wasn't going to prep the charms I'd be using on said run tonight. Spelling after midnight under a waning moon was asking for trouble. Besides, how I arranged my day was not his business.

Bothered, I looked at the back of the church, not wanting to be rude but not wanting my mom to play twenty questions with David, either. "I'll be right there, Mom!" I shouted, then turned to Jenks. "Will you see him out for me?"

"Sure thing, Rache." Jenks rose up to head height to accompany David into the foyer.

"'Bye, David," I said, and he gave me a raised-hand good-bye and put his hat on.

Why does it all happen at once? I thought, hustling to the kitchen. My mom visiting unannounced would top off an already perfect day. Tired, I entered the kitchen to find her with her head in my fridge. From the sanctuary came the boom of the front door closing.

"Mom," I said, trying to keep my voice pleasant. "It's great to see you. But it's business hours." My thoughts went to my bathroom, wondering if my undies were still atop the dryer.

Smiling, she straightened, peeking at me from around the door of the fridge. She was wearing sunglasses, and they looked really odd with her straw hat and sundress. *Sundress? She was in a sundress? It was below twenty out there.*

"Rachel!" Smiling, she shut the door and opened her arms. "Give me a hug, honey."

Thoughts whirling, I absently returned her embrace. Maybe I should call her psychologist and make sure she was still making her appointments. An odd smell clung to her, and as I pulled away, I said, "What is that you're wearing? It smells like burnt amber."

"That's because it is, love."

Shocked, my eyes went to her face. Her voice had dropped several octaves. Adrenaline shook me. I jerked back, only to find a white-gloved hand gripping my shoulder. I froze, unable to move as a ripple of ever-after cascaded over her, revealing Algaliarept. *Oh, crap. I was dead.*

"Good evening, familiar," the demon said, smiling to show me flat blocky teeth. "Let's find a ley line and get you home, hmm?"

"Jenks!" I shrieked, hearing my voice harsh with terror. Leaning back, I swung my foot up, kicking him square in the 'nads.

Al grunted, his red, goat-slitted eyes widening. "Bitch," he said, reaching down and grabbing my ankle.

Gasping, I went down as he yanked me onto my butt. I hit with a thump, panicking. As I kicked ineffectively at him, he dragged me out of the kitchen and into the hall.

"Rachel!" Jenks shrilled, black pixy dust sifting from him.

"Get me a charm!" I shouted as I grabbed the archway and hung on. *Oh God. He had me. If he got me to a line, he could physically drag me to the ever-after, me saying no or not.*

Arms tensing, I fought to hold onto the wall long enough for Jenks to open my charm cupboard and grab one. I didn't need a finger stick; my lip was already bleeding from the fall.

"Here," Jenks cried, hovering at ankle height to look me right in the eye. He had the cord to a sleep charm in his grip. His eyes were frightened and his wings were red.

"Don't think so, witch," Al said, giving me a jerk.

Pain sliced through my shoulder, and my grip was torn away. "Rachel!" Jenks exclaimed as my fingernails scraped the hardwood floor and then the carpet in the living room.

Al muttered Latin, and I cried out as an explosion blew the back door off its hinges.

"Jenks! Get out! Get your kids safe!" I shouted when cold air raced in to replace the air the explosion had blown out. Dogs barked as I slid down the stairs on my stomach. Snow, ice, and rock salt scraped my middle and my chin. I stared up at the shattered doorframe as David's silhouette showed black against the light. I held my hand out for the charm Jenks had dropped. "The charm!" I screamed when he clearly had no idea what I wanted. "Throw me the charm!"

Al came to a halt. His English riding boots making prints on the unshoveled walk, he turned. *"Detrudo,"* he said, clearly a trigger word for a curse imprinted on his memory.

I gasped as a black and red shadow of ever-after struck

David, throwing him into the far wall and out of my sight. "David!" I called as Al started dragging me again.

Wiggling, I twisted so I was on my butt and not my stomach. I cut a small swath through the snow behind Al as he pulled me kicking to the wooden gate at the front of the garden that led to the street. Al couldn't use the ley line in the graveyard to drag me into the ever-after, as it was entirely encircled by holy ground that he couldn't cross. The nearest ley line I knew about was eight blocks away. *I had a chance,* I thought, the cold snow soaking my jeans.

"Let go!" I demanded, kicking the back of Al's knees with my one free foot.

His leg buckled and he stopped, his irate look clear in the light from the streetlamp. He couldn't turn misty to avoid the strikes since I would be able to slip his grip. "What a canicula you are," he said, taking both ankles with one hand and continuing.

"I don't want to go!" I shouted, grabbing onto the edges of the gate as we passed through it. We jerked to a stop, and Al sighed.

"Let go of the fence," he said, sounding tired.

"No!" My muscles started to shake as I fought to keep unmoving while Al pulled. I had only one ley line charm imprinted on my subconscious, but trapping Al and me in a circle would get me nowhere. He could break it as easily as I, now that his aura would be tainting it.

A cry slipped from me when Al gave up trying to drag me through the gate and he picked me up and threw me over his shoulder. My breath exploded out of me as his muscle-hard shoulder cut into my middle. He stank of burnt amber, and I fought to get free.

"This would be a lot easier," he said as I jabbed my elbows between his shoulder blades to no effect, "if you would accept that I have you. Just say you'll come willingly, and I can pop us into a line from here and it will save you a lot of embarrassment."

"I'm not worried about embarrassment!" I stretched to

reach a passing limb of a tree, my breath coming out in relief as I snagged one. Al jerked back, pulled off balance.

"Oh, look," he said as he yanked me free and my palms came away scraped and bleeding. "Your wolfie friend wants to play."

David, I thought, twisting to see past Al's shoulder. As I struggled to breathe, I saw a huge shadow standing at the center of the lamp-lit, snow-packed street. My mouth dropped. He had Wered. He had Wered in less than three minutes. God, that must have hurt.

And he was huge, having retained his entire human mass. His head would come to my shoulder, I'd guess. Black silky fur, more like hair, shifted in the cold wind. His ears were flat against his head, and an impossibly low warning growl came from him. Feet the size of my spread hands dug into the snow as he barred our way. He gave an indescribably deep warning bark, and Al chuckled. Lights were coming on in adjacent houses and curtains were being peeked around. "She's legally mine," Al said lightly. "I'm carting her home. Don't even try."

Al started down the street, leaving me torn between screaming for help and admitting I was a gonner. A car was coming, its lights throwing everything into stark relief. "Good, doggie," Al muttered as we passed David with a good ten feet between us. Looking harsh in the light from the headlamps, David bowed his head, and I wondered if he had given up, knowing he could do nothing. But then his head came up and he started after us.

"David, there's nothing you can do! David, no!" I shrieked when his slow lope shifted into a full run. Eyes lost in a killing frenzy, he barreled right for me. Sure, I didn't want to be pulled into the ever-after, but I didn't want to be dead, either.

Swearing, Al turned around. *"Vacuefacio,"* he said, his white-gloved hand outstretched.

I twisted on his shoulder to see. A black ball of force shot from him, meeting David's silent attack two feet in front of us. David's huge feet skidded, but he ran right into it. Yelping, he rolled, tumbling into a snow pile. The scent of singed hair rose and was gone.

"David!" I cried, not feeling the cold that pinched me. "Are you all right?"

I yelped as Al dumped me on the ground, a blocky hand squeezing my shoulder until I cried out in pain. The thick sheet of compressed snow on the pavement melted up through me, and my rear went numb with hurt and cold. "Idiot," Al grumbled to himself. "You've got a familiar, why by your mother's ashes aren't you using her?"

He smiled at me, thick eyebrows high in anticipation. "Ready to work, Rachel, love?"

My breath froze in me. Panicking, I stared up at him, feeling my face go pale and my eyes go wide. "Please don't," I whispered.

He grinned all the wider. "Hold this for me," he said.

A scream of pain ripped from me as Al tapped a line, sending its strength thundering into me. My muscles jerked and a spasm shook me until my face hit the pavement. I was on fire, and I clenched into a fetal position, hands over my ears. Scream upon scream beat upon me. I couldn't block them out. They hammered at me, the only thing that was real besides the agony in my head. Like an explosion, the force of the line ran through me, settling into my center, spilling over to set my limbs on fire. My brain felt as if it had been dipped in acid, and all the time, that awful screaming racked my ears. I was on fire. I was burning.

I suddenly realized the screaming was coming from me. Huge, racking sobs took their place as I managed to stop. An eerie, keening wail rose, and I managed to stop that, too. Panting, I opened my eyes. My hands were pale and shaking in the light from the car. They weren't charred. The scent of burnt amber wasn't my skin peeling away. It was all in my head.

Oh God. My head felt like it was three places at once. I was hearing everything twice, smelling everything twice, and having no thoughts that weren't my own. Al knew everything I was feeling, everything I was thinking. I could only pray that I hadn't done this to Nick.

"Better?" Al said, and I jerked as if whipped, hearing his voice in my head as well as my ears. "Not bad," he said, yanking me unresisting to my feet. "Ceri passed out with only half that much, and it took her three months to stop making that awful noise."

Numb, I felt spittle slip from me. I couldn't remember how to wipe it away. My throat hurt and the cold air I sucked into me seemed to burn. I could hear dogs barking and a car engine. The light from its headlamps wasn't moving, and the snow sparkled. I hung loose in Al's grip, feet trying to move as he began walking again. He dragged me out from in front of the car, and in a slippery squeak of snow and ice, it sped away.

"Come along, Rachel, love," Al said in the new darkness, clearly in a good mood as he pulled me over a snowplowed hill and onto the shoveled walk. "Your wolf has given up, and unless you submit to me, we have a good bit of city to walk before I can get you to a ley line."

Stumbling, I lurched after Al, my feet in my socks long cold and unresponsive. His hand gripped my wrist in a shackle stronger than any metal. Al's shadow stretched behind us to where David panted, shaking his head as if to clear it. I could do nothing, feeling nothing as David's lips pulled back from his muzzle. Silently, he lunged. Numb and uncaring, I watched as if from a distance. Al, though, was very much aware.

"*Celero fervefacio!*" he exclaimed, angry, and I screamed as the curse burned through me. The force of Al's magic exploded from his outstretched hand and struck David. In a flash, the snow melted underneath the Were, and he writhed on the black circle of pavement. I screamed from the agony, catching it—smothering it—hearing it trail into the keen of a banshee.

"Please . . . no more," I whispered, spit falling from me to melt a spot of snow. I stared at the dirty white, thinking it was my soul, pitted and sullied, paying for Al's black magic. I couldn't think. The pain burned through me still, becoming a familiar hurt.

The sound of frightened people pulled my bleary gaze up. The neighborhood was watching from doors and windows. I'd probably make the news. A sharp bang drew my attention to the house we had passed, an elegant snow castle with turrets and towers gracing one corner of the yard. The light from the open door spilled over the trampled snow, falling almost to Al and me. I caught my breath at Ceri standing in the threshold, Ivy's crucifix about her neck. Her nightgown flowed to the porch, white and billowy. Her unbound hair floated about her, coming almost to her waist. Her posture was stiff with anger. "You," she said, her voice ringing clear over the snow.

From behind me came a warning yip, and I felt a tug of a pull. Through Al's knowledge, I instinctively knew that Ceri had set a circle around Al and me. A futile sob escaped me, but I fastened on the feeling like a hungry cur on trash. I had felt something that wasn't from Al. The demon's own emotion of annoyance was quick behind my depression, covering it up until I forgot what I felt like. From Al, I knew the circle was useless. You can make a circle without drawing it first, but only a drawn circle is strong enough to hold a demon.

Al didn't even bother to slow down, dragging me into the sheet of ever-after.

My breath hissed in as the force Ceri had put in the circle flowed into me. I screamed as a new wave of fire coated my skin. It ran from where I first touched the field, flowing like liquid to cover me. Pain searched for my center. It found it, and I screamed again, twisting out of Al's grip as it found my chi full and bursting. The ever-after rebounded, scouring through me to settle in the only place it could force room: my head. Sooner or later it would be too much and I'd go insane.

I clenched into myself. The rough sidewalk scraped my

thigh and shoulder as I convulsed. Slowly it became bearable, and I was able to stop screaming. The last one trailed off into a moan that silenced the dogs. *Oh God, I was dying. I was dying from the inside out.*

"Please," I begged Ceri, knowing she couldn't hear me. "Don't do that again."

Al yanked me upright. "You're an *excellent* familiar," he encouraged, his face split in a wide grin. "I'm so proud of you. You managed to stop screaming again. I think I'll make you a cup of tea when we get home and let you nap before I show you off to my friends."

"No . . ." I whispered, and Al chuckled at my defiance even before the word escaped me. I could have no thoughts without him knowing them first. Now I realized why Ceri had numbed her emotion, preferring to have none rather than share them with Al.

"Wait," Ceri said, her voice ringing clear over the snow as she ran down the porch steps, past the chain-link fence, and into the yard before us.

I sagged in Al's grip as he stopped to look at her. Her voice flowed over me, soothing my skin and mind alike. My eyes warmed at the hint of respite from the pain, and I almost sobbed in relief. She looked like a goddess. She granted release from pain.

"Ceri," Al said warmly, his attention only half on David as he circled us, his hackles raised and a frightening savagery in his eyes. "You're looking well, love." His eyes traveled over the elaborate castle of snow behind her. "Miss your homeland?"

"I am Ceridwen Merriam Dulciate," she said, the command in her voice like a whip. "I'm not your familiar. I have a soul. Give me the respect that calls for."

Al snickered. "I see you found your ego. How does it feel to be growing old again?"

I saw her stiffen. She came to stand before us, and I could see her guilt. "I don't fear it anymore," she said softly, and I wondered if an unaging life was what Al had lured her into being his familiar with. "It's the way of the world. Let Rachel Mariana Morgan go."

Al threw his head back and laughed, showing his thick, flat teeth to the cloudy sky. "She is mine. You're looking well. Care to come back? You could be sisters. How nice is that?"

Her mouth twitched. "She has a soul. You can't force her."

Panting, I hung from where Al held me. If he got me into a line, whether I had a soul or not wouldn't matter. "Yes, I can," Al said, cementing it into fact. His brow furrowed, and he jerked his attention to David. I had seen him circling us in a wide path, trying to make a physical circle with his foot-steps with which he could bind Al. The demon's eyes narrowed. *"Detrudo,"* he said, gesturing.

I gasped, jerking as a thread of ever-after flowed from me to work Al's charm. Head erect, I choked back whatever awful sound was going to come out of my raw throat. I managed to keep silent as it raced from me, but all my efforts to stay quiet did no good when a wave of ever-after surged in from a line to replace what Al had used. Again fire immolated my center, overflowing and making my skin burn, finally settling in my thoughts. I couldn't think. There was nothing but hurt in me. I was burning. My very thoughts, my soul, were burning.

Shocked, I fell to my knees, the pain from the icy side-walk going almost unnoticed as a cry of misery escaped me. My eyes were open, and Ceri cringed, standing barefoot before us in the snow. A shared pain was mirrored in her eyes, and I fastened on them, finding peace in their green depths. She had survived this. I could survive this. I would survive this. *God, help me find a way to survive this.*

Al laughed as he felt my resolve. "Good," he encouraged. "I appreciate your effort to be silent. You'll get there. Your god can't help you, but call for him anyway. I'd like to meet him."

I took a shuddering breath. David was a shaking puddle of

silky fur in the snow some distance from where he had been. I was screaming when the spell hit him and didn't see him knocked aside. Ceri went to him when he rose, grasping his muzzle in both hands and peering into his eyes. She looked dwarfed beside him, his absolute blackness looking dangerous and somehow right beside her frailty, dressed in flowing white. "Give this to me," she whispered as she gazed unafraid into his eyes, and David's ears pricked.

Dropping his face, she paced forward until she was standing where David's footprints left off. Keasley joined her, buttoning his thick fabric coat as he moved from my right to halt beside her. He took her hand, murmuring, "It's yours," before letting go, and they both stepped back.

I wanted to weep but didn't have the strength. They couldn't help me. I admired Ceri's confidence, her proud and impassioned stance, but it was misplaced. I might as well be dead.

"Demon," she said, her voice chiming thorough the still air like a bell. "I bind you."

Al jerked as a sheet of smokey blue ever-after blossomed over us, and his face reddened. *"Es scortum obscenus impurua!"* he shouted, letting me go. I stayed where I fell, knowing he wouldn't have released me if I could escape. "How dare you use what I taught you to bind me!"

Panting, I pulled my head up, only now realizing why she had touched David and then Keasley. David had started the circle, Ceri had made a second portion of it, and Keasley had made the third. They had given her permission to bind their paths together as one. The circle had been made; he was caught. And as I watched him pace to the edge of the bubble and a victorious Ceri, I thought it wouldn't take much for him to decide to kill me out of spite.

"Moecha putida!" he shouted, hammering on the force between them. "Ceri, I will tear your soul from you again, I swear it!"

"Et de," she said, her narrow chin high and her eyes glinting, *"acervus excrementum.* You can jump to a line from

here. Leave now before the sun rises so we can all go back to bed."

Algaliarept took a slow breath, and I shuddered at the bound anger in the movement. "No," he said. "I'm going to widen Rachel's horizons, and you will listen to her scream as she learns to take the full capacity of what I demand."

He could draw more through me? I thought, feeling my lungs press together as I temporarily lost the will to breathe. *There was worse than this?*

Ceri's confidence faltered. "No," she said. "She doesn't know how to store it properly. Any more, and her mind will bend. She'll be insane before you teach her how to make your tea."

"You don't need to be sane to make tea or do my toast upon one side," he snarled. Snatching my arm, he jerked me unresisting to my feet.

Ceri shook her head, standing in the snow as if it were summer. "You're being petty. You've lost her. She outsmarted you. You're a sore loser."

Al pinched my shoulder, and I gritted my teeth, refusing to cry out. It was only pain. It was nothing compared to the steady burning of the ever-after he was forcing me to hold for him. "Sore loser!" he shouted, and I heard the cries of fear from the people in the shadows. "She can't hide on holy ground forever. If she tries, I'll find a way to use her through the lines."

Ceri glanced at David, and I closed my eyes in despair. She thought he could do it. God help me. It was only a matter of time before he figured out how. My gamble to save my soul was going to fail. "Go away," she said, pulling her attention from David. "Go back to the ever-after and leave Rachel Mariana Morgan in peace. No one here has called you."

"You can't banish me, Ceri!" he raged, jerking me upright until I fell into him. "My familiar opened a summoning path for me to follow when she tapped a line. Break this circle and let me take her as is my right!"

Ceri took an exultant breath. "Rachel! He acknowledged you called him. Banish him!"

My eyes widened.

"No!" Algaliarept shouted, sending a flow of ever-after into me. I nearly passed out, the waves of pain washing through me building upon themselves until there was nothing left but agony. But I took a breath, smelling the stink of my burned soul.

"Algaliarept," I choked out, my voice a ragged gasp. "Return to the ever-after."

"You little bitch!" he snarled, backhanding me. The force of the blow picked me up, throwing me into Ceri's wall. I landed in a crumpled heap, unable to think. My head hurt and my throat was raw. The snow under me was cold. I snuggled into it, burning.

"Go away. Go away *now*," I whispered.

The overwhelming ever-after energy humming through my brain vanished in a clock-tick. I moaned at its absence. I heard my heart beat, pause, and beat again. It was all I could do to keep breathing, empty with just my own thoughts in my head. It was gone. The fire was gone.

"Get her out of the snow," I heard Ceri say urgently, her voice easing into me like ice water. I tried to open my eyes, failing. Someone picked me up, and there was the warmth of body heat. It was Keasley, a small part of me decided, as I recognized the smell of redwood and cheap coffee. My head thumped into him and my chin dropped to my chest. I felt small cool hands upon my forehead, and with Ceri singing to me, I felt myself shift into movement.

Nineteen

"**O**h God," I whispered, my words sounding as raw as my throat felt. It was a raspy utterance, more like gravel in a tin pail than a voice. My head hurt, and a wet washcloth smelling of Ivory soap was over my eyes. "I don't feel so good."

Ceri's cool hand touched my cheek. "I'm not surprised," she said wryly. "Keep your eyes shut. I'm going to change your compress."

Around me was the soft breathing of two people and a very big dog. I vaguely remembered being carried in, wavering on passing out but never quite managing it, hard as I tried. I could tell by the smell of my perfumes that Keasley had put me in my room, and the pillow under my head had a familiar, comfortable feel. The heavy weight of the afghan I kept at the foot of my bed was draped over me. *I was alive. Go figure.*

Ceri lifted the damp washcloth from me, and despite her warning, I cracked my lids. "Ow . . ." I moaned as the light from a candle on the dresser seemed to pierce my eyes, going all the way to the back of my skull and ricocheting. My headache tripled.

"She told you to keep your eyes shut," Jenks said sardonically, but the relief in his voice was obvious. The click of David's nails intruded, shortly followed by a warm snuff in my ear.

"She's fine," Ceri said softly, and he retreated.

Fine? I thought, concentrating on my breathing until the light bouncing around in my head lost momentum and died. *This was fine?*

The throbbing in my head retreated to a mild agony, and when I heard a soft puff of breath and the biting scent of blown-out candle reached me, I opened my eyes again.

In the streetlight leaking past my curtains, I could see Ceri on a kitchen chair beside my bed. A pan of water was on her lap, and I cringed when she set it on Ivy's vampire dating guide, out where everyone could see it. On my other side stood Keasley, a hunched shadow. Perched on the bedpost, Jenks glowed a dull amber, and lurking in the background was David taking up half the floorspace with his wolf bulk.

"I think we're back in Kansas, Toto," I murmured, and Keasley harrumphed.

My face was damp and cold, and a draft from the broken door mixed with the musty smell of the heater blowing from the vent. "Jenks!" I croaked when I remembered the wash of winter air that had hit him. "Are your kids all right?"

"Yeah, they're fine," he said, and I slumped back to the pillow. My hand crept up to hold my throat. It felt as if it was bleeding inside.

"David?" I questioned softer. "How about you?"

His panting increased as he pushed Keasley out of the way to snuff warm and moist in my ear. His jaws opened. Ceri gasped when David gripped my entire face in his mouth.

Adrenaline cut through the pain. "Hey!" I exclaimed, struggling as he gave me a gentle shake and let go. Heart pounding, I froze at the soft growl rumbling up and the wet nose nudging my cheek. Making a doggie huff, he padded into the hall.

"What in hell does that mean?" I said, heart jackhammering against my chest.

Jenks rose in a sprinkling of pixy dust that made me squint. It wasn't bright, but my eyes hurt that bad. "He's glad you're okay," he said, his tiny features serious.

"This is okay?" I said, and from the sanctuary came an odd, yodeling bark of laughter.

My throat hurt, and I held a hand to it as I sat up. There was Were spit on my face, and I wiped it off with the damp washcloth and set it over the edge of the pan. My muscles hurt. Hell, everything hurt. And I hadn't liked my head being in David's mouth at all.

The sound of manicured nails clacking on the floorboards drew my attention to the dark hallway as he trotted past headed for the back of the church. His backpack and clothes were in his mouth, and his coat trailed behind like a downed animal.

"Jenks," Ceri said softly. "See if he's going to change here or if he'd like some help getting his things in his satchel."

Jenks rose up, falling back at a short negative bark from the living room.

Jaw clenched against a Texas-sized headache, I decided it was likely he'd change back before leaving. It was illegal to Were in public outside of the three days around the full moon. Once the restriction had only been tradition; now it was law to make humans feel better. What Weres did in their own homes was their own business. I was confident no one would say anything about him shifting to help save me from a demon, but he couldn't drive his car in the shape he was in, and catching a ride on a bus wasn't going to happen.

"Well," Keasley said as he sat on the edge of my bed, "let's take a look at you."

"Ow . . ." I exclaimed when he touched my shoulder and the bruised muscle sent a stab of pain through me. I pushed his hand off me, and he shifted closer.

"I'd forgotten what a pain-in-the-butt patient you are," he said, reaching out again. "I want to know where you're hurting."

"Stop," I croaked, trying to slap his knobby arthritic hands. "My shoulder hurts where Al pinched it. My hands hurt where I scraped them, my chin and stomach hurt where he dragged me down the steps. My knees hurt from . . ." I hesitated. ". . . falling in the road. And my face hurts where Al slapped me." I looked at Ceri. "Do I have a black eye?"

"You will in the morning," she said softly, wincing in sympathy.

"And my lip is cut," I finished, touching it. The faint scent of bane joined the smell of snow. David was turning back, nice and slow. He'd have to after the hurt he must have endured to shift so quickly before. I was glad he had some bane. The herb was a mild pain depressant and sedative to make it easier. Too bad it only worked on Weres.

Keasley groaned as he rose. "I'll get you a pain amulet," he said, shuffling into the hallway. "Mind if I make some coffee? I'm staying until your roommate is back."

"Make it two amulets," I said, not knowing if it would help my head. Pain amulets worked only on physical pain, and I had a feeling this was more of an echo left from channeling so much ley line force. *Was this what I'd done to Nick?* No wonder he had left.

I squinted when the light flicked on in the kitchen and a slice of it spilled into my room. Ceri watched me carefully, and I nodded to tell her it was okay. Patting my hand atop the coverlet, she murmured, "Tea would be easier for you to stomach than coffee." Her solemn green eyes went to Jenks. "Will you stay with her?"

"Yeah." His wings flashed into motion. "Baby-sitting Rachel is what I do third best."

I sneered at him, and Ceri hesitated. "I won't be long," she said, rising to leave in the soft sound of bare feet on wood.

The comfortable rhythm of conversation drifted in from the kitchen, and I awkwardly pulled my afghan up about my shoulders. Every muscle ached as if I had been in a fever. My feet were cold in my soggy socks, and I was probably making a damp spot on my bed from my snow-wet clothes. Depressed, my eyes landed on Jenks atop the bedpost at my feet.

"Thanks for trying to help," I said. "You sure you're okay? He blew the door right off."

"I should have been faster with that amulet." His wings turned a dismal blue.

I shrugged, immediately wishing I hadn't when my shoulder started throbbing. *Where was Keasley with my charms?* "They might not even work on demons."

Jenks flitted close to land on the bump of my knee. "Damn, Rache. You look like crap."

"Thanks."

The heavenly scent of coffee started to mix with the musty heater. A shadow eclipsed the light from the hallway, and I creakily turned to see Ceri. "Eat these while your tea is brewing," she said, setting down a plate with three of Ivy's cookies on them.

My lips curled down in a frown. "Do I have to?" I complained. "Where's my amulet?"

"Where's my amulet?" Jenks mocked in a high falsetto. "God, Rachel. Suck it up."

"Shut up," I muttered. "You try channeling a demon's ley line and see if you even survive. I bet you'd explode in a flash of pixy dust, you little twit."

He laughed, and Ceri frowned at us as if we were children. "I've got it right here," she said, and I leaned forward so she could drape the cord over my head. A blessed relief soaked in to ease my muscles—Keasley must have invoked it for me—but my headache remained, all the worse now that there was nothing to distract me from it.

"I'm sorry," Ceri said. "It's going to take a good day." When I didn't say anything, she shifted to the door, adding, "I'll get your tea." She walked out, a scuffing pulling my gaze up. "Excuse me," she murmured, gazing at the floor when she almost ran into David. The Were looked tired, seeming older as he adjusted the collar of his coat. His stubble was thicker, and the thick spice of bane was heavy on him. "Would you like some tea?" she said, and my eyebrows rose as her usual confidence shifted to meek awe.

David shook his head, accepting her submissive mien with a grace that made him seem noble. Head still lowered, she edged past him and went into the kitchen. Jenks and I exchanged wondering looks as he came in and dropped his backpack. Nodding to Jenks, he pulled the kitchen chair farther away from me and sat down, leaning back with his arms crossed and eyeing me speculatively from under his cowboy hat.

"You want to tell me what that was all about before I go?" he said. "I'm starting to think there's a good reason no one will insure you."

I made an embarrassed face and took a cookie. "Remember that demon that testified to put Piscary behind bars?"

His eyes widened. "Son of my mother's bitch!"

Jenks laughed, his voice tinkling like wind chimes. "Damn stupid of her if you ask me."

Ignoring Jenks, I met David's shocked look: part worry, part pain, part disbelief. "He came to collect his due for services rendered," I said. "Which he got. I'm his familiar, but I still have my soul, so he can't cart me off to the ever-after unless I let him." I looked to the ceiling, wondering what kind of a runner I was going to be if I couldn't tap a line after sunset without bringing demons down on me.

David made a soft whistle. "No tag is worth that."

My eyes flicked to his. "Ordinarily I'd agree with you, but at the time, Piscary was trying to kill me and it seemed like a good idea."

"Good idea, hell. It was damn stupid," Jenks muttered, clearly of the belief that if he had been there, things never would have degraded that far. He might have been right.

Feeling as if I had a hangover, I took a bite of cookie. The dry things made me hungry and nauseated at the same time. "Thank you for helping me," I said, brushing the crumbs away. "He would have had me if you hadn't done something. Are you going to be okay? I've never seen anyone Were that fast before."

Leaning forward, he shifted his backpack to rest between his feet. I watched his eyes stray to the door, and I knew he wanted to leave. "My shoulder hurts, but I'll be all right."

"I'm sorry." I finished the first cookie and started on another. It seemed as if I could feel it starting to hum through me. "You ever need anything, you tell me. I owe you big. I know how bad it hurts. Last year I went from witch to mink in three seconds. Twice in one week."

His breath hissed and lines appeared in his brow. "Ouch," he said, respect in his eyes.

I smiled, a new warmth growing in me. "You aren't kidding. But you know, it's likely going to be the only time I'll ever be that skinny and have a fur coat."

A faint smile came over him. "Where does the extra mass go, anyway?"

There was only one cookie left, and I forced myself to eat it slowly. "Back to a ley line."

His head bobbed. "We can't do that."

"I noticed. You make one hell of a big wolf, David."

His smile widened. "You know what? I changed my mind. Even if you ever want to go into insurance, don't call me."

Jenks dropped to the empty plate so I wouldn't have to keep shifting my head to see both of them. "That will be the day," he snickered. "I can just see Rachel in a gray business suit with a briefcase, her hair in a bun and glasses on her nose."

I laughed, immediately falling into a coughing jag. Arms clasped about me, I hunched into myself, shaking with rough, hacking coughs. My throat felt like it was on fire, but that paled next to the throbbing ache in my head that exploded at the sudden movement. That pain amulet bumping about my neck wasn't doing much good.

David patted my back in concern. The hurt from my shoulder broke through the amulet, and my stomach roiled. Eyes watering, I fended him off. Ceri came in, making soft admonishments as she set a mug of tea down and put a hand on my shoulder. Her touch seemed to calm the spasm, and gasping, I let her ease me back into the pillows she propped up behind me. Finally I stopped and met her gaze.

Her shadowy face was pinched in concern. Behind her,

Jenks and David watched. I didn't like David seeing me like this, but it wasn't as if I had much choice. "Drink your tea," she said, holding it up to me and putting my hand around it.

"My head hurts," I complained, taking a sip of the bland brew. It wasn't real tea, but something with flowers and weeds in it. What I wanted was a cup of that coffee, but I didn't want to hurt Ceri's feelings. "I feel like run-over crap," I complained.

"You look like run-over crap," Jenks said. "Drink your tea."

It was tasteless but soothing. I took another swallow, scraping up a smile for Ceri. "Mmmm. Good," I lied.

She straightened, clearly pleased as she picked up the washbasin. "Drink it all. Do you mind if Keasley tacks a blanket over your door to stop the draft?"

"That would be great. Thanks," I said, but she didn't leave until I took another sip.

Her shadow left the hall, and my smile fell into a grimace. "This stuff is tasteless," I whispered. "Why does everything good for me have to be tasteless?"

David glanced at the empty doorway and the light spilling in. Jenks flew to land on his shoulder as the Were unzipped his backpack. "I've got something that might help," David said. "My old partner used to swear by it. Begged me for some when he partied-too-hearty."

"Whoa!" Hand over his nose, Jenks flitted upward. "How much bane you got in there, Johnny Appleseed?"

David's smile grew sly. "What?" he said, his brown eyes innocent. "It's not illegal. And it's organic. No carbs, even."

The familiar spicy scent of bane rose thicker in the small room, and I wasn't surprised when David brought out a cellophane bag with a zippy top. I recognized the name brand: Wolf's Head Organic. "Here," he said as he took the cup out of my hand and set it on my bedside table.

Hiding what he was doing from the hallway, he shook a good tablespoon into my drink. Running his eyes over me, he shook in a little more. "Try it now," he said, handing it to me.

I sighed. Why was everyone giving me stuff? All I wanted was a sleep charm or maybe one of Captain Edden's strange aspirins. But David looked so hopeful, and the smell of bane was more appealing than rosehips, that I stirred it with my pinky. The crushed leaves sank to leave the tea a richer color. "What good will this do?" I asked as I took a sip. "I'm not a Were."

David dropped the bag into his backpack and zipped it shut. "Not much. Your witch metabolism is too slow for it to really work. But my old partner was a witch, and he said it helped with his hangovers. It's got to taste better, if nothing else."

He stood to leave, and I sipped again, agreeing. My jaw relaxed; I hadn't even known I had been clenching it. Warm and smooth, the bane tea slipped down my throat with a mixed taste of ham broth and apples. My muscles seemed to unknot, like taking a shot of tequila. A sigh slipped from me, and the soft weight of Jenks landing on my arm pulled my eyes to his.

"Hey, Rache? You okay?"

I smiled and took another swallow. "Hi, Jenks. You're all sparkly."

Jenks's face blanked, and David looked up from working the buttons closed on his coat. His brown eyes were questioning.

"Thanks, David," I said, hearing my voice slow, precise, and low. "I owe you, okay?"

"Sure." He picked up his backpack. "You take care of yourself."

"I will." I gulped half my tea, and it slid down to make a warm spot in me. "I don't feel too bad right now. Which is good, seeing as I have a date with Trent tomorrow, and if I don't go, his security officer is gonna kill me."

David jerked to a stop in the threshold. From beyond him came the *tap-tap-tap* of Keasley hammering a blanket over the door. "Trent Kalamack?" the Were questioned.

"Yeah." I took another drink, swirling the tea with my

pinky until the bane made a whirlpool and shifted the brew even darker. "He's going to talk to Saladan. His security officer is making me go with him." I squinted up at David, the light from the hallway seeming bright but not painful. I wondered where David's tattoos were. Weres always had tattoos, don't ask me why.

"Have you ever met Trent?" I asked.

"Mr. Kalamack?" David rocked back into the room. "No."

I squirmed under my afghan and focused on my cup. David's partner was right. This stuff was great. I didn't hurt anywhere. "Trent is a prick," I said, remembering what we were talking about. "I've got the goods on him, and he's got the goods on me. But I don't have anything on his security officer, and if I don't do this, he's going to tell."

Jenks hovered, making an uncertain swoop from David to the door and back to me. David eyed him, then asked, "Tell what?"

I leaned closer, my eyes widening as my tea threatened to slop when I moved faster than I thought I should. Frowning, I finished it off, not minding the bits of leaves that came with it. Smiling, I leaned close, enjoying the smell of musk and bane. "My secret," I whispered, wondering if David would let me hunt for his tattoos if I asked. He looked great for an older guy. "I've got a secret, but I'm not going to tell you."

"I'll be back," Jenks said, swooping close. "I want to know what she put in that tea."

He zipped out, and I blinked, watching the sparkles of his pixy dust settle. I'd never seen so many before, and they were the colors of the rainbow. Jenks must have been worried.

"Secret?" David prompted, but I shook my head and the light seemed to brighten.

"I'm not going to tell. I don't like the cold."

David put his hands on my shoulders and eased me into the pillows. I smiled up at him, happy when Jenks flew in. "Jenks," David said softly. "Has she been bitten by a Were?"

"No!" he protested. "Unless it was before I met her."

My eyes had slid shut, and they opened when David

shook me. "What?" I protested, pushing at him when he peered at me, his liquid brown eyes too close to mine. Now he reminded me of my dad, and I smiled at him.

"Rachel, honey," he said. "You been bitten by a Were?"

A sigh came from me. "Nope. Never you and never Ivy. No one bites me but mosquitoes, and I squish them. Little bastards."

Jenks hovered backward and David drew away. I closed my eyes, listening to them breathe. It seemed awfully loud. "Shhhh," I said. "Quiet."

"Maybe I gave her too much," David said.

Ceri's soft padding of feet seemed loud. "What . . . What did you do to her?" she asked, her voice sharp, pulling my eyes open.

"Nothing!" David protested, his shoulders hunched. "I gave her some bane. It shouldn't have done this. I've never seen it do this to a witch before!"

"Ceri," I said, "I'm sleepy. Can I go to sleep?"

Her lips pursed, but I could tell she wasn't angry with me. "Yes." She tugged the coverlet to my chin. "Go to sleep."

I slumped back, not caring that I was still wearing wet clothes. I was really, really tired. And I was warm. And my skin was tingling. And I felt like I could sleep for a week.

"Why didn't you ask me before you gave her bane?" Ceri asked sharply, her words a whisper but very clear. "She's already on Brimstone. It's in the cookies!"

I knew it! I thought, trying to open my eyes. *Boy, I was going to let Ivy have it when she got home.* But she wasn't, and I was tired, so I did nothing. I'd had it with people getting me drunk. I swear, I wasn't going to eat anything I didn't make myself ever again.

The sound of David's chuckle seemed to set my skin to tingle where the coverlet didn't come between him and me. "I got it now," he said. "The Brimstone upped her metabolism to where the bane is going to do some real good. She's going to sleep for three days. I gave her enough to knock a Were out for a full moon."

A jerk of alarm went through me. My eyes flashed open. "No!" I said, trying to sit up as Ceri pushed me into the pillows. "I have to go to that party. If I don't, Quen will tell!"

David helped her, and together they kept my head on the pillow and my feet under the afghan. "Take it easy, Rachel," he soothed, and I hated that he was stronger than I. "Don't fight it, or it's going to come back up on you. Be a good little witch and let it work itself out."

"If I don't go, he'll tell!" I said, hearing my blood race through my ears. "The only thing I have on Trent is that I know what he is, and if I tell, Quen will freaking kill me!"

"What!" Jenks shrieked, his wings clattering as he rose.

Too late, I realized what I had said. *Shit.*

I stared at Jenks, feeling my face go white. The room went deathly still. Ceri's eyes were round with question, and David stared in disbelief. I couldn't take it back.

"You know!" Jenks shouted. "You know what he is, and you didn't tell me? You witch! You knew? You knew! Rachel! You . . . you . . ."

Disapproval was thick in David's eyes, and Ceri looked frightened. Pixy children peeked around the doorframe. "You knew!" Jenks yelled, pixy dust sifting from him in a golden sunbeam. His kids scattered in a frightened tinkling sound.

I lurched upright. "Jenks—" I said, hunching into myself as my stomach clenched.

"Shut up!" he shouted. "Just shut the hell up! We're supposed to be partners!"

"Jenks . . ." I reached out. I wasn't sleepy anymore, and my gut twisted.

"No!" he said, a burst of pixy dust lighting my dim room. "You don't trust me? Fine. I'm outta here. I gotta make a call. David, can I and my family bum a ride from you?"

"Jenks!" I tossed the covers from me. "I'm sorry! I couldn't tell you." *Oh God, I should have trusted Jenks.*

"Shut the hell up!" he exclaimed, then flew out, pixy dust flaming red in his path.

I stood to follow. I took a step, then reached for the door-frame, my head swinging to look at the floor. My vision wavered and my balance left me. I put a hand to my stomach. "I'm going to be sick," I breathed. "Oh God, I'm going to be sick."

David's hand was heavy on my shoulder. Motions firm and deliberate, he pulled me into the hall. "I told you it was going to come back up on you," he muttered while he pushed me into the bathroom and elbowed the light on. "You shouldn't have sat up. What is it with you witches? Think you know everything and never listen to a damn thing."

Needless to say, he was right. Hand over my mouth, I just made it to the toilet. Everything came up: the cookies, the tea, dinner from two weeks ago. David left after my first retch, leaving me alone to hack and cough my way into the dry heaves.

Finally I got control over myself. Knees shaking, I rose and flushed the toilet. Unable to look at the mirror, I rinsed my mouth out, gulping water right from the tap. I had thrown up all over my amulet, and I took it off, rinsing it under a steady stream of water before setting it beside the sink. All my hurts came flowing back, and I felt like I deserved them.

Heart pounding and feeling weak, I splashed water off my face and looked up. Past my raggedy looking reflection, Ceri stood in the doorway, her arms clasped about her. The church was eerily silent. "Where's Jenks?" I rasped.

Her eyes fell from mine, and I turned around. "I'm sorry, Rachel. He left with David."

He left? He couldn't leave. It was freaking twenty out.

There was a soft scuff, and Keasley shuffled to stand beside her.

"Where did he go?" I asked, shivering as the lingering bane and Brimstone churned inside.

Ceri's head drooped. "He asked David to take him to a friend's house, and the entire sídh left in a box. He said he couldn't risk his family anymore, and . . ." Her gaze went to

Keasley, her green eyes catching the fluorescent light. "He said he quit."

He left? I lurched into motion, headed for the phone. Didn't want to risk his family, my ass. He had killed two fairy assassins this spring, letting the third live as a warning to the rest. And it wasn't the cold. The door was going to be fixed, and they could always stay in Ivy's or my room until it was. He left because I had lied to him. And as I saw Keasley's wrinkled grim face behind Ceri's, I knew I was right. Words had been said that I hadn't heard.

Stumbling into the living room, I looked for the phone. There was only one place he'd go: the Were who had de-spelled my stuff last fall. I had to talk to Jenks. I had to tell him I was sorry. That I had been an ass. That I should have trusted him. That he was right to be angry with me and that I was sorry.

But Keasley intercepted my reach, and I drew back at his old hand. I stared at him, cold in the thin protection the blanket had put between me and the night. "Rachel . . ." he said as Ceri drifted to a melancholy stop in the hall. "I think . . . I think you should give him a day at least."

Ceri jerked, and she looked down the hallway. Faint on the air I heard the front door open, and the blanket moved in the shifting air currents.

"Rachel?" came Ivy's voice. "Where's Jenks? And why is there a Home Depot truck unloading sheet plywood in our drive?"

I sank down onto a chair before I fell over. My elbows went on my knees, and my head dropped into my hands. The Brimstone and bane still warred within me, making me shaky and weak. Damn. What was I going to tell Ivy?

Twenty

The coffee in my oversized mug was cold, but I wasn't going to go into the kitchen for more. Ivy was banging around there, baking more of her vile cookies despite us having already gone over that I wasn't going to eat them and was madder than a troll with a hangover that she'd been slipping me Brimstone.

The clatter of my pain amulet against the complexion charm hiding my bruised eye intruded as I set my mug aside and reached for the desk lamp. It had gotten dusky while Ceri tried to teach me how to store line energy. Cheery yellow light spilled over the plants strewn on my desk, the glow just reaching Ceri sitting on a cushion she had brought over from Keasley's. We could have done this in the more comfortable living room, but Ceri had insisted on hallowed ground despite the sun being up. And it was quiet in the sanctuary. Depressingly so.

Ceri sat cross-legged on the floor to make a small figure in jeans and a casual shirt under the shadow of the cross. A pot of tea sat beside her, steaming though my own mug was long cold. I had a feeling she was using magic to keep it warm, though I had yet to catch her at it. A delicate cup was cradled reverently in her thin hands—she had brought that from Keasley's, too—and Ivy's crucifix glimmered about her neck. The woman's hands were never far from it. Her fair hair had been plaited by Jenks's eldest daughter that morning, and she looked at peace with herself. I loved seeing her like this, knowing what she had endured.

There was a thump from the kitchen followed by the clatter of the oven door shutting. A frown crossed me, and I turned to Ceri as she prompted, "Are you ready to try again?"

Setting my sock-footed feet firmly on the floor, I nodded. Quick from practice, I reached out with my awareness and touched the line out back. My chi filled, taking no more or less than it ever did. The energy flowed through me much like a river flows through a pond. I had been able to do this since I was twelve and accidentally threw Trent into a tree at his father's Make-A-Wish camp. What I had to do was pull some of that energy out of the pond and lift it to a cistern in my mind, so to speak. A person's chi, whether human, Inderlander, or demon, could hold only so much. Familiars acted as extra chi that a magic user could draw on as his or her own.

Ceri waited until I gestured I was ready before she tapped the same line and fostered more into me. It was a trickle instead of Algaliarept's deluge, but even so, my skin burned when my chi overflowed and the force rippled through me, seeking somewhere to puddle. Going back to the pond and river analogy, the banks had overflowed and the valley was flooding.

My thoughts were the only place it could settle, and by the time it found them, I had made the tiny three-dimensional circle in my imagination that Ceri had spent most of the afternoon teaching me how to craft. Shoulders easing, I felt the trickle find the small enclosure. Immediately the warm sensation on my skin vanished as the energy my chi couldn't hold was drawn into it like mercury droplets. The bubble expanded, glowing with a red smear that took on the color of my and Al's aura. Yuck.

"Say your trigger word," Ceri prompted, and I winced. It was too late. My eyes met hers, and her thin lips twitched. "You forgot," she accused, and I shrugged. Immediately she stopped forcing energy into me, and the excess ran out in a brief spark of heat back to the line. "Say it this time," she said tightly. Ceri was nice, but she wasn't a particularly patient teacher.

Again she made ley line energy overflow my chi. My skin warmed, the bruise from where Algaliarept slapped me throbbing. The amperage, if you will, was a touch more than usual, and I thought that it was Ceri's not-so-subtle encouragement to get it right this time.

"Tulpa," I whispered, hearing it in my mind as well as my ear. The word choice wasn't important. It was building the association between the word and the actions that were. Latin was generally used, as it was unlikely that I would say it accidentally, triggering the spell by mistake. The process was identical to when I had learned to make an instant circle. The word tulpa wasn't Latin—it hardly qualified as English—but how often was it used in conversation?

Faster this time, the energy from the line found my enclosure and filled it. I pulled my gaze to Ceri and nodded for more. Green eyes serious in the dim light from the heat lamp on my desk, she returned it. My breath seeped out and my focus blurred when Ceri upped the level and a flash of warmth tingled over my skin. "Tulpa," I whispered, pulse quickening.

The new force found the first. My spherical protection circle within my unconsciousness expanded to take it in. Again my focus cleared, and I nodded to Ceri. She blinked when I gestured for more, but I wasn't going to let Al knock me out with an overload of force. "I'm fine," I said, then stiffened when the bruised skin around my eye throbbed, burning with the sensation of a sunburn even through the pain amulet. "Tulpa," I said, slumping as the heat vanished. *See,* I told my frazzled brain. *It's an illusion. I'm not really on fire.*

"That's enough," Ceri said uncomfortably, and I pulled my chin up from my chest. The fire was gone from my veins, but I was exhausted and my fingers were trembling.

"I don't want to sleep tonight until I can hold what he pushed into me," I replied.

"But, Rachel . . ." she protested, and I raised a hand slowly in denial.

"He's going to come back," I said. "I can't fight him if I'm convulsing in pain."

Face pale, she bobbed her head, and I jerked as she forced more into me. "Oh God," I whispered, then said my trigger word before Ceri could stop. This time I felt the energy flow like acid through me, following new channels, pulled by my word rather than finding its way to my bubble by accident. My head jerked up. Eyes wide, I stared at Ceri as the pain vanished.

"You did it," she said, looking almost frightened as she sat cross-legged before me.

Swallowing, I pulled my legs under me so she wouldn't see my knees tremble. "Yeah."

Unblinking, she held her cup in her lap. "Let it go. You need to recenter yourself."

I found my arms were wrapped around myself. Forcing them down, I exhaled. Letting go of the energy spindled in my head sounded easier than it was. I had enough force in me to throw Ivy into the next county. If it didn't flow back to my chi and then the line using the gently seared channels that Ceri had been burning through my nervous system, it was really going to hurt.

Steeling myself, I set my will around the bubble and squeezed. Breath held, I waited for the pain, but the ley line energy smoothly returned to my chi and then the line, leaving me shaking from spent adrenaline. Enormously relieved, I brushed my hair out of my eyes and put my gaze on Ceri. I felt awful: tired, exhausted, sweaty, and shaking—but satisfied.

"You're improving," she said, and a thin smile crossed me.

"Thanks." Taking my mug, I took a sip of cold coffee. She was probably going to ask me to pull it off the line by myself next; I wasn't yet ready to try. "Ceri," I said as my fingers trembled. "This isn't that hard compared to the benefits. Why don't more people know this?"

She smiled, her dusky shape in the shadow of the lamp going sage looking. "They do in the ever-after. It's the first thing—no, the second thing—that a new familiar is taught."

"What's the first?" I asked before I remembered I really didn't want to know.

"The death of self-will," she said, and my expression froze at the ugliness in how casually she said it. "Letting me escape, knowing how to be my own familiar, was a mistake," she said. "Al would kill me if he could to cover it up."

"He can't?" I said, suddenly frightened that the demon might try.

Ceri shrugged. "Maybe. But I have my soul, black as it is. That's what's important."

"I suppose." I didn't understand her cavalier attitude, but I hadn't been Al's familiar for a millennium. "I don't want a familiar," I said, glad Nick was so distant he couldn't feel any of this. I was sure if he was close enough, he would've called to make sure I was okay. I think.

"You're doing well." Ceri sipped her tea and glanced at the dark windows. "Al told me it took me three months to get to where you are now."

I looked at her, shocked. There was no way I could be better than her. "You're kidding."

"I was fighting him," she said. "I didn't want to learn, and he had to force me into it, using the absence of pain as a positive reinforcement."

"You were in pain for three months?" I said, horrified.

Her eyes were on her thin hands, laced about her teacup. "I don't remember it. It was a long time ago. I do remember sitting at his feet every night, his hand soft on my head while he relaxed as he listened to me cry for the sky and trees."

Imagining this beautiful wisp of a woman at Algaliarept's feet suffering his touch was almost too much to bear. "I'm sorry, Ceri," I whispered.

She jerked, as if only now realizing she had said it aloud. "Don't let him take you," she said, her wide eyes serious and solemn. "He liked me, and though he used me as they all use their familiars, he did like me. I was a coveted jewel in his belt, and he treated me well so I would be useful and at his side for a longer time. You, though . . ." Her head bowed, breaking our eye contact and pulling her braid over her shoulder. "He will torment you so hard and so fast that you won't have time to breathe. Don't let him take you."

I swallowed, feeling cold. "I wasn't planning on it."

Her narrow chin trembled. "You misunderstand. If he comes for you and you can't fight him off, make him so angry that he kills you."

Her sincerity struck me to the core. "He's not going to give up, is he?" I said.

"No. He needs a familiar to keep his standing. He won't give up on you unless he finds someone better. Al is greedy and impatient. He'll take the best he can find."

"So all this practice is making me a more attractive target?" I said, feeling sick.

Ceri squinted apologetically. "You need it to keep him from simply stunning you with a massive dose of ley line force and dragging you into a line."

I gazed at the darkening windows. "Damn," I whispered, not having considered that.

"But being your own familiar will help in your profession," Ceri said persuasively. "You'll have the strength of a familiar without the liabilities."

"I suppose." I set my mug aside, gaze unfocused. It was getting dark, and I knew she wanted to be home before the sun set. "Do you want me to try it alone?" I prompted hesitantly.

Her attention flicked to my hands. "I'd advise a small rest. You're still shaking."

I looked at my fingers, embarrassed that she was right. Curling them into a fist, I gave her a sheepish smile. She took a sip of her tea—clearly willing herself to be patient when I had no control over the situation—and I jumped when she whispered, *"Consimilis calefacio."*

She had done something; I had felt a drop in the line, even though I wasn't connected to it. Sure enough her gaze meeting mine was bright in amusement. "You felt that?" she said around a beautiful laugh. "You're getting very attached to your line, Rachel Mariana Morgan. It belongs to the whole street, even if it is in your backyard."

"What did you do?" I asked, not wanting to delve into what she had meant by that. She held her cup up in explanation, and my smile grew. "You warmed it up," I said, and she bobbed her head. Slowly my smile faded. "That's not a black charm, is it?"

Ceri's face lost its expression. "No. It's common ley line magic that acts on water. I will not add to the smut on my soul, Rachel. I'll be hard pressed to get rid of it as it is."

"But Al used it on David. It almost cooked him," I asserted, feeling sick. People were mostly water. Heat that up and you could cook them from the inside. *God, I was sick for even thinking of it.*

"No," she reassured me. "It was different. This one works only on things without auras. The curse strong enough to break through an aura is black and needs a drop of demon blood to twist. The reason David survived was because Al was drawing on a line through you, and he knew you couldn't handle the lethal amount—yet."

I thought about that for a moment. If it wasn't black, there was no harm in it. And being able to warm up my coffee without the microwave would blow Ivy away. "Is it hard to do?"

Ceri's smile blossomed. "I'll walk you through it. Give me a moment; I have to remember how to do it the long way," she said, extending her hand for my mug.

Oh, gotta slow to the witch's pace, I thought, leaning forward and handing it to her. But seeing as it was most likely the charm she used three times a day to cook Al's meals, she could probably do it in her sleep.

"It's sympathetic magic," she explained. "There's a poem to help remember the gestures, but the only two words you *have* to say are Latin. And it needs a focal object to direct the magic where to go," she explained, and took a sip of my cold coffee, making a face. "This is swill," she muttered, her words awkward as she spoke around the drop on her tongue. "Barbaric."

"It's better when it's hot," I protested, not having known you could hold a focal object in your mouth and still have it be effective. She could do the spell without it, but then she would have to throw the spell at my cup. This was easier, and less likely to spill my coffee, too.

Her face still showing her distaste, she raised her thin, expressive hands. "From candles burn and planet's spin," she said, and I moved my fingers, mimicking her gesture—I suppose if you used your imagination, it kind of looked like lighting a candle, though how her suddenly dropping hand related to spinning planets was beyond me. "Friction is how it ends and begins."

I jumped when she brought her hands together to make a loud pop, simultaneously saying, *"Consimilis."*

Similar, I thought, thinking it might be a catch phrase for sympathetic magic. And the pop might be an audible show of air molecules undergoing friction. In sympathetic magic, it didn't matter how nebulous the relationship was as long as it was real.

"Cold to hot, harness within," she continued, making another unfamiliar gesture, but I recognized the next finger movement from when I used a ley line charm to break the Howlers' bat in practice. Perhaps it was the motion that tapped into the focal object for direction. Huh. Maybe there was some sense to this ley line stuff after all.

"Calefacio!" she said happily, invoking the charm and setting it all into motion.

I felt a mild drop through me as the charm pulled energy from the line to excite the water molecules in the cup, warming the coffee. "Wow," I breathed when she handed me back my mug, softly steaming. "Thanks."

"You're welcome," she said. "You have to regulate the ending temperature yourself by how much line energy you put into it."

"The more energy, the hotter it gets?" I took a careful sip, deciding it was perfect. It must have taken her years to gain this much proficiency.

"Depending on the amount you have to warm up," Ceri whispered, her eyes distant in memory. "So be careful with your bathwater until you know what you're doing." Visibly pulling herself back to the present, she turned to me. "Are you settled now?"

Adrenaline zinged through me, and I set my warm coffee down. *I can do this. If Ceri can warm her tea and spindle line energy in her head, then so can I.*

"Fill your center," she encouraged. "Then pull some from it as if you're going to work a spell as you say your invocation word."

I tucked a curl behind my ear and settled myself. Exhaling, I closed my eyes and I tapped the line, feeling the pressures equalize in an instant. Setting my mind to the poised calmness I cultivated when I said a ley line charm, a curious, new sensation tingled through me. A tinge of energy flowed in from the line, replacing what I had unconsciously pulled from my chi. *Tulpa,* I thought, hope bringing me tight.

My eyes flew open as a wash of force flowed in from the line to replace what had darted from my chi to my head. In a torrent, the line raced through me and settled in my thoughts. My enclosure expanded to take it in. Shocked, I did nothing to stop it.

"Enough!" Ceri cried, rising to her knees. "Rachel, let go of the line!"

I jerked, pulling my focus from the ley line. There was a brief swish of warmth through me as a dribble of force backwashed from my thoughts to my chi, topping it off. Breath held, I froze in my chair, staring at her. I was afraid to move, there was so much energy in my head.

"Are you all right?" she said, not settling back down, and I nodded.

From the kitchen came a faint, "You okay in there?"

"We're fine!" I carefully shouted back, then looked at Ceri. "We're fine, right?"

Green eyes wide, she bobbed her head, not dropping my gaze for an instant. "You're holding a lot of energy outside your center," she said. "But I've noticed your chi doesn't hold as much as mine. I think . . ." She hesitated. "I think an elf's chi can hold more than a witch's, but witches seem to be able to hold more in their thoughts."

I could taste the energy in me, tinfoil-like on my tongue. "Witches make better batteries, huh?" I quipped weakly.

She laughed, her clear voice going up to the dusky rafters. I wished there were pixies up there to dance amid the sound. "Maybe that's why witches abandoned the ever-after sooner than elves," she said. "Demons seem to prefer witches over elves or humans for their familiars. I thought it was because there were so few of us, but maybe not."

"Maybe," I said, wondering how long I could hold all this force without spilling it. My nose tickled. I desperately didn't want to sneeze.

Ivy's boots in the hallway intruded, and we both turned as she strode toward us with her purse over her shoulder and a plate of cookies in her hand. "I'm headed out," she said lightly, tossing her hair over her shoulder. "Want me to walk you home, Ceri?"

Immediately Ceri stood. "That's not necessary."

Ire flickered in Ivy's eyes. "I know it's not necessary."

Ivy's plate of steaming cookies hit the desktop before me in a harsh clatter. My eyebrows rose, and I swung my feet to the floor. Ivy wanted to talk to Ceri alone—about me. Bothered, I tapped my fingernails in a sharp staccato. "I'm not eating those," I said flatly.

"It's medicinal, Rachel," she said, her voice heavy with threat.

"It's Brimstone, Ivy," I shot back. Ceri shifted from foot to foot in obvious discomfort, but I didn't care. "I can't believe you gave me Brimstone," I added. "I arrest people who do Brimstone; I don't share rent with them." *I was not going to tag Ivy. I didn't care if she broke every law in the I.S. handbook. Not this time.*

Ivy's stance went aggressive, her hip cocked and her lips almost bloodless. "It's medicinal," she said sharply. "It's specially processed and the amount of stimulant in it is so low you can't even smell it. You can't smell Brimstone, can you? Can you?"

The ring of brown about her pupils had shrunk, and I dropped my gaze, not wanting to trip her into pulling an aura. Not now, with the sun almost down. "There was enough in it to jerk the bane into play," I said sullenly.

Ivy, too, calmed, knowing she had reached her limits. "That wasn't my fault," she said softly. "I never gave you enough to even trigger a Brimstone dog."

Ceri raised her narrow chin. There was no remorse in her green eyes. "I apologized for that," she said tightly. "I didn't know it was illegal. It wasn't the last time I gave it to someone."

"See?" Ivy said, gesturing to Ceri. "She didn't know, and that insurance guy was only trying to help. Now shut up, eat your cookies, and stop making us feel bad. You've got a run tomorrow and you need your strength."

Leaning back in my swivel chair, I pushed the plate of vamp cookies away. I wasn't going to eat them. I didn't care that what I had kept down yesterday had upped my metabolism so my black eye was already turning yellow and my cut lip was healed. "I'm fine."

Ivy's usually placid face clouded over. "Fine," she said sharply.

"Fine," I shot back, crossing my legs and turning so I was eyeing her askance.

Ivy's jaw clenched. "Ceri, I'll walk you home."

Ceri glanced between us. Face empty of emotion, she bent to get her teapot and cup. "I'll take care of my dishes first," she said.

"I can do that," I rushed to say, but Ceri shook her head, watching her feet so as not to spill as she made her way to the kitchen. I frowned, not liking her doing domestic work. It was too much like what I imagined Algaliarept had forced on her.

"Let her do it," Ivy said when the sound of Ceri's steps ended. "It makes her feel useful."

"She's royalty," I said. "You do know that, don't you?"

Ivy glanced into the dark hallway as the sound of running water filtered out. "Maybe a thousand years ago. Now she's nothing, and she knows it."

I made a puff of air. "Don't you have any compassion? Doing my dishes is degrading."

"I have a lot of compassion." A flicker of anger set Ivy's thin eyebrows high. "But the last time I looked, there weren't any openings for princesses in the want ads. What is she supposed to do to give her life meaning? There aren't any treaties for her to make, no rulings to judge, and her biggest decision is to have eggs or waffles for breakfast. There's no way to give herself a feeling of worth with her old royalty crap. And doing dishes isn't degrading."

I leaned back in my chair in a show of acquiescence. She was right, but I didn't like it. "So you have a run?" I prompted when the silence stretched.

Ivy sent one shoulder up and down. "I'm going to talk to Jenks."

"Good." I met her eyes, relieved. *Something we could talk about without arguing.* "I stopped at that Were's house this afternoon. The poor guy wouldn't let me in. The pixy girls had been at him. His hair was solid cornrows." I had woken up one morning with my hair braided into the fringe of my afghan. Matalina had made them apologize, but it took me forty minutes to untangle myself. I would give just about anything to wake up like that again.

"Yeah, I saw him," Ivy said, and I sat up from my slouch.

"You've been over there?" I asked, watching Ivy get her coat from the foyer and return. She slipped it on, the short leather jacket making a soft hush of silk against silk.

"I've been over there twice," she said. "The Were won't let me in, either, but one of my friends is taking him out on a date so Jenks will have to answer the door, the little prick.

Typical little man. He has an ego the size of the Grand Canyon."

I chucked, and Ceri came in from the back. Her borrowed coat was over her arm and the shoes that Keasley bought her were in her grip. I wasn't going to tell her to put them on. She could walk in the snow barefoot as far as I was concerned. Ivy, though, gave her a pointed look.

"You going to be all right for a while?" Ivy asked as Ceri dropped her shoes to the floor and snugged her feet into them.

"Good God," I muttered, twisting the chair back and forth. "I'll be fine."

"Stay on holy ground," she added as she gestured for Ceri to head out. "Don't tap a line. Eat your cookies."

"Not going to happen, Ivy," I said. *Pasta. I wanted pasta in alfredo sauce.* That's what Nick had cooked up for me the last time Ivy was bent on shoving these things down my throat. I couldn't believe she'd been slipping me Brimstone. *Yes, I could.*

"I'll call you in about an hour to make sure you're all right."

"I won't answer," I said, irritated. "I'm going to take a nap." I stood and stretched until my sweater and halter top rose to show my belly button. It would have gotten a wolf whistle from Jenks, and the silence in the rafters was depressing.

Ceri came forward with her cushion to give me a hug good-bye. It startled me, and I hesitantly returned it. "Rachel can take care of herself," she said proudly. "She's been holding enough ever-after to blow a hole in the roof for the last five minutes and has forgotten about it."

"Holy crap!" I exclaimed, feeling my face warm. "I am, aren't I!"

Ivy sighed as she strode to the church's front door. "Don't wait up for me," she called over her shoulder. "I'm having dinner with my folks and won't be home until after sunup."

"You should let it go," Ceri said as she edged after Ivy.

"At least when the sun is down. Someone else might summon him, and if they don't banish him properly, he'll come looking for you. He might try to knock you out by adding to what you're holding now." She shrugged in a very modern gesture. "But if you stay on holy ground, you should be all right."

"I'll let it go," I said absently, my thoughts whirling.

Ceri smiled shyly. "Thank you, Rachel," she said softly. "It's good to feel needed."

I jerked my attention back to her. "You're welcome."

The scent of cold snow filtered in. I looked up seeing Ivy standing impatiently in the threshold of the open door, the fading light making her a threatening silhouette in tight leather. "'By-y-y-y-ye, Rachel," she prompted mockingly, and Ceri sighed.

Turning, the slender woman made her unhurried way to the door, kicking off her shoes at the last moment and going barefoot out onto the icy cement steps.

"How can you stand the cold?" I heard Ivy say before the door shut behind them.

I soaked in the silence and the dusky light. Reaching over, I clicked off the desk lamp and it seemed to brighten outside. I was alone—for what was probably the first time—in my church. No roommate, no boyfriend, no pixies. Alone. My eyes closed, and I sat on the slightly raised stage and breathed. I could smell plywood over the almond scent of Ivy's stupid cookies. A soft pressure behind my eyes reminded me I was still holding that ball of ever-after, and with a nudge of my will, I broke the three-dimensional circle in my thoughts and the energy flowed back to the line in a warm wash.

I opened my eyes and headed for the kitchen, my sock feet soundless. I wasn't going to take a nap; I was going to make brownies as part of Ivy's present. There was no way I could compete with thousand-dollar perfume: I had to take the handmade-goodie track.

Detouring into the living room, I searched for the remote.

The smell of plywood was almost an assault, and I glanced at the window Ivy had sketched on the panel, freehanding the view of the graveyard. I clicked on the stereo and Offspring's "Come Out and Play" spilled out. Grinning, I cranked it. "Wake the dead," I said, tossing the remote and dancing into the kitchen.

While the bouncy music lured me into a better mood, I pulled out my dented spell pot, which I couldn't use for spelling anymore, and the recipe book I had swiped from my mom. Thumbing through it, I found Grandma's fudgy brownie recipe penciled in beside the gourmet recipe that tasted like cardboard. Timing my motions with the music, I got out the eggs, sugar, vanilla, and dumped them on the center island counter. I had the chocolate chips melting on the stove and the evaporated milk measured out when the air shifted and the front door slammed. The egg in my hand slipped, cracking as it hit the counter.

"Forget something, Ivy?" I shouted. Adrenaline stabbed through me as my gaze went from the broken egg to everything scattered over the kitchen. I'd never get it hidden before she made it back here. *Couldn't that woman stay away for even an hour?*

But it was Kisten's voice that answered.

Twenty-one

"It's me, Rachel," Kisten called, his voice faint over the music blaring from the living room. I froze, the memory of the kiss he'd given me keeping me where I stood. I must have looked like an idiot when he turned the corner and stopped in the threshold.

"Ivy's not here?" he said, his eyes giving me the once-over. "Shoot."

I took a breath to settle myself. "Shoot?" I questioned, sliding the cracked egg off the counter and into the bowl. *I didn't think anyone said shoot anymore.*

"Can I say shit?"

"Hell, yes."

"Shit, then." His gaze went from me to the kitchen, lacing his hands behind his back as I picked the bigger chunks of shell out.

"Hey, would you, ah, turn the music down for me?" I said, sneaking a glance at him when he nodded and walked out. It was Saturday, and he was dressed casually in leather boots and faded jeans that were nice and tight. His short leather coat was open, and a burgundy silk shirt showed a wisp of chest hair. *Just enough,* I thought as the music softened. I could smell his coat. I was a sucker for the scent of leather. *This might be a problem.*

"Are you sure Ivy didn't send you over to baby-sit?" I

questioned as he returned and I wiped the egg slime off on a damp dishcloth.

He chuckled and sat in Ivy's chair. "No." He hesitated. "Is she going to be gone for a while, or can I wait?"

I didn't look up from the recipe, not liking how he had said that. There had been more inquiry in his voice than the question warranted. "Ivy went to talk to Jenks." I ran my finger down the page without looking at the words. "Then she's having dinner with her folks."

"Sunup," he murmured, and I felt my warning flags go up. All of them.

The clock above the sink ticked, and I took the melted chocolate off the stove. I wasn't about to stand with my back to him, so I set it on the counter between us, crossing my arms in front of me and putting my backside against the sink. Watching me, he tossed his hair out of his eyes. I took a breath to tell him to go, but he interrupted.

"Are you all right?"

I stared blankly at him, then remembered. "Oh! The demon—thing," I muttered, embarrassed as I touched the pain charms about my neck. "You heard about that, huh?"

He smiled with half his mouth. "You made the news. And I had to listen to Ivy for three solid hours while she bitched about not being here at the time."

Going back to my recipe, I rolled my eyes. "Sorry. Yeah. I'm okay. A few scrapes and bruises. Nothing major. But I can't tap a line after sundown anymore." I didn't want to tell him I wasn't entirely safe after dark either, unless I was on holy ground . . . which the kitchen and living room weren't. "It's really going to put a crimp in my runs," I said sourly, wondering how I was going to get around this latest mountain. Oh well. It wasn't as if I relied on ley line magic. I was an earth witch after all.

Kisten didn't seem to think it mattered much either, if his casual shrug meant anything. "I'm sorry to hear Jenks left," he said, stretching his legs out and crossing his boots at his ankles. "He was more than an asset to your company. He's a good friend."

My face screwed up into an unpleasant expression. "I should have told him what Trent was when I figured it out."

Surprise cascaded over him. "You know what Trent Kalamack is? No shit?"

Jaw clenched, I dropped my eyes to the recipe book and nodded, waiting for him to ask it.

"What is he?"

I stayed silent, my eyes fixed on the page. The soft sound of him moving pulled my gaze up.

"Never mind," he said. "It doesn't matter."

Relieved, I gave the chocolate a clockwise stir. "It matters to Jenks. I should have trusted him."

"Not everyone needs to know everything."

"You do if you're four inches tall with wings."

He got up, drawing my attention as he stretched. With a soft, satisfied sound, his shoulders eased and he collapsed in on himself. Taking his coat off, he headed to the fridge.

I tapped the spoon on the side to flick most of the chocolate off. My brow furrowed. Sometimes it was easier to talk to a stranger. "What am I doing wrong, Kisten?" I said, frustrated. "Why do I drive the people I like away?"

He came out from behind the fridge door with the bag of almonds I'd bought last week. "Ivy's not leaving."

"Those are mine," I said, and he paused until I gestured sourly that he could have them.

"I'm not leaving," he added, mouth gently moving as he ate one.

I exhaled noisily, dumping the measured sugar into the chocolate. He looked really good over there, and memories kept intruding: thoughts of us dressed up and enjoying ourselves, the spark his black eyes drew through me when Saladan's heavies lay broken in the street, Piscary's elevator with me wrapped around him wanting to feel him taking everything I had. . . .

The crunch of the sugar against the pan was loud as I stirred. *Damn vamp pheromones.*

"I'm glad Nick left," Kisten said. "He wasn't good for you."

I kept my head down, but my shoulders tensed. "What do you know about it?" I said, tucking a long red curl behind my ear. I looked up, finding him calmly eating my almonds. "Nick made me feel good. I made him feel good. We had fun together. We liked the same movies, the same places to eat. He could keep up with me when we ran at the zoo. Nick was a good person, and you have no right to pass judgment on him." I snatched a damp dishcloth, wiping up my spilled sugar and shaking it into the sink.

"You may be right," he said as he jiggled a handful of nuts into his palm and rolled the bag shut. "But I find one thing fascinating." He put a nut between his teeth and crunched through it noisily. "You put him in the past tense."

My mouth dropped open. Torn between anger and shock, my face went cold. In the living room, the music changed to something fast and bouncy—and totally inappropriate.

Kisten cracked the fridge open, set the nuts back into the door, and closed it. "I'll wait for Ivy for a while. She might come back with Jenks—if you're lucky. You have a tendency to demand more of a person than most are willing to give." He shook the nuts still left in his hand as I sputtered. "Kind of like a vampire," he added as he picked up his coat and walked out.

My hand was dripping, and I realized I was squeezing the dishcloth so hard that water was seeping out. I threw it into the sink, furious and depressed. Not a good combination. From the living room, happy pop music bounced and skittered. "Will you turn that off!" I shouted. My jaw ached where I was clenching it, and I forced my teeth to part when the music stopped. Fuming, I measured out the sugar and dumped it in. I reached for the spoon, a sound of frustration coming from me as I remembered I had already added the sugar. "Damn it back to the Turn," I muttered. Now I'd have to make a double batch.

Spoon held tightly, I tried to stir it in. Sugar went everywhere, spilling over the edge. My teeth gritted, and I stomped back to the sink for the dishcloth.

"You don't know squat," I whispered as I scraped the spilled sugar into a little pile. "Nick might come back. He said he was. I have his key."

I pushed the gathered sugar into the cup of my hand, hesitating before I dumped it into the bowl with the rest. Brushing the last of the grit from my fingers, I looked at the dark hallway. Nick wouldn't give me his key if he wasn't coming back.

Music started up, soft with a steady beat. My eyes narrowed. I never said he could put something else in. Angry, I took a step toward the living room, then jerked to a halt. Kisten had left in the middle of a conversation. He had taken food with him. Crunchy food. According to Ivy's dating book, that was a vampiric invitation. And following him would be saying I was interested. Even worse, he knew I knew.

I was still staring at the hallway when Kisten walked past. He backpedaled to a stop as he saw me there with a blank look on my face.

"I'll wait in the sanctuary," he said. "Is that okay with you?"

"Sure," I whispered.

His eyebrows rose, and with that same little smile, he ate an almond. "Okay." Kisten vanished down the dark hallway, his boots silent on the hardwood floor.

I turned away and stared at the night-blackened window. I counted to ten. I counted to ten again. I counted to ten a third time, finding myself in the hallway by the time I reached seven. *I'll go in, say my piece, and leave,* I promised myself when I found him at the piano, his back to me as he sat on the bench. He pulled himself straight as my feet scuffed to a halt.

"Nick is a good man," I said, my voice shaking.

"Nick is a good man," he agreed, not turning around.

"He makes me feel wanted, needed."

Kisten slowly spun. His stubble caught the faint light filtering in from the street. The outline of his wide shoulders tapered down to his slim waist, and I mentally shook myself at how good he looked. "He used to." His low, smooth voice sent a shiver through me.

"I don't want you to talk about him anymore," I said.

He gazed at me for a heartbeat, then said, "Okay."

"Good." I took a quick breath, turned and walked out.

My knees were shaking, and listening for any steps behind me, I took a right into my room. Heart pounding, I reached for my perfume. The one that hid my scent.

"Don't."

Gasping, I turned, finding Kisten behind me. Ivy's bottle slipped from my fingers. His hand darted out, and I jumped as it enfolded mine, imprisoning the precious bottle safe within my grip. I froze. "I like the way you smell," he whispered, far, far too close.

My stomach clenched. I could risk bringing Al down on me by tapping a line to knock him unconscious, but I didn't want to. "You need to get out of my bedroom," I said.

His blue eyes looked black in the dim light. The faint glow from the kitchen made him an alluring, dangerous shadow. My shoulders were so tense they hurt as he opened my hand and took the perfume from me. The click as it hit my dresser jerked me straight. "Nick isn't coming back," he said, unaccusing and blunt.

My breath slipped from me, and I closed my eyes. *Oh God.* "I know."

My eyes jerked open when he took my elbows. I froze, waiting for my scar to flash into play, but it didn't. He wasn't trying to bespell me. A foolish part of me respected that, and like an idiot, I did nothing instead of telling him to get the hell out of my church and away from me.

"You need to be needed, Rachel," he said, inches away as

his breath shifted my hair. "You live so brightly, so honestly, that you need to be needed. You're hurting. I can feel it."

"I know."

His solemn eyes took on a shade of pity. "Nick is human. No matter how he tries, he'll never understand you entirely."

"I know." I swallowed hard. There was a wet warmth in my eyes. My jaw tightened until my head hurt. *I will not cry.*

"He can't give you what you need." Kisten's hands slipped to my waist. "He'll always be just a little afraid."

I know. My eyes closed, opening as I let him pull me closer.

"And even if Nick learns to live with his fear," he said earnestly, his eyes asking me to listen, "he won't ever forgive you for being stronger than he is."

A lump formed in my throat. "I . . . I have to go," I said. "Excuse me."

His hands fell from me, and I pushed past him and into the hall. Confused and wanting to scream at the world, I strode into the kitchen. I stopped, seeing among the pots and flour a huge aching emptiness that had never been there before. Arms wrapped about myself, I lurched into the living room. I had to get the music off. It was beautiful. I hated it. I hated everything.

Snatching up the remote, I pointed it at the player. Jeff Buckley. I couldn't handle Jeff in the state I was in. Who in hell put Jeff Buckley in my player? Clicking it off, I tossed the remote to the couch. Adrenaline jerked me straight as the remote hit, not the suede of Ivy's couch, but someone's hand.

"Kisten!" I stammered as he turned the music back on, watching me with half-lidded eyes. "What are you doing?"

"Listening to music."

He was calm and wire-tight, and panic struck me at his calculating surety. "Don't sneak up on me like that," I said, my breath coming short. "Ivy never sneaks up on me."

"Ivy doesn't like who she is." His eyes were unblinking. "I do."

He reached out. Breath coming in a quick surge, I knocked his arm aside. Tension sang through me as he jerked me forward, holding me to him. Panic, then anger, flashed. There wasn't a twinge from my scar. "Kisten!" I exclaimed, trying to move. "Let me go!"

"I'm not trying to bite you," he said softly, his lips brushing my ear. "Stop it."

His voice was firm, soothing. There was no blood lust in it. My thoughts flashed back to waking up in his car to the sound of singing monks. "Let go!" I demanded, strung out and feeling like I was either going to hit him or start to cry.

"I don't want to. You're hurting too much. How long has it been since someone held you? Touched you?"

A tear leaked out and I hated that he saw it. Hated he knew I was holding my breath.

"You need to feel, Rachel." His voice grew soft, pleading. "This is killing you slowly."

I swallowed the lump in my throat. He was seducing me. I wasn't such an innocent that I knew he wouldn't try. But his hands upon my arms were warm. And he was right. I needed another's touch, ached for it, damn me to hell. I had almost forgotten how it felt to be needed. Nick had given that back to me, that tiny thrill of excitement knowing someone was wanting to touch you, wanting you and you alone to touch him.

I had endured more short-term relationships than a socialite has shoes. Either it was my I.S. job, or my wacko mother pushing for commitment, or that I attracted jerks who simply saw a redhead as a potential notch on their broomstick. Maybe I was a crazy bitch demanding trust without being able to give it. I didn't want another one-sided relationship, but Nick was gone and Kisten smelled good. He made me feel the pain less.

My shoulders eased, and he exhaled as he felt me stop fighting him. Eyes closing, I dropped my forehead into his shoulder as my folded arms made a small space between us. The music was soft and slow. I wasn't crazy. I could trust. I did trust. I had trusted Nick, and he had left.

"You'll leave," I breathed. "They all leave. They get what they want, and they leave. Or they find out what I can do, and then they leave."

His arms about me tightened for an instant, then relaxed. "I'm not going anywhere. You already scared the hell out of me when you took Piscary down." He buried his nose in my hair and breathed in my scent. "And I still am here."

Lulled by his body warmth and his touch, my tension tricked away. Kisten altered my balance—and I moved with him. Moving, hardly moving, our weight shifted as the slow and seductive music lured me into swaying with him.

"You can't hurt my pride," Kisten whispered, his fingers tracing the middle of my back. "I've lived my entire life with people stronger than I. I like that, and have no shame in being the weaker one. I'll never be able to cast a spell, and I don't give a shit that you can do something I can't."

The music and our almost-not-moving started a warm spot in me. Licking my lips, I slipped my arms from between us to find they felt natural about his waist. My heartbeat quickened and my eyes were wide as I stared at the wall, my breath slipping in and out of me in an unreal evenness. "Kisten . . ."

"I'll always be here," he said softly. "You can never fill my need, never drive me away, no matter how much you give me. The good or the bad. I'll always be hungry for emotion, always and forever, and I can feel you hurting. I can turn it to joy. If you'll let me."

I swallowed as he drew us to a stop. He pulled back, and with a gentle touch on my jaw, he tilted my head so he could see my eyes. The pulsing beat of the music pattered on my mind, numbing and soothing. His gaze was heady. "Let me do this," he whispered, deeply dangerous. But with his words, he put me in a position of power. I could say no.

I didn't want to.

My thoughts pinged through me too fast to be realized. His hands felt good, and his eyes held passion. I wanted what he could give me—what he promised. "Why?" I whispered.

His lips parted and he breathed, "Because I want to. Because you want me to."

I didn't look from him. His pupils never shifted, never grew. My grip on him became firmer as my arms pressed into him. "There will be no sharing of blood, Kisten. Ever."

His breath came and went, and his hands tightened. Expression dusky with the knowledge of what was to come, he leaned closer. "One," he said as he kissed the corner of my mouth. "Step." He kissed the other side. "At a time," he continued as he kissed me gently, so gently it made me ache for more. "My love," he finished.

A stab of desire went right to my core. My eyes closed. *Oh God. Save me from myself.*

"I make no promises," I whispered.

"I don't ask for any," he said. "Where are we going?"

"I don't know." My hands drifted downward from his waist. We were swaying to the music again. I felt alive, and as we almost-danced, a hint of fire came from my demon scar.

"Can I do this?" Kisten asked, moving closer so more of our bodies touched. I knew he was asking my permission to play upon my scar, to willingly let him bespell me. That he asked gave me a feeling of security I knew was probably false.

"No. Yes. I don't know." *So torn.* It felt good, just my body touching his, his arms about my waist, a new demand in their strength. "I don't know. . . ."

"Then I won't." *Where were we going?* Exhaling, he ran his hands down my arms, lacing his fingers in mine. Gently he pulled my hands to the small of his back, holding them there as we swayed, shifting to the slow, seductive music.

A shiver rose inside me. The scent of leather grew thick and warm. Where he touched sent a sliver of heat to tingle my fingers. My head dropped into the hollow between his neck and shoulder. I wanted to put my lips there, knowing what he would feel, knowing how he would taste if I dared. But I didn't, contenting myself to send my breath there instead, afraid of what he would do if my lips touched him.

Heart pounding, I moved his hands to the small of my

back and I left them there, moving, pressing, massaging. My hands rose to twine my fingers behind his head. My thoughts touched upon us in the elevator when I thought Piscary was going to kill me. It was too much to resist, the memory of my demon scar alive and alight.

"Please," I whispered, my lips brushing his neck to make him tremble. His torn earlobe was inches from me, tempting. "I want you to." Pulling my gaze up, I searched his eyes, seeing but not fearing the narrowing band of blue. "I trust you. But I don't trust your instincts."

A deep understanding and relief pinched his eyes. His hands dropped lower, caressing until they found the top of my legs, then reversed their motion, moving, always moving, as we swayed. "I don't trust them either," he said, fake accent utterly gone. "Not with you."

My breath caught as his fingers traced from my back to my front, a whisper against my jeans. Tugging at the top button. Hinting. "I'm wearing caps," he said. "The vampire has been defanged."

Startled, my lips parted as he smiled, showing me that his sharp canines were indeed capped. It sent a surge of heat through me, disquieting and thought provoking. Sure, he couldn't draw blood, but now I'd let him explore a hell of a lot more of me. And he knew it. But safe? No. He was more dangerous now than if he hadn't capped his teeth.

"Oh God," I whispered, knowing I was lost as he nuzzled his head into the hollow of my shoulder and gently kissed me. Eyes closing, I sent my fingers into his hair, clenching as his kiss shifted, moving to the very edge of my collarbone where my scar started.

Waves of demand pulsed from it, and my knees buckled.

"Sorry," Kisten breathed huskily as he caught my elbows and kept me upright. "I didn't know it was that sensitive. Just how much saliva did you get dosed with?"

His lips were off my neck and by my ear. Almost panting, I leaned into him. The blood in me pounded, wanting me to do something. "I almost died," I said. "Kisten . . ."

"I'll be careful," he said, the tenderness going right to my core. I willingly followed his lead as he sat me on the couch, nestling me between the back and the arm. Taking his hands, I pulled Kisten down beside me. My scar was tingling and waves of promise scoured me. *Where were we going?*

"Rachel?"

I heard the same question in his voice, but I didn't want to answer. Smiling, I pulled him closer across the couch. "You talk too much," I whispered, and covered my mouth with his.

A soft sound came from him as his lips pushed back, his stubble rough. Fingers spaced wide across my cheek, he held me still as I pulled his weight farther down upon me. Nudging my hip, he made room for his knee between me and the back of the couch.

My skin tingled where his fingers touched my jaw. I slipped a hesitant tongue between his lips, and my breath came quick as he darted his tongue deep into me. He tasted faintly of almonds, and when he moved to draw away, I twined my fingers at the nape of his neck to keep him there just a moment longer. He made a surprised sound, pushing more aggressively. Now I pulled back, running my tongue across the smoothness of his teeth as I went.

Kisten shuddered, the tremor felt clearly as he supported his weight over me. I didn't know how far I wanted to go. But this? This was good. I couldn't lead him on, promising more than I could give. "Wait . . ." I said reluctantly, meeting his gaze.

But seeing him above me, breathless with his passion held in check, I hesitated. His eyes were black, heady with desire and need. I searched for and found a carefully checked blood lust. His shoulders were tense under his shirt, a hand was firm against my side, his thumb massaging under my halter. The look of wanting in him sent adrenaline to my core, rousing me more than his rough and gentle touch that rose higher to find my breast. *Oh, to be wanted, needed.*

"What?" he said, poised and waiting.

The hell with it. "Never mind," I said, playing with the hair about his ear.

His soft hand under my halter top went still. "You want me to stop?"

A second stab of feeling struck though me. I felt my eyes close. "No," I breathed, hearing a hundred well-thought-out convictions die in that word. Heart pounding, I slipped my amulets from me and dropped them to the carpet—I wanted to feel everything—but it wasn't until I reached for his belt buckle that he understood.

A low guttural sound escaped him, and he dropped his head to mine. His weight was a welcomed warmth pressing on me as his lips found my demon scar and gently mouthed it.

Fire spilled like molten stone through me to my groin, and I gasped as the sensation rebounded and multiplied. The dull aches from my recent demon attack mutated into pleasure, courtesy of the old vampire saliva he was playing upon. I couldn't think. I couldn't breathe. My hands jerked out from where I had been trying to undo his pants, and I clutched his shoulder. "Kisten," I breathed when I was able to take a shuddering breath.

But he didn't let up, pushing me down until my head was on the arm of the couch. My fingers dug into him as gentle teeth replaced his lips. A groan escaped me, and he worked the scar, his teeth soft and his breath harsh. I wanted him. I wanted all of him.

"Kisten . . ." I pushed at him. I had to ask first. I had to know.

"What?" he said flatly as he pushed my shirt and halter out of the way and his fingers found my breast and began moving, promising more.

In the gap between us, I finally got his belt undone. I gave a tug, and I heard a rivet snap through. His head dropped back to me, and before he could find my neck again and send me into an unaware ecstasy, I undid his zipper and sent my hands searching. *God save me,* I thought as I found him, the smooth skin tight under my questing fingers. "You've had sex with a witch before?" I whispered, pushing his jeans down and running my hand across his backside.

"I know what I'm getting into," he said breathily.

I felt myself melt into the couch as my thoughts and shoulders eased. My hands found him again, and he exhaled long and slow. "I didn't want to assume—" I said, then gasped as he dropped his weight lower and pulled my shirt up. "I didn't want you to be surprised. . . . Oh God. Kisten," I panted, almost frantic with need as his lips moved from under my jaw to my collarbone and then to my breast. Waves of promise rose high, and I arched my back as he pulled, his hands warm against my skin. *Where was he? I couldn't reach that far.*

He silenced my whisper as he lifted his face and kissed me. Now I could reach, and my breath slipped from me in bliss as I grasped him and sent my fingers moving lower. "Kisten . . ."

"You talk too much," he said, his lips moving against my skin. "You ever have sex with a vamp?" he said, his eyes half closed, watching me.

I exhaled as he turned his attention to my neck again. His fingers traced the path his lips were going to take, and waves of ecstasy rolled through me when they did. "No," I panted as I yanked his jeans down. I'd never get them off over his boots. "Anything I should be aware of?"

He ran his hands under my breast, again tracing the path his lips soon followed. Back arched, I tried not to moan with need as I reached down, trying to find all of him. "We bite," he said, and I cried out when he did just that, gently pinching me between his teeth.

"Get my pants off before I kill you," I panted, almost insane with desire.

"Yes, ma'am," he growled, and his stubble scraped me as he pulled away.

I took a much needed deep breath, following him up to push him back down and straddle him. His hands worked my zipper as I fumbled with the buttons of his shirt. A sigh escaped me when I got the last one undone and sent my hands over him, my fingers tracing up and across the definition of his abs and chest. I leaned over him, my hair hiding what I was doing as my lips hop-skipped from his middle to the hollow at his neck. I lingered there, hesitantly, daring to run my teeth against his skin, pulling against it with a slight pressure. Under me, he shivered, and his hands, working my jeans down my hips, shook.

Eyes wide, I pulled away, thinking I had gone too far.

"No," he whispered, putting his hands on my waist to keep me there. His face was strained with emotion. "Don't stop. It's . . . I won't break your skin." His eyes flashed open. "Oh God, Rachel. I promise I won't break your skin."

The passion in his voice struck me. Abandoning myself, I pinned him to the couch, knees to either side. Lips searching, I found his neck, turning my kisses into something more substantial. His heavy breaths and light hands drove my desire into pulsing demands, pounding through me in time with my heartbeat. Teeth replaced my lips, and his breath grew ragged.

His hands grasped my waist, and I was lifted up enough that I could push my jeans off. They caught on my socks, and with a cry of impatience, I pulled my lips from him long enough to kick them off. Then I was back, my skin warm where it touched him under me. I leaned over him, holding his neck unmoving as I used my teeth against his skin instead of my lips.

Kisten's breath came in a shuddering sound. "Rachel," he breathed, his hands firm against my middle as he sent his hand downward, searching.

A low sound, barely audible, came from me as his fingers brushed me. In his touch, I felt his need flash into demand. My eyes closed and I sent one hand downward, finding him.

Feeling him against me, I shifted forward, then back. Our breath slipped out in tandem as we joined. Heavy and potent, my want and relief rose. He slipped deep inside me. *Soon, God help me, if it wasn't soon, I was going to die.* His soft breathing rose to swirl in my thoughts, sending surges from my neck to my groin.

My heart pounded, and his fingers traced my neck, resting

atop my pulsing skin. We moved together, a pace steady with promise. His free arm wrapped about me, holding me closer, its weight both imprisoning and secure.

"Give me this," he whispered, drawing me closer, and I willingly bent to his will, letting his lips find my demon scar.

My breath came in a loud gasp. I shuddered, our rhythm shifting. He held me close as the waves of desire built upon themselves. His lips on my neck became teeth, hungry, demanding. There was no pain, and I urged him to do what he would. A small part of me knew if he hadn't his caps, I would have been bitten. It only drove me to a more desperate need. I heard myself cry out, and his grip trembled, becoming tighter.

Wild with passion, I clutched his shoulders. It was there, I only needed to catch it. My breath came fast against his neck. There was nothing but him, and me, and our bodies moving together. His rhythm shifted, and feeling his passions beginning to crest, I found his neck and sent my teeth into him again.

"Harder," he whispered. "You can't hurt me. I promise you can't hurt me."

It tipped me over the edge, and as I played pretend with my vampire, I lunged hungrily into him with no thought of what I'd leave behind.

Kisten groaned, his arms tightening around me. His head pushed mine aside, and with a guttural sound, he buried his face in my neck.

I cried out as his lips found my scar. Fire struck my body alight. With that, fulfillment crashed upon me and I climaxed. Wave after wave rose, each building on the one before. Kisten shuddered, his motion under me ceasing as his passions crested an instant after my own. My breath came in a pained sound and I trembled, unable to move, fearing and wanting the last tingling jolts. "Kisten?" I managed as they faded to nothing and I found myself panting against him.

His grip about me hesitated and his hands fell away. My forehead dropped to his chest, and I took a shaking breath, exhausted and spent. I could do nothing as I lay atop him, my eyes half closed. Slowly I realized my back was cold and that Kisten's hand was tracing a warm path up and down my spine. I could hear his heartbeat and smell our scents mingling. Muscles trembling with fatigue, I pulled my head up to find his eyes shut and a contented smile on him.

My breath caught. *Holy shit. What had I just done?*

Kisten's eyes opened, finding mine. They were clear and blue, the black of his pupil normal and calming. "Now you're afraid?" he said. "It's a little late for that."

His gaze lingered on my black eye—only now seeing it with my amulets on the floor. I pulled myself up from him, immediately falling back as it was cold. My limbs started shaking. "Um, that was fun," I said, and he laughed.

"Fun," he said, running a finger down my jawline. "My wicked witch thought that was *fun*." His smile wouldn't leave him. "Nick was a fool to let you go."

"What do you mean?" I said, shifting to move, but his hands held me to him.

"I mean," he said softly, "that you are the most erotic woman I've ever touched. That you're both a wide-eyed innocent and an experienced slut all at the same time."

I stiffened. "If this is your attempt at pillow talk, it sucks eggs."

"Rachel," he cajoled, the heavy look of satisfied tenderness the only thing keeping me where I was. *That and I didn't think I could stand up quite yet.* "You have no idea how arousing it is to have your tiny little teeth on me, struggling to break through, tasting without tasting. An innocent, experienced and hungry all at the same time."

I raised my eyebrows, blowing a strand of hair out of my eyes. "You had this all planned, didn't you?" I accused. "Thought you could come in here and seduce me like you do everyone else?" It wasn't as if I could be angry, lying atop him as I was, but I tried.

"No. Not like everyone else," he said, the glint in his eyes going right to my core. "And yes, I came over here fully intending to seduce you." He lifted his head and whispered in my ear, "It's what I'm good at. Just like you're good at evading demons and kicking ass."

"Kicking ass?" I questioned as he dropped his head back to the arm of the couch. His hand was exploring again, and I didn't want to move.

"Yeah," he said, and I jumped as he found a ticklish spot. "I like a woman who takes care of herself."

"Not much of a white knight on a horse, huh?"

He raised one eyebrow. "Oh, I could," he said. "But I'm a lazy son of a bitch."

I laughed at that, and he joined me with his own chuckle as his grip about my waist tightened. With a little lurch, he lifted me from him. "Hold on," he said as he stood, swinging me into the cradle of his arms as if I was a five-pound bag of sugar. With his vamp strength, he held me with one arm and hoisted his pants up loose about his hips. "Shower?"

My arms were laced about his neck, and I inspected it for bite marks. There wasn't a one, though I knew I had bit down hard enough to leave them. I also knew without looking that he hadn't made a visible mark on me despite his roughness. "That sounds great," I said as he shuffled forward, his jeans still unzipped.

"I'll get you a shower," he said as I looked behind me to my amulets, pants, and one sock strewn on the floor. "And then we'll open all the windows and air the church out. I'll help you finish making your fudge, too. That will help."

"It's brownies."

"Even better. That uses the oven." He hesitated before my bathroom door, and feeling cared for and wanted in his arms, I pushed it open with my foot. The man was strong. I'd give him that. This was as satisfying as the sex. Well, almost.

"You have scented candles, don't you?" he asked as I flicked on the light with my toe.

"I have two X-chromosomes," I said dryly as he set me atop the washer and pulled off my last sock. "I have a candle or two." *He was going to help me into the shower? How sweet.*

"Good. I'll get one going in the sanctuary. Tell Ivy you put it there in the window for Jenks, and you can keep it going until sunup."

A whisper of unease pulled me straight, and my motions grew slow as I pulled my sweater over my head and dropped it onto the washer. "Ivy?" I questioned.

Kisten leaned against the wall and took off his boots. "You don't mind telling her?"

His boot thumped into the far wall, and my face went cold. *Ivy. Scented candles. Airing out the church. Making brownies to scent the air. Washing his scent off me. Swell.*

Smiling his bad-boy smile, Kisten padded to me in his socks and open jeans. His wide hand cupped my jaw and he leaned close. "I don't mind if she knows," he said, and I didn't move, enjoying the warmth. "She's going to find out eventually. But I'd break it to her gently if I were you, not dump it on her." He gave me a soft kiss on the corner of my mouth. His hand trailed reluctantly from me as he backed up and opened the door to the shower.

Crap, I'd forgotten about Ivy. "Yeah," I said distantly, recalling her jealousy, her dislike of surprises, and how badly she reacted to both. "You think she's going to be upset?"

Kisten turned, his shirt off and water beading on his hand from feeling the temperature. "Upset? She's going to be as jealous as a green apple that you and I have a physical way to express our relationship and she doesn't."

Frustration filled me. "Damn it, Kisten. I'm not going to let her bite me so she knows I like her. Sex and blood. Blood and sex. It's the same thing, and I can't do that with Ivy. I'm not wired that way!"

He shook his head, a sad smile on him. "You can't say blood and sex are the same thing. You've never given blood to another. You have nothing to base your view on."

I frowned. "Every time a vamp puts his eyes on me looking for a snack, it feels sexual."

He came forward, wedging his body between my knees, pressing close up to the washer. His hand went out, and he pushed my hair back over my shoulder. "Most living vampires who are looking for a quick fix find a willing partner faster when they stir them sexually. But Rachel, the meaning behind the giving and receiving blood isn't supposed to be based on sex but respect and love. That you can't be moved by the promise of great sex is why Ivy gave up that tack with you so quickly. But she's still hunting you."

I thought of all the facets of Ivy that Skimmer's appearance had forced me to openly acknowledge. "I know."

"Once she gets over her initial anger, I think she'll be all right with us dating."

"I never said I was dating you."

He smiled knowingly and touched my cheek. "But if I took your blood, even in accident or a moment of passion?" Kisten's blue eyes pinched in worry. "One scratch and she'd stake me. The entire city knows she's put a claim on you, and God help the vamp that gets in her way. I took your body. If I touch your blood, I'm dead twice."

I went cold. "Kisten, you're scaring me."

"You should be scared, little witch. She's going to be the most powerful vampire in Cincinnati someday, and she wants to be *your* friend. She wants you to be *her* savior. She thinks you'll either find a way to kill the vamp virus in her so she can die with her soul intact, or be her scion so she can die knowing that you'll be there to take care of her."

"Kisten. Stop."

Smiling, he kissed my forehead. "Don't worry. Nothing has changed from yesterday. Tomorrow will be the same. She's your friend, and she won't ask anything you can't give."

"That doesn't help."

He shrugged, and with a last touch on my side, he took a step back. Steam billowed out from the crack in the door as Kisten shimmied out of his jeans and leaned into the shower to adjust the temperature again. My eyes ran from his well-toned calves to his tight behind to his broad back, lightly muscled. All thoughts of Ivy's coming anger vanished. *Damn.*

As if feeling my eyes on him, he turned, catching me ogling him.

The steam eddied about him. Drops of moisture from the showerhead clung to his stubble. "Let me help you get your camisole off," he said, the timbre of his voice shifting.

I ran my eyes down him again, grinning as I brought my gaze up. *Double damn.*

He slipped his hands behind my back, and with a little help on my part, he nudged me forward to the edge of the dryer and slipped my halter top off. Wrapping my legs around him, I laced my hands behind his neck and tucked my chin into the hollow of his neck. God help me, he was beautiful. "Kisten?" I questioned as he nuzzled my hair out of the way and found the ticklish spot behind my ear. A warm feeling started in my middle, stemming from where his lips touched me, demanding I recognize it. Accept it. Call it a good thing.

"Do you still have that tight leather biker outfit?" I asked, kind of embarrassed.

Lifting me off the washer and carrying me into the shower, he laughed.

Twenty-two

I smiled as the music ended, to leave a comfortable silence. The ticking of the clock above the sink became loud in the candlelit air. My eyes went to the hand jerking about the dial. It was creeping up on four in the morning, and I had nothing to do but sit and daydream about Kisten. He had left about three to handle the crowd at Piscary's, leaving me warm, content, and happy.

We had spent the entire early evening together eating BLTs and junk food, ransacking Ivy's and my music collection and then using her computer to burn a CD of our favorites. In retrospect, I think it had been the most enjoyable evening of my entire adult life as we laughed over each other's memories and I realized I enjoyed sharing more than my body with him.

Every candle I owned was lit as insurance that I'd be able to pick the time I told Ivy about my new arrangement with Kisten, and their glow added to the peace instilled by the soft burble of potpourri over the stove and the slight lethargy from the pain amulet about my neck. The air smelled of ginger, popcorn, and brownies, and as I sat at Ivy's table with my elbows to either side of me, I played with my amulets and wondered what Kisten was doing.

Much as I didn't want to admit it, I really liked him, and that I could have gone from fear to dislike to attraction and interest in less than a year left me concerned and embarrassed. It wasn't like me to overlook my healthy distrust of vampires because of a tight butt and a charming demeanor.

Living with a vampire might have something to do with it, I thought, dipping my hand into the nearby bowl of popcorn and eating a piece because it was there, rather than out of any need to satisfy hunger. I didn't think my new attitude was because of my scar; I had liked Kisten before the sex, or there wouldn't have been any—and he hadn't played upon it to influence me, either.

Wiping my fingers free of the salt, I stared into nothing. I had been thinking of Kisten differently since he'd dressed me up and made me feel good. *Maybe,* I thought, picking out another kernel. Maybe I could find something with a vampire that I'd never been able to hold on to with a witch, warlock, or human.

Chin in the cup of my palm, I sent my fingers lightly over the demon scar as I recalled his careful attention as he shampooed my hair and soaped my back, and how good it felt to be able to return the favor. He had let me hog the showerhead most of the time. That kind of stuff was important.

The sound of the front door opening jerked my attention to the clock. *Ivy was home? Already?* I had wanted to be tucked in bed pretending sleep when she came in.

"You up, Rachel?" she said, loud enough to be heard and soft enough to not wake me.

"Kitchen," I called back. Nervous, I glanced at the potpourri. It was enough. Kisten had said it was. Standing, I flicked on the overhead light and resettled myself. As the fluorescent bulbs flickered on, I tucked my amulets behind my sweater and listened to her thump about in her room. Her steps in the hall were quick and stilted.

"Hi," I said when she walked in, a vision of tight leather and tall boots. A black satchel was over one arm, and a silk-wrapped package about the size of a broken fishing pole was in her hand. My eyebrows rose as I realized she had put on makeup. Her image was both professional and sexy. Where was she going this late? And dressed like that?

"What happened with dinner with the folks?" I prompted.

"Change of plans." Setting her stuff beside me on the table, she crouched to dig in a lower drawer. "I came to get a few things, then I'm gone." Still at knee level, she smiled at me to show teeth. "I'll be back in a couple of hours."

"Okay," I said, slightly confused. She looked happy. She actually looked happy.

"It's cold in here," she said as she pulled out three of my wooden stakes and set them clattering on the counter by the sink. "It smells like you had the windows open."

"Um, it must be from our plywood door." My brow furrowed as she stood, tugging the hem of her leather jacket down. Crossing the room with a speed just shy of eerie, she unzipped the satchel and jammed the stakes into it. I silently watched her, wondering.

Ivy hesitated. "Can I use them?" she asked, mistaking my silence for disapproval.

"Sure. Keep them," I said, wondering what was up. I hadn't seen her in this much leather since she took that run to liberate a vamp child from a jealous ex. And I really didn't want a stake back if it had been used.

"Thanks." Boot heels clacking on the linoleum, she went to the coffeemaker. Her oval face creased in annoyance as she peered at the empty carafe.

"You have a run?" I asked.

"Sort of." Her enthusiasm dimmed, and I watched her throw the old grounds away.

Curiosity got the better of me, and I flicked back the silk covering to see what was under it. "Holy crap!" I exclaimed as I found a shiny length of steel smelling faintly of oil. "Where did you get a sword!"

"Nice, isn't it." Not turning, she added three scoops of coffee to the filter and set it to brew. "And you can't trace it like bullets or charms."

Oh, such a warm and fuzzy thought. "Can you use it?"

Ivy pushed herself from the counter. I leaned back in my chair as she shook the wrap off, grasping the handle of the thin sword and pulling it from the back sheath. It came free with a whisper of ringing steel that tickled my inner ear. Like collapsing silk, her posture melted into a classic pose, her free arm arched over her head and her sword arm bent and extended. Her face was empty as she looked at the wall, her black hair swinging to a slow stop.

I had a freaking vampire samurai warrior for a roommate. This was getting better and better. "And you know how to use it, too," I said faintly.

She flashed me a smile as she stood and wedged it back into its sheath. "I took lessons from fifth grade through high school," she said as she set it on the table. "I grew so fast that it was hard to keep my balance. I kept running into things. Mostly people who irritated me. Adolescence is when the faster reflexes kick in. The practice helped, and I stuck with it."

I licked the salt off my fingers and pushed the popcorn away. I was willing to bet the classes had a good section devoted to self-control. Feeling more relaxed since the candles seemed to be working, I stretched my legs out under the table, wanting some of the coffee. Ivy rummaged in an upper cupboard to bring out her thermos. I eyed the dripping coffee, hoping she wasn't going to take it all.

"Well," she said as she filled the metal vacuum bottle with hot water to warm it up. "You look like the vamp who bled the cat."

"Beg pardon?" I said, stomach clenching.

She turned and dried her hands off on a dishcloth. "Did Nick call?"

"No," I said flatly.

Her smile widened. Swinging her hair out of her way, she said, "Good." Then, softly, she repeated, "That's good."

This was not where I wanted the conversation to go. Rising, I wiped my palms on my jeans and padded in my bare feet to turn the flame up under the potpourri. Ivy yanked open the fridge and came out with the cream cheese and a bag of bagels. The woman ate as if calories couldn't stick to her. "No Jenks?" I asked, though the answer was obvious.

"No Jenks. He did talk to me, though." Her eyes were pinched with frustration. "I told him I knew what Trent was, too, and to get over it. Now he won't talk to me, either." She popped the lid on the cream cheese and scraped a knifeful across her bagel. "Do you think we should put an ad in the paper?"

My head rose. "To replace him?" I stammered.

Ivy took a bite and shook her head. "Just shake him up," she said around her full mouth. "Maybe if he sees our ad for pixy backup, he'll talk to us."

Frowning, I sat down in my spot and slouched, extending my legs to put my bare feet on her unused chair. "I doubt it. It would be just like him to tell us to take a flying leap."

Ivy lifted one shoulder and let it fall. "It's not like we can do anything until spring."

"I suppose." God, this was depressing. I had to find a way to apologize to Jenks. Maybe if I sent him a clown-delivered telegram. Maybe if I was the clown. "I'll talk to him again," I said. "Take him some honey. Maybe if I get him drunk, he'll forgive me for being such an ass."

"I'll pick some up while I'm out," she offered. "I saw some gourmet honey made from Japanese cherry blossoms." Dumping the water from the thermos, she refilled it with the entire carafe of coffee, sealing the heavenly scent in metal and glass.

Biting back my disappointment, I pulled my feet off her chair. Obviously she had been thinking about how to soothe Jenks's pride as well. "So where are you going this late with a thermos of coffee, a bag of stakes, and that sword?" I asked.

Ivy leaned against the counter with the sleek grace of a black panther, the half-eaten bagel perched on her finger-tips. "I have to lean on some uppity vamps. Keep them up past their bedtime. The sword is for show, the stakes to remember me by, and the coffee is for me."

I made a face, imagining just how nasty it could be to have Ivy keep you up. Especially if she applied herself. But then my eyes widened as I put two and two together. "You're doing this for Piscary?" I said, sure I was right when she turned to look out the window.

"Yup."

Silently I waited, hoping she'd say something. She didn't. I ran my attention over her, taking in her closed posture. "Your dad worked something out?" I hinted.

She sighed and turned to me. "As long as I handle Piscary's affairs, the bastard won't be dipping into my head." She looked at her half-eaten bagel. Frowning, she clacked her boots to the trash and threw it away.

I said nothing, surprised she had capitulated so easily. Apparently hearing in my silence an accusation that wasn't there, her smooth face went ashamed. "Piscary agreed to let me continue using Kisten as my frontman," she said. "He likes the notoriety, and anyone who is important will know that whatever he says is really coming from me—I mean, Piscary. I don't have to do anything unless Kisten runs into something he can't handle. Then I'll go in as the muscle to bail him out."

My memories returned to Kisten taking down seven witches with the ease and nonchalance of breaking a candy bar. I couldn't imagine anything he couldn't handle, but then again, he wouldn't be able to go up against undead vampires without leaning on Piscary's strength. "And you're okay with this?" I said stupidly.

"No," she said, crossing her arms before her. "But it's what my dad came up with, and if I can't accept how he helped me, I shouldn't have asked for it."

"Sorry," I muttered, wishing I had kept my mouth shut.

Apparently mollified, Ivy crossed the kitchen and put the thermos in with the stakes. "I don't want Piscary in my head," she said, giving her satchel a shake to settle everything before zipping it closed. "As long as I do what he says, he'll stay out; and he'll leave Erica alone. Kisten should be his scion, not me," she muttered. "He wants it."

I absently agreed, and her fingers on the bag went still, her face carrying a shadow of the pain I recognized from the night Piscary had raped her in more ways than one. A chill struck through me as her nostrils flared and her focus went distant. "Kisten was here," she said softly.

My skin tightened. *Damn. I hadn't been able to keep it from her for even a night.* "Uh, yeah," I said as I pulled myself straighter in my chair. "He was here looking for you." *About half the day ago.* The chill inside me deepened when her focus narrowed, reading my unease. Her head shifted to look at the potpourri on the stove. *Double damn.*

Lips pressed tight, she walked out, heels clacking.

The wood chair scraped loudly as I stood. "Um, Ivy?" I called, following her out.

My breath caught and I jerked to a stop when I almost ran into her in the dark hallway on her way back from the sanctuary. "Excuse me," she muttered, shifting around me with a vamp's speed. Her posture was tense, and in the light leaking in from the kitchen, I could see her eyes were dilated. *Crap. She was vamping out.*

"Ivy?" I said to the empty hall, as she had walked into the living room. "About Kisten—"

My words choked off and I halted, my feet edging the gray carpet in the candlelit living room. Ivy stood with a ridged stiffness before the couch. The couch Kisten and I had had sex on. Emotions cascaded over her, frightening in their rapidity: dismay, fear, anger, betrayal. I jumped when she jerked into motion, jabbing at the CD-check button.

The five CDs came rolling halfway out. Ivy stared at them, stiffening. "I'll kill him," she said, her fingers touching Jeff Buckley.

Shocked, I opened my mouth to protest, finding my words dying to nothing at the anger, black and heavy, in her tight expression.

"I'll kill him twice," she said. She knew. Somehow she knew.

My heart pounded. "Ivy," I started, hearing the fear in my voice. And with that, I jerked her instincts into play. Gasping, I backpedaled, far too slow.

"Where is it?" she hissed, her eyes wide and wild as she reached for me.

"Ivy . . ." My back hit the wall of the hallway, and I knocked her hand aside. "He didn't bite me."

"Where is it!"

Adrenaline surged. Smelling it, she jerked her hand out, reaching. Her eyes were black and lost. It was only our former sparring that kept her grip from landing as I blocked her reach and dove under her arm to come to a stand in the middle of the candlelit living room.

"Back off, Ivy!" I exclaimed, trying not to fall into a defensive crouch. "He didn't bite me!" But I didn't have time to breathe before she was on me, jerking the collar of my sweater.

"Where did he bite you?" she said, her gray voice trembling. "I'll kill him. I'll freaking kill him! I can smell him all over you!"

Her hand jerked to the hem of my sweater.

It tripped me over the panic line, and instinct took over. "Ivy! Stop!" I shouted. Frightened, I tapped the line. She reached for me, face twisted in anger. The line filled my chi, wild and out of control. A burst of energy flamed from my hands, burning them, as I hadn't harnessed it with a charm.

We both cried out as a black and gold sheet of ever-after expanded from me, knocking Ivy back into the plywood door. She slid to the floor in an awkward heap, her arms over her head and her legs askew. The windows shook at the boom. I rocked back, then caught my balance. Anger replaced my fear. I didn't care if she was all right or not.

"He didn't bite me!" I shouted, spitting my hair out of my mouth as I stood over her. "Okay? We had sex. All right? God help you, Ivy. It was only sex!"

Ivy coughed. Red-faced and gasping, she found her breath. The plywood sheet behind her was cracked. Shaking her head, she peered up at me, clearly not focusing yet. She didn't get up. "He didn't bite you?" she rasped, her face shadowy in the candlelight.

My legs trembled from adrenaline. "No!" I exclaimed. "You think I'm stupid?"

Clearly shaken, she looked askance at me. Taking a slow breath, she wiped her lower lip with the back of her hand. My gut tightened as it came away red with blood. Ivy stared at it, then gathered her legs under her and got to her feet. I breathed easier when she reached for a tissue, wiping her hand off and crumpling it into a ball.

She reached out, and I sprang back. "Don't touch me!" I said, and she raised a hand in acquiescence.

"Sorry." She looked at the cracked plywood, then winced as she felt her back. Carefully she tugged her coat down. Eyes going to mine, she took a slow breath. My heart pounded in time to the pain in my head. "You slept with Kisten and he didn't bite you?" she asked.

"Yes. And no, he didn't bite me. And if you *ever* touch me again, I'm walking out the front door, forever. Damn it, Ivy. I thought we were clear on this!"

I expected an apology or something, but all she did was eye me speculatively and ask, "Are you sure? You might not even notice if he cut your inner lip."

Goose bumps rose, and I ran my tongue across the inside of my mouth. "He wore caps," I said, feeling ill for how easily he could have tricked me. But he hadn't.

Ivy blinked. Slowly she sat on the edge of the couch, her elbows on her knees and her forehead cupped in the cradle of her hands. Her thin body looked vulnerable in the light from the three candles on the table. Crap. It suddenly occurred to me that not only did she want a closer relationship with me, but that Kisten was her old boyfriend. "Ivy? Are you okay?"

"No."

I cautiously sat on the chair across from her, the corner of the table between us. By any standards, this was a complete shitfest. I cursed silently, then reached out. "Ivy. God, this is awkward."

She jumped at the weight of my hand on her arm, looking up with frighteningly dry eyes. I pulled back, laying my hand like a dead thing in my lap. I knew I shouldn't touch her when she wanted more. But to sit and do nothing was so cold.

"It just kind of happened."

Ivy touched her lip to see that it had stopped bleeding. "It was just sex? You didn't give him your blood?"

The vulnerability in her voice struck me. My head bobbed. I felt like a doll, my eyes wide and my thoughts empty. "I'm sorry," I said. "I didn't think you and Kisten . . ." I hesitated. This wasn't about the sex, but the blood she thought I had given him. "I didn't think you and Kisten had a formal relationship anymore," I fumbled, unsure if I was putting it right.

"I don't share blood with Kisten but for the rare occasion when he's been dumped and needs some TLC," she said, her gray silk voice soft. Still she wouldn't look up. "Blood is not sex, Rachel. It's a way to show you care for someone. A way to show . . . you love them."

It was barely a whisper. My breath grew fast. I felt we were balanced on a knife's edge, and it scared the crap out of me. "How can you say sex isn't blood, when you'll have sex with anyone?" I said, adrenaline making my voice harsher than I intended. "Good God, Ivy, when was the last time you had sex *without* blood?"

Only now did she bring her head up, shocking me with the fear in her eyes. She was afraid, and not because she thought I'd given my blood to Kisten. She was afraid of the answers I was demanding. I don't think she had faced them before, even in the chaos her desires had left her in. I felt hot, then cold. Pulling my knees to my chin, I tucked my bare heels against me.

"Okay," she said with the last of her exhaled breath, and I knew the next thing she said would be stark honesty. "You have a good point. I usually include blood with sex. I like it that way. It's a rush. Rachel, if you would only . . ." she said, her hands coming up from her knees.

I felt myself pale. I shook my head, and she changed her mind about what she was going to say. She seemed to deflate, all the tension pooling out of her. "Rachel, it's not the same," she finished weakly, brown eyes pleading.

My thoughts went to Kist. The twinge from my scar dove to my groin and brought my breath even faster. Swallowing, I forced the feeling from me. I pulled back, glad the table was between us. "That's what Kisten says, but I can't separate it. And I don't think you can either."

Ivy's face went red, and I knew I was right.

"Damn it, Ivy. I'm not saying it's wrong they're the same," I said. "Hell, I've been living with you for seven months. Don't you think by now you'd know if I thought it was? But that's not the way I'm put together. You're the best friend I've ever had, but I'm not going to share a pillow with you, and I'm never going to let anyone taste my blood." I took a breath. "I'm not put together that way, either. And I can't live my life avoiding a real relationship with someone because it might hurt your feelings. I told you it's not going to happen between us, and it's not. Maybe . . ." I felt sick. "Maybe I should move out."

"Move out?"

It was a breathy sound of dismay, and the warmth of tears stung my eyes. I stared at the wall, jaw clenched. The last seven months had been the most frightening, scary, and best months of my life. I didn't want to leave—and not just because she was protecting me from another vampire biting and claiming me—but staying here wasn't fair to either of us if she couldn't let it go.

"Jenks is gone," I said, my voice low so it wouldn't shake. "I just slept with your old boyfriend. It's not fair to stay here if there is never going to be anything more than friendship between us. Especially now that Skimmer is back." I looked at the broken door, hating myself. "We should just call everything quits."

God, why was I almost crying? I couldn't give her any more, and she desperately needed it. Skimmer could; Skimmer wanted to. I should leave. But when I looked up, I was shocked to see the candlelight glinting upon a ribbon of moisture under her eye.

"I don't want you to go," she said, and the lump in my throat thickened. "A good friendship is reason enough to stay, isn't it?" she whispered, her eyes so full of pain that a tear leaked out of me.

"Damn it," I said, wiping a finger under my eye. "Look what you made me do."

I jerked when she reached across the table and took my wrist. My eyes were riveted to hers as she pulled it to her and touched my tear-damp fingertips to her lips. Her eyes closed and her lashes fluttered. A zing of adrenaline struck me. My pulse quickened, the memory of vampire-induced ecstasy high in my thoughts. "Ivy?" I said weakly, pulling away.

She let go. My heart pounded as she took a slow breath, tasting the air with her senses, running my emotions through her incredible brain, reading the balance of what I might and might not do. I didn't want to know what her calculations totaled to.

"I'll pack my things," I said, frightened that she might know more about me than I did.

Her eyes opened. I thought I saw a faint glimmer of strength. "No," she said, the first hint of her iron will returning. "We're both crap when we're alone, and I'm not just talking about the stupid firm. I promise I won't ask anything of you except to be my friend. Please . . ." She took a breath. "Please don't go because of this, Rachel. Do what you want with Kist. He's a good man and I know he won't hurt you. Just . . ." She held her breath, her determination faltering. "Just be here when I come home tonight?"

I nodded. I knew she wasn't just asking about tonight. And I didn't want to leave. I loved it here: the kitchen, the witch's garden, the cool-factor of living in a church. That she valued our friendship meant a lot to me, and after avoiding true friendship for years because of what had happened to my dad, having a best friend meant a lot to me too. She had once threatened to withdraw her desperately needed protection from me if I left. This time, she hadn't. I was afraid to look for the reason, afraid that it might stem from that tiny thrill I had felt when she had tasted my tears.

"Thank you," she said, and I froze as she leaned forward over the table to give me a quick hug. The scent of almonds and leather filled my senses. "If Kisten can convince you that blood isn't sex," she said, "promise to tell me?"

I stared at her. The memory of Skimmer kissing her flashed through me and was gone.

Apparently satisfied, she let go, stood, and went into the kitchen.

"Ivy," I breathed, too numb and strung out to speak louder, knowing she could hear me. "How many rules are we breaking?"

She hesitated as she appeared in the hallway, satchel and sword in hand, shifting from foot to foot and not answering me. "I'll be back after sunrise. Maybe we can have a late dinner? Gossip about Kisten over lasagna? He's actually a nice guy—he'll be good for you." Giving me an awkward smile, she left.

Her voice had held a faint ribbon of regret, but I didn't know if it was for having lost me or Kisten. I didn't want to know. I stared at the carpet, not seeing the candles or smelling the scent of wax and perfume as the faint boom of the door shifted the air. How had my life gotten this screwed up? All I had wanted to do was quit the I.S., help a few people, make something of myself and my degree. Since then I had found and driven away my first real boyfriend in years, insulted a pixy clan, become Ivy's golden ring, and had sex with a living vampire. That wasn't even counting the two death threats I'd survived or the precarious situation with Trent. What the hell was I doing?

Rising, I stumbled into the kitchen, face cold and legs feeling like rubber. Looking up at the sound of running water, I froze. Algaliarept was at the sink filling the teapot, its tarnished copper beading with condensation.

"Good evening, Rachel," he said, smiling to show me flat teeth. "Hope you don't mind me making a pot of tea. We have a lot to do before the sun comes up."

Oh God. I'd forgotten about that.

Twenty-three

"**D**amn!" I swore, backpedaling. The sanctuary. If I could reach holy ground, he couldn't touch me. I shrieked as a heavy hand fell on my shoulder. Spinning, I clawed at his face. It went misty, and I lurched when his grip vanished. In an instant he had my ankle and jerked me off my feet. "Let go!" I shouted when I hit the floor, my voice harsh as I kicked him.

He spun me sliding into the fridge. His long face took on a sun-starved complexion and his red goat eyes turned eager over his smoked glasses. I scrambled up, and he lunged, grabbing me with his white-gloved hand and giving me a shake to rattle my teeth. He shoved me, and I landed against the center island counter like a rag doll. Turning, I put my back against it, wide-eyed and heart beating fast. I was so stupid. I was *so stupid!*

"If you run again, I'll call you in breach of our agreement," he said calmly. "That's your warning. Please run. It will make everything so-o-o-o much simpler."

Shaking, I held onto the counter for balance. "Go away," I said. "I didn't summon you."

"It's not that simple anymore," he said. "It took me a day in the library, but I found precedence." His precise accent became even more officious, and he put the back of his knuckles to his velvet green frock and quoted, " 'If said familiar is stationed at a beta site by way of loan or similar event, the master may seek the familiar out to perform duties.' You opened the door by tapping a line," he added. "And since I have a task for you, I'm here until you finish it."

I felt sick. "What do you want?" There was a spell pot on my counter full of an amber liquid smelling of geranium. I hadn't counted on him bringing his work to me.

"What do you want—master," Al prompted, smiling to show me his thick, blocky teeth.

I tucked my hair behind my ear. "I want you to get the hell out of my kitchen."

His smile never flickered as, with a powerful motion, he backhanded me. I stifled a gasp, lurching for balance. Adrenaline surged as he gripped my shoulder, keeping me upright.

"Funny, funny girl," he murmured, his British elegance chilling me and his beautiful chiseled looks turning harsh. "Say it."

The sharp taste of blood edged my tongue. My back pressed into the counter painfully. "What do you want, oh gracious master from my ass."

I didn't have time to duck as the flat of his hand swung. Pain shocked through my cheek, and I hit the floor. Al's silver-buckled boots edged my vision. He was wearing white stockings, and there was lace where they met the bottom of his trousers.

Nausea rose. I touched my cheek, feeling it burn and hating him. I tried to rise, unable to when he put a foot on my shoulder and forced me down. Hating him all the more, I tossed my hair aside so I could see him. *What difference did it make?* "What do you want, master?"

I felt like I was going to vomit.

His thin lips curled up in a smile. Tugging the lace from his sleeves, he bent to solicitously help me up. I refused, but he yanked me up so fast that I found myself pressed against him, breathing in the scent of crushed velvet and burnt amber. "I want this," he whispered, running a hand up under my sweater, searching.

My heart raced. Stiffening, I clenched my teeth. *I'll kill him. Somehow, I'll kill him.*

"Such a touching conversation with your roommate," he said, and I twitched, as his voice had shifted to Ivy's. Ever-after zinged through me as his appearance shifted while still touching me. Red goat eyes stared at me from Ivy's perfect face. Lean and tight, the image of her body wrapped in leather pressed against me, pinning me to the counter. The last time, he had bitten me. *Oh, God. Not again.*

"But maybe you want this instead," he said with her gray silk voice, and sweat started at the small of my back. Her long straight hair brushed my cheek, the silky whisper pulling an unstoppable shiver from my skin. Feeling it where our bodies touched, he leaned close until I recoiled.

"Don't pull away," he said with her voice, and my resolve grew. He was slime. He was a bastard. I'd kill him for this. "I'm sorry, Rachel. . . ." he breathed, long fingers burning into tingles where they touched, tracing a line from my shoulder to my hip. "I'm not angry. I understand you're afraid. But the things I could teach you—if you knew the heights of passion we could find." His breath shuddered. Ivy's arms were around me cool and light—gentling me to him against my will. I could smell her rich scent of dark incense and ash. He had her perfectly.

"Let me show you?" the vision of Ivy whispered, and I closed my eyes. "Just a taste . . . I know I can change your mind."

It was pleading, heavy with her vulnerable desires. It was everything she hadn't said, everything she wouldn't. My eyes opened as my scar flashed to life. *God, no.* Fire raced to my groin. Knees buckling, I tried to push away. Demon-red eyes shifted to a liquid brown, and his grip grew firmer, pulling me closer until his breath came and went on my neck. "Gently, Rachel," her voice whispered. "I could be so gentle. I could be everything a man can't be. Everything you want. Just one little word, Rachel. Tell me you will?"

I couldn't . . . I couldn't deal with this right now. "Didn't you have something for me to do?" I said. "The sun will be up soon and I need to get to bed."

"Slowly," he crooned, Ivy's breath smelling of oranges. "There's only one first time."

"Let go of me," I said tightly. "You aren't Ivy and I'm not interested."

Ivy's passion-filled black eyes narrowed, but Al's attention was over my shoulder and I didn't think it was anything I had said. He let go of me, and I stumbled to catch my balance. A shimmer of ever-after cascaded over him, melting his features back to his usual vision of a young British lord of the eighteenth century. The glasses were back to hide his eyes, and he adjusted them on his thin-bridged nose. "How grand," he said, his accent shifting as well. "Ceri."

There was the distant boom of the front door crashing open. "Rachel!" came her voice, high and frightened. "He's this side of the lines!"

Heart pounding, I spun. I took a breath to warn her, but it was too late. My outstretched hand fell as she lurched into the room, her simple white dress furling about her bare feet as she stopped in the archway. Green eyes wide and soulful, she put a hand to her chest atop Ivy's crucifix. "Rachel . . ." she breathed, dismay slumping her shoulders.

Al took a step and she spun in a dancer's circle, toe pointed and unbound hair furling. She recited an unheard poem laced with darkness, and a ripple of line energy cascaded between us. White-faced and holding her arms, she stared at him, trembling within her small circle.

The stately demon beamed, adjusting the lace about his collar. "Ceri. How splendid to see you. I miss you, love," he almost purred.

The young woman's chin trembled. "Banish him, Rachel," she said, her fear obvious.

I tried to swallow, failing. "I tapped a line. He found precedence. He has a task for me."

Her eyes widened. "No . . ."

Al frowned. "I haven't been in the library in a thousand years. They were whispering behind my back, Ceri. I had to renew my card. It was most embarrassing. Everyone knows you're gone. Zoë is making my tea. It's the most awful tea I've ever had—he can't hold the sugar spoon with only two digits. Do come back." His pleasant face creased into a smile. "I'll make it worth your soul."

Ceri jerked. Chin high, she said haughtily, "My name is Ceridwen Merriam Dulciate."

A rough sound of mirth escaped him. Taking off his glasses, he leaned an elbow against the counter. Mocking gaze on mine, he murmured, "Ceri, be a dear and make a spot of tea?"

My face went slack as Ceri dropped her head and took a step. Al chuckled when she made a cry of self-disgust and stopped at the edge of her circle. Tiny fists clenched, she fumed.

"Old habits die hard," he mocked.

Bile bubbled up. Even now she was his. "Leave her alone," I snarled.

From nowhere, a white-gloved hand struck me. I spun into the counter, jaw burning. Gasping, I hunched over it with my hair falling about my face. I was getting tired of this.

"Don't hit her!" Ceri said, her voice high and virulent.

"Does it bother you?" he said lightly. "Pain moves her more than fear. Which is good—pain keeps a person alive longer than fear."

My hurt turned to anger. Eyebrows high, he dared me to protest as I found my breath. His goat eyes slid to the head-sized vat he had brought with him. "Let's get started, shall we?"

I looked at the pot, recognizing the brew by the smell. It

was the one to make a person into a familiar. Fear chilled me, and I wrapped my arms about myself. "I'm already coated with your aura," I said. "Making me take more isn't going to make a difference."

"I didn't ask for your opinion."

I sprang back as he moved. Grinning, he extended the basket that had appeared in his hand. I could smell wax. "Set the candles," he ordered, amused at my quick reaction.

"Rachel . . ." Ceri whispered, but I couldn't look at her. I had promised to be his familiar, and now I would be. Miserable, my thoughts went to Ivy as I set the milky green candles at the spots marked by black nail polish. Why couldn't I make good choices?

My grip on the last candle trembled. It had gouges on it, as if something had tried to break the circle by going through it. Something with big nasty claws.

"Rachel!" Al barked, and I jumped. "You didn't set them with their place names."

Still holding the last candle, I stared blankly. Past him, Ceri nervously licked her lips.

"You don't know their place names," Al added, and I shook my head, not wanting to be hit again, but Al only sighed. "I'll set them myself when I light them," he grumbled, his pale face taking on a ruddy tinge. "I expected more of you than this. Apparently you've been spending most of your time with earth magic, neglecting your ley line arts."

"I'm an earth witch," I said. "Why would I bother?"

Ceri jerked as Al threatened to smack me again, her almost translucent hair swirling. "Let her go, Algaliarept. You don't want her for a familiar."

"Offering to take her place?" he mocked, and I took a fearful breath that she might.

"No!" I shouted, and he laughed.

"Don't fret, Rachel, love," he crooned, and I flinched when he ran a gloved finger across my jawline, tracing the path down my arm to my hand to take the last candle from me. "I keep my familiars until something better comes along, and despite you being as ignorant as a frog, you're capable of holding almost twice the line energy that she can." He leered. "Lucky you."

Clapping his white-gloved hands once, he spun to make his coattails furl. "Now. Watch closely, Rachel. You'll be lighting my candles tomorrow. These are words that move mortals and gods alike, making all equal and capable of keeping my circle whole against even Newt."

Swell.

"*Salax,*" he said as he lit the first candle from the pencil-thick red taper that had appeared in his gloved hand. "*Aemulatio,*" he said as he lit the second. "*Adfictatio, cupidus,* and my favorite, *inscitia,*" he said as he lit the last one. Smiling, the still-glowing taper vanished. I felt him tap a line, and with a translucent swirl of red and black, his circle rose to arch closed over our heads. My skin prickled from its strength, and I clasped my arms about myself.

These are a few of my favorite things, I heard patter through my mind, and I stifled a hysterical giggle. I was going to be a demon's familiar. There was no way out of it now.

Al's head jerked up at the ugly choking sound, and Ceri's face went still. "Algaliarept," she pleaded. "You're pushing her too hard. Her will is too strong to bend easily."

"I'll break my familiars the way I see fit," he said calmly. "A little grounding, and she'll be as right as rain in the desert." One hand on his hip and the other cupping his chin, he eyed me speculatively. "Time for your bath, love."

Algaliarept snapped his fingers with a showman's flair. His hand opened, and a cedar-slatted bucket appeared hanging from it. My eyes widened as he threw its contents at me.

Cold water smacked into me. My breath whooshed out in an affronted yelp. It was saltwater, stinging my eyes and dribbling into my mouth. Reality washed through me, clearing my head. He was making sure I didn't have any potions in me to contaminate the coming spell. "I don't use potions, you big green turd!" I shouted, shaking my arms in my sodden sleeves.

"See?" Al was clearly pleased. "All better."

The slight ache of my ribs intruded as my pain charm broke. Most of the water was soaking my spell book library. If I survived this, I'd have to air them all out. What a jerk.

"Ooooh, your eye is doing nicely," he said as he reached forward to touch it. "Eating your roommate's Brimstone, are we? Wait until you try the real stuff. It will knock your socks off."

I jerked back when his gloved hand brushed my skin with the scent of lavender, but Al's hand dropped lower to grasp my hair. Shrieking, I swung my foot up. He caught it, moving faster than I could follow. Ceri watched in pity as I fought, helpless. Holding my foot high, he forced me against the counter. His glasses had been knocked aside, and he smiled at me with a domineering delight. "The hard way," he whispered. "Marvelous."

"No!" I exclaimed as a pair of sheers suddenly glinted in his hand.

"Hold still," he said, dropping my foot and pinning me against the counter.

I wiggled and spit at him, but he had me against the counter and I could do nothing. I panicked as I heard metal sheering. He let go by turning misty, and I fell to the floor.

Hand clutching my hair, I scrambled to my feet. "Stop it! Just stop it!" I shouted, alternating my attention between his glee and the chunk he had cut from my hair. Damn it, it was at least four inches long. "Do you know how long it takes to grow my hair out!"

Al gave Ceri a sidelong glance as the scissors disappeared and he dropped my hair into the potion. "She's worried about her hair?"

My gaze shot to the red strands floating on top of Al's brew, and as I stood there in my soggy sweater, I went cold. That vat of potion wasn't for Al to give me more of his aura. It was for me giving him mine. "Oh, hell no!" I exclaimed, backing up. "I'm not giving you my aura!"

Al plucked a ceramic spoon from the rack hanging over

the center island counter and pushed the strands of hair down. He had a refined elegance in his velvet and lace, every inch of him as trim and debonair as inhumanly possible. "Is that a refusal, Rachel?" he murmured. "Please tell me it was?"

"No," I whispered. There was nothing I could do. Nothing.

His smile went wider. "Now your blood to quicken it, love."

Pulse pounding, I looked from the needle between his finger and thumb to the vat. If I ran, I was his. If I did this, he could use me through the lines. Damn, damn, and double damn.

Numbing my thoughts, I took the tarnished silver needle. My mouth went dry as its heavy weight filled my grip. It was as long as my palm and elaborately tooled. The tip was copper so the silver wouldn't interfere with the charm. Peering closer, I felt my stomach turn. There was a naked twisted body writhing around the barrel. "God save me," I whispered.

"He's not listening. He's too busy."

I stiffened. Al had come up behind me and was whispering in my ear.

"Finish the potion, Rachel." His breath was hot on my cheek, and I couldn't move as he pulled my hair back. A shudder rippled through me as he tilted his head and bent closer. "Finish it . . ." he breathed, his lips brushing my skin. I could smell starch and lavender.

Teeth gritted, I gripped the needle and stabbed it into me. My held breath came out, and I held it again. I thought I heard Ceri crying.

"Three drops," Al whispered, nuzzling my neck.

My head hurt. Blood pounding, I held my finger over the vat and massaged three drops into it. The scent of redwood rose, briefly overpowering the cloying stench of burnt amber.

"Mmmm, richer." His hand wrapped around mine, taking the needle back. It vanished in a smear of ever-after, and his grip shifted to my bleeding finger. "Give me a taste?"

I jerked back as far from him as I could, my arm stretched out between us. "No."

"Leave her alone!" Ceri pleaded.

Slowly Al's grip loosened. He watched me, a new tension rising in him.

I wrestled my hand away and put another step between us. I clutched my arms about me, cold despite the heater blowing on my bare feet.

"Get on the mirror," he said, his face expressionless behind his smoked glasses.

My gaze shot to it waiting for me on the floor. "I—I can't," I whispered.

His thin lips pressed together, and I gritted my teeth to keep silent when he picked me up and set me on it. I inhaled, eyes widening when I felt like I slipped two inches into the mirror. "Oh God, oh God," I moaned, wanting to reach for the counter, but Al was in the way, grinning.

"Push your aura off," he said.

"I can't," I panted, feeling myself hyperventilate.

Al pulled his glasses down his thin nose and looked at me over them. "Doesn't matter. It's dissolving like sugar in the rain."

"No," I whispered. My knees started shaking and the pounding in my head worsened. I could feel my aura slipping away and Al's taking a stronger hold on me.

"Capital and fine," Al said, his goat eyes on the mirror.

My gaze followed his, and I clutched at my stomach. I could see myself in it. My face was covered in Al's aura, black and empty. Only my eyes showed, a faint glow flickering about them. It was my soul, trying to make enough aura to put between Al's aura and me. It wasn't enough as the mirror sucked it all up and I could feel Al's presence sink into me.

I found I was panting. I imagined what it must have been like for Ceri, her soul utterly gone and Al's aura seeping into her like this all the time, alien and wrong.

I shook. Hands clasped over my mouth, I looked frantically for something to throw up in. Gagging, I lurched off the mirror. I would not spew. I wouldn't.

"Marvelous," Al said as I hunched over, my teeth clenched and my bile rising. "You got all of it. Here. I'll just slip it into the vat for you."

His voice was cheery and bright, and as I peered at him from around my hair, Al dropped the mirror into the potion. The brew flashed to clear. Just like I knew it would.

Ceri was sitting on the floor, crying with her head on her knees. She pulled her head up, and I thought she looked all the more beautiful for her tears. I only looked ugly when I cried.

I jumped when a thick yellowed tome hit the counter beside me. The light through the window was starting to brighten, but the clock said it was only five. Almost three hours before the sun would rise to end this nightmare, unless Al ended it sooner.

"Read it."

Looking down, I recognized it. It was the book I had found in my attic, the one that Ivy claimed wasn't among the ones she planted up there for me, the very same one that I had given to Nick to hold for me after I accidentally used it to make him my familiar and the same book that Al had tricked away from us. The one Algaliarept wrote to make people into demon familiars. *Shit.*

I swallowed hard. My fingers looked pale as I put them on the text, running down to find the incantation. It was in Latin, but I knew the translation. "Some to you, but all to me," I whispered. "Bound by ties made so by plea."

"Pars tibi, totum mihi," Al said, grinning. *"Vinctus vinculuis, prece fractis."*

My fingers started shaking. "Moon made safe, ancient light made sane. Chaos decreed, taken tripped if bane."

"Luna servata, lux sanata. Chaos statutum, pejus minutum. Go on. Finish."

There was only one line left. One line, and the spell would be complete. Nine words, and my life would be a living hell whether I was on this side of the lines or not. I took a breath. Then another. "Lee of mind," I whispered. My voice trembled, and it was getting harder to breathe. "Bearer of pain. Slave until the worlds are slain . . ."

Al's grin widened and his eyes flashed black. *"Mentem tegens, malum ferens,"* he intoned. *"Semper servus. Dum duret—mundus."*

With an eager impatience, Al pulled his gloves from his hands and plunged his hands into the vat. I jerked. A twang reverberated through me, followed by gut-wrenching dizziness. Black and smothering, the charm wrapped about my soul, numbing me.

Red-knuckled hands dripping, Al steadied himself against the counter. A shimmer of red cascaded over him, and his image blurred before settling. He blinked, seemingly shaken.

I took a breath, then another. It was done. He had my aura for good—all but what my soul was desperately trying to replace to insinuate between my being and Al's aura still coating me. Maybe in time it would get better, but I doubted it.

"Good," he said, tugging his sleeves down and wiping his hands off on a black towel that had appeared in his grip. White gloves materialized, hiding his hands. "Good and done. Capital."

Ceri cried softly, but I was too drained to even look at her.

My cell phone chirped from my bag on the far counter, sounding absurd.

The last of Al's fleeting disquiet vanished. "Oh, do let me answer," he said, breaking the circle as he went to get it.

I shuddered as I felt a slight pull from my empty center as the energy went back through Al and into the line it originated from. Al's eyebrows were high in delight when he turned with my cell phone in his gloved hand. "I wonder who it is?" he simpered.

Unable to stand any longer, I slipped to the floor, my back to the counter as I hugged my knees. The vent air was warm on my bare feet, but my damp jeans soaked up the cold. I was Al's familiar. Why was I even bothering to keep the air moving in and out of my lungs?

"That's why they take your soul," Ceri whispered. "You can't kill yourself if they have your will."

I stared, only now understanding.

"Hello-o-o-o?" Al purred, leaning against the sink, the pink cylinder looking odd against his old world charm. "Nicholas Gregory Sparagmos! What a delight!"

My head came up. "Nick?" I breathed.

Al held a long hand over the receiver and simpered. "It's your boyfriend. I'll field it for you. You look tired." Wrinkling his nose, he turned to the phone. "Feel that, did you?" he said cheerfully. "Something missing, now is there? Be careful what you wish for, little wizard."

"Where's Rachel!" came Nick's voice, thin and tinny. He sounded panicked, and my heart sank. I reached out, knowing Al wouldn't give the phone to me.

"Why, she's at my feet," Al said, grinning. "Mine, all mine. She made a mistake, and now she's mine. Send her flowers for her grave. It's all you can do."

The demon listened for a moment, emotions flickering over him. "Oh, don't be making promises you can't keep. It is so-o-o-o lower class. As it happens, I'm not in need of a familiar anymore, so I won't be responding to your little summons; don't call me. She saved your soul, little man. Too bad you never told her how much you loved her. Humans are so stupid."

He broke the connection with Nick in mid-protest. Snapping the phone closed, he dropped it back in my bag. It started ringing immediately, and he tapped it once. My phone played its obnoxious good-bye song and shut off.

"Now." Al clapped his hands. "Where were we? Ah yes. I'll be right back. I want to see it work." Red eyes glowing in delight, he vanished with a small shift of air.

"Rachel!" Ceri cried. She fell into me, dragging me out of the broken circle. I pushed at her, too depressed to try to get away. It was coming. Al was going to fill me with his force, making me feel his thoughts, turning me into a copper-top battery that could make his tea and do his dishes. The first of my helpless tears dribbled out, but I couldn't find the will to hate myself for them. I knew I should be crying. I had gambled my life to put Piscary away and lost.

"Rachel! Please!" Ceri pleaded, her grip on my arm hurting as she tried to drag me. My damp feet made a squeaking noise, and I pushed at her, trying to get her to stop.

A red bubble of ever-after popped into existence where Al had pinged out. The air pressure violently shifted, and both Ceri and I clasped our hands to our ears.

"Damn it all to heaven and back!" Al swore, his velvet green frock open and in disarray. His hair was wild and his glasses were gone. "You did everything right!" he shouted, gesturing violently. "I've got your aura. You've got mine. Why can't I reach you through the lines!"

Ceri knelt behind me, her arm protectively about me. "It didn't work?" she quavered, pulling me back a little more. Her wet finger traced a quick circle about us.

"Do I look like it worked?" he exclaimed. "Do I look happy to you?"

"No," she breathed, and her circle expanded about us, black-smeared but strong. "Rachel," she said, giving me a squeeze. "You're going to be okay."

Al went still. Deathly quiet, he turned, his boots making a soft sound against the flooring. "No, she isn't."

My eyes widened at his frustrated anger. *Oh God. Not again.*

I stiffened as he tapped a line and sent it crashing into me. With it came a whisper of his emotion, satisfied and anticipatory. Fire coursed through me, and I screamed, pushing Ceri away. Her bubble burst in a glittering sensation of hot needles, adding to my agony.

Curled into a fetal position, I frantically thought the word, *Tulpa,* slumping in relief as the torrent coursed through me and settled in the sphere in my head. Panting, I slowly pulled my head up. Al's confusion and frustration filled me. My anger grew until it overshadowed his emotions.

Al's thoughts in mine shifted to stark surprise. Vision blurring as what I was seeing conflicted with what my brain said was true, I stumbled to my feet. Most of the candles were out, knocked over to make puddles of wax and scenting the air with smoke. Al felt my defiance through our link, and his face turned ugly when my pride for having learned to store energy seeped into him. "Ceri . . ." he threatened, his goat eyes narrowing.

"It didn't work," I said, my voice low as I watched him from around my stringy wet hair. "Get out of my kitchen."

"I'm going to have you, Morgan," Al snarled. "If I can't take you by right, I'll by god beat you into submission and pull you in, broken and bleeding."

"Oh yeah?" I came back with. I glanced at the pot that had held my aura. His eyes widened in surprise as he knew my thought the instant I had it. The bond now went both ways. He had made a mistake.

"Get out of my kitchen!" I exclaimed, dumping the line energy he had forced me to hold back through our familiar link and into him. I jerked upright as it all flowed from me and into him, leaving me empty. Al stumbled backward, shocked.

"You *canicula!*" he cried, his image blurring.

Staggering to remain upright, he tapped the line, adding more force.

Eyes narrowing, I set my thoughts to loop it right back at him. Whatever he was going to send into me was going to end up right back in him.

Al choked as he sensed what I was going to do. There was a sudden wrench in my gut and I stumbled, catching myself against the table as he broke the live connection between us. I stared at him across the kitchen, breath rough. This was going to be settled right here and now. One of us was going to lose. And it wasn't going to be me. Not in my kitchen. Not tonight.

Al put one foot behind him, taking a deceptively relaxed stance. He ran a hand over his hair, smoothing it. His round smoked glasses appeared, and he buttoned his frock. "This isn't working," he said flatly.

"No," I rasped. "It isn't."

Safe in her circle, Ceri snickered. "You can't have her, Algaliarept, you big stupid," she mocked, making me wonder at her word choice. "You made the familiar gate swing both ways when you forced her to give you her aura. You're her familiar as much as she is yours."

Al's momentary placid face blossomed into anger. "I've used this spell a thousand times to milk auras, and this has never happened before. And I am *not* her familiar."

I watched, feeling tense and ill as a three-legged stool appeared behind Al. It looked like something Attila the Hun would have used, with a red velvet cushion and horsehair fringe going to the floor. Not bothering to see if it was behind him, he sat, his expression puzzled.

"That's why Nick called," I said, and Al gave me a patronizing look. When he took my aura, it broke the bond I had with Nick. He had felt it. *Aw, crap. Al was my familiar?*

Ceri gestured that I should join her in her circle, but I couldn't chance that Al might hurt her in the instant it would take to reform it. Al, though, was preoccupied with his own thoughts.

"This isn't right," he mumbled. "I've done this before with hundreds of witches with souls and it's never forged a bond this strong. What's so different about . . ."

My stomach dropped as all visible emotion drained from him. He glanced at the clock above the sink, then me. "Come here, little witch."

"No."

He pressed his lips together and stood.

Gasping, I backpedaled, but he had my wrist and pulled me to the island counter. "You've done this spell before," he said as he squeezed my pricked finger, making it bleed again. "When you made Nicholas Gregory Sparagmos your familiar. It was your blood in the brew, little witch, that invoked it?"

"You know it was." I was too drained to be frightened anymore. "You were there." I couldn't see his eyes, but my reflection in his glasses looked ugly and pale with wet stringy hair.

"And it worked," he said thoughtfully. "It didn't just bind you, it bound you tight enough for you to draw a line through him?"

"That's why he left," I said, surprised I could still feel the pain.

"Your blood kindled the spell fully. . . ." Speculation was thick in his goat eyes as he looked at me from over his glasses. He drew my hand up, and though I tried to wiggle free of him, he licked the blood from my finger with a cold, tingling sensation. "So subtly scented," he breathed, his eyes never leaving mine. "Like perfumed air your lover has walked through."

"Let go," I said, pushing at him.

"You should be dead," he said, his voice full of wonder. "How is it that you're still alive?"

Jaw clenched, I worked at his grip on me, trying to get my fingers between him and my wrist. "I work hard at it." With a gasp, I fell back as he released his hold.

"You work hard at it." Smiling, he took a step back and gave me a once-over. "The mad have a grace all their own. I must go start a study group."

Frightened, I hunched over my wrist and held it.

"And I will have the likes of you as my own, Rachel Mariana Morgan. Count on it."

"I'm not going into the ever-after," I said tightly. "You'll have to kill me first."

"You don't have a choice," he intoned, chilling me. "You tap a line when the sun is down, and I'll find you. You can't make the circle that can keep me out. If you aren't on holy ground, I'll beat you silly and drag you into the ever-after. And from there, you will not escape."

"Try it," I threatened, reaching behind me to find the meat-tenderizing hammer hanging on the overhead rack. "You can't touch me unless you go solid, and it's going to hurt, red man."

Brow furrowed in concern, Al hesitated. The thought flitted through me that it must be like swatting at a wasp. Timing is everything.

Ceri was wearing a smile I didn't understand. "Algaliarept," she said softly. "You made a mistake. She found a loophole in your contract, and now you'll accept it and leave Rachel Mariana Morgan alone. If you don't, I'm going to start a school on holding line energy."

The demon's face went blank. "Ah, Ceri? Wait a moment, love."

Hammer in hand, I backed up until her bubble was cold at my back. Her hand reached out, and I jumped when she pulled me in, her circle flashing up almost before I knew it had fallen. My shoulders eased at the shimmer of black between us and Al. There was only the faintest glimmer of pale blue from her damaged aura visible through the smut Al had left on her. I patted her hand as she gave me a relieved, sideways hug. "Is that a problem?" I asked, not understanding why Al was so upset.

Ceri was positively smug. "I escaped him knowing how. He'll get in trouble for it. Big trouble. I'm surprised he hasn't been called up on it yet. But then, no one knows." She turned her mocking green eyes on Al. "Yet."

I felt an odd stab of alarm as I took in the savage satisfaction on her. She had known this all along, simply waiting until the information could best be used. The woman was more contriving than Trent, and she didn't seem to have a problem gambling with people's lives, either, mine included. Thank God she was on my side. *She was, wasn't she?*

Al raised a protesting hand. "Ceri, we can talk about this."

"In a week," she said confidently, "there won't be a ley line witch in Cincinnati that won't know how to be their own familiar. In a year, the world will be closed to you and your kind, and *you* will have to answer for it."

"Is it that big of a deal?" I asked as Al adjusted his glasses and shifted from foot to foot. It was cold away from the vent, and I shivered in my damp clothes.

"It's harder to lull a person into foolish choices if they can fight back," Ceri said. "If it gets out, their pool of potential familiars will be weak and undesirable in a matter of years."

My mouth dropped open. "Oh."

"I'm listening," Al said, sitting with an uncomfortable stiffness.

Hope so strong it was almost painful raced through me. "Take your demon mark off me, break the familiar bond, agree to leave me alone, and I won't tell."

Al snorted. "Not shy about asking for things, are you?"

Ceri gave my arm a warning squeeze and let go. "Let me do this. I've written most of his nonverbal contracts the last seven hundred years. Can I speak for you?"

I looked at her, her eyes alight and savage with her need for revenge. Slowly I set the hammer down. "Sure," I said, wondering just what, exactly, I had saved from the ever-after.

She pulled herself straighter, an official air falling over her. "I propose that Al will take his mark off you and break the familiar bonds between you both, in return for your solemn vow to not teach anyone how to hold line energy. Furthermore, you and your kin by blood or the laws of man shall remain free of reprisal from the demon known as Algaliarept and his agents in this world or the ever-after from now until the two worlds collide."

I tried to find enough spit to swallow, failing. I never would have thought of that.

"No," Al said firmly. "That's three things to my one, and I'll not lose my hold on the likes of her completely. I want a way to recoup my loss. And if she crosses the lines, I don't care what agreement we have, she's mine."

"Can we force him?" I said softly. "I mean, we do have him over a barrel?"

Al chuckled. "I could call Newt in to arbitrate if you like. . . ."

Ceri went pale. "No." Taking a steadying breath, she looked at me, her confidence cracked but not shattered. "What of the three can you bear to keep?"

I thought of my mother and my brother Robbie. Nick. "I want him to break the familiar bonds," I said, "and I want him to leave me and my kin by blood or law alone. I'll keep the demon mark and settle up later."

Algaliarept brought his foot up and propped his ankle atop a bent knee. "Clever, clever witch," he agreed. "If she breaks her word, she forfeits her soul."

Ceri's eyes went serious. "Rachel, if you teach *anyone* how to hold line energy, your soul belongs to Algaliarept. He can pull you into the ever-after at his will and you are his. Do you understand?"

I nodded, believing for the first time that I might see the sunrise again. "What happens if he breaks his word?"

"If he harms you or your kin—by his own volition—Newt will put Algaliarept in a bottle and you have a genie. It's standard boilerplate, but I'm glad you asked."

My eyes widened. I looked from Al to her. "No shit?"

She smiled at me, her hair floating as she tucked it behind an ear. "No shit."

Al harrumphed, and we jerked our attentions back to him. "What about you?" he said, clearly annoyed. "What do you want for keeping your mouth shut?"

The satisfaction of getting something back from her former captor and tormentor was in Ceri's eyes. "You will take back the stain on my soul that I took in your stead, and you will not seek reprisal against me or my kin in body or law from now until the two worlds collide."

"I'm not taking back a thousand years of curse imbalance," Al said indignantly. "That's why you were my damn familiar." He put both feet on the floor and leaned forward. "But I won't have it said I'm not agreeable. You keep the smut, but I'll let you teach one person how to hold line energy." A smile, contriving and satisfied, filled his unholy eyes. "One child. A girl child. Your daughter. And if she tells anyone, her soul is forfeit to me. Immediately."

Ceri paled, and I didn't understand. "She can tell one of her daughters, and so on," she countered, and Al smiled.

"Done." He stood. The glow of ever-after energy hovered about him like a shadow. Lacing his fingers together, he cracked his knuckles. "Oh, this is grand. This is good."

I looked at Ceri in wonder. "I thought he'd be upset," I said softly.

She shook her head, clearly worried. "He still has a hold on you. And he's counting on one of my kin to forget the seriousness of the arrangement and make a mistake."

"The familiar bonds," I insisted, glancing at the dark window. "He breaks them now?"

"The time of dissolution was never stated," Al said. He was touching the things he had brought into my kitchen, making them disappear in a smear of ever-after.

Ceri drew herself up. "It was tacitly implied. Break your hold, Algaliarept."

He looked over his glasses at her, smiling when he put a hand before and behind him and made a mocking bow. "It is a small thing, Ceridwen Merriam Dulciate. But you can't think less of me for trying."

Humming, he adjusted his frock. A bowl cluttered with bottles and silver implements appeared on the island counter. There was a book atop it all, small with a handwritten title, the script elegant and looping. "Why is he so happy?" I whispered.

Ceri shook her head, the tips of her hair moving after her head stopped. "I've only seen him like this when he discovers a secret. I'm sorry, Rachel. You know something that makes him very happy."

Swell.

Holding the book at reading height, he rifled through it, a scholarly air about him. "I can break a familiar bond as easy as snapping your neck. You, though, will have to do it the hard way; I'm not going to waste a stored curse on you. And since I'll not have you knowing how to break familiar bonds, we will add a little something. . . . Here it is. Lilac wine. It starts with lilac wine." His eyes met mine over the book. "For you."

A flash of cold went through me as he beckoned me out of the circle, a small, smoky purple bottle appearing behind his long fingers.

I took a quick breath. "You'll break the bonds and leave?" I said. "Nothing extra?"

"Rachel Mariana Morgan," he admonished. "Do you think so little of me?"

I glanced at Ceri, and she nodded for me to go. Trusting her, not Al, I stepped forward. She broke the circle as I did, setting it in place immediately behind me.

He uncorked the bottle, pouring out a glimmering drop of amethyst into a tiny cut crystal cup the size of my thumb. Putting a gloved finger to his thin lips, he extending it. Grimacing, I took it. My heart pounded. I had no choice.

Coming close with an eagerness I didn't trust, he showed me the open book. It was in Latin, and he pointed at a hand-written set of instructions. "See this word?" he said.

I took a breath. *"Umb—"*

"Not yet!" Al shouted, making me start, heart pounding. "Not until the wine coats your tongue, stupid. My god, you think you'd never twisted a curse before!"

"I'm not a ley line witch!" I exclaimed, my voice harsher than it probably should be.

Al's eyebrows rose. "You could be." His eyes went to the glass in my grip. "Drink it."

I glanced at Ceri. At her encouragement, I let the tiny amount pass my lips. It was sweet, making my tongue tingle. I could feel it seeping into me, relaxing my muscles. Al tapped the book, and I looked down. *"Umbra,"* I said, holding the drop on my tongue.

The wild sweetness went sour. "Auck," I said, leaning forward to spit it out.

"Swallow . . ." Al warned softly, and I started when he clamped a hand under my chin and tilted my head back so I couldn't open my mouth.

Eyes tearing, I swallowed. My pounding heart echoed in my ears. Al leaned closer, his eyes going black as he loosened his grip on me and my head drooped. My muscles went loose and watery, and when he let go of me, I fell to the floor.

He didn't even try to catch me, and I landed in a pained crumple. My head hit the floor and I took a quick breath. Closing my eyes, I gathered myself, wedging my palms under me and sitting up. "Thanks a hell of a lot for the warning," I said angrily, looking up and not finding him.

Confused, I stood to find Ceri sitting at the table with her head in her hands and her bare feet tucked under her. The fluorescent light was off, and a single white candle sent a soft glow into the gloom of a cloudy dawn. I stared at the window. *The sun was up? I must have passed out.* "Where is he?" I breathed, blanching when I saw it was almost eight.

She pulled her head up, shocking me with how weary she seemed. "You don't remember?"

My stomach rumbled, and there was an uneasy lightness to it. "No. He's gone?"

She turned to face me squarely. "He took back his aura. You took back yours. You broke the bond with him. You cried and called him a son of a bitch and told him to leave. He did—after he struck you so hard you lost consciousness."

I felt my jaw, then the back of my head. It felt about the same: really, really bad. I was damp and cold, and I got up, clasping my arms around me. "Okay." I felt my ribs, deciding nothing was broken. "Anything else I ought to know?"

"You drank an entire carafe of coffee in about twenty minutes."

That might explain the shakes. It had to be that. Outsmarting demons was becoming old hat. I sat beside Ceri, exhaling in a long breath. Ivy would be home soon. "You like lasagna?"

A smile blossomed over her. "Oh, yes, please."

Twenty-four

My sneakers were silent on the flat carpet of Trent's back hallways. Both Quen and Jonathan were with me, leaving me trying to decide if they were escort or prison guard. We had already woven through the Sunday-silent public areas of his offices and conference rooms that Trent hid his illegal activities behind. Publicly, Trent controlled a good portion of the transportation that ran through Cincinnati, coming in from all directions and leaving the same: railways, roadways, and even a small municipal airport.

Privately, Trent ran a good deal more, using those same transportation systems to get his illegal genetic products out and expanding his Brimstone distribution. That Saladan was cutting into his business in his hometown probably cheesed the man off to no end. It was a finger in the air if anything was. And tonight ought to be an education as Trent either broke that finger off and jammed it into one of Saladan's convenient orifices or took a hit. I didn't like Trent, but I'd keep him alive if it was the latter.

Though I don't know why, I thought as I followed Quen. It was barren down here, lacking even the institutional holiday decorations that graced the front. The man was slime. He had hunted me down like an animal the time he caught me stealing evidence from his secondary office, and my face warmed when I realized we were in the hallway that led to that very room.

A half step ahead of me, Quen was tense, dressed in his vaguely uniformlike black body stocking. He had a snug black and green jacket on over it today, making him look like Scotty might beam him up at any moment. My hair brushed my neck, and I purposely shifted my head to feel the tips tickle my shoulders. I had gotten it cut that afternoon to match the chunk Al had taken out, and the cream rinse the stylist had used wasn't doing much to tame it.

My garment bag with the outfit Kisten had picked out for me was over my shoulder, back from the cleaners. I had even remembered the jewelry and boots. I wasn't going to put them on until I knew I was taking this run. I suspected Trent might have other ideas—and my jeans and sweatshirt with the Howlers' logo looked out of place beside Jonathan's tailored elegance.

The distasteful man hung an irritating three steps behind us. He had met us at the steps of Trent's main building and remained a silent, accusing, professionally cold presence since. The man was six-ten if he was a foot, his features pointy and sharp. An aristocratic, hawklike nose gave him an air of smelling something offensive. His eyes were a cold blue, and his carefully styled black hair was graying. I hated him, and I was trying really hard to overlook that he had tormented me when I was a mink trapped in Trent's office for three unreal days.

Warming at the memory, I took off my coat as we walked, struggling, as neither man offered to take my garment bag. There was a definite moistness to the air the farther back we went. Faint to the point of being almost subliminal was the sound of running water, piped in from who knew where. My steps slowed when I recognized the doorway to Trent's secondary office. Behind me, Jonathan stopped. Quen continued without pause, and I hurried to catch up.

Jonathan clearly wasn't pleased. "Where are you taking her?" he asked belligerently.

Quen's steps grew stiff. "To Trenton." He never turned around or changed his pace.

"Quen . . ." Jonathan's voice was thick in warning. I glanced mockingly back, pleased to see his long wrinkled face showing worry rather than his perpetual stuck-up sneer. Brow furrowed, Jonathan hastened forward as we halted before the arched wooden door at the end of the hall. The overly tall man pushed in front, placing a hand atop the heavy metal latch as Quen reached for it. "You aren't taking her in there," Jonathan warned.

I shifted my garment bag in a sound of sliding nylon, my eyes going from one to the other as the political currents passed between them. Whatever was behind the door was good.

The smaller, more dangerous man narrowed his eyes, and the pox scars went white in his suddenly red face. "She is going to keep him alive tonight," he said. "I'm not going to make her change and wait for him in a secondary office like a paid whore."

Jonathan's blue eyes went even more determined. My pulse quickened, and I stepped out from between them. "Move," Quen intoned, his surprisingly deep voice resonating through me.

Flustered, Jonathan stepped back. Quen pulled it open, the muscles in his back tensing. "Thank you," he said insincerely as the door swung out, slow with inertia.

My lips parted; the door was a freaking six inches thick! The sound of running water chattered out, accompanied by the scent of wet snow. It wasn't cold, though, and I peered past Quen's narrow shoulders to see a soft mottled carpet and a wall paneled in a dark wood that had been oiled and rubbed until it glistened with golden depths. *This,* I thought as I followed Quen in, *had to be Trent's private quarters.*

The short hallway immediately expanded into a second-story walkway. My feet stopped as I looked out over the large room below us. It was impressive, maybe 130 feet long, half as much wide, and twenty feet tall. We had come out on the second floor, which hugged the ceiling. Below, amid the rich carpet and woods, were casually placed seating arrangements of couches, chairs, and coffee tables. Everything was in soft earth tones, accented with maroon and black. A fireplace the size of a fire truck took up one wall, but what drew my attention was the floor-to-ceiling window that stretched the entirety of the wall across from me, letting in the dusky light of early evening.

Quen touched my elbow, and I started down the wide carpeted stairs. I kept one hand on the banister since I couldn't look away from the window, fascinated. Window, not windows, as it seemed to be one plate of glass. I didn't think glass that large was structurally sound, but there it was, looking as if it was only a few millimeters thick with no distortion. It was as if nothing was there.

"It's not plastic," Quen said softly, his green eyes on the view. "It's ley line energy."

My eyes jerked to his, reading the truth in his eyes. Seeing my wonder, a faint smile edged his Turn-scarred features. "It's everyone's first question," he said, showing how he knew where my thoughts had been. "Sound and air are the only things to pass through."

"It must have cost a fortune," I said, wondering how they got the usual red haze of ever-after out of it. Beyond it was a stunning vista of Trent's private, snow-slumped gardens. A crag of stone rose almost as high as the roof, a waterfall cascading over it to leave thickening bands of ice to glint in the last of the day's light. The water pooled into a natural-looking basin that I would have bet wasn't, turning into a stream that meandered through the well-established evergreens and shrubs until it vanished.

A deck gray with age and swept clear of snow stretched between the window and the landscaping. As I slowly descended to the lower level, I decided the round disk of cedar flush with the deck and leaking steam was probably a hot tub. Nearby was a sunken area with seating for backyard parties. I had always thought Ivy's grill with its gleaming chrome and huge burners was over the top, but whatever Trent had was probably obscene.

My feet found the first floor, and my gaze dropped to my feet as it suddenly seemed I was walking on loam instead of carpet. "Nice," I breathed, and Quen indicated that I should wait at the nearest gathering of chairs.

"I'll tell him," the security officer said. He shot Jonathan what I thought was a warning look before he retraced his steps to the second floor to vanish into an unseen area of the house.

I laid my coat and garment bag on a leather couch and made a slow spin on my heel. Now that I was downstairs, the fireplace looked even bigger. It wasn't lit, and I thought I could probably stand up in the hearth without stooping. At the opposite end of the room was a low stage with built-in amps and a light display. A nice-sized dance floor spread before it, surrounded by cocktail tables.

Hidden and cozy under the shelter of the second-story overhang was a long bar, the well-oiled wood and chrome gleaming. There were more tables here, bigger and lower. Huge planters full of dark green foliage that could flourish in the dimmer light surrounded them to give a measure of privacy that the large open floor plan lacked.

The noise from the waterfall had quickly retreated into an unnoticed background babble, and the stillness of the room soaked into me. There were no attendants, no one moving through the room on other business, not even one holiday candle or dish of sweets. It was as if the room was caught under a storybook spell, waiting to be woken. I didn't think the room had been used for what it was designed for since Trent's father died. Eleven years was a long time to be silent.

Feeling peace in the quiet of the room, I took a slow breath and turned to find Jonathan eyeing me with obvious distaste. The faint tension in his jaw sent my eyes to where Quen had vanished. A faint smile quirked the corner of my mouth. "Trent doesn't know you two cooked this up, does he?" I said. "He thinks Quen is going with him tonight."

Jonathan said nothing, the twitch in his eye telling me I was right. Smirking, I dropped my shoulder bag to the floor beside the couch. "I bet Trent could throw a hell of a party," I prompted, hoping for something. Jonathan was silent, and I wove past a low coffee table to stand with my hands on my hips to look out the "window."

My breath made the sheet of ever-after ripple. Unable to resist, I touched it. Gasping, I jerked my hand back. An odd, drawing sensation pulled through me, and I clutched my hand within the other as if I'd been burned. It was cold. The sheet of energy was so cold that it burned. I looked behind me to Jonathan, expecting to see him smirking, but he was staring at the window, his long face slack in surprise.

My gaze followed his, my stomach tightening as I realized the window wasn't clear anymore, but swirling with amber shades of gold. Damn. It had taken on the color of my aura. Clearly Jonathan hadn't expected this. My hand ran through my short hair. "Ah . . . Oops."

"What did you do to the window?" he exclaimed.

"Nothing." I took a guilty step back. "I just touched it, that's all. Sorry."

Jonathan's hawklike features took on more ugliness. Steps long and jerky, he strode to me. "You hack. Look what you did to the window! I will not allow Quen to entrust Mr. Kalamack's safety to you tonight."

My face warmed, and finding an easy outlet for my embarrassment, I let it turn to anger. "This wasn't my idea," I snapped. "And I said I was sorry about the window. You should be lucky I'm not suing for pain and suffering."

Jonathan took a loud breath. "If he comes to any harm because of you, I'll—"

Anger flashed through me, fed by the memory of three days in hell as he tormented me. "Shut up," I hissed. Ticked that he was taller than me, I stepped up onto a nearby coffee table. "I'm not in a cage anymore," I said, keeping enough presence of mind not to poke him in the chest with a finger. His face went startled, then cloric. "The only thing between your head and my foot becoming real close and personal right now is my questionable professionalism. And if you *ever* threaten me again, I'll slam you halfway across the room before you can say number-two pencil. Got it, you tall freak of nature?"

Frustrated, he clenched his long thin hands tight.

"Go ahead, elf-boy," I seethed, feeling the line energy I had spindled in my head earlier almost spill over to fill my body. "Give me a reason."

The sound of a closing door jerked our attentions to the second-story walkway. Jonathan visibly hid his anger and took a step back. Suddenly I felt really stupid on top of the table. Trent came to a startled halt above us in a dress shirt and pants, blinking. "Rachel Morgan?" he said softly to Quen, standing beside and a little behind him. "No. This isn't acceptable."

Trying to scrape something from the situation, I threw one hand extravagantly into the air. Putting the other on my hip, I posed like a prop girl showing off a new car. "Ta-da!" I said brightly, very conscious of my jeans, sweatshirt, and the new haircut I wasn't particularly fond of. "Hi, Trent. I'm your baby-sitter tonight. Where do your folks hide the good booze?"

Trent's brow furrowed. "I don't want her there. Put on your suit. We leave in an hour."

"No, Sa'han."

Trent had turned to walk away, but he jerked to a stop. "Can I speak to you for a moment," he said softly.

"Yes, Sa'han," the smaller man murmured deferentially, not moving.

I hopped off the table. Did I know how to make a good first impression or what?

Trent frowned, his attention going from an unrepentant Quen to Jonathan's nervous stance. "You're both in on this," he said.

Jonathan laced his hands behind his back, subtly shifting himself another step from me. "I trust Quen's judgment,

Sa'han," he said, his low voice rising clear in the empty room. "I do not, however, trust Ms. Morgan's."

Affronted, I huffed at him. "Go suck on a dandelion, Jon."

The man's lips twitched. I knew he hated the shortened name. Trent, too, wasn't happy. Glancing at Quen, he started down the stairway with a fast, even pace, half dressed in his dark designer suit and looking like a cover model for GQ. His wispy blond hair had been slicked back, and his shirt pulled slightly across his shoulders as he descended to the lower floor. The spring in his step and the glint in his eye told me more clearly than anything that elves were at their best the four hours around sunup and sundown. A deep green tie was draped casually across the back of his neck, not yet fastened into place. God help me, but he looked good, everything anything of the female persuasion could ever want: young, handsome, powerful, confident. I wasn't pleased that I liked the way he looked, but there it was.

Question high in his expression, Trent shook his sleeves down and buttoned the cuffs with a preoccupied quickness as he came down the stairs. The top two buttons of his shirt were undone, making an intriguing sight. His head came up as he reached the lower landing, and he paused for a heartbeat when he saw the window.

"What happened to the ward?" he questioned.

"Ms. Morgan touched it." Jonathan had the smug glee of a six-year-old tattling on his older sibling. "I'd advise against Quen's plans. Morgan is unpredictable and dangerous."

Quen shot him a dark look that Trent missed since the man was buttoning the top of his shirt. "Lights full," Trent said, and I squinted when huge lights in the ceiling flickered on one by one to make it bright as day. My stomach clenched as I looked at the window. Crap. I had broken it but good. Even my streaks of red were in it, and I didn't like that the three of them would know I had that much tragedy in my past. But at least Al's black was gone. *Thank God.*

Trent came closer, his smooth face unreadable. The clean smell of aftershave drifted from him as he stopped. "It did this when you touched it?" he asked, his gaze going from my new haircut to the window.

"I, uh, yeah. Quen said it was a sheet of ever-after. I thought it was a modified protection circle."

Quen ducked his head and stepped closer. "It's not a protection circle, it's a ward. Your aura and the aura of the person who set it up must resonate to a similar frequency."

His young features creased in worry, Trent squinted at it. An unshared thought passed through him, and his fingers twitched. I eyed the tell, knowing he thought it more than odd, and significant. It was a notion that solidified when Trent glanced at Quen and something of a security nature passed between them. Quen made a small shrug, and Trent took a slow breath.

"Have someone from maintenance look at it," Trent said. Tugging at his collar, he added loudly, "Lights revert." I froze when the glare vanished and my eyes tried to adjust.

"I don't agree with this," Trent said in the soothing dimness, and Jonathan smiled.

"Yes, Sa'han," Quen said softly. "But you will take Morgan or you will not be going."

Well, well, well, I thought, as the rims of Trent's ears went red. I hadn't known Quen had the authority to tell Trent what to do. Clearly, though, it was a right seldom invoked, and never without consequences. Beside me, Jonathan looked positively ill.

"Quen . . ." Trent started.

The security officer took a firm stance, looking over Trent's shoulder at nothing with his hands laced behind his back. "My vampire bite makes me unreliable, Sa'han," he said, and I winced at his obvious pain of openly admitting it. "I'm no longer sure of my effectiveness."

"Damn it, Quen," Trent exclaimed. "Morgan has been bitten, too. What makes her any more sure than you?"

"Ms. Morgan has been living with a vampire for seven months and hasn't succumbed," Quen said stiffly. "She has developed a series of defensive strategies for combating a vamp trying to bespell her. I haven't, yet, and so I'm no longer reliable in questionable situations."

His scarred face was tight with shame, and I wished Trent would shut up and just go with it. This confession was killing Quen.

"Sa'han," he said evenly. "Morgan can protect you. I cannot. Don't ask me to do this."

I fidgeted, wishing I was somewhere else. Jonathan glared at me as if it were my fault. Trent's face was pained and worried, and Quen flinched when he put a comforting hand upon his shoulder. With a reluctant slowness, Trent let his hand fall away. "Get her a corsage and see if there's something suitable for her to wear in the green suite. She looks about the same size."

The flash of relief that crossed Quen was replaced by a deeper self-doubt that looked wrong and worrisome. Quen appeared broken, and I wondered what he was going to do if he felt he couldn't protect Trent anymore. "Yes, Sa'han," he murmured. "Thank you."

Trent's gaze fell on me. I couldn't tell what he was thinking, and I felt cold and uneasy. The feeling strengthened when Trent nodded once to Quen and said, "Do you have a moment?"

"Of course, Sa'han."

The two of them headed into one of the unseen downstairs rooms to leave me with Jonathan. The unhappy man gave me a look rife with disgust. "Leave your dress here," he said. "Follow me."

"I have my own outfit, thanks," I said picking up my shoulder bag, coat, and my garment bag from where I had left them and following him to the stairs. At the foot of the stairs, Jonathan turned. His cold eyes traveled over me and my garment bag, and he sniffed patronizingly.

"It's a nice outfit," I said, warming when he snickered.

He took the steps quickly, forcing me to scramble to keep up. "You can look like a whore if you like," he said. "But Mr. Kalamack has a reputation." He eyed me over his shoulder as he reached the top. "Hurry up. You don't have much time to get presentable."

Seething, I took two steps for every one of his as he cut a sharp right into a large common room holding a comfortable, more normal-sized living room. There was an efficiency at the back, and what looked like a breakfast nook. One of Trent's live-shot video feeds showed a second view of the dim garden. Several heavy-looking doors opened up onto the area, and I was guessing this was where Trent did his "normal" living. I became sure of it when Jonathan opened the first one to show a small sitting room opening onto an extravagant bedroom. It was decorated entirely in shades of green and gold, managing to look wealthy without dipping into gaudy. Another fake window past the bed showed the forest, dusky and gray with twilight.

I assumed that the other doors led to other such suites of rooms. All the wealth and privilege couldn't hide that the entire area was set up to be very defensible. There probably wasn't a real window in the place other than the one downstairs covered in ley line energy.

"Not that way," Jonathan all but barked as I took a step to the bedroom. "That's the bedroom. Stay out of it. The changing room is over here."

"Sorry," I said sarcastically, then hitched my garment bag higher atop my shoulder and followed him into a bathroom. At least I thought it was a bathroom. There were so many plants it was hard to tell. And it was the size of my kitchen. The multitude of mirrors reflected the lights that Jonathan flicked on until I was squinting. The glare seemed to bother him, too, since he worked the bank of switches until the multitude of bulbs reduced to one over the commode and one over the single sink and expansive counter. My shoulders eased in the dimmer light.

"This way," Jonathan said as he passed through an open archway. I followed, stopping short just inside. I suppose it was a closet, as there were clothes in it—expensive-looking women's clothes—but the room was huge. A rice-paper screen took up one corner with a vanity against the back of it. A small table with two chairs was tucked to the right of the door. To the left was a trifold mirror. All it needed was a wet bar. Damn. I was *so* in the wrong line of work.

"You can change here," Jonathan said through his nose. "Try not to touch anything."

Ticked, I dropped my coat on a chair and hung my garment bag on a convenient hook. Shoulders tight, I unzipped the bag and turned, knowing Jonathan was judging me. But my eyebrows rose at his surprised look while he took in the outfit Kisten had put together for me. Then his expression returned to its usual ice. "You aren't wearing that," he said flatly.

"Shove it up your ass, Jon," I snapped.

Movements stilted, he strode to a set of sliding mirror doors, opening them to pull out a black dress as if he knew exactly where it was. "You will wear *this,*" he said, thrusting it at me.

"I'm not wearing that." I tried to make my voice cold, but the dress was exquisite, made of a soft fabric cut low down the back and flatteringly high in the front and around the neck. It would fall to my ankles to make me look tall and elegant. Swallowing back my envy, I said, "It's cut too low in back to hide my splat gun. And it's too tight to run in. That's a lousy dress."

His extended arm dropped, and it was all I could do to keep from wincing when the beautiful fabric puddled on the carpet. "You pick one out, then."

"Maybe I will." I stepped hesitantly to the closet.

"The evening dresses are in that one," Jonathan said, sounding patronizing.

"Duh . . ." I mocked, but my eyes widened and my hand went out to touch. God help me, they were all beautiful, each having an understated elegance. They were organized by color, and matching shoes and purses were carefully arranged underneath. Some had hats in the rack above them. My shoulders slumped when I touched a flaming red dress, but Jonathan's whispered, "whore" encouraged me to keep moving. My eyes left it reluctantly.

"So, Jon," I said as he watched me shuffle through the dresses. "Either Trent is a cross-dresser or he enjoys bringing size eight tall women to his house wearing evening gowns and sending them home in rags." I eyed him. "Or does he just knock them up and knock them off?"

Jonathan's jaw clenched and his face flushed. "These are for Miss Ellasbeth."

"Ellasbeth?" My hands fell from a purple dress that would cost me a month of runs. *Trent had a girlfriend?* "Oh, hell no! I'm not wearing another woman's dress without asking."

He snickered, his long face taking on a hint of annoyance. "They belong to Mr. Kalamack. If he says you can wear them, you can."

Not fully reassured, I turned back to my search. But all my apprehensions vanished when my hands touched a soft filmy gray. "Oh, look at this," I breathed, pulling the top and skirt from the closet and holding them triumphantly up, as if he gave a flying flip.

Jonathan looked from the cabinet of scarves, belts, and purses he had just opened. "I thought we threw that out," he said, and I made a face, knowing he was trying to make me feel like it was ugly. It wasn't. The tight bustier and matching skirt were elegant, the fabric soft to the touch and thick enough for winter without being binding. It was a shimmering black once I got it into the light. The skirt went to the floor, but was split in a multitude of narrow bands from the knees so it would flutter about my ankles. And with the slits that high, my splat gun in its thigh holster would be an easy reach. It was perfect.

"Is it suitable?" I asked as I took it to the hanger and hung it over my outfit. I looked up when he was silent, finding his face twisted.

"It will do." He raised his watchband to his wrist, pushing a button and speaking into the spiffy-keen communicator I remembered was there. "Make the corsage black and gold," he muttered. Glancing at the door, he added to me, "I'll get the matching jewelry from the safe."

"I have my own jewelry," I said, then hesitated, not wanting to see what my imitation stuff would look like against fabric such as this. "But okay," I amended, unable to meet his eyes.

Jonathan harrumphed. "I'll send someone to do your makeup," he added as he walked out.

That was downright insulting. "I can touch up my own makeup, thank you," I said loudly after him. I was wearing mundane makeup atop the complexion spell that hid the remnants of my still healing black eye, and I didn't want anyone to touch it.

"Then I only have to get the stylist to do something with your hair," came echoing back.

"My hair is fine!" I shouted. I looked in one of the mirrors, touching the loose curls starting to frizz. "It's fine," I added, softer. "I just had it done." But all that I heard was Jonathan's sniggering laughter and the sound of a door opening.

"I'm not going to leave her alone in Ellasbeth's room," came Quen's gravely voice in answer to Jonathan's mutter. "She'd kill her."

My eyebrows rose. Did he mean I would kill Ellasbeth, or Ellasbeth would kill me? That kind of detail was important.

I turned when Quen's silhouette took up the doorway to the bathroom. "You baby-sitting me?" I said as I grabbed my slip and nylons and took the black dress behind the screen.

"Miss Ellasbeth isn't aware you're on the grounds," he said. "I didn't think it necessary to tell her, as she's returning home, but she's been known to change her plans without notice."

I eyed the rice paper between Quen and me, then kicked off my sneakers. Feeling vulnerable and short, I shimmied out of my clothes, folding them instead of letting them sit in a crumpled heap as I usually did. "You're really big on that need-to-know kick, aren't you?" I said, and I heard him speak softly to someone who had just come in. "What is it you aren't telling me?"

The second, unseen person left. "Nothing," Quen said shortly.

Yeah, right.

The dress was lined in silk, and I stifled a moan as it eased over me. I looked down at the hem, deciding that it would fall right when I put my boots on. Brow pinching, I hesitated. My boots weren't going to work. I'd have to hope Ellasbeth was a size eight shoe and that tonight's butt kicking could be accomplished in heels. The bustier gave me a smidgen of trouble, and I finally gave up trying to zip it the last inch.

I gave myself one last look, tucking my complexion amulet between me and my waistband. Splat gun in my thigh holster, I came round the screen. "Zip me up, honey?" I said lightly, earning what I thought was a seldom-given smile from Quen. He nodded, and I showed him my back. "Thanks," I said when he finished.

He turned to the table and chairs, stooping to pick up a corsage that hadn't been there when I went behind the screen. It was a black orchid bound with a gold and green ribbon. Straightening, he took the pin from it, hesitating as he looked at the narrow strap. Right off I knew his dilemma, and I wasn't going to help him a bit.

Quen's scarred face pinched. Eyes on my dress, his lips pressed together. "Excuse me," he said, reaching forward. I froze, knowing he wouldn't touch me unless he had to. There was enough fabric to attach it, but he would have to put his fingers between that pin and me. I exhaled, collapsing my lungs to give him a smidgen more room.

"Thank you," he said softly.

The back of his hand was cold, and I stifled a shiver. Trying not to fidget, I sent my attention to the ceiling. A faint smile crossed me, growing as he got the orchid fastened and stepped away with an exhalation of relief.

"Something funny, Morgan?" he said sourly.

I dropped my head, watching him from around my drooping bangs. "Not really. You reminded me of my dad—for a minute there."

Quen adopted a look both disbelieving and questioning. Shaking my head, I grabbed my shoulder bag from the table and went to sit at the vanity against the screen. "See, we had this big seventh-grade dance, and I had a strapless dress," I said as I brought out my makeup. "My dad wouldn't let my date pin the flower on, so he did it himself." My focus blurred, and I crossed my legs. "He missed my prom."

Quen remained standing. I couldn't help but notice he had put himself where he could see me and the door both. "Your father was a good man. He'd be proud of you tonight."

Quick and painful, my breath caught. Slowly I let it out, my hands resuming their primping. I really wasn't surprised Quen had known him—they were the same age—but it hurt nonetheless. "You knew him?" I couldn't stop myself from asking.

The look he gave me through the mirror was unreadable. "He died well."

Died well? God, what was it with these people?

Angry, I turned in my seat to see him directly. "He died in a cruddy little hospital room with dirt in the corners," I said tightly. "He was supposed to stay alive, damn it." My voice was even, but I knew it wouldn't stay that way. "He was supposed to be there when I got my first job, then lost it three days later after I slugged the boss's son when he tried to feel me up. He was supposed to be there when I graduated from high school and then college. He was supposed to be there to scare my dates into behaving so I wouldn't have to find my own way home from wherever the prick dumped me when he found I'd fight back. But he wasn't, was he? No. He died doing something with Trent's father, and no one has the balls to tell me what great thing it was that was worth screwing up my life for."

My heart pounded, and I stared at Quen's quiet, pox-scarred face. "You've had to be your own keeper for a long time," he said.

"Yeah." Lips pressed tight, I turned back to the mirror, my foot bobbing up and down.

"What doesn't kill you—"

"Hurts." I watched his reflection. "It hurts. It hurts a lot." My black eye throbbed under my higher blood pressure, and I reached to touch it. "I'm strong enough," I said bitterly. "I don't want to be any stronger. Piscary is a bastard, and if he gets out of prison, he's going to die twice." I thought of Skimmer, hoping she was as bad a lawyer as she was good a friend to Ivy.

Quen's feet shifted, but he didn't move. "Piscary?"

The question in his voice brought my gaze up. "He said he killed my dad. Did he lie to me?" *Need to know. Did I finally "need to know" according to Quen?*

"Yes and no." The elf's eyes flicked to the doorway.

I spun in the chair. He could tell me. I think he wanted to. "Well, which is it?"

Quen ducked his head and took a symbolic step back. "It's not my place."

Heart pounding, I stood, my hands clenched into fists. "What happened?" I demanded.

Again Quen looked toward the bathroom. A light flicked on and a beam spilled into the room to diffuse into nothing. An effeminate man's voice chattered seemingly to itself, filling the air with a bright presence. Jonathan answered back, and I looked at Quen in a panic, knowing he wouldn't say anything in front of him.

"It was my fault," Quen said softly. "They were working together. I should have been there, not your father. Piscary killed them as sure as if he had pulled the trigger."

Feeling unreal, I stepped close enough to see the sweat on him. It was obvious he had overstepped his bounds telling me even this much. Jonathan came in trailing a man dressed in tight black and shiny boots. "Oh!" the small man exclaimed, hustling to the vanity with his fishing-tackle boxes. "It's red! I *adore* red hair. And it's natural, too. I can tell from here. Come sit, dove. The things I can do for you! You won't recognize yourself."

I spun to Quen. Tired eyes haunted looking, he stepped away, leaving me breathless. I stood, staring, wanting more, knowing I wouldn't get it. Damn it, Quen's timing sucked, and I forced my hands to remain at my side instead of throttling him.

"Sit your fanny down!" the stylist exclaimed when Quen inclined his head at me and walked out. "I only have half an hour!"

Frowning, I gave Jonathan's mocking expression a tired look, then sat down in the chair and tried to explain to the man that I liked it the way it was, and could he just give it a quick brush through? But he hissed and shushed me, pulling out bottle after bottle of spray and odd-looking instruments whose use I couldn't even guess. I knew it was a battle already lost.

Twenty-five

Isettled into the seat of Trent's limo, crossing my legs and arranging one of the narrow panels of my skirt to cover my knee. The shawl I was using instead of a coat slid down my back, and I let it stay there. It smelled like Ellasbeth, and my subtler perfume couldn't compete.

The shoes were a half size too small, but the dress fit perfectly: the bustier tight but not confining, and the skirt riding high on my waist. My thigh holster was as subtle as dandelion fluff, completely unseen. Randy had styled my shorter hair up off my neck, binding it with thick gold wire and vintage beads into an elaborate coiffure that had taken the man twenty minutes of unending prattle to fix. But he was right. I felt completely unlike myself and *expe-e-e-ensive*.

This was the second limo I'd been in that week. Maybe it was a trend. If so, I could handle that. Jittery, I glanced at Trent staring out at the huge trees as we approached the gatehouse, their black trunks standing out against the snow. He seemed a thousand miles away, not even aware I was sitting next to him. "Takata's car is nicer," I said, breaking the silence.

Trent twitched, recovering smoothly. The reaction made him look as young as he was. "Mine's not a rental," he said.

I shrugged, foot jiggling as I looked out the smoked window.

"Warm enough?" he asked.

"What? Oh. Yes, thank you."

Jonathan drove us past the guardhouse without slowing, the rising bar reaching its apex the second we passed under it. It closed equally fast. I fidgeted, checking my clutch purse for my charms, feeling for the press of my splat gun, and touching my hair. Trent was looking out the window again, lost in his own world, which had nothing to do with me.

"Hey, sorry about the window," I said, not liking the silence.

"I'll send you a bill if it can't be fixed." He turned to me. "You look nice."

"Thank you." I sent my eyes over his silk-lined wool suit. He wasn't wearing an overcoat, and it was tailored to show off every inch of him. His boutonniere was a tiny black bud rose, and I wondered if he had grown it himself. "You wash up good yourself."

He gave me one of his professional smiles, but there was a new glint to it, and I thought it might actually have a tinge of real warmth.

"The dress is beautiful," I added, wondering how I was going to get through tonight without resorting to talk about the weather. I leaned to tug my nylons straight.

"That reminds me." Trent twisted to dip a hand into a pocket. "These go with it." He held out his hand, dropping a heavy set of earrings into my palm. "There's a necklace, too."

"Thanks." I tilted my head to take out my simple hoops, dropping them into my clutch purse and snapping it closed. Trent's earrings were a series of interlocking circles, and heavy enough to be real gold. I worked them into place, feeling their unfamiliar weight.

"And the necklace . . ." Trent held it up, and my eyes widened. It was gorgeous, made of interlaced rings the size of my thumbnail and matching the earrings. They made a delicate lace panel, and I would have labeled it goth but for its richness. A wooden pendant in the shape of the Celtic rune for protection hung from the nadir, and I hesitated in my reach. It was beautiful, but I suspected its peekaboo lace would make me a veritable vampire slut.

And Celtic magic gave me the willies. It was a specialized art, much of it depending upon one's belief, not if you did the spell right or not. More of a religion than magic. I didn't like mixing religion and magic—it made for terribly strong forces when something unmeasurable mixed its will with that of the practitioner's intent, making the results not necessarily in line with what was expected. It was wild magic, and I preferred mine nicely scientific. If you invoke the help of a higher being, you can't complain when things don't go to your plan, but to its.

"Turn around," Trent said, and my eyes darted to his. "I'll put it on you. It has to be snug for it to look right."

I was not about to show Trent I was squeamish, and as protection charms were fairly reliable, I took the simple fake gold cord from around my neck and dropped it into my clutch bag with my earrings. I wondered if Trent knew what wearing this was saying, deciding he probably did and thought it was a big joke.

Tension tightened my shoulders as I gathered strands of hair that Randy had pulled for effect. The necklace settled about my neck in a heavy feeling of security, still warm from his pocket.

Trent's fingers touched me, and I yelped in surprise as a surge of ley line energy rose through me and into him. The car swerved and Trent's fingers jerked away. The necklace hit the carpeted floor with a tinkle of metal. Hand to my throat, I stared at him.

He had put himself into the corner. The amber light from the ceiling glinted to make shadows on him. Eyeing me with a look of annoyance, he scooted forward and scooped the necklace from the floor, jiggling it until it hung properly across one hand.

"Sorry," I said, heart pounding and my hand still covering my neck.

Trent frowned, meeting Jonathan's gaze in the rearview mirror before gesturing for me to turn back around. I did, very conscious of him behind me. "Quen said you've been working on your ley line skills," Trent said while he draped the metal over me again. "It took me a week to learn how to keep my familiar's energy from trying to equalize when I touched another practitioner. Of course I was three at the time, so I had an excuse."

His hands fell from me, and I settled into the supple cushions. His expression was smug, his usual professionalism gone. It wasn't any of his business that this was the first time I had tried to spindle line energy in me as a matter of convenience. I was ready to bag it. My feet hurt, and thanks to Quen, I wanted to go home, eat a carton of ice cream, and remember my dad.

"Quen knew my dad," I said sullenly.

"So I hear." He looked not at me but the passing view as we made our way into the city.

My breath came faster, and I shifted in my seat. "Piscary said he killed my dad. Quen implied there was more to it than that."

Trent crossed his legs and unbuttoned his suit coat. "Quen talks too much."

Tension pulled my stomach tight. "Our fathers were working together?" I prompted. "Doing what?"

His lip twitched, and he ran a hand across his hair to make sure it was lying flat. From the driver's seat, Jonathan coughed in warning. *Right. Like his threats meant anything to me?*

Trent shifted in the seat to look at me, his face holding a shade of interest. "Ready to work with me?"

I cocked an eyebrow at him. *Work* with *me. Last time it was* work *for* me.

"No." I smiled though I wanted to step on his foot. "Quen seems to blame himself for my dad's death. I find that fascinating. Especially when Piscary claimed responsibility."

A sigh came from Trent. His hand went out to steady himself when we eased onto the interstate. "Piscary killed my father outright," he said. "Your father was bitten while trying to help him. Quen was supposed to be there, not your father.

That's why Quen went to help you subdue Piscary. He felt he needed to take your father's place, seeing as he believes it was his fault your father wasn't there to help you himself."

My face went cold, and I pushed myself back into the leather seat. I had thought Trent had sent Quen to help me; Trent had nothing to do with it. But a niggling thought surfaced through my confusion. "But my father didn't die of a vampire bite."

"No," Trent said carefully, his eyes on the growing skyline. "He didn't."

"He died when his red blood cells started attacking his soft tissues," I prompted, waiting for more, but Trent's posture went closed. "That's all I'm getting, isn't it?" I said flatly, and the man gave me half a smile, charming and sly.

"My offer of employment is ever open, Ms. Morgan."

It was hard, but I managed to keep a somewhat pleasant expression on my face as I slumped in the seat. I suddenly felt like I was being lulled, lured into places that I once vowed I'd never go: places like working for Trent, sex with a vampire, crossing the street without looking. All of them you could get away with, but eventually you were going to get blasted by a bus. *What in hell was I doing in a limo with Trent?*

We had passed into the Hollows, and I sat up, taking more interest. The holiday lights were thick, primarily green, white, and gold. The silence stretched. "So-o-o, who is Ellasbeth?"

Trent shot me a poisonous look, and I smiled sweetly. "Not my idea," he said.

How very interesting, I thought. *I found a nerve. Wouldn't it be fun to stomp on it?* "Old girlfriend?" I guessed brightly. "Live-in? Ugly sister you hide in the basement?"

Trent's expression had returned to its professional emptiness, but his restless fingers were ever-moving. "I like your jewelry," he said. "Maybe I should have had Jonathan put it into the house safe while we were gone."

I put a hand to his necklace, feeling it warm from my

body. "I was wearing crap, and you know it." Damn it, I had enough of his gold on me to make a set of false teeth for a horse.

"We can talk about Nick, then." Trent's soothing voice carried a derisive edge. "I'd much rather talk about Nick. It was Nick, wasn't it? Nick Sparagmos? He's moved out of the city, I hear, after you sent him into an epileptic seizure." Hands clasped at his knee, he gave me a telling look, pale eyebrows high. "What *did* you do to him? I never could find that out."

"Nick is fine." I pulled my hands down before they could play with my hair. "I'm watching his apartment while he's away on business." I looked out the window, reaching behind me to pull the shawl back up over my shoulders. He could sling mud better than the best rich-bitch at school. "We need to discuss what it is I'm supposed to be protecting you against."

From the driver's seat came Jonathan's snort. Trent, too, chuckled. "I'm not in need of protection," he said. "If I was, Quen would be here. You're a semifunctioning decoration."

Semifunctioning . . . "Yeah?" I shot back, wishing I could say I was surprised.

"Yeah," he said right back, the word sounding odd coming from him. "So sit where you're put and keep your mouth shut."

Face warming, I moved so that my knees almost touched his thigh. "Listen to me, Mr. Kalamack," I said sharply. "Quen is paying me good money to keep your ass above the grass, so don't leave the room without me and don't get into my line of sight with the bad guys. Got it?"

Jonathan turned into a parking lot, and I had to brace myself when he applied the brakes too sharply. Trent glanced at him, and I watched their gazes lock through the rearview mirror. Still angry, I looked out to find ugly piles of snow a good six feet high. We were down by the riverfront, and my shoulders tensed at the gambling boat with its stacks steaming slightly. Saladan's gambling boat? Again?

My thoughts went back to my night with Kisten and the guy in a tux who had taught me craps. *Shit.* "Hey, uh, do you know what Saladan looks like?" I asked. "Is he a witch?"

The hesitancy in my tone was probably what caught Trent's attention, and while Jonathan parked in the long spot reserved for a car of this length, he eyed me. "He's a ley line witch. Black hair, dark eyes, my age. Why? Are you worried? You should be. He's better than you."

"No." *Crap. Or should I say craps?* Grabbing my clutch purse, I slumped back into the cushions when Jonathan opened the door and Trent got out with a grace that had to be practiced. A blast of cold air replaced him, making me wonder how Trent could stand there as if it was summer. I had a feeling I'd already met Saladan. *Idiot!* I berated myself. But showing Lee I wasn't afraid of him after his failed little black charm would be extremely satisfying.

Becoming eager for the encounter, I slid across the bench seat to the open door, jerking back when Jonathan slammed it in my face. "Hey!" I shouted, adrenaline making my head hurt.

The door opened, and Jonathan gave me a satisfied smirk. "Sorry, ma'am," he said.

Past him was Trent, a tired look on his face. Holding my borrowed shawl close, I watched Jonathan as I slid out. "Why, thank you, Jon," I said brightly, "you freaking bastard."

Trent ducked his head, hiding a smile. I jerked the shawl higher, and making sure I kept my line energy where it was supposed to be, I took Trent's arm so he could help me up the icy ramp. He stiffened to pull away, and I grabbed his arm with my free hand, pinching my purse between us. It was cold, and I wanted to get inside. "I'm wearing heels for you," I muttered. "The least you can do is make sure I don't fall on my can. Or are you afraid of me?"

Trent said nothing, his posture shifting into an uneasy acceptance as we went, step for step, across the parking lot. He turned to look over his shoulder at Jonathan, indicating that he should stay with the car, and I simpered at the tall unhappy man, giving him Erica's crooked-bunny-ear kiss good-bye. It was fully dark now, and the wind blew bits of snow against my legs, bare but for my nylons. Why hadn't I insisted on borrowing a coat? I wondered. This shawl was worthless. And it stank like lilac. I hated lilac.

"Aren't you cold?" I questioned, seeing Trent seemingly as warm as if it was July.

"No," he said, and I remembered Ceri walking in the snow with a similar tolerance.

"Must be an elf thing," I muttered, and he chuckled.

"Yup," he said, my eyes jerking to his at the casual word. They were bright with amusement, and I glanced at the beckoning ramp.

"Well, I'm frozen through," I grumbled. "Can we move a little faster?"

He quickened his pace, but I was still shivering by the time we got to the entry door. Trent solicitously held it for me, ushering me in ahead of him. Letting go of his arm, I went inside, my hands clasping my upper arms to try to warm myself. I gave the doorman a brief smile, and got a stoic, blank look. Taking my shawl off, I held it between two fingers to the coat attendant, wondering if I could conveniently leave it here—by accident, of course.

"Mr. Kalamack and Ms. Morgan," Trent said, ignoring the guestbook. "We're expected."

"Yes, sir." The doorman gestured for someone to take his place. "Right this way."

Trent offered me his arm. I hesitated, trying to read his quiet face and failing. Taking a breath, I linked my arm in his. As my fingers brushed the top of his hand, I made a conscious effort to maintain my level of line energy when I felt a slight pull from my chi. "Better," he said, his eyes searching the busy game room as we followed the doorman. "You're improving by leaps and bounds, Ms. Morgan."

"Shove it, Trent," I said, smiling at the people who looked up when we entered. His hand was warm under my fingers, and I felt like a princess. There was a lull in the noise, and when the conversations rose again, they had an excitement that couldn't be laid entirely at the feet of gambling.

It was warm, and the air pleasantly scented. The disk hanging over the center of the room seemed quiet, but I imagined if I bothered to look at it with my second sight that it would be pulsating with that ugly purple and black. I glanced at my reflection to see if my hair was behaving under the stylist's sprays and wires, glad the yellow of my black eye was still hidden behind the mundane makeup. Then I looked again.

Damn! I thought, slowing. Trent and I looked fantastic. No wonder people were staring. He was trim and debonair, and I was elegant in my borrowed dress with my hair up off my neck and bound with that heavy gold wire. Both of us were confident, both of us were smiling. But even as I thought we made the perfect couple, I realized that though we were together, each of us was alone. Our strengths were not dependent upon each other, and while that wasn't bad, it didn't lend itself to being a couple. We were simply standing next to each other looking good.

"What is it?" Trent asked, gesturing that I should go up the stairs ahead of him.

"Nothing." Gathering my slit skirt as best I could, I went up the narrow carpeted stairway after the doorman. The sound of gaming people went faint, turning into a background hum to stir my subconscious. A cheer rose, and I wished I could be down there, feeling my heart pound in the breathless wait to see what the dice would show.

"I thought they'd search us," Trent said softly so the man escorting us couldn't hear.

I shrugged. "For what? Did you see that big disk on the ceiling?" He glanced behind us, and I added, "It's a huge spell damper. Kind of like the charms I used to have on my cuffs before you burned them all to hell, but it affects the whole boat."

"Didn't you bring a weapon?" he whispered as we reached the second floor.

"Yes," I said through my teeth, smiling. "And I could shoot someone with it, but the potions won't take effect until whoever it is leaves the boat."

"What good is it then?"

"I don't kill people, Trent. Get over it." *Though I might make an exception for Lee.*

I saw his jaw tighten and relax. Our escort opened a narrow door, gesturing for me to enter. I stepped in, finding Lee looking pleasantly surprised as he brought his attention from the paperwork on his desk. I tried to keep my expression neutral, the memory of that man writhing on the street under a black charm aimed at me making me angry and ill all at the same time.

A tall woman stood behind him, leaning to breathe upon his neck. She was leggy and lean, dressed in a black jumpsuit with bell-bottom hems. The neckline went almost to her navel. Vamp, I decided, when her eyes dropped to my necklace and she smiled to show me small, pointy canines. My scar twinged, and my anger slowed. Quen wouldn't have stood a chance.

Eyes alight, Lee rose and tugged the coat of his tux straight. Physically pushing the vampire out of his way, he came out from around the desk. Trent entered, and his gaze became even more animated. "Trent!" he exclaimed, striding forward with his hands extended. "How are you, old man!"

I stepped back as Trent and Lee warmly clasped hands. *You've got to be kidding me.*

"Stanley," he said, smiling, and it finished falling into place. *Stanley, long for Lee.*

"Damn!" Lee said, pounding Trent on the back. "How long has it been? Ten years?"

Trent's smile flickered, his annoyance at that back slap nearly undetectable but for the slight tightening in his eyes. "Almost that. You look good. Still hitting the waves?"

Lee ducked his head, a roguish grin turning him into a scalawag despite him being in a tux. "Now and again. Not as much as I like. My damn knee has been giving me trouble. But you look good. Got some muscle on you now. Not that skinny boy trying to keep up with me."

Trent's eyes flicked to mine, and I gave him a mute look. "Thanks."

"Word is you're getting married."

Married? I was wearing his fiancée's dress? Oh, this was getting better and better.

Lee brushed his hair out of his eyes and sat against the desk. The vamp behind him started to rub his shoulders in a sultry, whore-bitch sort of a way. She hadn't taken her eyes off me, and I didn't like it. "Anyone I know?" Lee prompted, and Trent's jaw clenched.

"A beautiful young woman named Ellasbeth Withon," he said. "From Seattle."

"Ah." Brown eyes wide, Lee smiled as if he was laughing at Trent. "Congratulations?"

"You've met her," Trent said sourly, and Lee chuckled.

"I've heard of her." He made a pained face. "Am I invited to the wedding?"

I puffed impatiently. I had thought we came here to knock heads, not have a reunion. Ten years would put them in their late teens. College? And I didn't like being ignored, but I supposed that was standard for hired help. At least whore-bitch hadn't been introduced either.

"Of course," Trent said. "The invitations will go out as soon as she decides between the eight options she's narrowed it down to," he said dryly. "I'd ask you to be my best man, if I thought you'd ever get on a horse again."

Lee pulled himself off the desk and out of the vamp's reach. "No, no, no," he protested, going to a small cabinet and bringing out two glasses and a bottle. "Not again. Not with you. My God, what did you whisper into that beast's ear, anyway?"

Trent smiled, a real one this time, and took the offered shot glass. "Fair is fair, surfer dude," he said, and I blinked at the accent he affected. "Seeing as you almost drowned me."

"Me?" Lee sat back on the desk, one foot off the floor. "I had nothing to do with that. The canoe had a leak. I didn't know you couldn't swim."

"That's what you keep saying." Trent's eye twitched. Taking a tiny sip, he turned to me. "Stanley, this is Rachel Morgan. She's my security tonight."

I beamed a false smile. "Hello, Lee." I held out my hand, careful to keep my ley line energy reined, though with the memory of that man's screams echoing through me, it was hard not to give him a jolt. "Nice to see the upstairs this time."

"Rachel," Lee said warmly, turning my hand to kiss the top of it instead of shaking it. "You can't imagine how bad I felt for getting you mixed up in that ugly business. I'm so pleased you came away from it unscathed. I trust you're being compensated properly tonight?"

I yanked my hand back before his lips touched it, making a show of wiping it off. "No apologies needed. But I'd be remiss for not thanking you for teaching me how to play craps." My pulse quickened and I stifled the urge to slug him. "Want your *dice back?*"

The vampire slid behind him, her hands going possessively atop his shoulders. Lee kept his smile in place, seemingly oblivious to my barb. *God, the man had been bleeding from his pores, and that had been aimed at me. Bastard.*

"The orphanage was most grateful for your donation," Lee said smoothly. "They put a new roof on with it, so I'm told."

"Fantastic," I said, honestly pleased. Beside me, Trent fidgeted, clearly dying to interrupt. "I'm always glad when I can help those less fortunate."

Lee took the vampire's hands in his and moved her to stand beside him.

Trent took my arm while they were distracted. "You bought the new roof?" he breathed.

"Apparently," I muttered, noting he was surprised about the roof, not the scuffle in the streets.

"Trent, Rachel," Lee said as he held the vampire's hand in his. "This is Candice."

Candice smiled to show her teeth. Ignoring Trent, she fixed her brown eyes on my neck, a red tongue edging the corner of her mouth. Exhaling, she eased closer. "Lee, sweetheart," she said, and I gripped Trent's arm tighter when her voice ran like ripples over my scar. "You told me I'd be entertaining a man." Her smile went predatory. "But this is okay."

I forced a breath. Waves of promise were coming from my neck, making my knees weaken. My blood pounded and my eyes almost slipped shut. I took a breath, then another. It took all my experience with Ivy to keep from responding. She was hungry, and she knew what she was doing. If she had been undead, I would have been hers. As it was, even with my scar she couldn't bespell me unless I let her. And I wasn't going to.

Aware of Trent watching, I gained control of myself, though I could feel the sexual tension rising in me like fog on a damp night. My thoughts slid to Nick, then Kisten, where they lingered to make things worse. "Candice," I said softly, leaning closer. *I wouldn't touch her. I wouldn't.* "It's nice to meet you. And I will break off your teeth and use them to pierce your belly button if you even as much as look at my scar again."

Candice's eyes flashed to black. The warmth in my scar died. Angry, she drew away, her hand atop Lee's shoulder. "I don't care if you are Tamwood's plaything," she said, trying to be all Queen of the Damned, but I lived with a truly dangerous vampire and her efforts were pathetic. "I can take you down," she finished.

My jaw clenched. "I live with Ivy. I'm not her plaything," I said softly, hearing a muted cheer from downstairs. "What does that tell you?"

"Nothing," she said, her pretty face going ugly.

"And nothing is exactly what you're going to get from me, so back off."

Lee stepped between us. "Candice," he said, putting a hand on the small of her back and pushing her to the door. "Do me a favor, sweetheart. Get Ms. Morgan some coffee, will you? She's working tonight."

"Black, no sugar," I said, hearing my voice rasp. My heart was pounding and sweat had broken out. Black witches I could handle. Skilled, hungry vampires were a little harder.

Unkinking my fingers from Trent's arm, I pulled away. His face was quiet as he looked at me and then the vamp Lee was escorting to the door. "Quen . . ." he whispered.

"Quen wouldn't have had a chance," I said, my heart slowing. If she had been an undead, neither would I. But Saladan wouldn't have been able to convince an undead vampire to back him, lest Piscary find out and kill him or her twice. There was honor among the dead. Or maybe it was just fear.

Lee said a few words to Candice, and the woman slunk out into the hall, giving me a sly smile before she left. Red heels were the last I saw of her. My thoughts spun when I noticed she had an anklet identical to Ivy's. There couldn't be more than one like that without a reason—perhaps Kisten and I ought to chat.

Not knowing what it meant, if anything, I sat in one of the green upholstered chairs before I fell over from the fading adrenaline. Hands clasped to hide their faint trembling, I thought of Ivy and the protection she gave me. No one had made a play for me like that in months, not since the vamp at the perfume counter had mistaken me for someone else. If I had to fight that off every day, it would only be a matter of time before I became a shadow of myself: thin, anemic, and belonging to someone. Or worse, belonging to anyone.

The sound of sliding fabric pulled my attention to Trent as he sat in the second chair. "You all right?" he breathed when Lee shut the door behind Candice with a firm thump.

His voice was soothing, surprising me. Forcing myself to straighten, I nodded, wondering why he cared, or even if he did. Exhaling, I forced my hands open and loose.

Bustling with efficiency, Lee edged back around his desk and sat. He was smiling to show his white teeth amid his suntanned face. "Trent," he said, leaning back in his chair. It was larger than ours, and I think it put him several inches taller. *Subtle.* "I'm glad you came to see me. We should talk before anything gets more out of hand than it has."

"Out of hand?" Trent didn't move, and I watched his concern for me melt into nothing. Green eyes hard, he set his shot glass on the desk between them, the soft click sounding louder than it should. Never looking from Saladan's sloppy grin, he took over the room. This was the man who killed his employees in his office and got away with it, the man who owned half the city, the man who thumbed his nose at the law, living above it in his fortress in the middle of an old-growth, planned-out forest.

Trent was angry, and I suddenly didn't mind that they were ignoring me.

"You derailed two of my trains, caused a near strike of my trucking line, and burned down my primary public relations effort," Trent said, a wisp of his hair starting to float.

I stared at him while Lee shrugged. *Primary public relations effort? It had been an orphanage. God, how cold could you be?*

"It was the easiest way to get your attention." Lee sipped his drink. "You've been inching your way past the Mississippi the last ten years. Did you expect anything less?"

Trent's jaw tightened. "You're killing innocent people with the potency of the Brimstone you're putting on the streets."

"No!" Lee barked, pushing the glass from him. "There are no innocents." Thin lips pressed together, he leaned forward, angry and threatening. "You crossed the line," he said, shoulders tense under his tux. "And I wouldn't be here culling your weak clientele if you stayed on your side of the river as agreed."

"My father made that agreement, not me. I've asked your father to lower the levels he allows in his Brimstone. People want a safe product. I give it to them. I don't care where they live."

Lee fell back with a sound of disbelief. "Spare me the benefactor crap," he simpered. "We don't sell to anyone who doesn't want it. And Trent? They want it. The stronger, the better. The death levels even out in less than a generation. The weak die off, the strong survive, ready and willing to buy more. To buy stronger. Your careful regulation weakens everyone. There's no natural balance, no strengthening of the species. Maybe that's why there are so few of you left. You've killed yourself by trying to save them."

I sat with my hands deceptively slack in my lap, feeling the tension rise in the small room. *Culling weak clientele? Strengthening the species?* Who in hell did he think he was?

Lee made a quick movement, and I twitched.

"But the bottom line," Lee said, easing back when he saw me move, "is that I'm here because you are changing the rules. And I'm not leaving. It's too late for that. You can hand everything over to me and graciously move off the continent, or I will take it, one orphanage, one hospital, one train station, street corner, and bleeding-heart innocent at a time." He took a sip of his drink and cradled it in his laced hands. "I like games, Trent. And if you remember, I won whatever we played."

Trent's eye twitched. It was his only show of emotion. "You have two weeks to get out of my city," he said, his voice a smooth ribbon of calm water hiding a deadly undertow. "I'm going to maintain my distribution. If your father wants to talk, I'm listening."

"Your city?" Lee flicked his eyes over me, then back to Trent. "Looks to me like it's split." He arched his thin eyebrows. "Very dangerous, very attractive. Piscary is in prison. His scion is ineffective. You're vulnerable from the veneer of honest businessman you hide behind. I'm going to take Cincinnati and the distribution net you have so painstakingly developed, and use it as it ought to be. It's a waste, Trent. You could control the entire Western Hemisphere with what you have, and you're pissing it away on half-strength Brimstone and biodrugs to dirt farmers and welfare cases that won't ever make anything of themselves—or anything for you."

A seething anger warmed my face. I happened to be one of those welfare cases, and though I would probably be shipped off to Siberia in a biocontainment bag if it ever got out, I bristled. Trent was scum, but Lee was disgusting. I opened my mouth to tell him to shut up about things he didn't understand when Trent touched my leg with his shoe in warning.

The rims of Trent's ears had gone red, and his jaw was tight. He tapped at the arm of the chair, a deliberate show of his agitation. "I do control the Western Hemisphere," Trent said, his low, resonating voice making my stomach clench. "And my welfare cases have given me more than my father's paying customers—Stanley."

Lee's tanned face went white in anger, and I wondered what was being said that I didn't understand. Perhaps it hadn't been college. Maybe they had met at "camp."

"Your money can't force me out," Trent added. "Ever. Go tell your father to lower his Brimstone levels and I'll back off from the West Coast."

Lee stood, and I stiffened, ready to move. He placed his hands spread wide, bracing himself. "You overestimate your reach, Trent. You did when we were boys, and nothing has changed. It's why you almost drowned trying to swim back to shore, and why you lost every game we played, every race we ran, every girl we made a prize." He was pointing now, underscoring his words. "You think you're more than you are, having been coddled and praised for accomplishments that everyone else takes for granted. Face it. You're the last of your kind, and it's your arrogance that put you there."

My eyes shifted between them. Trent sat with his legs comfortably crossed and his fingers laced. He was absolutely still. He was incensed, none of it showing but for the hem of his slacks trembling. "Don't make a mistake you can't walk away from," he said softly. "I'm not twelve anymore."

Lee backed up, a misplaced satisfaction and confidence in him as he eyed the door behind me. "You could have fooled me."

The door latch shifted and I jerked. Candice walked in, an institutional-white mug of coffee in her hand. "Excuse me," she said, her kitten-soft voice only adding to the tension. She slunk between Trent and Lee, breaking their gazes on each other.

Trent shook out his sleeves and took a slow breath. I glanced at him before reaching for the coffee. He looked shaken, but it was from repressing his anger, not fear. I thought of his biolabs and Ceri safely hiding with an old man across the street from my church. Was I making choices for her that she should be making for herself?

The mug was thick, the warmth of it seeping into my fingers when I took it. My lip curled when I realized she had put cream in it. Not that I was going to drink it. "Thanks," I said, making an ugly face right back at her when she took a sexually charged pose atop Lee's desk, her legs crossed at the knee.

"Lee," she said, leaning to make a provocative show. "There is a slight problem on the floor that needs your attention."

Looking annoyed, he pushed her out of his way. "Deal with it, Candice. I'm with friends."

Her eyes went black and her shoulders stiffened. "It's something you need to attend. Get your ass downstairs. It won't wait."

I flicked my gaze to Trent, reading his surprise. Apparently the pretty vamp was more than decoration. *Partner?* I wondered. She sure was acting like it.

She cocked one eyebrow at Lee in mocking petulance, making me wish I could do the same. I still hadn't bothered to learn how. "Now, Lee," she prompted, slipping off the desk and going to hold the door for him.

His brow furrowed. Brushing his short bangs from his eyes, he pushed his chair back with excessive force. "Excuse me." Thin lips tight, he nodded to Trent walked out, his feet thumping on the stairway.

Candice smiled predatorily at me before she slipped out after him. "Enjoy your coffee," she said, closing the door. There was a click as it locked.

Twenty-six

I took a deep breath, listening to the silence. Trent shifted his legs to put his ankle atop a knee. Eyes distant and worried, he chewed on a lower lip, looking nothing like the drug lord and murderer he was. Funny, you couldn't tell by looking.

"She locked the door," I said, jumping at the sound of my own voice.

Trent lifted his eyebrows. "She doesn't want you to wander. I think it's a good idea."

Snarky elf, I thought. Stifling a frown, I went to the small round window looking out across the frozen river. Using the flat of my hand, I wiped the condensation from it and took in the varied skyline. Carew Tower was lit up with holiday lights, glowing with the gold, green, and red film they covered the top floor windows with so they would shine like huge bulbs. It was clear tonight, and I could even see a few stars through the city's light pollution.

Turning, I put my hands behind my back. "I don't trust your friend."

"I never have. You'll live longer that way." Trent's tight jaw eased and the green of his eyes went a little less hard. "Lee and I spent our summers together when we were boys. Four weeks at one of my father's camps, four weeks at his family's beach house on a manmade island off the coast of California. It was supposed to foster goodwill between our families. He's the one who set the ward on my great window, actually." Trent shook his head. "He was twelve. Quite an accomplishment for him at the time. Still is. We had a party. My mother fell into the hot tub, she was so tipsy. I should replace it with glass now that we're—having difficulties."

He was smiling in a bittersweet memory, but I had stopped listening. Lee set the ward? It had taken the color of my aura, just like the disk in the game room. Our auras resonated to a similar frequency. Eyes squinting, I thought about our shared aversion to red wine. "He has the same blood disease I do, doesn't he?" I said. It couldn't be a coincidence. Not with Trent.

Trent's head jerked up. "Yes," he said cautiously. "That's why I don't understand this. My father saved his life, and now he's squabbling over a few million a year?"

Few million a year. Pocket change for the rich and filthy. Restless, I glanced at Lee's desk, deciding I had nothing to learn by sifting through the drawers. "You, ah, monitor the levels of Brimstone you produce?"

Trent's expression went guarded, then, as if making a decision, he ran a hand across his hair to make it lie flat. "Very carefully, Ms. Morgan. I'm not the monster you'd like me to be. I'm not in the business of killing people; I'm in the business of supply and demand. If I didn't produce it, someone else would, and it wouldn't be a safe product. Thousands would die." He glanced at the door and uncrossed his legs to put both feet on the floor. "I can guarantee it."

My thoughts went to Erica. The thought of her dying under the flag of being a weak member of the species was intolerable. But illegal was illegal. My hand smacked into his gold earrings as I tucked a strand of hair behind my ear. "I don't care how pretty the colors are that you paint your picture with, you're still a murderer. Faris didn't die because of a bee sting."

His brow furrowed. "Faris was going to give his records to the press."

"Faris was a frightened man who loved his daughter."

I put a hand on my hip and watched him fidget. It was very subtle: the tension in his jaw, the way he held his manicured fingers, the lack of any expression.

"So why don't you kill me?" I asked. "Before I do the same?" My heart pounded, and I felt as if I was at a cliff's edge.

Trent broke his persona of professional, well-dressed drug lord with a smile. "Because you won't go to the press," he said softly. "They will bring you down with me, and survival is more important than the truth to you."

My face warmed. "Shut up."

"It's not a failing, Ms. Morgan."

"Shut up!"

"And I knew eventually you'd work with me."

"I won't."

"You already are."

Stomach churning, I turned away. I gazed unseeing over the frozen river. A frown creased my brow. It was so silent I could hear the thumping of my heart—why was it that quiet?

I spun, hands gripping my elbows. Trent looked up from arranging the crease in his pants. His gaze was curious at the frightened look I knew I had. "What?" he said carefully.

Feeling unreal and disconnected, I took a step to the door. "Listen."

"I don't hear anything."

I reached out and wiggled the knob. "That's the problem," I said. "The boat is empty."

There was a heartbeat of silence. Trent rose, his suit making a pleasant hush. He looked more concerned than alarmed as he shook his sleeves down and came forward. Nudging me out of the way, he tried the handle.

"What, you think it's going to work for you when it won't work for me?" I said, grabbing his elbow and pulling him out from in front of the door. Balancing on one foot, I held my breath and kicked at the jamb, thankful that even luxury boats tried to keep everything as light as possible. My heel went right through the thin wood, my foot catching. The strips of my beautiful dress dangled and waved as I hopped ungainly backward to disentangle myself.

"Hey! Wait!" I exclaimed when Trent picked the splinters from the hole and reached through to unlock it from the outside. Ignoring me, he opened the door and darted into the hall.

"Damn it, Trent!" I hissed, snatching up my clutch purse and following him. Ankle hurting, I caught up with him at the foot of the stairs. Reaching out, I jerked him back, sending his shoulder into the wall of the narrow passage. "What are you doing?" I said, inches away from his angry eyes. "Is this how you treat Quen? You don't know what's out there, and if you die, I'm the one that's going to suffer, not you!"

He said nothing, his green eyes choleric and his jaw tight.

"Now get your scrawny ass behind mine, and keep it there," I said, giving him a shove.

Sullen and worried, I left him there. My hand wanted to reach for my splat gun, but as long as that purple disk was up and running, the potions in it wouldn't do anything but tick someone off as I got a nasty concoction of monkshood and spiderwort all over their nice dress clothes. A faint smile curved over my face. I didn't mind doing this the physical way.

What I could see of the room was empty. I listened, hearing nothing. Crouching to put my head at knee level, I peeked around the corner. I was down here for two reasons. First, if anyone was waiting to hit me, they'd have to adjust their swing, giving me time to get out of the way. Second, if I were hit, I wouldn't have so far to go to find the floor. But as I took in the elegant room, my stomach churned. The floor was littered with bodies.

"Oh my God," I said softly as I rose. "Trent, he killed them." *Was that it? Was Lee going to frame us for murder?*

Trent pushed past me, slipping my grasping reach easily. He crouched by the first body. "Knocked out," he said flatly, his beautiful voice turned to steel.

My horror turned to confusion. "Why?" I scanned the floor, guessing they had fallen where they stood.

Trent rose. His eyes went to the door. I agreed. "Let's get out of here," I said.

His steps behind me were quick as we hustled to the foyer to find it predictably locked. Through the frosted glass I could see cars in the parking lot, Trent's limo parked where we left it. "I got a bad feeling about this," I muttered, and Trent pushed me aside to look.

I stared at the thick wood, knowing I wouldn't be able to kick through that. Tense, I dug through my clutch purse. While Trent wasted his energy trying to break a window with a bar stool, I punched speed dial number one. "It's bulletproof glass," I said as the phone rang.

He lowered the stool and ran a hand over his wispy hair to make it perfect again. He wasn't even breathing hard. "How do you know?"

I shrugged, turning sideways for some privacy. "It's what I would have used." I returned to the gaming room as Ivy picked up. "Hey, Ivy," I said, refusing to lower my voice lest I give Mr. Elf the impression I hadn't planned this. "Saladan locked us in his gambling boat and ran away. Could you come on out and jimmy the door for me?"

Trent was peering out at the parking lot. "Jonathan is there. Call him."

Ivy was saying something, but Trent's voice was louder. I covered the receiver with a hand and said to Trent, "If he was still conscious, don't you think that he might be a little curious as to why Lee left and already have come to take a look?"

Trent's face went a little whiter.

"What?" I said as I focused back on Ivy. She was almost frantic.

"Get out!" she shouted. "Rachel, Kist had a bomb put on the boiler. I didn't know that's where you were going! Get out!"

My face went cold. "Um, I gotta go, Ivy. Talk to you later."

As Ivy yelled, I closed the cover to my phone and tucked it away. Turning to Trent, I smiled. "Kisten is blowing up Lee's boat as an object lesson. I think we need to leave."

My phone started ringing. I ignored it, and the call—Ivy?—was shunted into voice mail. Trent's confidence melted away to leave an attractive, well-dressed young man trying to show he wasn't afraid. "Lee wouldn't let anyone burn his boat," he said. "He doesn't work that way."

I clutched my arms about myself, scanning the room for something—anything—to help me. "He burned down your orphanage."

"That was to get my attention."

I looked at him, tired. "Would your *friend* let his boat burn and take you with it if Piscary was blamed for it? Heck of an easy way to take over the city."

Trent's jaw tightened. "The boiler room?" he asked.

I nodded. "How did you know?"

He headed for a small door behind the bar. "It's what I would have done."

"Swell." I followed him, my pulse quickening as I stepped around the unconscious people. "Where are we going?"

"I want to look at it."

I stopped dead in my tracks as Trent turned to go down a ladder backward. "You can dismantle a bomb?" It would be the only way to save everyone. There had to be a dozen people.

From the bottom of the ladder, Trent peered up at me, looking odd in his dress suit among the filth and clutter. "No. I just want to look at it."

"Are you nuts!" I exclaimed. "You want to look at it? We have to get out of here!"

Trent's upturned face was placid. "It might have a timer on it. Are you coming?"

"Sure," I said, stifling a laugh; I was pretty sure it would come out sounding hysterical.

Trent wove through the boat with a disturbing lack of urgency. I could smell hot metal and smoke. Trying not to snag my dress, I peered into the dimness. "There it is!" I shouted, pointing. My finger was shaking, and I dropped my hand to hide it.

Trent strode forward and I followed, hiding behind him when he crouched before a metal box with wires coming out of it. He reached to open it, and I panicked. "Hey!" I cried, grabbing his shoulder. "What the Turn are you doing? You don't know how to turn it off!"

He caught his balance without getting up, looking at me in annoyance, every hair on his head still perfect. "That's where the timer will be, Morgan."

I swallowed hard, peering over his shoulder as he carefully opened the lid. "How much time?" I whispered, my breath sending his wispy hair drifting.

He stood, and I took a step back. "About three minutes."

"Oh, hell no." My mouth went dry, and my phone started ringing. I ignored it. Leaning, I looked closer at the bomb, starting to feel a little unsteady.

Trent pulled on a watch fob to bring out an antique-looking timepiece and set the modern timer on it. "We've got three minutes to find a way off."

"Three minutes! We can't find a way off the boat in three minutes. The glass is bulletproof, the doors are thicker than your head, and that big purple disk will soak up any spell we throw at it!"

Trent's eyes were cold on me. "Get ahold of yourself, Morgan. Hysterics won't help."

"Don't tell me what to do!" I exclaimed, my knees starting to shake. "I think best when I'm having hysterics. Just shut up and let me have them!" Arms wrapped around myself, I glanced at the bomb. It was hot down there, and I was sweating. Three minutes. What in hell could you do in three minutes? Sing a little song. Dance a little dance. Make a little love. Find a new romance. *Oh God. I was making up poetry.*

"Maybe he has an escape route in his office?" Trent suggested.

"And that's why he locked us in there?" I said. "Come

on." I grabbed his sleeve and pulled. "We don't have enough time to find a way off." My thoughts went to the purple disk in the ceiling. I had influenced it once. Maybe I could bend it to my will. "Come on!" I repeated as his sleeve slipped through my fingers when he refused to move. "Unless you want to stay and watch numbers count down. I might be able to break the no-spell zone Lee has on his boat."

Trent rocked into motion. "I still say we can find a weak point in his security."

I headed up the ladder, not caring if Trent noticed I wasn't wearing undies or not. "Not enough time." Damn it, why didn't Kisten tell me what he was doing? I was surrounded by men who kept secrets from me. Nick, Trent, and now Kisten. Could I pick 'em or what? And Kist was killing people. I didn't want to like a guy who killed people. What was *wrong* with me?

Heart pounding as if marking the reducing seconds, we went back to the gaming room. It was silent and still. Waiting. My mouth twisted at the sight of the sleeping people. They were dead. I couldn't save them and Trent. I didn't even know how I was going to save myself.

The disk above me looked innocuous enough, but I knew it was still functioning when Trent glanced at it and paled. I guessed he was using his second sight. "You can't break that," he said. "But you don't need to. Can you make a protection circle big enough for both of us?"

My eyes widened. "You want to ride it out in a protection circle? You *are* crazy! The minute I hit it, down it goes!"

Trent looked angry. "How big, Morgan?"

"But I tripped the alarms last time just looking at it!"

"So what!" he exclaimed, his confidence cracking. It was nice to see him shaken, but under the circumstances, I couldn't enjoy it. "Trip the alarms! The disk doesn't stop you from tapping a line and making a spell. It only catches you when you do. Make the damned circle!"

"Oh!" I looked at him in understanding, my first wild

hope dying. I couldn't tap a line to make a protection circle. Not sitting on water as I was. "Um, you make it," I said.

He seemed to start. "Me? It takes me a good five minutes with chalk and candles."

Frustrated, I groaned. "What kind of an elf are you!"

"What kind of a runner are you?" he shot back. "I don't think your boyfriend will mind if you tap a line through him to save your life. Do it, Morgan. We're running out of time!"

"I can't." I spun in a tight circle. Through the unbreakable glass, Cincinnati glowed.

"Screw your damned honor, Rachel. Break your word to him or we're dead!"

Miserable, I turned back to him. *He thought I was honorable?* "That's not it. I can't draw on a line through Nick anymore. The demon broke my link with him."

Trent went ashen. "But you gave me a shock in the car. That was too much for what a witch can hold in his or her chi."

"I'm my own familiar, okay!" I said. "I made a deal with a demon to be its familiar so it would testify against Piscary, and I had to learn how to store ley line energy for it. Oh, I've got tons of energy, but a circle requires you stay connected to a line. I can't do it."

"You're a demon's familiar?" His face looked horrified, frightened, scared of me.

"Not anymore!" I shouted, angry to have to admit it had even happened. "I bought my freedom. Okay? Get off my case! But I don't have a familiar, and I can't tap a line over water!"

From my bag came the faint sound of my phone ringing. Trent stared at me. "What did you give it for your freedom?"

"My silence." My pulse hammered. What difference did it make if Trent knew? We were both going to die.

Grimacing as if having decided something, Trent took off his coat. Shaking his sleeve down, he undid the cuff link and pushed his sleeve past his elbow. "You aren't a demon's familiar?" It was a soft, worried whisper.

"No!" I was shaking. As I watched in slack-eyed confusion, he grabbed my arm just below the elbow. "Hey!" I shouted, pulling away.

"Deal with it," he said grimly. Gripping my arm harder, he used his free hand to force me to take his wrist in the same grip acrobats use when working the trapeze. "Don't make me regret this," he muttered, and my eyes widened when a rush of line energy flowed into me.

"Holy crap!" I gasped, almost falling. It was wild magic, having the uncatchable flavor of the wind. He had joined his will to mine, tapping a line through his familiar and giving it to me as if we were one. The line coming through him and into me had taken on a tinge of his aura. It was clean and pure with the taste of the wind, like Ceri's.

Trent groaned, and my eyes shot to his. His face was drawn and sweat had broken out on him. My chi was full, and though the extra energy was looping back to the line, apparently the stuff I had spindled already in my head was burning through him.

"Oh God," I said, wishing there was a way I could shift the balance. "I'm sorry, Trent."

His breath came in a ragged gasp. "Make the circle," he panted.

Eyes jerking to his timepiece swinging from its fob, I said the invocation. We both staggered as the force running through us ebbed. I didn't relax at all as the bubble of ley line energy blossomed about us. I glanced at his watch. I couldn't see how much time was left.

Trent tossed his hair from his eyes, not letting go of my arm. Eyes looking haggard, he ran his gaze over the gold smeared bubble over us to the people beyond. His expression went empty. Swallowing hard, he shifted his grip tighter. Clearly it wasn't burning him any longer, but the pressure would steadily build to its previous levels. "It's really big," he said, looking at the shimmer. "You can hold an undrawn circle this big?"

"I can hold it," I said, avoiding his eyes. His skin pressing against mine was warm and there were tingles coming from it. I didn't like the intimacy. "And I wanted it large so we have some leeway when the shock hits us. As soon as you let go or I touch it—"

"It falls," Trent finished for me. "I know. You're babbling, Morgan."

"Shut up!" I exclaimed, nervous as a pixy in a room full of frogs. "You may be used to having bombs blow up around you, but this is my first time!"

"If you're lucky, it won't be the last," he said.

"Just shut up!" I snapped. I hoped my eyes weren't as scared looking as his. If we survived the blast, there was still the aftermath to get through. Falling chunks of boat and icy water. Great. "Um, how long?" I asked, hearing my voice shake. My phone was ringing again.

He glanced down. "Ten seconds. Maybe we should sit down before we fall."

"Sure," I said. "That's probably a good ide—"

I gasped as a boom shook the floor. I reached for Trent, desperate that our grip on each other not break. The floor pushed up at us, and we fell. He clutched at my shoulder, pulling me into him to keep me from rolling away. Pressed against him, I could smell silk and aftershave.

My stomach dropped, and a flash of fire burst around us. I screamed as my ears went numb. In an unreal, soundless motion, the boat broke apart as we rose. The night became smears of black sky and red fire. The tingle of the circle breaking washed over me. Then we fell.

Trent's grip was torn away, and I cried out when fire raced over me. My explosion-numbed ears filled with water and I couldn't breathe. I wasn't burning, I was drowning. It was cold, not hot. Panicking, I fought against the heavy water pushing at me.

I couldn't move. I didn't know which way was up. The dark was full of bubbles and chunks of boat. A faint glow to my left caught my attention. I gathered myself and aimed for it, telling my brain it was the surface even though it seemed to be sideways, not up.

God, I hoped it was the surface.

I burst from the water, my ears still not working. The cold struck me, freezing. I gasped, the air like knives in my lungs. I took another thankful breath. I was so cold it hurt.

Pieces of boat were still falling, and I tread water, thankful that I wore a dress I could move in. The water tasted like oil, and the swallow I had taken in hung heavy in me.

"Trent!" I shouted, hearing it as if through a pillow. "Trent!"

"Here!"

I shook the wet hair from my eyes and turned. Relief went though me. It was dark, but through the floating ice and wood, I saw Trent. His hair was plastered against him, but he looked unhurt. Shivering, I kicked off the one heel that I still had on and started toward him. Bits of boat were making the odd splash. How could it still be falling? I wondered. There was enough flotsam between us to build two boats.

Trent started forward with a professional looking stroke. Apparently he had learned to swim. The glimmer of fire on the icy water brightened around us. Looking up, I gasped. Something big and burning had yet to come down.

"Trent!" I shouted, but he didn't hear me. "Trent, look out!" I screamed, pointing. But he wasn't listening. I dove, trying to escape.

I was flung as if smacked. The water around me turned red. I lost most of the air from my lungs when something hit me, bruising my back. The water saved me, though, and with my lungs aching and my eyes smarting, I followed my exhaled breath to the surface.

"Trent!" I called as I emerged from the icy water and into the burning cold of the night. I found him holding a cushion that was rapidly filling with water. His eyes met mine, unfocused. The light from the burning boat was dimming, and I swam for him. The dock was gone. I didn't know how we were going to get out of there.

"Trent," I said, coughing when I reached him. My ears were ringing, but I could hear myself. I spit the hair out of my mouth. "Are you okay?"

He blinked as if trying to focus. Blood seeped from under his hairline, making a brown streak in his fair hair. His eyes closed, and I watched in horror when his grip on the cushion went slack. "No, you don't," I said, reaching out before he could slip under.

Shivering, I wrapped an arm about his neck, tucking his chin against the inside of my elbow. He was breathing. My legs were going slow from the cold and my toes were cramping. I looked for help. Where in hell was the I.S.? Someone must have seen that explosion.

"Never around when you need them," I muttered, shoving a chunk of ice as large as a chair out of my way. "Probably out giving someone a ticket for selling expired charms." The dock was gone. I had to get us out of the water, but the break wall was three feet of concrete. The only way out was to get back onto the ice and walk to another dock.

A sound of desperation came from me as I struck out for the edge of the hole the blast had ripped in the ice. I'd never make it even with the slow current. The water was starting to creep higher up me, and my movements were slower and harder to make. I wasn't cold anymore, either, and that scared the hell out of me. I could probably make it . . . if I weren't dragging Trent.

"Damn it all to hell!" I shouted, using my anger to keep moving. I was going to die here, trying to save his ass. "Why didn't you tell me what you were doing, Kisten!" I exclaimed, feeling my tears like fire leaking out of me as I swam. "Why didn't I tell you where I was going?" I yelled back at myself. "I'm a dumbass. And your stupid watch is fast, Trent! Did you know that? Your stupid . . ." I took a sobbing breath. ". . . watch is fast."

My throat hurt, but the motion seemed to warm me. The water felt positively balmy now. Panting, I stopped swimming, treading water. My vision blurred when I realized I was almost there. A big chunk of ice was in my way, though, and I'd have to swim around it.

Taking a resolute breath, I shifted my leaden arm and kicked my legs. I couldn't feel them anymore, but I assumed they were moving since the eight-inch-thick shelf of ice seemed to be moving closer. The last of the light from the burning boat made little red smears on the ice as I reached out and touched it. My hand slid cleanly away to pull in snow, and I sank. Adrenaline pounded through me and I kicked back to the surface. Trent sputtered and coughed.

"Oh, Trent," I said, water filling my mouth. "I forgot you were here. You first. Come on. Up on the ice."

Using the questionable leverage of what looked like part of the casino's bar, I got Trent halfway up onto the frozen river. Tears slipped down my face as I was now able to use both arms to keep myself afloat. I hung for a moment, my hands unfeeling in the snow while I rested my head atop the ice. I was so tired. Trent wasn't drowning. I had done my job. Now I could save myself.

I reached up to pull myself onto the ice—and failed. Snow fell in to make puddles of slush. Switching tactics, I tried to lever my leg up. It wouldn't move. I couldn't move my leg.

"Okay," I said, not as scared as I thought I ought to be. The cold must have numbed everything—even my thoughts felt blurry. I was supposed to be doing something, but I couldn't remember what. I blinked as I saw Trent, his legs still in the water.

"Oh, yeah," I whispered. I had to get out of the water. The sky above me was black, and the night was silent but for the ringing in my ears and the faint sound of sirens. The light from the fires was dim and going dimmer. My fingers wouldn't work, and I had to use my arms like clubs to pull a chunk of boat closer. Concentrating to not lose my thought, I pushed it under to buoy me up. A groan slipped from me when, with its help, I managed to slip a leg up onto the ice. I rolled awkwardly and lay panting. The wind was like fire on my back, and the ice was warm. I'd done it.

"Where is everyone?" I breathed, feeling my flesh hard against the cold ice. "Where's Ivy? Where's the fire department? Where's my phone?" I giggled as I remembered it was at the bottom of the river with my purse, then sobered as I thought of the unconscious people drifting downward through the icy water in their best finery to join it. Hell, I'd kiss even Denon, my old, despised boss from the I.S., if he showed up.

That reminded me. "Jonathan," I whispered. "Oh, Jo-o-o-o-onathan," I sang. "Where are you? Come out, come out, wherever you are—you tall freak of nature."

I lifted my head, glad I was pointed in the right direction. Squinting past my stringy hair, I could see a light where the limo sat. The headlights were aimed at the river, shining to show the destruction and the sinking bits of boat. Jonathan's silhouette stood at the quay. I could tell it was him because he was the only person I knew who was that tall. He was looking the wrong way. He'd never see me, and I couldn't shout anymore.

Damn it. I was going to have to get up.

I tried. I really did. But my legs wouldn't work and my arms just lay there, ignoring me. Besides, the ice was warm, and I didn't want to get up. Maybe if I shouted he'd hear me.

I took a breath. "Jonathan," I whispered. Oh hell, this wasn't going to work.

I took another breath. "Jonathan," I said, hearing it around my ringing ears. I pulled my head up, watching as he didn't move to look. "Never mind," I said, letting my head fall back onto the ice. The snow was warm, and I pressed into it. "This is nice," I mumbled, but I don't think it made it past my thoughts into real words.

It felt as if the world was spinning, and I could hear the slosh of water. Snuggling into the ice, I smiled. I hadn't slept well for days. I exhaled, drifting off into nothing, enjoying the warmth of the sun that was suddenly shining on the ice. Someone curled their arms around me, and I felt my head thump into a soggy chest as I was lifted.

"Denon?" I heard myself murmur. "Come here, Denon. I owe you a big . . . kiss . . ."

"Denon?" someone echoed.

"I'll carry her, Sa'han."

I tried to open my eyes, swirling back into nothing when I felt myself move. I drowsed, not awake but not quite not asleep. Then I was still, and I tried to smile and go to sleep. But a faint pinch and throb kept intruding on my cheek, and my legs hurt.

Irritated, I pushed at the ice, finding it was gone. I was sitting up, and someone was slapping me. "That's enough," I heard Trent say. "You're going to leave a mark."

The pinch vanished to leave just the throbbing. *Jonathan was slapping me?* "Hey, you freakin' bastard," I breathed. "You hit me again and I'll take care of your family planning."

I could smell leather. My face screwed up as feeling started to come back into my legs and arms. Oh God, it hurt. I opened my eyes to find Trent and Jonathan peering down at me. Blood seeped from Trent's hairline and water dripped from his nose. Above their heads was the interior of the limo. I was alive? How did I get to the car?

"'Bout time you found us," I breathed, my eyes closing.

I heard Trent sigh. "She's okay."

I suppose. Maybe. Compared to being dead, I guess I was okay.

"Pity," Jonathan said, and I heard him shift away from me. "It would have simplified things if she wasn't. Not too late to slip her in the water with the rest."

"Jon!" Trent barked.

His voice was as hot as my skin felt. I was freaking burning up.

"She saved my life," Trent said softly. "I don't care if you like her or not, but she has earned your respect."

"Trenton—" Jonathan started.

"No." It was cold. "She has *earned* your respect."

There was a hesitation, and I would have drifted off to nothing if the pain in my legs would let me. And my fingers were on fire. "Yes, Sa'han," Jonathan said, and I jerked awake.

"Get us home. Call ahead and have Quen draw a bath for her. We have to get her warmer than this."

"Yes, Sa'han." It was slow and reluctant. "The I.S. is here. Why don't we leave her with them?"

I felt a small pull upon my chi as Trent tapped a line. "I don't want to be seen here. Just don't get in anyone's way and we won't be noticed. Hurry up."

My eyes wouldn't listen to me anymore, but I heard Jonathan get out and shut the door. There was another thump when he got in the driver's door and the car eased into motion. The arms around me tightened, and I realized I was in Trent's lap, the warmth of his body doing more than the air to warm me. I felt the softness of a blanket against me. I must have been swaddled up right tight; I couldn't move my legs or arms.

"I'm sorry," I murmured, giving up on trying to open my eyes. "I'm getting water all over your suit." Then I giggled, thinking that had sounded really pathetic. He was already soaked. "Your Celtic charm isn't worth a damn," I whispered. "I hope you kept your receipt."

"Shut up, Morgan," Trent said, his voice distant and preoccupied.

The car picked up speed, and the sound seemed to lull me. *I could relax,* I thought as I felt the tingling of circulation in my limbs. I was in Trent's car, wrapped in a blanket, and held in his arms. He wouldn't let anything hurt me.

He wasn't singing, though, I mused. *Shouldn't he be singing?*

Twenty-seven

The warm water I was sitting in was nice. I had been in it long enough to prune twice, but I didn't care. Ellasbeth's sunken tub was fab. I sighed, leaning my head back and staring at the ten-foot ceilings framed by the potted orchids lining the bathtub. Maybe there was something to this drug lord business if you got to have a tub like this. I'd been in it for over an hour.

Trent had called Ivy for me even before we reached the city's limits. I'd talked to her myself not too long ago, telling her I was okay and was soaking in warm water and wasn't getting out until hell froze over. She had hung up on me, but I knew we were okay.

Dragging my fingers through the bubbles, I adjusted Trent's borrowed pain amulet hanging about my neck. I didn't know who had invoked it; maybe his secretary? All my charms were at the bottom of the Ohio River. My smile faltered as I remembered the people I hadn't been able to save. I would not feel guilty that I breathed and they didn't. Their deaths were laid at Saladan's feet, not mine. Or maybe Kisten's. Damn it. What was I going to do about that?

I closed my eyes and said a prayer for them, but they jerked open when a faint cadence of brisk steps grew louder. They quickly grew closer, and I froze as a thin woman dressed smartly in a cream-colored suit clacked and clicked in over the bathroom tile unannounced. There was a department store bag over her arm. Her steely gaze was fixed on the doorway to the changing room, and she never saw me as she vanished into it.

It had to be Ellasbeth. Crap. What was I supposed to do? Wipe the bubbles from my hand and offer to shake hers? Frozen, I stared at the door. My coat was on one of the chairs and my garment bag was still hanging by the changing screen. Pulse quickening, I wondered if I could reach the green towel before she realized she wasn't alone.

The faint rustling stopped, and I shrank down into the bubbles when she strode back in, house afire. Her dark eyes were narrowed in anger and her high cheekbones were red. Posture stiff, she halted, bag still over her arm and apparently forgotten. Her thick, waving blond hair was held back to give her narrow face a stark beauty. Lips tight, she held her head high, her eyes fixing vehemently upon me as soon as she cleared the archway.

So that's what it looked like when hell froze over.

"Who are you?" she said, her strong voice domineering and cold.

I smiled, but I knew it looked rather sickly. "Ah, I'm Rachel Morgan. Of Vampiric Charms?" I started to sit up, then changed my mind. I hated the question that had crept into my tone, but there it was. 'Course it might have been there because I was naked except for bubbles, and she was standing in four-inch heels and a casually tasteful outfit that Kisten might pick out for me if he took me shopping in New York.

"What are you doing in my bathtub?" She gazed disparagingly at my healing black eye.

I reached for a towel and dragged it in with me, covering myself. "Trying to warm up."

Her mouth twitched. "I don't wonder why," she said sharply. "He's a cold bastard."

I sat up in a rush of water as she walked out. "Trenton!" her voice rang out, harsh against the peace I had been wallowing in.

My breath puffed out, and I looked at the soaked towel clinging to me. Sighing, I got up and opened the drain with my foot. The water swirling about my calves settled and began to escape. Ellasbeth had thoughtfully left all the doors open, and I could hear her shouting at Trent. She wasn't far away. Perhaps as close as the common room. Deciding that as long as I could hear her out there, it was probably safe enough to get dried off in here, I wrung out the soaked towel and grabbed two new ones from the warmer.

"God save you, Trenton," came her voice, bitter and abusive. "Couldn't you even wait until I was gone before bringing in one of your whores?"

I reddened and my motions to dry my arms grew rough.

"I thought you *had* left," Trent said calmly, not helping matters. "And she's not a whore, she's a business associate."

"I don't care what you call her, she's in my rooms, you bastard."

"There wasn't anywhere else to put her."

"There are eight bathrooms this side of the wall, and you put her in mine?"

I was glad my hair was somewhat dry, and that it smelled like Ellasbeth's shampoo made me feel all peachy-keen. Hopping ungainly on one foot, I tried to get my underwear on, thankful I had only been wearing the nylons that I brought from home when I went into the drink. My skin was still damp and everything was sticking. I almost went down when my foot got stuck halfway into my jeans leg, and lurching, I caught myself against the counter.

"Damn you, Trenton! Don't even try to say *that* is business!" Ellasbeth was shouting. "There's a naked witch in my bathtub, and you're sitting in your robe!"

"No, you listen to me." Trent's voice was iron hard, and I could hear his frustration even from two rooms away. "I said she's a business associate, and that's what she is."

Ellasbeth made a harsh bark of laugher. "From Vampiric Charms? She told me the name of her bloodhouse herself!"

"She's a runner, if it's any of your business," Trent said so coldly I could almost see his clenched jaw. "Her partner is a vampire. It's a play on words, Ellasbeth. Rachel was my security escort tonight, and she fell into the river saving my life. I wasn't going to drop her at her office half dead from hypothermia like an unwanted cat. You told me you were taking the seven o'clock flight out. I thought you were gone, and I wasn't about to put her in my rooms."

There was a moment of silence. I shimmied into my sweatshirt. Somewhere on the bottom of the river was several thousand dollars of soft ribbon gold from Randy's coiffure and one earring. At least the necklace had survived. Maybe the charm worked only on the necklace.

"You were on that boat. . . . The one that blew up . . ." It was softer, but there wasn't a hint of apology in her sudden concern.

In the silence, I fumbled at my hair, grimacing. Maybe if I had half an hour I could do something with it. Besides, there was no way to recover from the first stellar impression I'd made. Taking a steadying breath, I squared my shoulders and padded in my sock feet to the common room. Coffee. I could smell coffee. Coffee would make everything better.

"You can understand my confusion," Ellasbeth was saying as I hesitated by the door, unnoticed but able to see them. Ellasbeth stood beside the round table in the breakfast nook, looking meek in the way a tiger looks when it realizes it can't eat the man with the whip. Trent was seated, wearing a green robe edged in maroon. There was a professional-looking bandage on his forehead. He looked bothered—as he should with his fiancée accusing him of cheating.

"That's the closest to an apology I'm going to get, isn't it?" Trent said.

Ellasbeth dropped the department store bag and put a hand on her hip. "I want her out of my rooms. I don't care who she is."

Trent's eyes fell on mine as if drawn to them, and I winced apologetically. "Quen is taking her home after a light dinner," he said to her. "You're welcome to join us. As I said, I thought you had left."

"I changed to a vamp flight so I could shop longer."

Trent glanced back at me again to tell Ellasbeth that they weren't alone. "You spent six hours in the stores and have only one bag?" he said, the faintest accusation in his voice.

Ellasbeth followed his gaze to me, quickly masking her anger with a pleasant expression. But I could see her frustration. It remained to be seen how it would show itself. I was betting on hidden barbs and slights disguised as compliments. But I would be nice as long as she was.

Smiling, I came out in my jeans and Howlers sweatshirt. "Hey, uh, thanks for the pain amulet and letting me get cleaned up, Mr. Kalamack." I stopped beside the table, the awkwardness as thick and choking as bad cheesecake. "No need to bother Quen. I'll call my partner to come and get me. She's probably banging on your gatehouse already."

Trent made a visible effort to purge the anger from his posture. Elbows on the table so the sleeves of his robe fell to show the fair hair upon his arms, he said, "I'd rather have Quen take you home, Ms. Morgan. I don't particularly want to talk to Ms. Tamwood." He glanced at Ellasbeth. "Do you want me to call the airport for you, or are you staying another night?"

It was entirely devoid of any invitation. "I'll be staying," she said tightly. Bending at the waist, she picked up her bag and walked to her door. I watched her quick stilted steps, seeing in them a dangerous combination of callous disregard and ego.

"She's an only child, isn't she?" I said as the sound of her heels was lost on the carpet.

Trent blinked, his lips parting. "Yes, she is." Then he gestured for me to sit. "Please."

Not really sure I wanted to eat with the two of them, I gingerly sat on the chair opposite Trent. My gaze went to the fake window spanning the entirety of the wall that the small, nearby sunken living room took up. It was just after eleven according to the clocks I had seen, and it was dark with no moon. "Sorry," I said, my gaze flicking to the archway to El-lasbeth's rooms.

His jaw tightened for an instant, then relaxed. "Can I get you some coffee?"

"Sure. That would be great." I was almost faint from hunger, and the heat of my bath had drained me. I looked up with wide eyes as a matronly woman in an apron made her unhurried way out of the small kitchen tucked in at the back of the room. It was partially open to the seating arrangement, but I hadn't noticed her until now.

Giving me a smile that encompassed all her face, the woman set a mug of that heavenly scented coffee in front of me before topping off Trent's smaller teacup with an amber brew. I thought I could smell gardenias, but I wasn't sure. "Bless you," I said as I wrapped my hands around it and breathed in the steam.

"You're welcome," she said with the professional warmth of a good waitress. Smiling, she turned to Trent. "What will it be tonight, Mr. Kalamack? It's almost too late for a proper dinner."

As I blew on the surface of my coffee, my thoughts went to the different schedules of witches and elves, thinking it interesting that one of our species was awake at all times and that dinner happened about the same time for both of us.

"Oh, let's make it light," Trent said, clearly trying to ease the mood. "I have about three pounds of Ohio River sitting in me somewhere. How about a breakfast instead? The usual, Maggie."

The woman nodded, the white hair clipped close to her head not moving at all. "And how about you, dear?" she asked me.

I glanced between Trent and the woman. "What's the usual?"

"Four eggs over easy and three slices of rye toast done on one side."

I felt myself blanch. "That's eating light?" I said before I could stop my mouth.

Trent arranged his jammies' collar, peeking from behind his robe. "High metabolism."

My thoughts went back to how he and Ceri never seemed to get cold. The temperature of the river, too, hadn't affected him. "Um," I said as I realized she was still waiting. "The toast sounds good, but I'll pass on the eggs."

Eyebrows high, Trent took a sip of his tea, eyeing me over the rim. "That's right," he said, his voice unaccusing. "You don't tolerate them well. Maggie, let's go with waffles."

Shocked, I leaned back in my chair. "How did you . . ."

Trent shrugged, looking good in his bathrobe and bare feet. He had nice feet. "You don't think I know your medical history?"

My wonder died as I recalled Faris dead on his office floor. *What in hell was I doing here eating dinner with him?* "Waffles would be great."

"Unless you'd like something more traditional for dinner. Chinese doesn't take long. Would you rather have that? Maggie makes fabulous wontons."

I shook my head. "Waffles sound good."

Maggie smiled, turning to putter back into the kitchen. "Won't be but a moment."

I put my napkin in my lap, wondering how much of this let's-be-nice-to-Rachel scene was because Ellasbeth was in the next room listening and Trent wanted to hurt her for accusing him of cheating. Deciding I didn't care, I put my elbows on the table and took a sip of the best coffee I'd ever tasted. Eyes closing in the rising steam, I moaned in delight. "Oh God, Trent," I breathed. "This is good."

The sudden thump of heels on carpet pulled my eyes open. It was back.

I straightened in my chair as Ellasbeth came in, her dress coat open to show a starched white shirt and a peach-colored scarf. My gaze went to her ring finger and I blanched. You could run a city on the sparkle that thing put out.

Ellasbeth sat beside me, a shade too close for my liking.

"Maggie?" she said lightly. "I'll have tea and biscuits, please. I ate while out."

"Yes, ma'am," Maggie said as she leaned through the open archway. Her tone lacked utterly in any warmth. Clearly Maggie didn't like Ellasbeth, either.

Ellasbeth fixed a smile to her face, setting her long, fragile-looking fingers on the table to best show off her engagement ring. *Bitch.* "Seems we got off the horse on the wrong side, Ms. Morgan," she said cheerfully. "Have you and Trenton known each other long?"

I didn't like Ellasbeth. I think I'd be pretty upset myself if I came home and found a girl in Nick's bathtub, but after seeing her shouting at Trent, I couldn't find any sympathy for her. Accusing someone of cheating is harsh. My smile faltered as I realized I had almost done the same thing to Nick. I had accused him of dumping me, asking if there was someone else. There was a difference, but not much. Shit. I had to apologize. That he hadn't told me where he'd been going the last three months while avoiding me didn't seem like enough reason anymore. At least I hadn't called him any names. Jerking myself from my thoughts, I smiled at Ellasbeth.

"Oh, Trent and I go back a long way," I said lightly, twirling a curl of my hair about my finger and remembering its new shortness. "We met at camp as children. Sort of romantic when you think about it." I smiled at Trent's suddenly blank look.

"Really?" She turned to Trent, the hint of a tiger growling in her voice's soft cadence.

Sitting up, I tucked my legs under me to sit cross-legged, running my finger across the rim of the mug suggestively. "He was such a cub when he was younger, full of fire and spirit. I had to fight him off, the dear boy. That's where he got that scar on his lower arm."

I looked at Trent. "I can't believe you haven't told Ellasbeth! Trent, you aren't still embarrassed about that, are you?"

Ellasbeth's eye twitched, but her smile never faltered.

Maggie set a delicate looking cup full of an amber liquid by her elbow and quietly walked away. Her carefully shaped eyebrows high, Ellasbeth took in Trent's silent posture and his lack of denial. Her fingertips made one rolling cadence against the table in agitation. "I see," she said, then stood. "Trenton, I do believe I will catch a flight out tonight after all."

Trent met her gaze. He looked tired and a bit relieved. "If that is what you want, love."

She leaned close to him, her eyes on me. "It's to give you the chance to settle your affairs—sweetness," she said, her lips shifting the air about his ear. Still watching me, she lightly kissed his cheek. There was no feeling in her eyes beyond a vindictive glint. "Call me tomorrow."

Not a flicker of emotion crossed Trent. Nothing. And its very absence chilled me. "I'll count the hours," he said, his voice giving no clue either. Both of their eyes were on me as his hand rose to touch her cheek, but he didn't kiss her back. "Should Maggie pack up your tea?"

"No." Still watching me, she straightened, her hand lingering possessively on his shoulder. The picture they made was both beautiful and strong. And united. I remembered the reflection of Trent and me at Saladan's boat. Here was the bond that had been lacking between us. It wasn't love, though. It was more of . . . My brow furrowed. . . . a business merger?

"It was a pleasure meeting you, Rachel," Ellasbeth said, pulling my thoughts back to the present. "And thank you for accompanying my fiancé tonight. Your services are undoubtedly well-practiced and appreciated. It's a shame he won't be calling upon them again."

I leaned across the table to shake her offered hand with a neutral pressure. I think she had just called me a whore—again. I suddenly didn't know what was going on. *Did he like her, or didn't he?* "Have a nice flight out," I said.

"I will. Thank you." Her hand slipped from mine and she drew a step back. "Walk me to the car?" she asked Trent, her voice smooth and satisfied.

"I'm not dressed, love," he said softly, still touching her. "Jonathan can take your bags."

A flicker of annoyance crossed her, and I flashed her a catty smile. Turning, she walked out to the hallway overlooking the great room. "Jonathan?" she called, her heels clacking.

My God. The two played mind games with each other as if it was an Olympic sport.

Trent exhaled. Putting my feet on the floor, I made a wry face. "She's nice."

His expression went sour. "No she isn't, but she's going to be my wife. I'd appreciate it if you wouldn't imply anymore that we are sleeping together."

I smiled, a real one this time. "I just wanted her to leave."

Maggie bustled close, putting down table settings and taking away Ellasbeth's teacup and saucer. "Nasty, nasty woman," she muttered, her motions quick and sharp. "And you can sack me if you want, Mr. Kalamack, but I don't like her and I never will. You watch. She'll bring some woman with her who will take over my kitchen. Rearrange my cupboards. Push me out."

"Never, Maggie," Trent soothed, his posture shifting to a companionable ease. "We all have to make the best of it."

"Oh, worra, worra, worra," she mumbled as she made her way back into the kitchen.

Feeling more relaxed now that Ellasbeth was gone, I took another sip of that wonderful coffee. "*She's* nice," I said, looking at the kitchen.

His green eyes boyishly soft, he nodded. "Yes, she is."

"She's not an elf," I said, and his eyes jerked to mine. "Ellasbeth is," I added, and his look went closed again.

"You're getting uncomfortably adept, Ms. Morgan," he said, leaning away from me.

Putting my elbows to either side of the white plate, I rested my chin on the bridge my hands made. "That's Ellasbeth's problem, you know. She feels like she is a broodmare."

Trent shook out his napkin and put it on his lap. His robe was slowly coming undone to show a pair of executive-looking pajamas. It was somewhat of a disappointment—I'd been hoping for boxers. "Ellasbeth doesn't want to move to Cincinnati," he said, unaware that I was sneaking glances at his physique. "Her work and friends are in Seattle. You wouldn't be able to tell by looking at her, but she's one of the world's best nuclear transplant engineers."

My surprised silence brought his attention up, and I stared at him.

"She can take the nucleus of a damaged cell and transplant it into a healthy one," he said.

"Oh." Beautiful and smart. She could be Miss America if she learned how to lie better. But it sounded really close to illegal genetic manipulation to me.

"Ellasbeth can work from Cincinnati as easily as Seattle," Trent said, mistaking my silence for interest. "I've already financed the university's research department to update their facilities. She's going to put Cincinnati on the map for her developments, and she's angry that she's being forced to move instead of me." He met my questioning eyes. "It's not illegal."

"Tomato, tomatto," I said, leaning back when Maggie set a crock of butter and a pitcher of steaming syrup on the table and walked away.

Trent's green eyes met mine and he shrugged.

The scent of cooking batter drifted close, heady with promise, and my mouth watered as Maggie returned with two steaming plates of waffles. She set one before me, hesitating to make sure I was pleased. "This looks wonderful," I said, reaching for the butter.

Trent adjusted his plate while he waited for me. "Thanks, Maggie. I'll take care of the settings. It's getting late. Enjoy the rest of your evening."

"Thank you, Mr. Kalamack," Maggie said, clearly pleased as she rested a hand atop his shoulder. "I'll clean up the spills before I go. More tea or coffee?"

I looked up from pushing the butter to Trent. They were both waiting for me. "Um, no," I said as I glanced at my mug. "Thank you."

"This is fine," Trent echoed.

Maggie nodded as if we were doing something right before she returned to the kitchen humming. I smiled when I recognized the odd lullaby, "All the Pretty Little Horses."

Lifting a lid to a covered container, I found it full of crushed strawberries. My eyes widened. Tiny whole ones the size of my pinky nail made a ring around the rim as if it was June, not December, and I wondered where he had gotten them. I eagerly ladled berries on top of my waffle, looking up when I realized Trent was watching me. "You want some of these?"

"When you're done with them."

I went to take another scoop, then hesitated. Dropping the spoon back in, I pushed them across the table. The small noise of clinking silverware seemed loud as I poured the syrup. "You do know the last man I saw in a robe, I beat into unconsciousness with a chair leg," I quipped, desperate to break the silence.

Trent almost smiled. "I'll be careful."

The waffle was crisp on the outside and fluffy on the inside, easily cut with a fork. Trent used a knife. I carefully put the perfect square into my mouth so I wouldn't dribble. "Oh God," I said around my full mouth and giving up on manners. "Is it because we almost died that this tastes so good, or is she the best cook on earth?"

It was real butter, and the maple syrup had the dusky flavor that said it was a hundred percent real. Not two percent, not seven percent; it was real maple syrup. Remembering the stash of maple candy I once found while searching Trent's office, I wasn't surprised.

Trent put an elbow on the table, his eyes on his plate. "Maggie puts mayonnaise in them. It gives them an interesting texture."

I hesitated, staring at my plate, then deciding if I couldn't taste it, there wasn't enough egg to worry about. "Mayonnaise?"

A faint sound of dismay came from the kitchen. "Mr.

Kalamack . . ." Maggie came out, wiping her hands on her apron. "Don't be giving my secrets away, or you'll find tea leaves in your brew tomorrow," she scolded.

Leaning to look over his shoulder, he widened his smile to become an entirely different person. "Then I'll be able to read my fortune. Have a good night, Maggie."

Harrumphing, she walked out, passing the sunken living room and making a left turn at the walkway overlooking the great hall. Her steps were almost soundless, and the closing of the main door was loud. Hearing running water in the new silence, I ate another bite.

Drug lord, murderer, bad man, I reminded myself. But he wasn't talking, and I was starting to feel uncomfortable. "Hey, I'm sorry about the water in your limo," I offered.

Trent wiped his mouth. "I think I can handle a little dry cleaning after what you did."

"Still," I said as my gaze slid to the crock of strawberries. "I'm sorry."

Seeing my eyes flick from the fruit to him, Trent made a questioning face. He wasn't going to offer them to me, so I reached out and took them. "Takata's car isn't nicer than yours," I said, upending the container over the remains of my waffle. "I was just jerking you around."

"I figured that out," he said wryly. He wasn't eating, and I looked up to see him with knife and fork in hand, watching me scrape the last of the strawberries out with my butter knife.

"What?" I said as I put the crock down. "You weren't going to have any more."

He carefully cut another square of waffle. "You've been in contact with Takata, then?"

I shrugged. "Ivy and I are working security at his concert next Friday." I wedged a small bite into my mouth and closed my eyes as I chewed. "This is really good." He didn't say anything, and my eyes opened. "Are you—ah—going?"

"No."

Turning back to my plate, I glanced at him from around

my hair. "Good." I ate another bite. "The man is something else; when we talked, he was wearing orange pants. And he's got his hair out to here." I gestured, showing Trent. "But you probably know him. Personally."

Trent was still working on his waffle with the steady pace of a snail. "We met once."

Content, I slid all the strawberries off the remnants of my waffle and concentrated on them. "He picked me up off the street, gave me a ride, dumped me off on the expressway." I smiled. "At least he had someone bring my car along. Have you heard his early release?" *Music. I could always keep the conversation going if it was about music. And Trent liked Takata. I knew that much about him.*

" 'Red Ribbons'?" Trent asked, an odd intentness to his voice.

Nodding, I swallowed and pushed my plate away. There were no more strawberries, and I was full. "Have you heard it?" I asked, settling back in my chair with my coffee.

"I've heard it." Leaving a shallow wedge of waffle un-eaten, Trent set his fork down and pushed it symbolically away. His hands went to his tea and he leaned back in his chair. I went to take a sip of coffee, freezing as I realized Trent had mirrored both my posture and my motion.

Oh, crap. He likes me. Mirroring motions was classic in the body language of attraction. Feeling as if I'd stumbled into somewhere I didn't want to go, I intentionally leaned forward and put the flat of my arm on the table, my fingers encircling my warm mug of coffee. *I wouldn't play this game. I wouldn't!*

" 'You're mine, yet wholly you,' " Trent said dryly, clearly oblivious to my thoughts. "The man has no sense of discretion. It's going to catch up with him someday."

Eyes distant and unaware, he put the flat of his arm on the table. My face went cold and I choked, but it wasn't because of what he had done. It was because of what he had said. "Holy crap!" I swore. "You're a vamp's scion!"

Trent's eyes jerked to mine. "Excuse me?"

"The lyrics!" I sputtered. "He didn't release those. It's on the vamp track only undead vampires and their scions can hear. Oh my God! You've been bitten!"

Lips pressed together, Trent picked up his fork and cut a triangle of waffle, using it to sop up the last of the syrup on his plate. "I'm not a vampire's scion. And I've never been bit."

My heart pounded and I stared. "Then how do you know them? I heard you. I heard you say them. Straight off the vamp track."

He arched his thin eyebrows at me. "How do you know about the vamp track?"

"Ivy."

Trent rose. Wiping his fingers clean, he tightened his robe and crossed the room to the casual living-room pit with the wall-sized TV and stereo. I watched him pluck a CD from atop a shelf and drop it into a player. While it spun up, he punched in a track and "Red Ribbons" came from hidden speakers. Though it was soft, I could feel the base line thumping into me.

Trent showed a tired acceptance as he turned with a set of wireless headphones. They were professional looking, the type that fit over your ears instead of resting on them. "Listen," he said, extending them to me. I drew back suspiciously, and he wedged them on my head.

My jaw dropped and my eyes flew to his. It was "Red Ribbons," but it wasn't the same song. It was incredibly rich, seeming to go right to my brain, skipping my ears. It echoed within me, swirling behind and through my thoughts. There were impossible highs, and rumbling lows that set my tongue tingling. It was the same song, but there was so much more.

I realized I was staring at my plate. What I had been missing was beautiful. Pulling in a breath of air, I drew my head up. Trent had sat again, watching. Stunned, I reached to touch the headphones, reassuring myself that they were really there. The vamp track was indescribable.

And then the woman started to sing. I looked at Trent, feeling panicked, it was so beautiful. He nodded with a Cheshire cat smile. Her voice was lyrical, both rough and tragic. It pulled emotion from me I wasn't aware I could feel. A deep painful regret. Unrequited need. "I didn't know," I whispered.

As I listened to the end, unable to take the headphones off, Trent took our plates to the kitchen. He came back with an insulated pot of tea, topping off his cup before sitting down. The track ended, leaving only silence. Numb, I slid the headphones off and set them by my coffee.

"I didn't know," I said again, thinking that my eyes must look haunted. "Ivy can hear all that? Why doesn't Takata release them sounding like that?"

Trent adjusted his position in his chair. "He does. But only the undead can hear it."

I touched the headphones. "But you—"

"I made them after finding out about the vamp track. I wasn't sure they would work with witches. I gather by your expression that they did?"

My head bobbed loosely. "Ley line magic?" I questioned.

A smile, almost shy, flickered over him. "I specialize in misdirection. Quen thinks it a waste of time, but you'd be surprised what a person will do for a pair of those."

I pulled my eyes from the headphones. "I can imagine."

Trent sipped his tea, leaning back in speculation. "You don't . . . want a pair, do you?"

I took a breath, frowning at the faint taunt in his voice. "Not for what you're asking, no." Setting my mug of coffee at arm's length, I stood. His earlier behavior of mimicking my motions was suddenly abundantly clear. He was an expert in manipulation. He had to know what signals he was sending. Most people didn't—at least consciously—and that he had tried to lay the groundwork to try to romance my help when money wouldn't buy it was contemptible.

"Thanks for dinner," I said. "It was fabulous."

Surprise brought Trent straight. "I'll tell Maggie you enjoyed it," he said, his lips tightening. He'd made a mistake, and he knew it.

I wiped my hands off on my sweatshirt. "I'd appreciate that. I'll get my things."

"I'll tell Quen you're ready to go." His voice was flat.

Leaving him sitting at the table, I walked away. I caught a glimpse of him as I turned and went into Ellasbeth's rooms. He was touching the headphones, his posture unable to hide his annoyance. The bandage on his head and his bare feet made him look vulnerable and alone.

Stupid lonely man, I thought.

Stupid ignorant me for pitying him.

Twenty-eight

I scooped my shoulder bag up from the bathroom floor,
making a slow circuit to be sure I'd gotten everything.
Remembering my garment bag, I went to retrieve it and my
coat from the changing room. My jaw dropped at the open
phone book on the low table and my face flamed. She had it
open to escorts, not independent runners. "She thinks I'm a
hooker," I muttered, ripping the page out and jamming it into
my jeans pocket. Damn it, I didn't care that we both did legit
escort service occasionally, Ivy was going to take it out.
Ticked, I shrugged into my ugly coat with the fake fur about
the collar, snatched up my unworn outfit, and left, almost
running into Trent on the open walkway. "Whoa! Sorry," I
stammered, taking two steps back.

He tightened the tie on his robe, his eyes empty. "What
are you going to do about Lee?"

The night's events rushed back, making me frown.
"Nothing."

Trent rocked back, surprise making him look young.
"Nothing?"

My focus blurred as I recalled the people scattered where
they fell past my saving. Lee was a butcher. He could have
gotten them out but had left them so it would look like a hit by
Piscary. Which it was, but I couldn't believe that Kisten
would do that. He must have warned them. He had to have.
But Trent was standing before me, his green eyes questioning.

"It's not my problem," I said, and pushed past him.

Trent was right behind me, his bare feet silent. "He tried to kill you."

Not slowing, I said over my shoulder, "He tried to kill you. I got in the way." *Twice.*

"You're not going to do anything?"

My gaze went to the huge window. It was hard to tell in the dark, but I thought it was clear again. "I wouldn't say that. I'm going to go home and take a nap. I'm tired."

I headed for that six-inch-thick door at the end of the walkway. Trent was still behind me. "You don't care he's going to flood Cincinnati with unsafe Brimstone, killing hundreds?"

My jaw tightened as I thought of Ivy's sister. The jarring from my steps went up my spine. "You'll take care of him," I said dryly. "Seeing as it touches your *business interests.*"

"You have no desire to seek revenge. None whatsoever."

His voice was thick with disbelief, and I stopped. "Look. I got in his way. He's stronger than me. You, on the other hand . . . I'd just as soon see you fry, elf-boy. Maybe Cincinnati would be better without you."

Trent's smooth face went blank. "You don't seriously believe that."

Shifting my garment bag, I exhaled. "I don't know what I believe. You aren't honest with me. Excuse me. I have to go home and feed my fish." I walked away, headed for the door. I knew the way to the front, and Quen would probably catch up with me somewhere in between.

"Wait."

The pleading tone in his voice pulled me to a stop, my hand touching the door. I turned as Quen appeared at the foot of the stairway, his face worried and threatening. Somehow, I didn't think it was because I was about to go wandering through the Kalamack compound, but of what Trent might say. My hand fell from the doorknob. *This might be worth staying for.*

"If I tell you what I know of your father, will you help me with Lee?"

At the ground floor, Quen shifted. "Sa'han—"

Trent's brow furrowed defiantly. *"Exitus acta probat."*

My pulse quickened and I adjusted the fake fur collar of my coat. "Hey! Keep it English, boys," I snapped. "And the last time you said you would tell me about my dad, I came away with his favorite color and what he liked on his hot dog."

Trent's attention went to the floor of the great room and Quen. His security officer shook his head. "Would you like to sit down?" Trent said, and Quen grimaced.

"Sure." Eyeing him warily, I retraced my steps and followed him to the ground floor. He settled himself in a chair tucked between the window and a back wall, his comfortable posture telling me this was where he sat when he was in this room. He had a view of the dark waterfall, and there were several books, their ribbon bookmarks giving evidence of past afternoons in the sun. Behind him on the wall were four tattered Visconti tarot cards, each carefully protected behind glass. My face went cold as I realized that the captive lady on the Devil card looked like Ceri.

"Sa'han," Quen said softly. "This is not a good idea."

Trent ignored him, and Quen retreated to stand behind him, where he could glower at me.

I put my garment bag over a nearby chair and sat, my legs crossed at the knees and my foot bobbing impatiently. Helping Trent with Lee would be a small thing if he told me anything of importance. Hell, I was taking the bastard out myself as soon as I got home and whipped up a few charms. Yeah, I was a liar, but I was always honest with myself about it.

Trent edged to the end of his seat, his elbows on his knees and his gaze on the night. "Two millennium ago, the tide turned in our effort to reclaim the ever-after from the demons."

My eyes widened. Foot stilling, I took my coat off. This might take a while to get to my dad. Trent met my gaze, and seeing my acceptance of this roundabout way, he eased back in a squeak of leather. Quen made a pained sound deep in his throat.

"The demons saw their end coming," Trent said softly. "In an unusual effort of cooperation, they set aside their internal squabblings for supremacy and worked to twist a curse upon all of us. We didn't even realize it had happened for almost three generations, not recognizing the higher fatality percentage of our newborn for what it was."

I blinked. The demons were responsible for the elves' failure? I thought it had been their habit of hybridizing with humans.

"Infant mortality increased exponentially each generation," Trent said. "Our tenuous grip on victory slipped from us in tiny coffins and the sound of mourning. Eventually we realized they had twisted a curse on us, changing our DNA so that it spontaneously broke, each generation becoming progressively worse."

My stomach roiled. Genetic genocide. "You tried to repair the damage by hybridizing with humans?" I asked, hearing the smallness of my voice.

His eyes flicked from the window to me. "That was a last ditch effort to save something until a way could be developed to fix it. It was ultimately a disaster, but it did keep us alive until we improved the genetic techniques to arrest and ultimately repair most of the degradation. When the Turn made it illegal, the labs went underground, desperate to save the few of us who managed to survive. The Turn scattered us, and I find a confused child about every other year."

Feeling unreal, I whispered, "Your hospitals and orphanages." I had never guessed there was a motive other than public relations behind them.

Trent smiled faintly upon seeing the understanding in my eyes. Quen looked positively ill, his wrinkles sliding into each other, his hands behind his back, staring at nothing in a silent protest. Trent eased forward again. "I find them sickly and dying, and they're always grateful for their health and the chance to seek out more of their kin. It's been a thin line the last fifty years. We're balanced. This next generation will save or damn us."

The thought of Ceri intruded, squelched. "What does this have to do with my dad?"

A quick nod bobbed his head. "Your father was working with mine trying to find an old sample of elven DNA in the ever-after that we could use as a pattern. We can fix what we know is wrong, but to make it better, to bring the infant mortality down to where we can survive without medical help, we needed a sample from someone that died before the curse was twisted. Something that we can pattern the repairs upon."

A sound of disbelief escaped me. "You need a sample over two thousand years old?"

He lifted one shoulder in a half shrug. His shoulders didn't seem as wide in the robe, and he looked comfortably vulnerable. "It's possible. There were many pockets of elves that practiced mummification. All we need is one cell even marginally perfect. Just one."

My eyes flicked to a stoic Quen, then him. "Piscary almost killed me trying to find out if you hired me to go into the ever-after. It's not to happen. I'm not going there." I thought of Al waiting for me, my agreement worthless on his side of the lines. "No way."

An apologetic slant came into Trent's eyes as he watched me from across the coffee table. "I'm sorry. I didn't mean for Piscary to focus on you. I would have rather told you the entire story last year when you quit the I.S., but I was concerned . . ." He took a slow breath. "I didn't trust you to keep your mouth shut about our existence."

"You trust me now?" I said, thinking of Jenks.

"Not really, but I have to."

Not really, but I have to. What the hell kind of an answer is that?

"We're too few to let the world know we exist," Trent was saying, his eyes on his laced fingers. "It would be too easy for a zealot to pick us off, and I have enough trouble with Piscary trying to do just that. He knows the threat we will pose to his standing if our numbers increase."

My mouth twisted and I pushed back into the leather. Politics. It was always political. "Can't you just untwist the curse?"

His face was weary as he turned to the window. "We did when we discovered what had happened. But the damage remains, and would be worsening if we didn't find every elven child and fix what we can."

My lips parted in understanding. "The camp. That's why you were there?"

He shifted reluctantly in his chair, looking suddenly nervous. "Yes."

I pressed back farther into the cushions, not knowing if I wanted him to answer my next question. "Why . . . why was I at that camp?"

Trent's stiff posture eased. "You have a somewhat unusual genetic defect. A good five percent of the witch population has it—a recessive gene which is harmless unless they pair up."

"One in four chance?" I guessed.

"If both parents have it. And if the two recessive genes pair up, it kills you before your first birthday. My father managed to keep it suppressed in you until you were old enough to handle a full course of treatment."

"He did this a lot?" I asked, my stomach knotting. I was alive because of illegal genetic manipulation. It was what I had guessed, but now I knew for sure. Maybe I shouldn't let it bother me. The entire elf race relied on illegal medicine to remain in existence.

"No," Trent said. "Records indicate that with very few exceptions, he allowed infants with your affliction to die, their parents not knowing there was a cure. It's rather expensive."

"Money," I said, and Trent's jaw clenched.

"If the decision was based on money, you wouldn't have seen your first birthday," he said tightly. "My father didn't take one cent for saving your life. He did it because he was friends with your father. You and Lee are the only two running about under the sun that he pulled back from that death, and that was because of friendship. He didn't take a dime for saving either of you. Personally, I'm starting to think he made a mistake."

"This isn't making me want to help you," I said snidely, but Trent gave me a tired look.

"My father was a good man," he said softly. "He wouldn't refuse to help your father save your life when your father had already devoted his life to help him save our entire race."

Frowning, I put a hand to my stomach. I didn't like what I was feeling. My father didn't sacrifice his life in exchange for mine—which was a good thing. But he wasn't the upright, honest, hardworking I.S. runner I had thought. He had willingly helped Trent's father with his illegal activities long before I got sick.

"I'm not a bad person, Rachel," Trent said. "But I will eliminate anyone who threatens to stop the flow of money coming in. My research to repair the damage the demons did to my people's genome isn't cheap. If we could find an old enough sample, we could fix it completely. But it has degraded to the point where we don't know even the color of the pieces anymore."

My thoughts lighted on Ceri, and I steeled my face. The thought of her and Trent meeting was intolerable. Besides, she was only a thousand years old.

Trent's smooth features went tired with a worry far beyond his years. "If the money stops, the next generation of elves will start to slip again. Only if we find a sample from before the curse was twisted can we fix it completely and my species will have a chance. Your father thought it was a task worth dying for."

My eyes flicked to the tarot card with Ceri's likeness and I kept my mouth shut. Trent would use her like a tissue and throw her away.

Trent leaned back, his gaze going sharp on mine. "Well, Ms. Morgan," he said, managing to appear in control even wearing a robe and pj's. "Have I given you enough?"

For a long moment I looked at him, watching his jaw slowly tighten when he realized I was balancing and not knowing which way I was going to jump. Feeling cocky and self-assured, I raised my eyebrows. "Oh hell, Trent. I was going after Lee anyway. What do you think I was doing in your bathtub for two hours? Washing my hair?"

I had no choice but to tag Lee after he tried to blow me up. If I didn't, every mark I put behind bars was going to come out gunning for me.

Trent's face went annoyed. "You've got it figured out already, don't you?" he asked, irritation thick in his river-gray voice.

"Mostly." I beamed, and Quen sighed, clearly having seen beforehand that I was going to snooker his boss but good. "I just need to call my insurance agent and set it up."

Knowing I had gotten the better of Trent was worth more than he could ever line my pockets with, and I snorted when Quen whispered, "Her insurance agent?"

Still sitting, I pointed a finger at Trent. "I've got two things for you to do. Two things, then you back off and let me work. I'm not doing this as a committee. Understand?"

Eyebrows high, Trent said flatly, "What do you want?"

"First, I want you to go to the FIB and tell them Lee knocked out all those people and locked the doors knowing there was a bomb on the boat."

Trent laughed, his warm voice taking on a biting edge. "What is that going to get you?"

"They'll go looking for him. He'll go underground. A warrant will be filed, and with that, I have a legal right to pick him up."

Trent's eyes widened. Behind him, Quen nodded. "That's why . . ." Trent murmured.

I couldn't help my smile. "You can run from the law, but

standing up your insurance adjustor?" I shook my head. "Not a good idea."

"You're going to get in to kill him posing as an insurance agent?"

I wished I could say I was surprised. *God, he was so arrogant.* "I don't kill people, Trent. I haul their asses to lockup, and I need a reason for keeping him there. I thought he was your friend."

A hint of uncertainty flickered over Trent. "I thought he was, too."

"Maybe his girlfriend knocked him on the head and forced him into leaving?" I said, not believing it. "Wouldn't you feel bad if you killed him, then found out he had tried to save you?"

Trent gave me a weary look. "Always seeing the best in a person, Ms. Morgan?"

"Yeah. Except with you." I started making a mental list of who I had to tell I was alive: Kisten, Jenks—if he'd listen— Ceri, Keasley . . . Nick? Oh God, my mom. *That one ought to be fun.*

Pushing his fingers into his forehead, Trent sighed. "You have no idea how this works."

Affronted, I puffed at him and his smarter-than-thou attitude. "Work with me here, huh? Letting the bad guy live might be good for your soul."

He didn't look convinced; he looked patronizing. "Letting Lee live is a mistake. His family won't like him in jail. They'd rather have him dead than be an embarrassment."

"Well isn't that just too bad. I'm not going to kill him, and I'm not going to let you kill him, either, so sit down, shut up, hold on, and watch how real people solve problems."

Trent shook his head to make his hair float about his red-rimmed ears. "What's arresting Lee going to get you? His lawyers will have him out before he can sit on a jail-cell cot."

"Voice of experience?" I mocked, seeing as I almost had him there last fall.

"Yes," he said darkly. "The FIB has my fingerprints on file, thanks to you."

"And the I.S. has a sample of my DNA for identification purposes. Suck it up."

Quen made a soft sound, and I suddenly realized we were arguing like children.

Looking peeved, Trent settled back in his chair and laced his fingers over his middle. Fatigue pulled at him. "Admitting I was on that boat is going to be difficult. We weren't seen leaving. And it would be hard to explain how we survived and everyone else died."

"Be inventive. Maybe the truth?" I said cockily. *Pushing Trent's buttons was kinda fun.* "Everybody knows he's trying to jerk Cincinnati out from under you and Piscary. Go with it. Just leave me dead in the river."

Trent eyed me carefully. "You're going to tell your FIB captain you're alive, yes?"

"That's one of the reasons you're going to file with the FIB and not the I.S." My gaze went to the stairway as Jonathan's tall form started down it. He seemed irritated, and I wondered what was up. No one said anything as he approached, and I wished I hadn't pushed Trent so far. The man didn't look happy. It would be just like him to kill Lee out from under me. "You want Saladan out of the city?" I said. "I'll do that for you for free. All I want is you to file a complaint and pay for the lawyer to keep him in prison. Can you do that for me?"

His face went empty as thoughts he didn't want to share with me passed through his mind. Nodding slowly, he beckoned Jonathan closer.

Taking that as a yes, I felt my shoulders ease. "Thanks," I muttered as the tall man bent to whisper in Trent's ear and Trent's gaze shot to me. I strained to hear, getting nothing.

"Keep him at the gate," Trent said, glancing at Quen. "I don't want him on the grounds."

"Who?" I said, wondering.

Trent stood and tightened the tie on his robe. "I told Mr.

Felps I'd arrange for your return, but he seems to think you're in need of rescuing. He's waiting for you at the gatehouse."

"Kisten?" I stifled a jerk. I'd be glad to see him, but I was afraid of the answers he would have for me. I didn't want him to have planted that bomb, but Ivy had said he did. *Damn it, why did I always fall for the bad boys?*

While the three men waited, I stood and gathered my things, hesitating before I stuck my hand out. "Thank you for your hospitality . . . Trent," I said, pausing only briefly as I tried to decide what to call him. "And thanks for not letting me freeze to death," I added.

A soft smile quirked the corners of his lips at the hesitation, and he met my firm grip with his own. "It was the least I could do, seeing as you kept me from drowning," he answered. His brow furrowed, clearly wanting to say more. Breath held, he changed his mind and turned away. "Jonathan, will you accompany Ms. Morgan to the gatehouse? I want to talk to Quen."

"Of course, Sa'han."

I glanced back at Trent as I followed Jonathan to the stairs, my mind already on what I had to do next. I'd call Edden first, at his home number, soon as I got to my Rolodex. He might still be up. Then my mother. Then Jenks. This was going to work. It had to.

But as I quickened my pace to keep up with Jonathan, a wash of concern went though me. Sure, I was going to get in to see Saladan, but then what?

Twenty-nine

Kisten had the heat on full, and the warm air shifted a strand of my shorter hair to tickle my neck. I reached to turn it down, thinking he was laboring under the false assumption that I was still suffering from hypothermia and warmer was better. It was stifling, the sensation only strengthened by the darkness we drove through. I cracked the window and eased back as the cold night slipped in.

The living vamp snuck a look at me, jerking his gaze back to the headlight-lit road as soon as our eyes met. "Are you okay?" he asked for the third time. "You haven't said a word."

Shaking my open coat to make a draft, I nodded. He had gotten a hug at Trent's gate, but it was obvious he felt the hesitation. "Thanks for picking me up," I said. "I wasn't too keen on Quen taking me home." I ran my hand across the door handle of Kisten's Corvette, comparing it to Trent's limo. I liked Kisten's car better.

Kisten blew out his breath in a long exhalation. "I needed to get out. Ivy was driving me crazy." He glanced away from the dark road. "I'm glad you told her as soon as you did."

"You talked?" I asked, surprised and a little worried. *Why couldn't I like nice men?*

"Well, she talked." He made an embarrassed noise. "She threatened to cut off both my heads if I jerked your blood out from under her."

"Sorry." I looked out the window, becoming more upset. I didn't want to have to walk away from Kisten because he had meant for those people to die in some stupid power struggle they weren't aware of. He took a breath to say something, and I interrupted with a quick, "Would you mind if I used your phone?"

His expression wary, he pulled his shiny phone from a belt holster and handed it to me. Not particularly happy, I called information and got the number for David's company, and for a few dollars more, they connected me. Why not? It wasn't my phone.

While Kisten silently drove, I worked my way through their automated system. It was almost midnight. He ought to have been in, unless he was on a run or had gone home early. "Hi," I said when I finally got a real person. "I need to talk to David Hue?"

"I'm sorry," an older woman said with an overabundance of professionalism. "Mr. Hue isn't here presently. Can I give you to one of our other agents?"

"No!" I said before she could dump me back into the system. "Is there a number I can reach him at? It's an emergency." *Note to self: never, ever throw anyone's card away again.*

"If you'd like to leave your name and number—"

What part of "emergency" didn't she understand? "Look," I said with a sigh. "I really need to talk to him. I'm his new partner, and I lost his extension. If you could just—"

"You're his new partner?" the woman interrupted. The shock in her voice gave me pause. Was David that hard to work with?

"Yeah," I said, flicking a glance at Kisten. I was sure he could hear both ends of the conversation with his vamp ears. "I really need to talk to him."

"Ah, can you hold for a moment?"

"You bet."

Kisten's face brightened in the glare of oncoming cars. His jaw was fixed and his eyes were riveted to the road.

There was a crackling of the phone being passed, then a cautious, "This is David Hue."

"David," I said, smiling. "It's Rachel." He didn't say anything, and I rushed to keep him on the line. "Wait! Don't hang up. I've got to talk to you. It's about a claim."

There was the sound of a hand going over the phone. "It's okay," I heard him say. "I'll take this one. Why don't you make an early night of it? I'll close down your computer."

"Thanks, David. I'll see you tomorrow," his secretary said faintly, and after a long moment, his voice came back on the line.

"Rachel," he said warily. "Is this about the fish? I've already filed the claim. If you've perjured me, I'm going to be very upset."

"What is it with you thinking the worst of me?" I questioned, miffed. My eyes slid to Kisten as he gripped the wheel tighter. "I made a mistake with Jenks, okay? I'm trying to fix it. But I've got something you might be interested in."

There was a short silence. "I'm listening," he said cautiously.

My breath puffed out in relief. Fidgeting, I dug for a pen in my shoulder bag. Opening my datebook, I clicked my pen open. "Ah, you work by commission, right?"

"Something like that," David said.

"Well, you know that boat that exploded?" I snuck a glance at Kisten. The light from the oncoming traffic made little glints in his stubble as he clenched his jaw.

There was a rattling of computer keys in the background. "Still listening . . ."

My pulse quickened. "Does your company own the policy on it?"

The sound of keys quickened and vanished. "Seeing as we insure everything Piscary isn't interested in, probably." There was another spurt of tapping keys. "Yes. We have it."

"Great," I sighed. *This was going to work.* "I was on it when it exploded."

I heard the squeak of a chair through the line. "Somehow that doesn't surprise me. You saying it wasn't an accident?"

"Ah, no." I flicked a glance at Kisten. His knuckles gripping the wheel were white.

"Really." It wasn't a question, and the sound of tapping keys started up again, shortly followed by the hum of a printer.

I shifted in Kisten's heated leather seats and stuck the end of the pen in my mouth. "Would I be correct that your company doesn't pay out when property is destroyed—"

"Because of acts of war or gang-related activity?" David interrupted. "No. We don't."

"Fantastic," I said, not thinking it necessary to tell him I was sitting next to the guy who had arranged the whole thing. *God, please let Kisten have an answer for me.* "How would you like me to come down there and sign a paper for you?"

"I'd like that really fine." David hesitated, then added, "You don't strike me as the kind of woman who commits acts of random kindness, Rachel. What do you want out this?"

My gaze ran down Kisten's clenched jaw to his strong shoulders, then lingered on his hands gripping the wheel as if he was trying to squeeze the iron out of it. "I want to be with you when you go out to adjust Saladan's claim."

Kisten jerked, apparently only now understanding why I was talking to David. The silence on the other end of the line was thick. "Ah . . ." David murmured.

"I'm not going to kill him; I'm going to arrest him," I quickly offered.

The thrum of the engine rumbling up through my feet shifted and steadied.

"It's not that," he said. "I don't work with anyone. And I'm not working with you."

My face burned. I knew he thought very little of me after finding I had kept information from my own partner. But it was David's fault it came out. "Look," I said, turning away from Kisten as he stared at me. "I just saved your company a wad of money. You get me in when you go to adjust his claim, then back out of the way and let me and my team work." I glanced at Kisten. Something had shifted in him. His grip on the wheel was loose and his face was empty.

There was a short silence. "And afterward?"

"Afterward?" The moving lights made Kisten's face un-readable. "Nothing. We tried working together. It didn't work out. You get an extension on finding a new partner."

There was a long silence. "That's it?"

"That's it." I clicked my pen closed and threw it and my datebook into my bag. *Why did I even try to be organized?*

"Okay," he finally said. "I'll bark down the hole and see what comes up."

"Fantastic," I said, genuinely glad, though he seemed less than pleased. "Hey, in a few hours I'm going to have died in that explosion, so don't worry about it, okay?"

A tired sound escaped him. "Fine. I'll call you tomorrow when the claim comes in."

"Great. I'll see you then." David's lack of excitement was depressing. The phone clicked off without him saying good-bye, and I closed it and handed it back to Kisten. "Thanks," I said, feeling very awkward.

"I thought you were turning me in," Kisten said softly.

Mouth falling open, I stared, only now understanding his previous tension. "No," I whispered, feeling afraid for some reason. He had sat there and done nothing as he thought I was turning him in?

Shoulders stiff and eyes on the road, he said, "Rachel, I didn't know he was going to let those people die."

My breath caught. I forced it out, then took another. "Talk to me," I said, feeling light-headed. I stared out the window, hands in my lap and my stomach clenched. *Please, let me be wrong this time?*

I looked across the car, and after his eyes flicked to the rearview mirror, he pulled off to the side of the road. My gut clenched. Damn it, why did I have to like him? Why couldn't I like nice men? Why did the power and personal strength that attracted me always seem to translate into callous disregard for other people's lives?

My body shifted forward and back when he came to a sudden halt. The car shook as traffic continued to pass us at eighty miles an hour, but here it was still. Kisten shifted in his seat to face me, reaching over the gearshift to cradle my hands in my lap. His day-old stubble glinted in the lights from the oncoming traffic across the median, and his blue eyes were pinched.

"Rachel," he said, and I held my breath hoping he was going to tell me it had all been a mistake. "I arranged to have that bomb strapped to the boiler."

I closed my eyes.

"I didn't intend for those people to die. I called Saladan," he continued, and I opened my eyes when a passing truck shook us. "I told Candice there was a bomb on his boat. Hell, I told her where it was and that if they touched it, it would detonate. I gave them plenty of time to get everyone off. I wasn't trying to kill people, I was trying to make a media circus and sink his business. It never occurred to me he would walk away and leave them to die. I misjudged him," he said, a bitter recrimination in his voice, "and they paid for my shortsightedness with their lives. God, Rachel, if I even guessed he would do that, I'd have found another way. That you were on that boat . . ." He took a breath. "I almost killed you. . . ."

I swallowed hard, feeling the lump in my throat grow less. "But you've killed people before," I said, knowing the problem wasn't tonight but a history of belonging to Piscary and having to carry out his will.

Kisten leaned back though his hands never left mine. "I killed my first person when I was eighteen."

Oh God. I tried to pull away, but he gently tightened his grip. "You need to hear this," he said. "If you want to walk away, I want you to know the truth so you don't come back.

And if you stay, then it's not because you made a decision based on too little information."

Steeling myself, I looked at his eyes, gauging them sincere, and perhaps carrying a hint of guilt and past hurt. "You've done this before," I whispered, feeling afraid. I was one in a string of women. They had all left. Maybe they were smarter than me.

He nodded, his eyes closing briefly. "I'm tired of being hurt, Rachel. I'm a nice guy who just happened to kill his first person at eighteen."

I swallowed, taking my hands back under the pretense of tucking my hair behind an ear. Kisten felt me draw away and turned to look out the front window, placing his hands back on the wheel. I had told him not to make my decisions for me; I suppose I deserved every sordid detail. Stomach twisting, I said, "Go on."

Kisten stared at nothing as the traffic passed, accentuating the point of stillness in the car. "I killed my second about a year later," he said, his voice flat. "She was an accident. I managed to keep from ending anyone else's life again until last year when—"

I watched him as he took a breath and exhaled. My muscles trembled, waiting for it.

"God, I'm sorry, Rachel," he whispered. "I swore I'd try to never have to kill anyone again. Maybe that's why Piscary doesn't want me as his scion now. He wants someone to share the experience, and I won't do it. He was the one who actually killed them, but I was there. I helped. I held them down, kept them busy while he gleefully butchered them one by one. That they deserved it hardly seems justification anymore. Not with the way he did it."

"Kisten?" I said hesitantly, pulse fast.

He turned, and I froze, trying not to be frightened. His eyes had gone black in the memory. "That feeling of pure domination is a twisted, addictive high," he said, the lost hunger in his voice chilling me. "It took me a long time to learn how to let go of that so I could remember the inhuman savagery of it, hidden by the jolt of pure adrenaline. I lost myself with Piscary's thoughts and strength flooding me, but I know how to wield it now, Rachel. I can be both his scion and a just person. I can be his enforcer and a gentle lover. I know I can walk the balance. He's punishing me right now, but he'll take me back. And when he does, I'll be ready."

What the hell was I doing here?

"So," I said, hearing my voice tremble. "That's it?"

"Yeah. That's it," he said flatly. "The first was under Piscary's orders to make an example of someone luring underage kids. It was excessive, but I was young and stupid, trying to prove to Piscary that I'd do anything for him, and he took enjoyment from seeing me agonize about it later. The last time was to stop a new camarilla from forming. They were advocating a return to pre-Turn traditions of abducting people no one would miss. The woman." His eyes flicked to me. "That's the one that haunts me. That's when I decided to be honest when I could. I swore I'd never end another innocent's life again. It doesn't matter that she lied to me . . ." His eyes closed and his grip on the wheel trembled. The light from across the median showed the lines of pain on his face.

Oh God. He had killed someone in a passionate rage.

"And then I ended sixteen lives tonight," he whispered.

I was so stupid. He admitted to killing people—people the I.S. probably would thank him for getting rid of, but people nevertheless. I had come into this knowing he wasn't the "safe boyfriend," but I'd had the safe boyfriend and always ended up hurt. And despite the brutality he was capable of, he was being honest. People had died tonight in a horrible tragedy, but that hadn't been his intent.

"Kisten?" My eyes dropped to his hands, his short round nails carefully kept clean and close to his fingertips.

"I had the bomb set," he said, guilt making his voice harsh.

I hesitantly reached to take his hands from the wheel. My fingers felt cold against his. "You didn't kill them. Lee did."

His eyes were black in the uncertain light when he turned to me. I sent my hand behind his neck to pull him closer, and he resisted. He was a vampire, and that wasn't an easy thing to be—it wasn't an excuse, it was a fact. That he was being forthright meant more to me than his ugly past. And he had sat there while he thought I was turning him in and did nothing. He had ignored what he believed and trusted me. I would try to trust him.

I couldn't help but feel for him. Watching Ivy, I had come to the conclusion that being a master vampire's scion was very much like being in a mentally abusive relationship where love had been perverted by sadism. Kisten was trying to distance himself from his master's masochistic demands. He *had* distanced himself, he had distanced himself so far that Piscary had dumped him for a soul even more desperate for acceptance: my roommate. *Swell.*

Kisten was alone. He was hurting. He was being honest with me—I couldn't walk away. We had both done questionable things, and I couldn't label him as evil when I was the one with the demon mark. Circumstances had made our choices for us. I did the best I could. So did he.

"It wasn't your fault they died," I said again, feeling as if I had found a new way to see. Before me lay the same world, but I was looking around corners. *What was I becoming? Was I a fool to trust, or a wiser person finding the capacity to forgive?*

Kisten heard the acceptance of his past in my voice, and the relief reflected in his face was so strong that it was almost painful. My hand on his neck slid forward, drawing him closer over the console. "It's okay," I whispered as his hands slipped from my fingers and took my shoulders. "I understand."

"I don't think you can. . . ." he insisted.

"Then we'll deal with it when I do." Tilting my head, I

closed my eyes and leaned to find him. His grip on my shoulder eased, and I found myself reaching after him, drawn in as our lips touched. My fingers pressed into his neck, urging him closer. A jolt struck through me, bringing my blood to the surface, tingling through me as his kiss deepened, promising more. It didn't stem from my scar, and I drew his hand to it, almost gasping when his fingertips traced the light, almost unseen scar tissue. The thought of Ivy's dating guide flitted through me, and I saw it all in an entirely new way. *Oh God, the things I could do with this man.*

Maybe I needed the dangerous man, I thought as a wild emotion rose in me. Only someone who had done wrong could understand that, yes, I did questionable things too, but that I was still a good person. If Kisten could be both, then maybe that meant I could be, too.

And with that, I abandoned all pretense of thought. His hand feeling my pulse and my lips pulling on his, I sent my tongue hesitantly between his lips, knowing a gentle inquiry would strike a hotter chord than a demanding touch. I found a smooth tooth, and I curled my tongue around it, teasing.

Kisten's breath came fast and he jerked away.

I froze as he was suddenly not there, the heat of him still a memory on my skin. "I'm not wearing my caps," he said, the black swelling in his eyes and my scar pulsing in promise. "I was so worried about you, I didn't take the time to . . . I'm not . . ." He took a shaking breath. "God, you smell good."

Heart pounding, I forced myself back into my seat, watching him as I tucked my hair behind an ear. I wasn't sure I cared if he had his caps on or not. "Sorry," I said breathlessly, blood still pounding through me. "I didn't mean to go that far." *But you just sort of pull it out of me.*

"Don't be sorry. You're not the one who's been neglecting—things." Blowing his breath out, Kisten tried to hide his heady look of want. Under the rougher emotions was a soft look of grateful understanding and relief. I had accepted his ugly past, knowing his future might not be any better.

Saying nothing, he put the car in first and accelerated. I held the door until we slid back onto the road, glad nothing had changed though everything was different.

"Why are you so good to me?" he said softly as we picked up speed and passed a car.

Because I think I could love you? I thought, but I couldn't say it yet.

Thirty

My head came up at the faint sound of knocking. Giving me a warning look, Ivy stood, stretching for the kitchen's ceiling. "I'll get it," she said. "It's probably more flowers."

I took a bite of cinnamon toast and muttered around my full mouth, "If it's food, bring it back, will you?"

Sighing, Ivy walked out, both sexy and casual in her black exercise tights and a thigh-length baggy sweater. The radio was on in the living room, and I had mixed feelings about the announcer talking about the tragedy of the boat explosion early last night. They even had a clip of Trent telling everyone I had died saving his life.

This was really odd, I thought as I wiped butter from my fingers. Things had been showing up on our doorstep. It was nice to know I would be missed, and I hadn't known I had touched so many lives. It wasn't going to be pretty when I came out of the closet as being alive, though—kind of like standing someone up at the altar and having to give all the presents back. 'Course, if I died tonight, I'd go to my grave knowing just who my friends were. I kinda felt like Huck Finn.

"Yeah?" Ivy's wary voice came back through the church.

"I'm David. David Hue," came a familiar voice, and swallowing the last bite of toast, I ambled up to the front of the church. I was starving, and I wondered if Ivy was slipping

Brimstone into my coffee to try to build my body's reserves after that dunk in the river.

"Who is she?" Ivy asked belligerently as I entered the sanctuary and found them on the landing, the lowering sun coming in past their feet.

"I'm his secretary," a tidy woman at David's side said, smiling. "Can we come in?"

My eyes widened. "Whoa, whoa, whoa," I said, waving my hands in protest. "I can't watch two of you and bring in Lee."

David ran his eyes down my casual sweater and jeans, his eyes thick with a calculating evaluation. They lingered on my shortened hair, dyed a temporary brown just this after-noon as he had suggested over the phone. "Mrs. Aver isn't going to come with us," he said, making what was probably an unconscious nod of approval. "I thought it prudent that your neighbors see me arrive with a woman as well as leave with one. You're close to the same body build."

"Oh." *Idiot,* I thought. *Why didn't I think of that?*

Mrs. Aver smiled, but I could tell she thought I was an idiot, too. "I'll just pop into your bathroom and change, and then I'll go," she said brightly. Taking a step into the room, she set her slim briefcase beside the piano bench and hesitated.

Ivy started. "This way," she said, indicating that the woman should follow her.

"Thank you. You're so kind."

Making a small face for all the hidden undercurrents, I watched Mrs. Aver and Ivy leave, the former making a lot of noise in her bland black heels, the latter silent in her slip-pers. Their conversation ended with the click of my bath-room door shutting, and I turned to David.

He looked like a completely different Were outside of his spandex running pants and shirt. And nowhere near the same person the time I saw him leaning against a park tree in a duster that went to his boot tops and a cowboy hat pulled over his eyes. His heavy stubble was gone, to leave sun-roughed cheeks, and his long hair was styled and smelled of moss. Only the highest ranking Weres could carry off polish and not look like they were trying, but David managed it. The three-piece suit and manicured fingernails helped. He looked older than his athletic physique would testify, with a pair of glasses perched on his nose and a tie snugged up to his neck. Actually, he looked really good—in a professional, educated sort of way.

"Thanks again for helping me get in to see Saladan," I said, feeling awkward.

"Don't thank me," he said. "I'm getting a huge bonus." He set his expensive-looking suitcase on the piano bench. He seemed preoccupied—not angry with me, but wary and disapproving. It made me uncomfortable. Sensing me watching him, he looked up. "Mind if I do a little prep paperwork?"

I shifted back a step. "No. Go right ahead. You want some coffee?"

David looked at Jenks's desk and hesitated. Brow furrowing, he sat astride the piano bench and opened his briefcase up before him. "No thanks. We won't be here that long."

"Okay." I retreated, feeling his dissatisfaction heavy on me. I knew he didn't like that I had lied to my partner by omission, but all I needed was for him to get me in to see Lee. I hesitated at the top of the hallway. "I'll go change. I wanted to see what you were wearing."

David looked up from his paperwork, his brown eyes distant as he tried to do two things at once. "You'll be wearing Mrs. Aver's clothes."

My eyebrows rose. "You've done this before."

"I told you the job was a lot more interesting than you would think," he said to his papers.

I waited for him to say something more, but he didn't, so I went to find Ivy, feeling awkward and depressed. He hadn't said a word about Jenks, but his disapproval was clear.

Ivy was busy with her maps and pens when I entered, saying nothing as I poured a cup of coffee for me, and then her. "What do you think of David?" I asked, setting her cup beside her.

Her head went down and she tapped a colored pen on the table. "I think you'll be okay. He seems to know what he's doing. And it's not like I won't be there."

Leaning against the counter, I held my mug with both hands and took a long sip. Coffee slid down, easing my jitters. Something in Ivy's posture caught my attention. Her cheeks were a shade red. "I think you like him," I said, and her head jerked up. "I think you like older men," I added. "Especially older men in suits that bite and can plan better than you."

At that, she did flush. "And I think you should shut up."

We both started at the soft knock on the archway to the hall. It was Mrs. Aver, and it was embarrassing that neither of us had heard her come out of the bathroom. She was dressed in my robe, her clothes over one arm. "Here you go, honey," she said as handed me her gray suit.

"Thanks." I set my coffee down and took it.

"If you would, drop them off at Weres-'N-Tears dry cleaners. They do a good job getting out blood and stitching up small rips. Do you know where that is?"

I looked at the matronly woman standing before me in my fuzzy blue robe, her long brown hair down about her shoulders. She looked to be about the same size as me, if a bit hippy. My hair was a shade darker, but it was close enough. "Sure," I said.

She smiled. Ivy was back at her maps, ignoring us, her foot silently moving. "Great," the Were said. "I'm going to change and say 'bye to David before I leave on four feet." Flashing me a toothy grin, she sashayed to the hallway, hesitating. "Where's your back door?"

Ivy stood up with a noisy scrape of a chair. "It's broken. I'll get it for you."

"Thank you," she said with that same polite smile. They left, and I slowly I brought the woman's clothes to my nose. They were still warm from her body heat, and the faint scent of musk mixed with a light meadowy smell. My lips curved downward at the idea of wearing someone else's clothes, but the entire idea was to smell like a Were. And it wasn't as if she had brought me rags to put on. The lined wool suit must have cost her a bundle.

Steps slow and measured, I went to my room. That dating guide was still out on my dresser, and I looked at it with a mix of depression and guilt. What had I been thinking, wanting to read it again with the idea to drive Kisten wild? Miserable, I shoved it in the back of my closet. God help me, I was an idiot.

Resigned, I slipped out of my jeans and sweater. Soon the clack of nails in the hallway intruded, and as I put on my nylons, there was the pained sound of nails being pulled from wood. The new door wouldn't be in until tomorrow, and it wasn't as if she could slip out a window.

I was feeling very unsure about this, and it wasn't anything I could really pinpoint. *It wasn't going in charmless,* I thought as I shimmied into the gray skirt and tucked the white blouse in. Ivy and Kisten would be bringing in everything I needed; my duffel bag of spells was already packed and waiting in the kitchen. And it wasn't because I was going up against someone better in ley line magic. I did that all the time.

I shrugged into the jacket, slipping the warrant for Lee into an inner pocket. Wedging my feet into the low heels I had pulled from the back of my closet, I stared at my reflection. Better, but still it was me, and I reached for the contact lenses that David had couriered over earlier.

As I blinked and teared the thin brown bits of plastic into place, I decided that my unease was because David didn't trust me. He didn't trust my abilities, and he didn't trust me. I'd never had a partner relationship where I was the one under doubt. I had been thought of as an airhead before, and a flake, even incompetent, but never untrustworthy. I didn't like it. But looking back over what I had done to Jenks, it was probably deserved.

Movements slow and depressed, I styled my shorter hair up into a spare, businesslike bun. I put my makeup on heavy, using a base that was too dark, and so having to give my hands and neck a good layer as well. It covered my freckles, though, and with an unhappy feeling, I twisted my wooden pinky ring off; the charm was broken. With the darker makeup and the brown contact lenses, I looked different, but the clothes really turned the trick. And as I stood before my mirror and looked at myself in my dull boring suit and a dull boring hairstyle, and a dull boring look on my face, I didn't think even my mother would recognize me.

I dabbed a drop of Ivy's expensive perfume on me—the one that hid my scent—then followed it up with a splash of a musky perfume Jenks once said smelled like the underside of a log: earthy and rich. Clipping Ivy's phone onto my waist, I went into the hall, my heels making an unusual amount of noise. The soft sound of Ivy and David in conversation pulled me into the sanctuary, where I found them at her piano. I really wished Jenks were with us. It was more than needing him for reconnaissance and camera detail. I missed him.

David and Ivy looked up at the sound of my feet. Ivy's mouth dropped open. "Bite me and slight me," she said. "That is the most god-awful thing I think I've seen you wear. You actually look respectable."

I smiled weakly. "Thanks." I stood there gripping my hands in a fig-leaf posture as David ran his gaze over me, the slight easing of his brow the only sign of his approval. Turning away, he tossed his papers into his briefcase and snapped it shut. Mrs. Aver had left hers behind, and I picked it up when David indicated I should. "You'll bring my spells?" I asked Ivy.

She sighed, turning her gaze to the ceiling. "Kisten is on his way over. I'll go over it with him one more time, then we lock up the church and leave. I'll give you a ping when we're in place." She looked at me. "You do have my spare phone?"

"Ah . . ." I touched it on my waist. "Yes."

"Good. Go," she said as she turned and walked away. "Before I do something stupid like give you a hug."

Depressed and unsure, I headed out. David was behind me, his pace silent but his presence obvious by the faint scent of fern. "Sunglasses," he murmured when I reached for the door handle, and I paused to put them on. I pushed the door open, squinting from the late sun as I picked my way through the sympathy offerings ranging from professional flower arrangements to crayon-bright pages torn from coloring books. It was cold, the crisp air refreshing.

The sound of Kisten's car pulled my head up, and my pulse jackhammered. I froze on the steps and David almost ran into me. His foot bumped a squat vase, and it rolled down the steps to the sidewalk, spilling water and the single budded red rose it held.

"Someone you know?" he asked, his breath warm on my ear.

"It's Kisten." I watched him park and get out. *God, he looked good, all trim and sexy.*

David's hand went onto my elbow, pushing me into motion. "Keep going. Don't say anything. I want to see how your disguise holds up. My car is across the street."

Liking the idea, I continued down the stairs, stopping only to pick up the vase and set it on the lowest stair. It was actually a jelly-jar glass, with a pentagram of protection on it, and I made a soft sound of recognition as I tucked the red rose back into it and straightened. I hadn't seen one of those in years.

I felt a flutter in my stomach when Kisten's steps grew loud.

"Bless you," he said as he passed me, thinking I had put the flower there, not just picked it up. I opened my mouth to say something, closing it as David pinched my arm.

"Ivy!" Kisten shouted, hammering on the door. "Let's go! We're going to be late!"

David escorted me across the street and to the other side of his car, his hand firmly under my elbow—it was slick, and the heels I had on weren't made for ice. "Very nice," he said, sounding begrudgingly impressed. "But it's not as if you've slept with him."

"Actually," I said as he opened the door for me, "I have."

His eyes jerked to mine and a shocked look of revulsion crossed him. From inside the church came a faint, "You're fucking kidding! That was her? No fucking way!"

I pushed my fingers into my forehead. At least he didn't swear like that when I was around. My eyes went to David, the width of the door between us. "It's the species thing, isn't it?" I said flatly.

He said nothing. Jaw clenched, I told myself that he could think what he wanted. I didn't have to live up to his standards. Lots of people didn't like it. Lots of people didn't give a flip. Who I slept with should have nothing to do with our professional relationship.

Mood worsening, I got in and closed my door before he could do it. My belt clicked shut, and he slid behind the wheel and started his little gray car up. I didn't say a word as he pulled out and headed for the bridge. David's cologne became cloying, and I cracked the window.

"You don't mind going in without your charms?" David asked.

His tone lacked the expected disgust, and I seized on that. "I've gone in charmless before," I said. "And I trust Ivy to get them to me."

His head didn't move, though his eyes tightened in the corners. "My old partner never was without his charms. I'd laugh at him when we'd go in and he'd have three or four of them hanging around his neck. 'David,' he'd say, 'this one's for seeing if they're lying. This one's for knowing if they're under a disguise. And this one's for telling me if they're carrying a bunch of energy around in their chi and are ready to blast us all to hell.'"

I glanced at him, my mood softening. "You don't mind working with witches."

"No." He took his hand off the wheel when we rumbled over a railroad track. "His charms saved me a lot of pain. But I can't tell you the number of times he spent fumbling for the right spell when a good right cross would have settled things faster."

We crossed the river into Cincinnati proper, and the buildings made flickering come-and-go shadows on me. He was prejudiced only when sex came into the picture. I could handle that. "I'm not going in completely helpless," I said, warming slightly. "I can make a protection circle around myself if I have to. But I'm really an earth witch. Which might make things difficult as it's harder to bring someone in if you can't do the same magic." I made a face he didn't see. "Then again, there's no way I can beat Saladan at ley line magic, so it's just as well I'm not even going to try. I'll get him with my earth charms or my foot in his gut."

David brought the car to a slow halt at a red light. Face showing the first signs of interest, he turned to me. "I heard you brought down three ley line assassins."

"Oh, that." I warmed. "I had help with that. The FIB was there."

"You brought Piscary down yourself."

The light changed, and I appreciated him not creeping up on the car ahead of us until it moved. "Trent's security officer helped me," I admitted.

"He distracted him," David said softly. "You were the one who clubbed him into unconsciousness."

Pressing my knees together, I turned to look at him straight on. "How do you know?"

David's heavy jaw tightened and relaxed, but he didn't look from the street. "I talked to Jenks this morning."

"What!" I exclaimed, almost hitting my head on the ceiling. "Is he okay? What did he say? Did you tell him I was sorry? Will he talk to me if I call him?"

David glanced askance at me as I held my breath. Saying nothing, he made a careful turn onto the parkway. "No to everything. He's very upset."

I settled in my seat, flustered and worried.

"You need to thank him if he ever talks to you again,"

David said tightly. "He thinks the world of you, which is the main reason I didn't go back on my agreement to get you in to see Saladan."

My gut twisted. "What do you mean?"

He hesitated while he passed a car. "He's hurt you didn't trust him, but he didn't say one bad word about you, even stood up for you when I called you a flighty airhead."

My throat tightened and I stared out the passenger-side window. *I was such an ass.*

"He's of the backward opinion that he deserved being lied to, that you didn't tell him because you felt he couldn't keep his mouth shut and that you were probably right. He left because he thought he let you down, not the other way around. I told him you were a fool, and that any partner who lied to me would end up with their throat torn out." David made a puff of scorn. "He kicked me out. Four-inch man kicked me out. Told me if I didn't help you like I said I would, he'd track me down when the weather broke and give me a lobotomy when I slept."

"He could do it," I said, my voice tight. I could hear the threatened tears in it.

"I know he could, but that's not why I'm here. I'm here because of what he didn't say. What you did to your partner is deplorable, but so honorable a soul wouldn't think highly of someone who didn't deserve it. I can't see why he does, though."

"I've have been trying to talk to Jenks for the last three days," I said around the lump in my throat. "I'm trying to apologize. I'm trying to fix this."

"That's the other reason I'm here. Mistakes can be fixed, but if you do it more than once, it's no longer a mistake."

I said nothing, my head starting to hurt as we passed a river-overlook park and pulled onto a side street. David touched his collar, and I read in his body posture that we were almost there. "And it was sort of my fault it came out," he said softly. "Bane has a tendency to make you loose in the lips. I'm sorry about that, but it was still wrong of you."

It didn't matter how it came out. Jenks was furious with me, and I deserved it.

David signaled and turned into a cobbled drive. I tugged at my gray skirt and adjusted my jacket. Wiping my eyes, I sat upright and tried to look professional, not like my world was falling down around me and all I had to depend on was a Were who thought I was the lowest of the low. I'd have given anything to have Jenks on my shoulder making wise-cracks about my new haircut or how I smelled like the bottom of an outhouse. Anything.

"I'd keep my mouth shut if I were you," David said darkly, and I bobbed my head, thoroughly depressed. "My secretary's perfume is in the glove box. Give your nylons a good spray. The rest of you smells okay."

I obediently did as he said, my usual hot abhorrence to take direction from someone squelched in that he thought so little of me. The musty scent of the perfume overpowered the car, and David rolled his window down, grimacing. "Well, you did say . . ." I muttered when the cold air pooled at my ankles.

"It's going to be quick once we get in there," David said, his eyes watering. "Your vamp partner has five minutes tops before Saladan gets angry about the claim and kicks us out."

I held Mrs. Aver's briefcase on my lap tighter. "She'll be there."

David's only response was a muttered rumble. We wound up a short drive that looped about itself. It had been plowed and swept, and the red clay bricks were damp with snowmelt. At the top of it was a stately house painted white with red shutters and tall, narrow windows. It was one of the few older mansions that had been refurbished without losing its charm. The sun was behind the house, and David parked in the shadows behind a black pickup truck and cut the engine. A curtain at a front window shifted.

"Your name is Grace," he said. "If they want identification, it's in your wallet inside your briefcase. Here." He handed me his glasses. "Wear them."

"Thanks." I set the plastic lenses on my nose, learning that David was farsighted. My head started to hurt and I pulled them lower so I could look at the world over them instead of through them. I felt awful, the butterflies in my stomach as heavy as turtles.

A sigh shifted him, and he reached between our seats for his briefcase in the back. "Let's go."

Thirty-one

"**D**avid Hue," David said coolly, sounding bored and a little irritated as we stood in the entryway of the old mansion. "I have an appointment."

I, not we, I thought, keeping my eyes down and trying to stay in the background while Candice, the vamp that had been all over Lee on his boat, cocked her jeans-clad hip and looked at his business card. There were two more vamps behind her in black suits that screamed security. I didn't mind playing the meek subordinate; if Candice recognized me, it would get really bad, really quick.

"That was me you talked to," the shapely vampire said around a bothered sigh. "But after the recent ugliness, Mr. Saladan has retired to . . . a less public environment. He's not here, much less taking appointments." Smiling to show her teeth in a politically polite threat, she handed his card back. "I'll be glad to talk to you, though."

My heart pounded and I stared at the Italian tile. He was here—I could almost hear the rattle of chips—but if I didn't get in to see him, this was going to be a lot more difficult.

David looked at her, the skin about his eyes tightening, then picked up his briefcase. "Very well," he said shortly. "If I can't speak with Mr. Saladan, my company has no recourse but to assume our understanding of terrorist activity is correct and we will deny payment on the claim. Good day, ma'am." He barely glanced at me. "Come on, Grace. Let's go."

Breath catching, I felt my face pale. If we walked out of here, Kisten and Ivy would be headed into a trap. David's steps were loud as he went for the door, and I reached out after him.

"Candice," came Lee's irate, buttery voice from the second-story railing above the grand staircase. "What are you doing?"

I spun, David taking my elbow in warning. Lee stood by the upper landing, a drink in one hand, a folder and pair of wire-rimmed glasses in the other. He was wearing what looked like a suit without the coat, his tie loose about his neck but still tidy.

"Stanley, honey," Candice purred, falling into a provocative slump against the small table by the door. "You said no one. Besides, it's just a little boat. How much could it be worth?"

Lee's dark eyes pinched as he frowned. "Almost a quarter million—dear. They're insurance agents, not I.S. operatives. Do a spell check on them and show them up. They're required by law to keep everything confidential, including that they were even here." He looked at David and tossed his surfer-boy bangs out of his way. "Am I right?"

David smiled up at him with that shared, good-old-boys' look that I hated. "Yes, sir," he said, his voice echoing against the flat white of the open vestibule. "We couldn't do our work without that little constitutional amendment."

Lee put his hand up in acknowledgment, turned, and vanished down the open hall. A door creaked shut, and I jerked as Candice grabbed my briefcase. Adrenaline pulled me straight, and I clutched it to me.

"Relax, Grace," David said patronizingly as he took it from me and handed it to Candice. "This isn't unusual."

The two vamps in the background came forward, and I forced myself to not move. "You'll have to forgive my assistant," David said while he put our cases on the table by the door and opened first his and spun it around, then mine. "Breaking in a new assistant is hell."

Candice's expression went mocking. "Were you the one to give her the black eye?"

I flushed, my hand going to touch my cheekbone and my gaze falling to my ugly shoes. Apparently the darker makeup didn't work as well as I thought.

"You have to keep your bitches in line," David said lightly. "But if you hit them right, you only have to hit them once."

My jaw clenched, and I warmed as Candice laughed. I watched from under my lowered brow while a vamp pawed through my briefcase. It was full of stuff only an insurance adjustor would have: a calculator with more tiny buttons than a leprechaun's dress boots, notepads, coffee-stained folders, useless little calendars to stick on your fridge, and pens with smiley faces on them. There were receipts from places like sub shops and Office Depot. God, it was awful. She glanced at my fake business cards with an absent-minded interest.

While David's briefcase got the same scrutiny, Candice sauntered into a back room. She came back with a pair of wire-rimmed glasses, with which she made a show of scrutinizing us through. My heart pounded as she then brought out an amulet. It was glowing a warning red.

"Chad, honey," she murmured. "Back up. Your spell is interfering."

One of the vamps flushed and retreated. I wondered what Chad-honey had a spell for that would turn his ears that particular color. My breath slipped from me when the amulet shifted green, making me grateful that I'd gone in under a mundane disguise. Beside me, David's fingers twitched. "Can we move this faster?" he said. "I have other people to see."

Candice smiled and twirled the amulet on her finger. "Right this way."

With a quickness seemingly born from irritation, David

snapped his briefcase closed and dragged it from the small table. I did the same, relieved when the two vamps vanished into a back room following the smell of coffee. Candice headed up the stairs with a slow pace, her hips going as if they were going to gyrate off her. Trying to ignore her, I followed.

The house was old, and now that I was getting a better look at it, not well-maintained. Upstairs, the carpet was thinning, and the pictures hanging in the open hallway overlooking the vestibule were so ancient they probably came with the house. The paint above the wainscoting was that icky green popular before the Turn, and it looked repulsive. Someone with little imagination had used it to cover the eight-inch floorboards carved with ivy and hummingbirds, and I spared a pained thought at the grandeur hidden behind ugly paint and synthetic fibers.

"Mr. Saladan," Candice said in explanation as she opened a black-varnished door. Her smile was catty, and I followed David in, keeping my eyes down when I passed her. I held my breath, praying that she couldn't tell it was me, hoping she wouldn't come in. But why would she? Lee was an expert in ley line magic. He didn't need protection from two Weres.

It was a good-sized office done in oak paneling. High ceilings and the thick framework about the tall block of windows was the only evidence that the room had started out as a bedroom before becoming an office. Everything else had been covered and disguised with chrome and light oak that was only a few years old. I was a witch; I could tell.

The windows behind the desk went to the floor, and the low sun spilled in over Lee as he rose from his desk chair. A bar cart was in one corner, and an entertainment center took up most of the opposite wall. Two comfortable chairs were arranged before his desk, leaving one ugly one in a far corner. There was a huge wall mirror and no books. My opinion of Lee hit rock bottom.

"Mr. Hue," Lee said warmly as he extended his tanned hand over the expanse of the modern-looking desk. His suit coat was hanging from a nearby hat tree, but he had at least snugged his tie up. "I've been expecting you. Sorry about the mix-up downstairs. Candice can be protective at times. You can understand, seeing as boats seem to be exploding around me."

David chuckled, sounding a little like a dog. "Not a problem, Mr. Saladan. I won't take much of your time. It's a courtesy call to let you know how your claim is being processed."

Smiling, Lee held his tie to himself and sat, indicating we should do the same. "Can I get you a drink?" he asked as I settled myself in the supple leather chair and put my briefcase down.

"No, thank you," David said.

Lee hadn't given me more than a cursory glance, not even offering to shake my hand. The "men's club" air was thick enough to chew on, and whereas I normally would have charmingly asserted myself, this time I gritted my teeth and pretended I didn't exist like a good little bitch at the bottom of the hierarchy.

While Lee added ice to his drink, David donned a second pair of glasses and opened his briefcase atop his lap. His clean-shaven jaw was tight and I could smell his leashed excitement growing. "Well," he said softly, bringing out a sheaf of papers. "I regret to inform you that, after our initial inspection and our preliminary interviews with a survivor, my company has declined making a settlement."

Lee dropped a second cube of ice into his drink. "Excuse me?" He spun on a shiny heel. "Your *survivor* has too much at stake to come forth with any information contrary to it being an accident. And as for your inspection? The boat is at the bottom of the Ohio River."

David bobbed his head. "Quite so. But the boat *was* destroyed during a citywide power struggle, and thus its destruction falls under the terrorism clause."

Making a bark of disbelief, Lee sat behind his desk. "That boat is brand-new. I've only made two payments on it. I'm not going to take the loss. That's why I insured it."

David put a stapled pack of papers on the desk. Peering over his glasses, he dug out a second paper, closed his brief-case, and signed it. "This is also notice that your premiums on your other properties we insure will be increasing by fif-teen percent. Sign here, please."

"Fifteen percent!" Lee exclaimed.

"Retroactive to the beginning of the month. If you would like to cut me a check, I am prepared to accept payment."

Damn, I thought. David's company played hardball. My thoughts shifted from Lee to Ivy. This was going south really fast. Where was her call? They had to be in place by now.

Lee wasn't happy. Jaw tight, he laced his fingers together and set them on the desk. His face went red from behind his black bangs and he leaned forward. "You need to look in your briefcase, little pup, and find a check in there for me," he said, his Berkeley accent growing pronounced. "I'm not accustomed to being disappointed."

David snapped his briefcase shut and set it gently on the floor. "You need to broaden your horizons, Mr. Saladan. It happens to me all the time."

"Not me." Round face wrathful, Lee got to his feet. The tension rose. I eyed Lee, then David, looking confident even though he was seated. Neither man was going to back down.

"Sign the paper, sir," David said softly. "I'm just the mes-senger. Don't get the lawyers into this. Then they're the only ones who get any money and you become uninsurable."

Lee took a hasty breath, his dark eyes pinched in anger.

I jumped at the sudden ring of my phone. My eyes widened. It was playing the theme to the Lone Ranger. I scrambled to turn it off, not knowing how. *God help me.*

"Grace!" David barked, and I jumped again. The phone slipped from my fingers. I fumbled after it, face flaming. My emotions warred between panic that they were both looking at me and my relief that Ivy was ready.

"Grace, I told you to turn that phone off when we were in the drive!" David yelled.

He stood, and I looked at him in helplessness. He

snatched the phone out of my hands. The music cut off and he threw it back at me.

My jaw clenched as it hit my palm with a sharp snap. I'd had enough. Seeing my hot anger, David moved between me and Lee, gripping my shoulder in warning. Ticked, I knocked his arm away. But my anger caught when he smiled and winked at me.

"You're a good operative," he said softly as Lee punched a button on his intercom and had a hushed conversation with what sounded like a very upset Candice. "Most of the people I work with would have gone for my throat at the front door with that subordinate-bitch comment. Dig your feet in. We can get a few more minutes out of this conversation, and I still need him to sign my form."

I nodded, though it was hard. The compliment helped.

Still standing, Lee reached for his coat and slipped his arms into it. "I'm sorry, Mr. Hue. We will have to continue this at another opportunity."

"No, sir." David stood unmoving. "We will finish this now."

There was a commotion in the hallway, and I rose when Chad, the vampire with the charm, stumbled in. Seeing David and me, he swallowed down his first, probably frantic, words.

"Chad," Lee said, the faintest bother in his expression as he took in the vamp's disheveled appearance. "Will you see Mr. Hue and his assistant to their car?"

"Yes, sir."

The house was quiet and I stifled a smile. Ivy once took out an entire floor of FIB agents. Unless Lee had a hell of a lot of people hidden about, it wouldn't be long until I had my charms and Lee would be wearing handcuffs.

David didn't move. He stood before Lee's desk, his Were mien growing. "Mr. Saladan." He pushed the form forward with two fingers. "If you would?"

Red spots started on Lee's round cheeks. Taking a pen from an inner jacket pocket, he signed the paper, making his name big and unreadable. "Tell your superiors that I will be compensated for my loss," he said, leaving it on the desk for David to pick up. "It would be a shame if your company found itself in financial straits by a number of your more expensive properties becoming damaged."

David picked up the paper and tucked it in his briefcase. Standing beside and a little behind him, I felt his tension rise and saw him shift his balance to the balls of his feet. "Is that a threat, Mr. Saladan? I can transfer your claim to our complaint department."

A soft boom thumped against my inner ear, and Chad jiggled on his feet. It was a distant explosion. Lee looked at a wall as if he could see through it. My eyebrows rose. Ivy.

"Just one more signature." David brought out a trifolded paper from a coat pocket.

"Our time is done, Mr. Hue."

David stared at him, and I could almost hear the growl. "It won't take but—a moment. Grace, I need your signature, here. Then Mr. Saladan's . . . here."

Surprised, I stepped forward, head lowered to the paper David smoothed out on the desk. My eyes widened. It stated that I was a witness to seeing the bomb on the boiler. I thought it wrong that David's company was more worried about the boat than the people who died on it. But that was insurance for you.

I took the pen, glancing up at David. He made a small shrug, a new, hard glint to his eyes. Despite his anger, I think he was enjoying this.

Heart pounding, I signed it as Rachel. I listened for any sound of battle as I handed the pen to David. They had to be close, and there might not be any indication that they were in the house if all went well outside. Lee was tense, and my stomach tightened.

"And you, sir." It was sarcastic, and David turned the paper to him. "Sign, and I can close your file and you'll never have to see me again."

I wondered if that was his standard line as I reached into

an inner pocket of my borrowed jacket and pulled out the warrant Edden had brought over that afternoon.

Motions rough and belligerent, Lee signed the paper. Beside me, I heard the softest rumble of satisfaction from David. It was only then that Lee looked at my signature. The man went white under his tan. His thin lips parted. "Son of a bitch," he swore, his eyes rising to me, then Chad in the corner.

Smiling, I gave Lee my warrant. "This one's from me," I said cheerfully. "Thanks, David. Do you have what you need?"

David took a step back, tucking his form away. "He's all yours."

"Son of a bitch!" Lee said again, a disbelieving smile quirking his lips. "You just don't know when to stay dead, do you?"

My breath hissed in and I jerked as I felt him tap a line.

"Get down!" I shouted, shoving David out of the way and lurching back.

Pinwheeling, David hit the floor. I slid almost to the door. The air crackled and a thump reverberated through me. On all fours, I jerked my gaze to the ugly purple stain dripping to the floor. *What the Turn was that?* I thought, scrambling up and tugging my skirt to my knees.

Lee gestured to Chad, who looked cowed. "Well, get them!" he said, sounding disgusted.

Chad blinked, then strode to David.

"Not him, you idiot!" Lee shouted. "The woman!"

Chad yanked himself to a stop, turned, then reached for me. *Where in hell was Ivy?* My demon scar flamed to pleasure, and while it was rather distracting, I nevertheless had no problem jamming the heel of my palm into Chad's nose, jerking back when the cartilage tore. I hated the feel of breaking noses. It gave me the willies.

Chad cried out in pain, hunching over and holding his blood-soaked hands to his face. I followed him down, giving him an elbow on the back of his neck, which he conveniently put in my reach. In three seconds Chad was down.

Rubbing my elbow, I looked up to find David watching in wide-eyed interest. I was between Lee and the door. Smiling, I tossed the hair that had escaped my bun out of my eyes. Lee was a ley line witch; chances were that he was a coward when it came to physical pain. He wouldn't jump out that window unless he had to.

Lee thumbed an intercom. "Candice?" His voice was a mix of anger and threat.

Panting, I licked my thumb and pointed to Lee. "David, you might want to leave. This is going to be dicey."

My good mood grew when Kisten's voice came out of the speaker along with the pained sounds of a catfight. "Candice is busy, old man." I recognized the sound of Ivy's attack, and Kisten made a noise of sympathy. "Sorry, love. You shouldn't have strayed. Oh, that *had* to hurt." Then he was back, his fake accent heavy and amused. "Perhaps I could help you?"

Lee clicked off the intercom. He adjusted his coat, watching me. He looked confident. Not good. "Lee," I said, "we can do it easy, or hard."

There was a thumping of feet in the hallway, and I fell back to David when five men came spilling in. Ivy wasn't with them. Neither were my charms. They did have a lot of guns, though, all pointed at us. *Damn.*

Lee smiled and came out from behind his desk. "I'm all for easy," he said, so smug I wanted to slap him.

Chad was starting to move, and Lee nudged him in the ribs. "Get up," he said. "The Were has a paper in his jacket. Get it."

Stomach churning, I backed up as Chad staggered to his feet, blood dripping on his cheap suit. "Just give it to him," I warned when David tensed. "I'll get it back."

"No, I don't think you will," Lee said as David handed it to Chad and the vamp passed the now blood-smeared paper to Lee. White teeth gleaming, he tossed his hair and smiled. "Sorry to hear about your accident."

I glanced at David, hearing our coming death in his words.

Lee wiped the blood off on Chad's coat. Folding it twice, he tucked it in a jacket pocket. Headed for the door, he said casually, "Shoot them. Take out the bullets, then dump them under the ice downriver from the dock. Clean up the room. I'm going out for an early dinner. I'll be back in two hours. Chad, come with me. We need to talk."

My heart pounded and I could smell David's rising tension. His hands were opening and closing as if they hurt. Maybe they did. I gasped at the sound of safeties going off.

"Rhombus!" I shouted, my word lost in the thunder of weapons discharging.

I staggered as my thoughts tapped the nearest line. It was the university's, and it was huge. I smelled gunpowder. Straightening, I patted at myself frantically. Nothing hurt but my ears. David's face was white but there was no pain in his eyes. A shimmer of molecule-thin ever-after shone around us. The four men were straightening from their own crouches. I had gotten the circle up in time and their bullets had ricocheted right back at them.

"What do we do now?" one asked.

"Hell if I know," the tallest said.

From the floor of the vestibule came Lee's shout, "Just fix it."

"You!" came Ivy's faint demand. "Where's Rachel!"

Ivy! Frantic, I looked at my circle. It was a trap. "Can you take two of them?" I asked.

"Give me five minutes to Were, and I can take them all," David all but growled.

The noise of fighting drifted up. It sounded like there were a dozen people down there, and one angry vampire. One of the men looked at the others and ran out. Three left. The pop of a gun downstairs brought me straight. "We don't have five minutes. Ready?"

He nodded.

Face twisting, I broke my link to the line and the circle fell. "Go!" I exclaimed.

David was a blur beside me. I went for the smallest, knocking his weapon aside with a foot as he tried to backpedal. It was my training against his slower magic, and my training won. His gun skittered across the floor, and he dove for it. *Idiot.* Following him down, I elbowed his kidney. He gasped and turned to face me, far short of the gun. God, he looked young.

Teeth gritted, I picked up his head and slammed it into the ground. His eyes closed and his body went slack. Yeah, it was crude, but I was in kind of a hurry.

The crack of a weapon discharging pulled me around. "I'm fine!" David barked, popping up with a Were's quickness from a crouch and jabbing a small, powerful fist at the last witch standing. Eyes rolling to the back of his head, the witch dropped the gun from slack fingers and toppled to fall on the first man David had downed. Damn, he was fast!

My heart pounded and my ears rang. We had brought them down with only one shot fired. "You got two," I said, exhilarated at the joined effort. "Thanks!"

Breathing hard, David wiped his lip and swooped to get his briefcase. "I need my paper."

We stepped over the downed witches. David went out before me. He stopped, eyes narrowing at the man on the balcony taking aim at Ivy. Grunting, he swung his briefcase. It smacked into the witch's head. Staggering, the man turned. I spun on one foot, slamming my foot into his solar plexus. His arms pinwheeled as he fell back into the railing.

I didn't stop to see if he was down or not. Leaving David to wrestle for the gun, I ran down the stairs. Ivy was fending off Candice. My bag of charms was at Ivy's feet. There were three bodies sprawled on the tile floor. Poor Chad wasn't having a very good day.

"Ivy!" I called when she threw Candice into the wall and had a moment. "Where's Lee!"

Her eyes were black and her lips were pulled back from

her teeth. With a high scream of outrage, Candice came at her. Ivy jumped for the chandelier, her foot connecting with Candice's jaw to rock the vampire back. There was a creak from the ceiling.

"Look out!" I cried from the bottom step as Ivy swung to land with an unreal grace and the chandelier fell. It shattered, sending broken glass and crystal everywhere.

"Kitchen!" Ivy panted from a hunched crouch. "He's in the garage. With Kisten."

Candice looked at me, hatred in her black eyes. Blood ran from her mouth, and she licked it. Her gaze went to the duffel bag of spells. She tensed to run for it—and Ivy jumped.

"Go!" Ivy shouted, grappling with the smaller vampire.

I went. Heart pounding, I ran around the ruin of the chandelier, scooping up my charms in passing. From behind me came a scream of terror and pain. I skidded to a stop. Ivy had Candice pinned to the wall. My face went cold. I'd seen it before. *God help me. I'd lived it.*

Candice bucked and fought, a new frenzy in her motions as she tried to get free. Ivy held her still, as unmoving as a steel girder. Piscary's strength made her unstoppable, and Candice's fear was feeding her blood lust. A rattle of gunfire came from the unseen garage. I tore my gaze from them, frightened. Ivy had vamped out. Absolutely and totally. She had lost herself.

Mouth dry, I ran through the empty kitchen to the garage door. Candice screamed again, the terrifying sound ending in a gurgle. I hadn't wanted this. I hadn't wanted this at all.

I spun at a scuffling noise behind me, but it was David. His face was white, and he never slowed down as he paced to me. There was a weapon in his grip.

"Is she . . ." I asked, hearing my voice shake.

His hand went on my shoulder and he pushed me into motion. Lines marked his face, and he looked old. "Just go," he said raggedly. "She's got your back."

The sound of men's voices in the garage rose, then fell. There was a spat of gunfire. Crouched by the door, I shuffled through my duffel bag. I put a slew of amulets around my neck and tucked my cuffs into my waistband. My splat gun was heavy in my hand, fourteen little babies in a row ready for sleep in the reservoir, enough propellant to shoot them all.

David peeked around the door, then ducked back. "Five men with Saladan behind a black car on the far end of the garage. I think they're trying to get it started. Your boyfriend is around the corner. We can reach him with a quick run." He looked at me as I fumbled at my charms. "Good God! What are all those for?"

My boyfriend? I thought, crawling to the doorway with my charms dragging under me. *Well, I* had *slept with him.* "One is for pain," I whispered. "One is for slowing down bleeding. One is for detecting black charms before I walk into them, and one—"

My words cut off as the car started. *Shit.*

"Sorry I asked," David muttered, close behind me.

Heart pounding, I risked an upright, hunched walk, taking a deep breath of the dark, garage-cold air as I ducked behind a bullet-dinged silver Jag. Kisten's head swung up. He was on the floor with a hand pressed to his lower chest. Pain glazed his eyes, and his face was pale under his blond-dyed hair. Blood seeped from under his hand, and I went cold from more than the unheated garage. Four men were down beside him. One moved, and he kicked him in the head until he didn't move anymore.

"Better and better," I whispered, making my way to Kisten. The garage door whined into motion, and the shouts from the car were loud over the revving engine. But Kisten was the only thing I cared about right now.

"Are you okay?" I dropped two charms over his head. I felt sick. He wasn't supposed to have gotten hurt. Ivy wasn't supposed to have been tripped into draining someone. Nothing was supposed to have gone this way.

"Get him, Rachel," he said, managing a pained-looking grimace. "I'll live."

The car's tires squealed as it backed up. Panicking, I looked from Kisten to the car, torn.

"Get him!" Kisten insisted, his blue eyes crinkled in pain.

David eased Kisten to the garage floor. One hand pressing Kisten's hand against the wound, he sent the other searching his jacket. Pulling out his phone, David flipped it open and punched 911.

Kisten nodded, his eyes closing as I stood. The car had backed up into the turnaround spot and was jerking into motion. It stalled. Mad as all hell, I stomped out after it.

"Lee!" I shouted. The car's engine sputtered and caught, its wheels spinning on the wet cobbles. My jaw gritted. Tapping a line, I clenched my fist. Line energy coursed through me, filling my veins with the staggering feeling of strength. My eyes narrowed. "Rhombus," I said, fingers splayed as I gestured.

My knees buckled and I screamed when the pain from the line energy required to make such a large circle raged through me, burning when I couldn't channel it all at once. There was an ugly noise of folding metal and squealing tires. The sound raked through me, fixing in my memory to haunt my nightmares. The car had hit my circle, but the car broke, not me.

I caught my balance and continued forward as men piled out of the smashed vehicle. Never slowing, I took aim with my splat gun, squeezing the trigger with a methodical slowness. Two went down before the first of the bullets went cutting through the air beside my head.

"You shooting at me?" I screamed. "You shooting at me!" I dropped the gunman with a charm, leaving Lee and two men. One put his hands in the air. Lee saw him, then with no hesitation, shot him. The pop of the gun jerked through me as if I had been hit.

The witch's face went ashen, and he collapsed to the cobbled drive, leaning against the car and trying to hold his blood into him.

Anger shocked through me and I halted. Seething, I aimed at Lee and squeezed.

Drawing himself up, he whispered Latin and gestured. I lurched to the side, but he had been going for the ball and it deflected to the right. Still crouched, I shot again. Lee's eyes went patronizing as he deflected it too. The movements of his hands took on a more sinister mien, and my eyes widened. *Shit, I had to end this now.*

I lunged at him, yelping when the last vampire slammed into me. We went down in a tangle, me fighting furiously to keep him from getting a hold on me. With a last grunt and savage kick, I broke free, rolling to my feet. Panting, I backed away. My sparring with Ivy came back in a mixed slurry of hope and despair. I had never managed to best her. Not really.

Silent, the vampire attacked. I dove to the side, skinning my elbow as Mrs. Aver's suit tore through. He was on me, and I rolled, head covered with my arms, kicking him off when I caught my breath. The tingle of my circle zinged through me. I had run into it and it had fallen. Immediately I lost connection with the line, making me feel empty.

I jumped to my feet, swerving to avoid the vamp's leg swing. *Damn it, he wasn't even trying!* My splat gun was behind him, and when he came at me, I collapsed out of his reach, rolling to get it. Fingers grasping, my breath exploded out as the cool metal settled in my grip.

"Got you, you bastard!" I shouted, spinning to plug him right in the face.

His eyes widened, then rolled up. Stifling a shriek, I rolled out of the way as his momentum tipped him forward. There was a sodden thump as he hit the cobbled drive. Blood seeped out from under his cheek. He'd broken something.

"Sorry you work for such a dick," I breathed as I got up, then did a double take. My face went slack and I let my gun slip to dangle from a finger. I was surrounded by eight men, all of them a good ten feet back. Lee stood behind them, looking obnoxiously satisfied as he adjusted the button on his coat. I grimaced and tried to catch my breath. Oh yeah. I had broken the circle. *Shit on crap, how many times did I have to tag this guy?*

Panting and hunched in pain, I saw David and Kisten unmoving under three guns in the garage. There were eight surrounding me. Add in the five I'd just downed. Kisten had gotten at least four. Mustn't forget the original guys upstairs. I didn't even know how many Ivy had taken out. The man was ready for a freaking war.

Slowly I straightened. I could handle that.

"Ms. Morgan?" Lee's voice sounded odd among the dripping snowmelt coming off the garage's overhang. The sun was behind the house, and I shivered now that I wasn't moving. "Anything left in your little gun?"

I looked at it. If I had counted right—and I thought I had—there were eight charms in there. Eight charms that were useless as Lee could deflect them all. And even if he didn't, I stood little chance in taking that many men without getting nailed. *If I played by the rules . . .*

"I'm dropping the gun," I said, then carefully, slowly, opened the reservoir and dumped the blue splat balls out before I tossed it to him. Seven tiny spheres bounced, rolling in the cracks of the red cobbled drive to come to a stop. Seven in the open; one in my hand. *God, this had to work. Just don't bind my hands. I had to keep my hands.*

Shaking, I put my hands in the air and backed away, a tiny splat ball dropping down my sleeve to make a cold spot at my elbow. Lee gestured, and the surrounding men converged. One grabbed my shoulder, and I struggled not to hit him. *Placid, meek. No need to tie me up.*

Lee got in my face. "Stupid, stupid girl," he sneered, touching his forehead under his short dark bangs where a new cut spread.

He pulled his hand back, and I forced myself to not move, taking it as he backhanded me. Seething, I pulled myself straight where the momentum had shifted me. The surrounding men laughed, but my hands behind my back were moving, the splat ball rolling to find my palm as I finished. My eyes flicked from Lee to my splat balls on the cobbles. Someone bent to pick one up. "You're wrong," I said to Lee, breathing hard. "I'm a stupid, stupid witch."

Lee's attention followed mine to the splat balls. *"Consimilis,"* I said, tapping a line.

"Get down!" Lee exclaimed, pushing the men around him out of the way.

"Calefacio!" I shouted, elbowing the witch holding me and rolling to the ground. My circle snapped into existence around me with a quick thought. There was a sharp pop, and a scattering of blue-colored shrapnel peppered the outside of my bubble. The plastic balls had burst from the heat, sending superheated sleep potion everywhere. I looked up from between my arms. Everyone was down but Lee, having put enough men between him and the flying potions. In the garage, Ivy stood panting over the last three vamps. We had gotten them. All that was left was Lee. And he was mine.

A smile curved over me as I stood and broke my circle, taking the energy back into my chi. "Just you and me, surfer boy," I said, tossing the splat ball I had used for a focusing object and catching it. "Care to throw the dice?"

Lee's round face went still. He held himself unmoving, and then, without a glimmer of emotion, tapped a line.

"Son of a bitch," I swore, lunging. I slammed into him, knocking him flat on the cobbles. Teeth gritted, he gripped my wrist, squeezing until the splat ball rolled from me.

"You will shut up!" I shouted from atop him, jamming my arm into his throat so he couldn't speak. He fought me, bringing his hand up to smack my cheek.

My breath hissed out in a pained gasp as he hit the bruise Al gave me. Catching his wrist, I snapped my cuffs on him. Spinning him over, I wrenched his arm out from under him. Knee on his back, pinning him to the pavement, I snapped the other ring about his other wrist.

"I am tired of your crap!" I exclaimed. "Nobody tries to put a black charm on me, and nobody traps me in a boat with a bomb. Nobody! You hear me? Who in hell do you think you are, coming into my city and trying to take over?" Rolling him over, I snatched David's paper from behind his coat. "And this isn't yours!" I said, holding it high like a trophy.

"Ready for a little trip, witch?" Lee said, his eyes dark with hate and blood leaking from his mouth.

My eyes widened as I felt him pull more from the ley line he was already linked to. "No!" I shouted, realizing what he was doing. *The cuffs were FIB issue,* I thought, kicking myself. They were FIB issue, lacking the core of solid silver that the I.S. issue cuffs came standard with. He could jump. He could jump to a line if he knew how. And apparently he did.

"Rachel!" Ivy shrieked, her voice and the light cutting off with a terrifying suddenness.

A sheet of ever-after coated me. I choked, pushing Lee away, clawing at my mouth, unable to breathe. My heart beat wildly as his magic raced through me, etching the lines both physical and mental that defined me. The blackness of never flooded me, and I panicked as I felt myself exist in splinters everywhere but nowhere sure. I teetered on madness, unable to breathe, unable to think.

I screamed as I snapped back into myself with a wrench and the blackness retreated to the pit of my soul. I could breathe.

Lee kicked at me, and I rolled away to my hands and knees, thanking God I had them again. Cold rock bit through my nylons, and I sucked in the air, gasping, gagging at the choking smell of ash. The wind whipped my hair into my face. My exposed skin went icy. Heart pounding, I looked up, knowing by the ruddy light coating the rubble I knelt in that we weren't in Lee's drive anymore.

"Oh . . . crap," I whispered as I took in the setting sun glowing through the remains of shattered buildings.

I was in the ever-after.

Thirty-two

The frost-rimmed rocks beside me slid, and I jerked out of the way before Lee's foot could connect with my ribs again. Red and small, the sun crept behind the shadow of a broken building. It looked like Carew Tower. Nearby were the remnants of what might be a fountain. *We were at Fountain Square?* "Lee," I whispered, frightened. "We have to get out of here."

There was a *ping*, and Lee brought his arms out from behind his back. His suit was dirty and it looked out of place amid the destruction. The soft and certain clink of a falling rock pulled my head around, and he threw the handcuffs at it. We weren't alone. *Damn.*

"Lee!" I hissed. *Oh God. If Al found me, I was dead.* "Can you get us home?"

He smiled, brushing the hair out of his eyes. Slipping on the loose rubble, he scanned the ragged horizon. "You don't look well," he said, and I winced at how loud his voice was against the cold rocks. "First time in the ever-after?"

"Yes and no." Shivering, I got up and felt my scraped knees. I'd put a run in my nylons, and blood was seeping out. I was standing in a line. I could feel it humming, could almost see it—it was that strong. Clasping my arms about myself, I jerked at the sound of sliding rock. I wasn't thinking of tagging him; I was thinking of escape. But I couldn't travel the lines.

Another rock fell, bigger. I spun, eyes searching the frost-smeared rubble.

Hands on his hips, Lee squinted up at the red-bottomed clouds as if the cold didn't bother him. "Lesser demons," he said. "Fairly harmless unless you're hurt or ignorant."

I inched away from the fallen rock. "This isn't a good idea. Let's go back and we can finish this like normal people."

He brought his gaze to me. "What will you give me?" he mocked, thin eyebrows high.

I felt like the time my date drove me to a farmhouse and stranded me, telling me if I didn't put out, I could find my own way back. I broke his finger to get the key for his truck and cried all the way home. My mom called his mom and that was the end of it except for the endless ribbing I took at school. Maybe I'd have gotten some respect if my dad had beat up his dad, but that hadn't been an option at that point. I didn't think breaking Lee's finger would get me home this time. "I can't," I whispered. "You killed all those people."

Shaking his head, he sniffed. "You hurt my reputation. I'm going to be rid of you."

My mouth went dry when I realized where this was headed. He was going to give me to Algaliarept, the bastard. "Don't do this, Lee," I said, frightened. My head jerked up at the rapid scrabbling of claws. "We both owe him," I said. "He can take you just as easily."

Lee kicked chunks of rock from his feet to make a clear spot. "No-o-o-o, the word on both sides of the lines is he wants *you*." Eyes black in the red light, Lee smiled. "But just in case, I'm going to soften you up a little first."

"Lee," I whispered, hunched from the cold as he started to mutter Latin. The glow of the line energy in his hand lit his face with ugly shadows. I tensed in sudden panic. There was nowhere to run in the three seconds I had.

My breath caught at the sudden clatter of things hiding. I jerked my attention up to see a sphere of energy headed right for me. If I made a circle, Al would feel it. If I deflected it, Al would know. So like an idiot, I froze, and it smacked right into me.

Fire rippled over my skin. My head flung back, mouth open as I fought for air. It was simply line energy, overflowing my chi. *Tulpa,* I thought as I fell, giving it somewhere to go.

Immediately the fire died, racing to the sphere already up and waiting in my head. Something in me seemed to shift, and I knew I had made a mistake. The things around us squealed and vanished.

I heard a gentle pop. Heart pounding, I straightened. My breath caught, and I slowly let it out in a steaming ribbon of white moisture. Al's jaunty silhouette was black against the setting sun as he stood atop a broken building, his back to us.

"Shit," Lee swore. "What the hell is he doing here already?"

I spun to Lee and the soft hiss of metallic chalk against pavement. It was a ley line witch's version of duct tape, and it would make a very secure circle. My heart pounded as a shimmer of black and purple rose between us. Blowing hard, Lee tucked his chalk away and smiled confidently at me.

Shivering violently, I looked over the sunset-red slumps of broken rock. I didn't have anything to make a circle with. I was a dead witch. I was on Al's side of the lines; my previous contract didn't mean anything.

Al turned at the sensation of Lee's circle going up. But it was to my eyes that his fixed on. "Rachel Mariana Morgan," he drawled, clearly pleased as a cascade of ley line energy washed over him and his attire shifted to what I thought was an English riding outfit, complete with whip and shiny, calf-high boots. "What *did* you do to your hair?"

"Hi, Al," I said, backing up. I had to get out of there. *There's no place like home,* I thought, feeling the hum of the line I was standing in and wondering whether it would help if I clicked my heels. Lee had flown over the rainbow, why, oh why, the hell couldn't I?

Satisfaction all but glowed from Lee. My gaze went from

him to Al as the demon carefully picked his way down the slide of rubble to the floor of the large square.

The square, I thought, hope catching in my throat. Spinning, I tried to place myself, tripping as I pushed rocks with my foot, searching. If this was a mirror of Cincinnati, then this was Fountain Square. And if this was Fountain Square, then there was a humdinger of a circle all laid out between the street and the parking garage. But it was really, really big.

My breath came fast when my foot revealed a battered arc of purple inlay. *It was the same. It was the same!* Frantic, I realized Al was almost to the floor of the square. I quickly tapped the nearby line. It flowed into me with the mirror-bright taste of clouds and tinfoil. *Tulpa,* I thought, desperate to gather enough power to close a circle this size before Al realized what I was doing.

I stiffened as a torrent of line energy flooded me. Groaning, I dropped to one knee. His aristocratic face going slack, Al drew himself upright. He saw my intent in my eyes. "No!" he cried, lunging forward as I reached to touch the circle and say my word of invocation.

A gasp slipped from me as, with the feeling of being poured out of myself, a shimmering wave of translucent gold swam up from the ground, bisecting rocks and slumped rubble, arching to a humming close high over my head. Staggering, I fell back, my mouth gaping open as I stared up at it. *Holy crap, I had closed Fountain Square circle.* I had closed a circle thirty feet across that had been designed for seven witches to set comfortably, not one. Though apparently one could do it if properly motivated.

Al skidded to a halt, arms swinging to avoid running into the circle. A faint bong of reverberation echoed in the dusky air, crawling over my skin like dust. My eyes widened and I stared. Bells. Big, deep, resonant bells. There really were bells, and my circle had rung them.

Adrenaline shook my knees, and they rang again. Al stood to look peeved a mere three feet from the edge, head cocked and thin lips pressed tight as he listened to the third peal die away. The power of the line running through me ebbed, settling into a soft hum. The silence of the night was frighteningly profound.

"Nice circle," Al said, sounding impressed, bothered, and interested. "You're going to be grand fun at tractor pulls."

"Thanks." I twitched when he took off his glove and tapped my circle to make rippled dimples waver across it. "Don't touch it!" I blurted, and he chuckled—tapping, tapping, ever moving, looking for a weak spot. It was a huge circle; he might find one. *What had I done?*

My hands tucked into my armpits for warmth, I looked at Lee, still in his circle, doubly safe within mine. "We can still get out of here," I said, hearing my voice tremble. "Neither one of us needs to be his familiar. If we—"

"How stupid can you be?" Lee edged his foot across his circle, dissolving it. "I want to be rid of you. I want to pay off my demon scar. Why, on God's green earth, would I save you?"

Shivering, I felt the wind bite at me. "Lee!" I said, turning to keep Al in my sight as he moved to the back of my circle, still testing. "We have to get out of here!"

His small nose wrinkling at the scent of burnt amber, Lee laughed. "No. I'm going to beat you into a pulp, and then I'm going to give you to Algaliarept, and he's going to call my debt paid." Cocky and self-assured, he looked at Al, who had stopped pushing at my circle and was now standing with a beatific smile. "Is that satisfactory?"

A lump of fear settled heavy in my belly as a wicked, contriving smile spread over Al's chiseled face. An elaborately detailed rug and a maroon velvet chair from the eighteenth century appeared behind him, and still smiling, Al settled himself, the last of the sun making him a red smear among the broken buildings. Crossing his legs, he said, "Stanley Collin Saladan, we have an agreement. Give me Rachel Mariana Morgan, and I will indeed call your debt paid."

I licked my lips, and they went cold in the bitter wind. Around us came the soft scrabblings as things crept closer, called by me ringing the city's bells and lured by the promise of darkness. A soft plink of stone brought me spinning around. *Something was in here with us.*

Lee smiled, and I wiped my hands off on my borrowed dress suit and stood straighter. He was right to feel confident—I was an earth witch without her charms up against a ley line master—but he didn't know everything. Al didn't know everything. Hell, I didn't know everything, but I knew something they didn't. And when that ugly red sun set behind the broken buildings, it wasn't going to be me who was Al's familiar.

I wanted to survive. Right now it didn't matter if giving Lee to Al in my stead was right or not. Later, when I was curled up with a cup of cocoa and shaking with the memory of this, would be soon enough to decide. But to win, I'd first have to lose. This was really going to hurt.

"Lee," I said, trying one last time. "Take us out of here!" *God, please let me be right!*

"You're such a girl," he said, tugging his dirt-stained suit straight. "Always whining and expecting to be rescued."

"Lee! Wait!" I shouted as he took three steps and threw a ball of purple haze.

I dove to the side. It skimmed past at chest height to hit the remnants of the fountain. With a rumble, a section of it cracked and broke away. Dust rose, red in the darkening air.

When I turned, Lee had my business card in his grip—the one I had given the bouncer at his boat. *Shit. He had a focusing object.* "Don't," I said. "You won't like how it ends."

Lee shook his head, his lips moving as he whispered. *"Doleo,"* he said clearly, the invocation word vibrating the air, and with my card in his grip, he gestured.

Jerking straight, I caught my harsh gurgle before it came from me. Gut-twisting pain doubled me over. Breathing through it, I staggered to my feet. I couldn't think to come back with anything. I staggered forward to try to free myself from pain. If I could hit him, it might stop. If I could get my card, he couldn't target me but would have to throw his spells.

I crashed into Lee. We went down, stones jabbing me. Lee kicked out, and I rolled as Al applauded, white-gloved hands a soft patting. Pain clouded me; thinking was impossible. *Illusion,* I told myself. It was a ley line charm. Only earth magic could inflict real pain. *It was an illusion.* Panting, I forced the charm from me with pure will. I wouldn't feel it.

My bruised shoulder throbbed, hurting worse than it actually did. I fastened on the real pain, willing the phantom agony away. Hunched, I saw Lee from around my hair, now completely fallen out of that stupid bun. *"Inflex,"* Lee said, grinning as his moving fingers finished his spell, and I cringed, waiting for something to happen, but nothing did.

"Oh, I say!" Al exclaimed from his rock. "First rate. Capital!"

I wove on my feet, fighting the last shadows of pain. I was in the line again. I could feel it. If I knew how to trip the lines, I could end this right now. *Bibbity bobbity boo,* I thought. *Alakazam.* Hell, I'd even twitch my nose if I thought it would work. But it didn't.

The rustle around me grew. They were becoming bolder as the sun threatened to set. A rock fell behind me, and I spun. My foot slipped. Crying out, I went down. Nausea hit me as my ankle twisted. Gasping, I clutched at it, feeling tears of pain start.

"Brilliant!" Al applauded. "Bad luck is extremely difficult. Take the charm off her. I don't want a klutz in my kitchen."

Lee gestured and a brief whirlwind smelling of burnt amber lifted through my hair. My throat tightened as the charm broke. My ankle throbbed and the cold rocks bit at me. He had cursed me with bad luck? *Son of a bitch . . .*

Jaw gritted, I reached for a rock to pull myself up. I had blasted Ivy before with raw ever-after, and I didn't need a focusing object if I threw it at him. Anger growing, I pulled upright, reaching into my memory for the how of it. It had always been instinctive before. The fear and anger helped, and as I staggered to my feet, I pushed the ever-after from my chi into my hands. They burned, but I held it, pulling more energy off the line until my outspread hands felt like they were charring. Furious, I compressed the raw energy in my hands to baseball size. "Bastard," I whispered, stumbling as I threw it at him.

Lee dived to the side, and my gold ball of ever-after hit my circle. My eyes widened when a cascade of tingles raced through me as my bubble broke.

"Damn it all to hell!" I shouted, not having thought ahead enough to realize my aura-laced spell would break my circle. Terrified, I spun to Al, thinking if I couldn't get it back up in time I'd be fighting both of them. But the demon was still seated, staring over my shoulder with his goat-slitted eyes wide. He looked over his glasses, mouth hanging open.

I spun in time to see my spell hit a nearby building. A faint *boom* shook my feet. I put a hand to my mouth as a chunk the size of a bus flaked off and fell with an unreal slowness.

"You stupid witch," Lee said. "It's coming right for us!"

I turned and ran, hands reaching as I scrabbled my way across the rubble, hands numb on the frost-cracked rocks. The ground shook, dust rose thick in the air. I staggered and fell.

Hacking and coughing, I got up, shaking. My fingers hurt and I couldn't move them. I turned to find Lee on the other side of the new rockfall, hatred and a touch of fear in his eyes.

Latin came from him. My eyes were fixed upon the card in his moving fingers, heart pounding as I waited, helpless. He gestured, and my card burst into flame.

It flashed like gunpowder. I cried out and turned away, hands over my eyes. The shrieks of the minor demons beat upon me. I reeled backward, balance gone. Red smears coated my vision. My eyes were open and tears streamed down my face, but I couldn't see. I couldn't see!

There was the sound of sliding rocks, and I yelped as someone cuffed me. I blindly lashed out, almost falling as the heel of my hand met nothing. Fear settled into me, debilitating. I couldn't see. He had taken my sight!

A hand shoved me over, and I fell, swinging my leg. I felt it hit him, and he went down. "Bitch," he gasped, and I shrieked when he yanked out a handful of my hair and scrabbled away.

"More!" Al said cheerfully. "Show me your best!" he encouraged.

"Lee!" I cried. "Don't do this!" The red wasn't clearing. *Please, please let it be illusion.*

Dark words came from Lee, sounding obscene. I smelled a strand of my hair burn.

My heart clenched in sudden doubt. I wasn't going to make it. He was going to all but kill me. There was no way to win this. Oh, God . . . what had I been thinking?

"You gave her doubt," Al said wonderingly from the blackness. "That's a very complex charm," he breathed. "What else? Can you divine?"

"I can look backward," Lee said nearby, panting.

"Oh!" Al said gleefully. "I have a marvelous idea! Make her recall her father's death!"

"No . . ." I whispered. "Lee, if you have any compassion. Please."

But his hated voice started whispering, and I groaned, falling into myself as a mental pain cut through the physical. My dad. My dad gasping his last. The feel of his dry hand in mine, the strength gone. I had stayed, refusing to leave for anything. I was there when his breaths stopped. I was there when his soul was freed, leaving me to fend for myself far, far too early. It had made me strong, but it had left me flawed.

"Dad," I sobbed, my chest hurting. He had tried to stay,

but couldn't. He had tried to smile, but it was broken. "Oh, Dad," I whispered, softer as the tears welled. I had tried to keep him there with me, but I hadn't been able to.

A black depression rose from my thoughts, pulling me into myself. He had left me. I was alone. He had gone. No one had ever come close to filling the void. No one ever would.

Sobbing, the miserable memory of that awful moment when I realized he was gone filled me. It wasn't when they pulled me from him at the hospital, but two weeks later when I broke the school's eight hundred meters record and I looked into the stands for his proud smile. He was gone. And that was when I knew he was dead.

"Brilliant," Al whispered, his cultured voice soft beside me.

I did nothing as a gloved hand curved under my jaw and tilted my head up. I couldn't see him as I blinked, but I felt the warmth of his hand. "You broke her utterly," Al said in wonder.

Lee's breathing was harsh. Clearly it had taken a lot out of him. I couldn't stop crying, the tears dribbling down my cheeks, cold in the wind. Al let go of my jaw, and I curled into a ball in the rubble at his feet, uncaring of what might happen next. *Oh God, my dad.*

"She's yours," Lee said. "Take my mark off."

I felt Al's arms go around me, lifting me up. I couldn't help but press into him. I was so cold, and he smelled like Old Spice. Though I knew it was Al's twisted cruelty, I clutched at him and sobbed. I missed him. God, I missed him. "Rachel," came my dad's voice, pulled from my memory, and I cried all the harder. "Rachel," it came again. "Is there nothing left?"

"Nothing," I said around my sobbing breaths.

"Are you sure?" my dad said, gentle and caring. "You tried so hard, my little witch. You really fought him with everything and failed?"

"I failed," I said between my sobs. "I want to go home."

"Shhhh," he soothed, his hand cool against me in my darkness. "I'll get you home and put you to bed."

I felt Al shift into motion. I was broken, but I wasn't done. My mind rebelled, wanting to sink deeper into nothingness, but my will survived. It was either Lee or me, and I wanted my cup of cocoa on Ivy's couch and a theme book of rationalizations.

"Al," I whispered. "Lee should be dead." It was easier to breathe. The memory of my father's death was slipping back into the hidden folds of my brain. They had been buried there so long that they found their places easily, one by one filed away for lonely nights by myself.

"Hush, Rachel," Al said. "I see what you intended by letting Lee trounce you, but you can kindle demon magic fully. There has never been a witch that can do that." He laughed, his glee chilling me. "And you're mine. Not Newt's, not anyone else's but mine."

"What about my demon mark?" Lee protested, several steps back, and I wanted to cry for him. He was so dead, and he didn't know it yet.

"Lee can," I whispered. I could see the sky. Blinking profusely, I saw a dark shadow of Al holding me silhouetted against the red-smeared clouds. Relief slipped into me, pushing out the last of my doubt to leave a shimmer of hope underneath. Ley line charms of illusion only worked short-term unless they were given a permanent place to reside in silver. "Taste him," I said. "Taste his blood. Trent's father fixed him, too. He can kindle demon magic."

Al jerked to a stop. "Bless me thrice. There are two of you?"

I shrieked as I fell, crying out as my hip hit a rock.

From behind me, I heard Lee's shout of fear and shock. Turning where Al had dropped me, I peered over the rubble and rubbed my eyes to make out Al drawing a sharp nail across Lee's arm. Blood welled, and I felt sick. "I'm sorry, Lee," I whispered, hugging my knees to myself. "I'm so sorry."

Al made a low sound deep in his throat of pleasure. "She's right," he said as he brought a finger from his lips. "And you're better at ley line magic than she is. I'll take you instead."

"No!" Lee screamed, and Al jerked him closer. "You wanted her! I gave you her!"

"You gave her to me, I took off your demon mark, and now I'm taking you. You can both kindle demon magic," Al said. "I could spend decades fighting a scrawny, high-maintenance familiar like her and never wedge the spells you already know into her cotton-fluffed head. Ever try twisting a demon curse?"

"No!" Lee cried, fighting to get away. "I can't!"

"You will. Here," Al said, dropping him down onto the ground. "Hold this for me."

I covered my ears and curled into myself as Lee screamed, then screamed again. It was high and raw, scraping across my skull like a nightmare. I felt like I was going to vomit. I had given Lee to Al to save my life. That Lee tried to do the same to me didn't make me feel better.

"Lee," I said, tears leaking out. "I'm sorry. God, I'm sorry."

Lee's voice cut off as he passed out. Al smiled, turning on a heel to me. "Ta, love. I don't like to be on the surface when it gets dark. All the best of luck to you."

My eyes widened. "I don't know how to get home!" I cried.

"Not my problem. 'Bye now."

I sat up, chilled as the stones I was sitting on seemed to soak into me. Lee came to with an ugly gibbering sound. Tucking him under an arm, Al gave me a nod and vanished.

A stone slid down to roll to my feet. I blinked, wiping my eyes to only get rock dust and chips of stone in them. "The line," I whispered, remembering. Maybe if I got into the line. Lee had jumped from outside of a line, but maybe I had to learn to walk before I could run.

A movement at the edge of my awareness caught my attention. Heart pounding, I whipped my head around, seeing nothing. Steadying myself, I wedged myself up, gasping when white-hot knives stabbed my ankle to take my breath away. I slipped back to the ground. Jaw gritted, I decided I would just crawl over there.

I reached out, seeing Mrs. Aver's business suit coated in the dust and frost it had scraped from the surrounding rocks. Gripping an outcrop, I pulled myself forward, managing a halfway upright position. My body was shaking with cold and fading adrenaline. The sun was almost down. A sliding of rocks urged me on. They were getting closer.

A soft pop pulled my head up. A tumble of pebbles and rocks came from everywhere as the lesser demons scrambled into hiding. My breath slipped from me as, from around my hair, I saw a small figure in dark purple sitting cross-legged before me, a narrow staff as long as I was tall laying across its lap. A robe draped it. Not a bathrobe, but a classy mix of a kimono and something a desert sheik would wear, all billowy with the suppleness of linen. A round hat with straight sides and a flat top was perched on its head. Squinting in the fading light, I decided there was an inch or so of air between the gold trim and the ground. *Now what?*

"Who in hell are you?" I said, pulling myself forward another step, "and will you be taking me home instead of Al?"

"Who in hell are you?" it echoed, its voice a mix of rough lightness. "Yes. That fits."

It wasn't hitting me with that carved black stick, or putting a charm on me, or even making ugly faces, so I ignored it and dragged myself forward another foot. There was a crackle of paper, and wondering, I tucked David's trifolded paper into my waistband. *Yeah, he'd probably want this back.*

"I'm Newt," it said, seemingly disappointed I was ignoring it. There was a rich accent that I couldn't place, an odd way of saying the vowels. "And no, I'm not taking you home. I already have a demon familiar. Algaliarept is right; you're almost worthless right now."

A demon for a familiar? Ooooh, that had to be good.

Grunting, I pulled myself forward. My ribs hurt, and I pressed a hand into them. Panting, I looked up. A smooth face, not young, not old—sort of . . . nothing—met me. "Ceri is afraid of you," I said.

"I know. She's very perceptive. Is she well?"

Fear slid through me. "Leave her alone," I said, jerking back as it pushed my hair out of my eyes. Its touch seemed to sink into me though I felt fingertips firm on my forehead. I stared at its black eyes as it peered at me, unruffled and curious.

"Your hair ought to be red," it said, smelling of crushed dandelions. "And your eyes are green like my sisters', not brown."

"Sisters?" I wheezed, considering I might give it my soul if it would give me a pain amulet. God, I hurt all over, inside and out. I sat back on my heels out of its reach. Newt had an eerie grace, its outfit giving no hint to gender. There was a necklace of black gold about its neck—again, the design neither masculine nor feminine. My gaze dropped to its bare feet, hovering above the rubble. They were narrow and slim, somewhat ugly. Masculine? "Are you a boy or a girl?" I finally asked, not sure.

Newt's brow furrowed. "It makes a difference?"

Muscles trembling, I pulled my hand to my mouth and sucked at a spot where the rock had pinched me. *It did to me.* "Don't get me wrong, but why are you just sitting there?"

The demon smiled, making me think the reason couldn't be good. "There are a few side bets as to whether you will learn how to use the lines before sunset. I'm here so no one cheats."

A stab of adrenaline cleared my head. "What happens when the sun goes down?"

"Anyone can have you."

A rock slid from a nearby pile, and I pushed into motion. "But you don't want me."

It shook its head, drifting back. "Maybe if you told me

why Al took the other witch instead of you, I might. I . . . don't remember."

Newt's voice sounded worried, making me wonder. Too much ever-after in the brainpan perhaps? I didn't have time to deal with a crazy demon, no matter how powerful it was. "Read the papers. I'm busy," I said, pulling myself forward.

I jerked when a boulder the size of a car fell two feet in front of me. The ground shook and bits of rock chips stung my face. I stared at it, then Newt, who was smiling as it adjusted its grip on its staff to look pleasant and innocuous. My head hurt. *Okay, maybe I had a little time.* "Ah, Lee can kindle demon magic," I said, not seeing any reason to tell it I could too.

Newt's black eyes widened. "Already?" it said, then its face clouded, not angry with me, but at itself. I waited for it to move the rock. It didn't. Taking a deep breath, I started to go around Newt, as it seemed the demon had forgotten I was there. The sense of danger flowing from the slight figure was growing, building on itself to tighten my gut and make my skin crawl. I was getting the distinct impression that I was still alive because a very powerful demon was curious, nothing more.

Hoping Newt would forget about me, I inched myself forward, trying to ignore the pain in my ankle. I slipped, sucking in my breath as the flat of my arm hit a rock, sending a shiver of pain up it. The boulder was right in front of me, and gathering myself, I wedged my knees under me. My ankle was burning agony as I gained my feet and held the rock for balance.

There was a brush of air, and Newt was beside me. "Do you want to live forever?"

The question sent a shiver through me. Damn it, Newt was becoming more interested, not less. "No," I whispered. Hand outstretched, I limped from the rock.

"I didn't either, until I tried it." The redwood staff clunked to the ground as Newt moved to keep even with me, black eyes eerily more alive than anyone else's I'd ever seen. My skin crawled. Something was wrong with Newt—really wrong. I couldn't put my finger on it until I realized that the minute I took my attention from Newt, I forgot what the demon looked like. Apart from those eyes.

"I know something Algaliarept doesn't," Newt said. "I remember now. You like secrets. You're good at keeping them, too. I know all about you; you're afraid of yourself."

I gritted my jaw as my ankle gave a twinge as I slipped on a rock. The line was just ahead. I could feel it. The sun had sunk below the horizon, halfway gone. It took seven minutes to sink once it touched the earth. Three and a half minutes. I could hear a gathering of breath from the lesser demons. *God, help me find a way out of this.*

"You should be afraid of you," Newt said. "Want to know why?"

I pulled my head up. Newt was bored out of his or her mind and looking for amusement. I didn't want to be interesting. "No," I whispered, becoming more frightened.

An evil smile crossed Newt, emotions shifting faster than a vampire hyped up on Brimstone. "I think I will tell Algaliarept a joke. And when he's done ripping that witch apart for what he lost, I'll trade for that mark you owe him and make it mine."

I started to shake, unable to stop my hands from trembling. "You can't do that."

"I can. I might." Newt twirled the staff idly, hitting a rock so it ricocheted into the dark. There was a catlike yelp of pain and a scattering of sliding rock. "And then I'll have two," the demon said to itself, "because you won't be able to figure out how to travel the lines and will have to buy a trip out of here. From me."

There was a cry of outrage from the watchers behind the rocks, quickly squelched.

Horrified, I came to a jerky stop, feeling the line right ahead of me.

"You want to survive," Newt intoned, its voice dropping in pitch. "You'll do anything for it. Anything."

"No," I whispered, terrified because Newt was right. "I saw Lee do it. I can do it too."

Black eyes glinting, Newt set the butt of its staff down. "You won't figure it out. You won't believe; not yet. You have to make a deal . . . with me."

Frightened, I wavered on my feet, and with the next step, I stumbled into the line, feeling as if it was a stream, warm and generous, filling me up. Almost panting, I teetered, seeing the eyes around me narrow with greed and anger. I hurt. I had to get out of there. The power of the line hummed through me, peaceful and comforting. *There's no place like home.*

Newt's expression went mocking, its pupil-black eyes spiteful. "You can't do it."

"I can," I said, my vision darkening as I almost passed out. From the deepest shadows glittered green eyes. Close. Very close. The power of the line hummed through me. *There's no place like home, there's no place like home, there's no place like home,* I thought desperately, pulling energy into me, spindling it in my head. I had traveled the lines with Lee. I had seen how he had done it. All it took was him thinking about where he wanted to be. I wanted to be home. Why wasn't it working?

My knees shook as the first dark shape came out to stand with an unreal thinness, slow and hesitant. Newt looked at it, then turned slowly to me, one eyebrow raised. "One favor, and I'll send you back."

Oh God. Not another one. "Leave me alone!" I shouted, the rough edges of a rock scraping my fingers as I flung it at an approaching form and almost fell over. A gasp sounding like a sob came from me as I caught my balance. The lesser demon ducked, then straightened. Three more pairs of eyes glowed behind it.

I jumped as Newt suddenly was before me. The light was gone. Black eyes slammed into me, delving into my soul and clenching until fear squeezed out to bubble up. "You can't do it. No time to learn," Newt said, and I shuddered. Here was power, raw and swirling. Newt's soul was so black it was almost unseen. I could feel its aura press against me, starting to slip into mine with the force of Newt's will. It could take me over if it wanted. I was nothing. My will was nothing.

"Owe me or die in this squalid pile of broken promises," Newt said. "But I can't send you through the lines with a thin tie called home. Home won't do it. Think on Ivy. You love her more than that damn church," it said, its honesty more cutting than any physical pain.

Crying out in angry, high voices, the shadows bunched and lunged.

"Ivy!" I shouted, accepting the bargain and willing myself to her: the smell of her sweat when we sparred, the taste of her Brimstone cookies, the sound of her steps, and the rise of her eyebrows when she was trying not to laugh.

I recoiled as Newt's black presence was suddenly in my head. *How many mistakes can one life survive?* echoed crystallinelike in my mind, but whose thought it was I didn't know.

Newt pressed the air from my lungs, and my mind shattered. I was everywhere and nowhere. The perfect disconnection of the line raced through me, making me exist in every line on the continent. *Ivy!* I thought again, starting to panic until I remembered her, fastening on her indomitable will and the tragedy of her desires. *Ivy. I want to go to Ivy.*

With a savage, jealous thought, Newt snapped my soul back together. Gasping, I covered my ears as a loud pop shook me. I fell forward, my elbows and knees smacking into gray tile. People screamed, and I heard the crash of metal. Papers flew, and someone shouted to call the I.S.

"Rachel!" Ivy cried.

I looked up past my falling hair to see I was in what looked like a hospital hallway. Ivy was sitting in an orange plastic chair, her eyes red and her cheeks blotchy, shock in her wide brown eyes. David was beside her, dirty and disheveled, Kisten's blood on his hands and chest. A phone rang and went unanswered.

"Hi," I said weakly, my arms starting to tremble. "Uh, could one of you maybe check me in? I don't feel so good."

Ivy stood, reaching out. I tipped forward. My cheek hit the tile. The last thing I remember was my hand touching hers.

Thirty-three

"Coming!" I called out, my pace quickening as I strode through the dusky sanctuary to the door, my snow boots thumping to leave small inverse divots of snow behind. The huge dinner bell that was our doorbell clanked again, and I picked up the pace. "I'm coming. Don't ring the bell again or the neighbors will call the I.S., for God's sake."

The reverberations were still echoing when I reached for the handle, the nylon of my coat making a sliding sound. My nose was cold and my fingers were frozen, the warmth of the church not having had enough time to warm them up. "David!" I exclaimed, opening the door to find him on the softly lit stoop.

"Hi, Rachel," he said, looking comfortably attractive with his glasses, long coat, thick stubble, and his cowboy hat dusted with snow. The bottle of wine in his hand helped. An older man stood beside him in a leather jacket and jeans. He was taller than David, and I eyed his lightly wrinkled but trim physique in question. A wisp of snow-white hair peeped from under his hat. There was a twig in his grip, unquestionably a symbolic offering for the solstice bonfire out back, and I realized he was a witch. *David's old partner?* I thought. A limo idled softly behind them, but I was guessing they had come in the blue four-door parked in front of it.

"Rachel," David said, drawing my gaze back to them. "This is Howard, my old partner."

"Pleased to meet you, Howard," I said, extending my hand.

"The pleasure is mine." Smiling, he slipped off a glove to extend a softly wrinkled, freckled hand. "David told me all about you, and I invited myself. I hope you don't mind."

"Not at all," I said earnestly. "The more, the merrier."

Howard pumped my hand up and down three times before releasing it. "I had to come," he said, green eyes glinting. "The chance to meet the woman who can outrun David *and* put up with his working style doesn't come along very often. You two did good with Saladan."

His voice was deeper than I expected, and the feeling of being evaluated strengthened. "Thank you," I said, mildly embarrassed. I shifted back from the doorway in invitation. "We're all back by the fire. Come on in. It's easier to go through the church than stumble through the garden the back way."

Howard slipped inside in a whiff of redwood while David knocked the snow from his boots. He hesitated, looking up at the new sign above the door. "Nice," he said. "Just get it?"

"Yeah." Mood going soft, I leaned out to look up at it. The deeply engraved brass plaque had been bolted to the front of the church above the door. It had come with a light, and the single bulb lit the stoop in a soft glow. "It's a solstice gift for Ivy and Jenks."

David made a sound of approval laced with understanding. I flicked my attention from him back to the sign. VAMPIRE CHARMS; LLC. TAMWOOD, JENKS, AND MORGAN. I loved it, and I hadn't minded paying extra to make it a rush order. Ivy's eyes had gotten very wide when I pulled her out on the stoop that afternoon to see it. I thought she was going to cry. I'd given her a hug right there on the landing as it was obvious she wanted to give me one but was afraid I'd take it the wrong way. She was my friend, damn it. I could hug her if I wanted.

"I'm hoping it helps stop the rumors about me being dead," I said, ushering him in. "The paper was really quick to print my obituary, but because I'm not a vamp, they won't put anything in the risen-again announcements unless I pay for it."

"Imagine that," David said. I could hear the laughter in his voice, and I gave him a dry look as he stomped his boots a final time and came in. "You look good for a dead witch."

"Thanks."

"Your hair is almost back to normal. How about the rest of you?"

I shut the door, flattered at the sound of concern in his voice. Howard stood in the middle of the sanctuary, his eyes ranging over Ivy's piano and my desk. "I'm doing okay," I said. "My stamina is shot, but it's coming back. My hair, though?" I tucked a curl of reddish-brown hair behind an ear and the soft knit hat my mother had given me that afternoon. "The box said it washes out in five shampoos," I said sourly. "I'm still waiting."

Somewhat peeved at the reminder of my hair, I led the way into the kitchen, the two men trailing behind. Actually, my hair was the least of my worries. Yesterday I had found a scar with a familiar circle-and-slash pattern on the arch of my left foot; Newt's claim of a favor. I owed two demons, but I was alive. I was alive and was no one's familiar. And finding the mark there had been better than waking up with a big N tattooed on my forehead.

David's steps faltered as he saw the plates of goodies laid out on the table. Ivy's workspace had been pushed into a three-by-three-foot section, the rest was full of cookies, fudge, cold cuts, and crackers. "Help yourself," I said, refusing to get worked up about things currently out of my control. "Do you want to nuke your wine before we go out?" I asked, eating a slice of salami. "I've got a pitcher to warm it up in." I could use my new charm, but it wasn't reliable, and I was tired of burning my tongue.

The clunk of the wine as it hit the table was loud. "You drink it warm?" David said, sounding appalled as he looked at the microwave.

"Ivy and Kisten do." Seeing the Were hesitate, I gave the pot of spiced cider on the stove a quick stir. "We can warm up half and put the rest in a snow bank if you want," I added.

"Sure," David said, his short fingers manipulating the foil-wrapped top.

Howard began filling a plate, but at David's pointed look, he started. "Mmmm!" the older witch said abruptly, plate in hand. "Mind if I go out back and introduce myself?" He wiggled the twig sandwiched between his hand and the foam plate in explanation. "I haven't been to a solstice burning in a long time."

A smile came over me. "Go right on out. The door is through the living room."

David and Howard exchanged another look, and the witch found his way. I heard a soft rise of voices in greeting as he opened the door. David exhaled slowly. Something was up.

"Rachel," he said. "I've got a paper for you to sign."

My smile froze. "What did I do?" I blurted. "Was it breaking Lee's car?"

"No," he said, and my chest tightened when his eyes dropped. *Oh God. It must be bad.*

"What is it?" I set the spoon in the sink and turned, gripping my elbows.

David unzipped his coat and pulled out a trifolded paper and handed it to me. Taking his bottle, he started to open it. "You don't have to sign it if you don't want to," he said, glancing at me from under his cowboy hat. "I won't be offended. Really. You can say no. It's okay."

I went cold, then hot, as I read the simply worded statement, wonder in me as I looked up and met his anxious eyes. "You want me to be a member of your pack?" I stammered.

"I don't have one," he rushed to explain. "You'd be the only one in it. I'm a registered loner but my company won't fire someone with tenure if they're an alpha male or female."

I could say nothing and he rushed to fill the silence.

"I, uh, feel bad for trying to bribe you," he said. "It's not like we're married or anything, but it gives you the right to get your insurance through me. And if either of us is hospitalized, we have access to the medical records and have a say as to what happens if the other is unconscious. I don't have anyone to make those kind of decisions for me, and I'd rather have you than a court or my siblings." He shrugged with one shoulder. "You can come to the company picnic, too."

My gaze fell to the paper, then rose to his stubbled face, then back to the paper. "What about your old partner?"

He peeked over the paper to look at the print. "It takes a female to make a pack."

"Oh." I stared at the form. "Why me?" I asked, honored he'd ask but bewildered. "There must be lots of Were women who would jump at the chance."

"There are. And that's just it." Dropping back, he rested against the island counter. "I don't want a pack. Too much responsibility. Too many ties. Packs grow. And even if I went into this with another Were with the understanding that it was an agreement on paper and nothing else, she would expect certain things, and so would her kin." He looked at the ceiling, his eyes showing his age. "And when those things weren't provided, they would start to treat her like a whore instead of an alpha bitch. I won't have that problem with you." He met my eyes. "Will I?"

I blinked, starting slightly. "Ah, no." A smile quirked the corner of my mouth. *Alpha bitch? That sounded about right.* "Gotta pen?" I asked.

David exhaled with a soft puff, relief in his eyes. "We need three witnesses."

I couldn't stop grinning. Wait until I told Ivy. She'd have kittens.

We both spun to the window as a whoosh of flame and a shout rose high. Ivy threw a second bough of evergreen on the bonfire, and the fire billowed up again. She was taking to my family's tradition of a solstice fire with an unsettling enthusiasm.

"I can think of three people off the top of my head," I said, jamming it into a back pocket.

David nodded. "We don't have to do it tonight. But the fiscal year is coming up, and we'll want to file it before then so you can start your benefits and get a line in the new catalog."

I was on tiptoe to reach a pitcher for the wine, and David reached up and got it for me. "There's a catalog?" I asked as I dropped to my heels.

His eyes were wide. "You want to remain anonymous? That costs extra, but okay."

I shrugged, not knowing. "What's everyone going to say when you show up at the company picnic with me?"

David poured half the wine into the pitcher and set it to heat in the microwave. "Nothing. They all think I'm rabid anyway."

The smile wouldn't leave me as I ladled out a mug of spiced cider. His motive might be slanted—wanting the extra security for his job—but we would both benefit. So it was with a much improved mood that we headed for the back door, his warmed wine and half-empty bottle in his hands, and my spiced cider in mine. The heat of the church had taken the chill from me, and I led the way into the living room.

David's steps slowed while he took in the softly glowing room. Ivy and I had decorated, and purple, red, gold, and green were everywhere. Her leather stocking had looked lonely on the mantel, so I had bought a red and green knit one with a bell on the toe, embracing any holiday that got me presents. Ivy had even hung a little white stocking for Jenks that she had taken from her sister's doll collection, but the jar of honey wouldn't come close to fitting in it.

Ivy's Christmas tree glowed in the corner, looking ethereal. I'd never had one before, and I felt honored she had let me help her decorate it with tissue-paper-wrapped ornaments. We had made a night of it as we listened to music and ate the popcorn that never made it onto a string.

There were only two things under it: one for me, one for

Ivy, both from Jenks. He was gone, but his presents to us had been left behind in opposite bedrooms.

I reached for the handle of the new door, a lump in my throat. We had opened them already—neither one of us were good at waiting. Ivy had sat and stared at the Bite-me-Betty doll, her jaw clenched and her breathing almost nonexistent. I hadn't been much better, all but crying upon finding the pair of cell phones in their foam box. One was for me, the other, much smaller one, was for Jenks. According to the receipt still in the box, he had activated it last month and even put himself on speed dial on mine.

Yanking open the door, I held it for David, my jaw clenched. I'd get him to come back. If I had to hire a pilot to write my apology in the sky, I would get him to come back.

"David," I said as he passed. "If I give you something, will you take it to Jenks?"

He glanced at me from the first step down. "Maybe," he said warily.

I grimaced. "It's just some seeds. I couldn't find anything in my language of flowers book that said, 'I'm sorry. I'm an ass,' so I went with forget-me-nots."

"Okay," he said, sounding more sure. "I can do that."

"Thanks." It was a whisper, but I was sure he heard me over the calls at his arrival.

I took the heated wine from David and placed it near the fire. Howard looked content talking to Keasley and Ceri, sneaking unsure glances at Takata lurking in the more-certain shadows of the oak tree. "Come on over," I said to David as Kisten tried to get his attention. Ivy's sister was prattling next to him, and he looked exhausted. "I want you to meet Takata."

The midnight air was crisp, almost painfully dry, and I smiled at Ivy when I saw her trying to explain to Ceri the art of making a s'more. The puzzled elf didn't understand how layering chocolate between a sugary grain product and spun confection could possibly taste good. Her words, not mine. I was sure her opinion would change after she ate one.

I felt Kisten's eyes on me from around the lowering flames and I stifled a shiver. The come-and-go light played on his face, not unattractively thinner after his stint in the hospital. My thoughts of Nick had waned to a soft ache under the living vamp's attentions. Kist was here, and Nick wasn't. The reality was, Nick hadn't truly been here for months. He hadn't called or sent a solstice card, and he had intentionally left no way for me to reach him. It was time to move on.

Takata shifted his perch atop the picnic table in case we wanted to sit. The concert earlier tonight had gone off without a hitch, and since Lee wasn't around, Ivy and I watched from backstage. Takata had dedicated "Red Ribbons" to our firm, and half the crowd had waved their lighters in tribute thinking I was still dead.

I had only been joking when I invited him to my bonfire, but I was glad he came. He seemed to relish that no one was fawning over him as he sat contentedly in the background. I recognized that distant look on his lined face from when Ivy was planning a run, and wondered if his next album might have a song about sparks among the frost-blackened arms of an oak.

"Takata," I said as we approached, and he came back to himself. "I'd like you to meet David Hue. He's the insurance adjustor who helped me get to Saladan."

"David," Takata said, taking off his glove before extending his thin long hand. "Nice to meet you. It looks like you escaped unscathed from Rachel's latest run."

David smiled warmly without showing his teeth. "Pretty much," he said as he released his hand and rocked back a step. "Though I wasn't sure when those handguns showed up." Making a mock shudder, he shifted so his front would be warmed by the flames. "Too much for me," he said softly.

I was glad he wasn't wide-eyed and stammering, or squealing and jumping up and down like Erica had done until Kisten collared her and dragged her away.

"David!" Kisten called when my thoughts pulled my eyes

to him. "Can I talk to you about my boat? How much do you think it would cost to insure her through you?"

A sound of pain slipped from David. "The price of being in insurance," he said softly.

My eyebrows rose. "I think he just wants to get someone between him and Erica. The girl does *not* shut up."

David pushed himself into motion. "You won't leave me alone too long will you?"

I grinned. "Is that one of my responsibilities as a member of your pack?" I said, and Takata's eyes widened.

"As a matter of fact, it is." Raising his hand to Kisten, he ambled to him, stopping to nudge a log back into the flames with the toe of his boot as he went. Howard was laughing at him from across the fire, his green eyes glinting.

I looked to find Takata's thick eyebrows high. "Member of his pack?" he questioned.

Nodding, I sat beside Takata on top of the picnic table. "For insurance purposes." Setting my spiced cider down, I put my elbows on my knees and sighed. I loved the solstice, and not just for the food and parties. Cincinnati dropped all of its lights from midnight until sunrise, and it was the only time I ever saw the night sky as it was supposed to be. Anyone thieving during the blackout was dealt with hard, curtailing any problems.

"How are you doing?" Takata said, surprising me. I had almost forgotten he was there. "I heard you were hospitalized."

I smiled sheepishly, knowing I was starting to look tired after screaming for two-plus hours at Takata's concert. "I'm okay. They weren't ready to release me, but Kisten was just down the hall, and after they caught us, ah, experimenting with the controls for the bed, they decided we both were well enough to be on the streets." *Crabby old night nurse. By the amount of fuss she made, one would have thought we were committing some kind of kinky—well, crabby old night nurse, anyway.*

Takata eyed me as I flushed and pulled my knit hat down lower over my ears. "There's a limo out front," I said to change the subject. "Want me to tell them to go away?"

His gaze went up into the black branches. "They can wait. They have food in there."

Nodding, I relaxed. "You want some warm wine?"

He started, his wide eyes looking shocked. "No. No thanks."

"More spiced cider, then?" I offered. "Here. I haven't had any of mine."

"Just put a swallow in there," he said, extending his empty cup, and I poured half of my drink into his. I felt kinda special, sitting next to Takata with half my drink in his mug, but I stiffened as a faint twang reverted through me. I froze, not knowing what it was, and Takata's eyes met mine.

"You felt it too?" he said, and I nodded, feeling uneasy and a little worried.

"What was it?"

Takata's wide mouth turned into a huge smile as he laughed at me. "The circle at Fountain Square. Happy Solstice." He raised his cup, and I automatically touched mine to it.

"Happy Solstice," I echoed, thinking it odd that I had felt it. I never had before. But then, maybe having closed it myself once made me sensitive to it.

Feeling as if all was right with the world, I sipped my cider, finding David's eyes pleading with me over the rim of my mug. Erica's mouth was going nonstop, and Kisten was gripping his shoulder, trying to have a conversation around her. "Excuse me," I said as I slid from the table. "David needs rescuing."

Takata chuckled, and I made my unhurried way past the fire. Though he never stopped talking to David, Kisten's eyes were on me, and I felt a warm spot start in my middle.

"Erica," I said, coming even with them. "Takata wants to play a song for you."

Takata jerked upright, giving me a panicked look when the young woman squealed. Both Kisten and David slumped in relief as she darted around the fire to him. "Thank God,"

Kisten whispered, and I sat down in her spot. "That girl never shuts up."

Snorting, I eased closer, pushing into his thigh, hinting. He curved an arm around me, as I wanted, pulling me close. Kisten exhaled softly, and a shiver rippled over me. I knew he felt it when my scar started tingling. "Stop it," I whispered, embarrassed, and his grip tightened.

"I can't help it," he said on an intake of breath. "When is everyone going to be leaving?"

"Sunup," I said, setting my drink down. "Absence makes the heart grow fonder."

"It's not my heart that misses you," he breathed, and a second shiver passed through me.

"So," Kisten said loudly when David started to look uncomfortable. "Rachel tells me you asked her to be your absent partner so you could get two salaries and she could get a good rate on her insurance."

"Ah, yes . . ." David stammered, looking down so his hat hid his eyes. "About that . . ."

I jumped as Kisten's cold hand worked its way under my coat and touched the skin at my waist. "I like that," he murmured, not talking about how his fingers were tracing small circles to warm my middle. "Inventive. My kind of man."

David's head came up. "Would you excuse me," he muttered, sending a quick hand to fiddle with his glasses. "I haven't said hello to Ceri and Keasley yet."

I chuckled, and Kisten pulled me closer. "You do that, Mr. Peabody," Kisten said.

The short Were jerked to a stop, gave him a warning frown, then continued, stopping to get a glass of his wine on the way.

My smile slowly faded. The scent of leather became obvious, mixing with the hard aroma of burning ash, and I snuggled closer into Kisten. "Hey," I said softly, my gaze fixed on the fire. "David wants me to sign a paper. Make me part of his pack."

His breath caught. "You're kidding," he said, pushing me away so he could focus on me. His blue eyes were wide and his face surprised and wondering.

Looking at my cold fingers, I slipped them into his. "I'd like you to witness it."

"Oh." His gaze went to the fire and he shifted his arm to lean a smidgen away.

I grinned in understanding and laughed. "No, you idiot," I said, pushing on his arm. "It's a pack membership, not an interspecies bond. I'm not marrying the guy, for the Turn's sake. It's only a legal agreement so I can get my insurance through him and his company won't fire him. He'd ask a Were woman, but he doesn't want a pack, and that's what he'd get if he asked one."

Kisten exhaled long and slow, and I could feel the softness return to his grip. "Good," he said, pulling me closer. "'Cause you're my alpha bitch, babe, and no one else's."

I gave him a telling look, which was hard to do seeing as I was almost in his lap. "Babe?" I said dryly. "You know what I did to the last guy who called me that?"

Kisten jerked me closer. "Maybe later, love," he whispered to start a delicious tingle in me. "We don't want to shock your friends," he added, and I followed his gaze to where Howard and Keasley were laughing while Ceri tried to eat her s'more without getting messy.

"Will you witness the paper for me?" I asked.

"Sure." His grip around me tightened. "I think making ties is a good thing." His arm slipped from me, and I followed his gaze to see Ivy glaring at us. "Ivy might not, though."

Suddenly concerned, I pulled away. Ivy got to her feet, and with steps quick and long, she strode up the porch steps and into the church. The back door shut hard enough to make the wreath fall off.

Not noticing, Erica sprang into a flurry of motion to move a bench closer to the fire. The conversation grew excited, and Keasley and Ceri drifted over when Takata finally pulled out the guitar he brought with him but had been ignoring. He settled himself, long fingers moving slowly from the cold as he strummed. It was nice. Really nice. The only thing missing was Jenks's wiseass remarks and a sprinkling of pixy dust.

I sighed, and Kisten's lips brushed my ear. "You'll get him back," he breathed.

Surprised he knew where my thoughts were, I said, "Are you sure?"

I felt him nod. "Come springtime and he can get out again, he'll be back. He thinks too much of you to not listen once his pride starts to heal. But I know all about big egos, Rachel. You're going to have to grovel."

"I can do that," I said in a small voice.

"He thinks it's his fault," Kisten continued.

"I'll convince him otherwise."

His breath was a puff behind my ear. "That's my girl."

I smiled at the stirring of feelings he was instilling in me. My gaze went to the shadow of Ivy in the kitchen, then back to the impromptu music. One down. Two more to go. And they were likely going to be the hardest ones. It wasn't as if I could ask Ceri or Keasley. There was a spot on that form for a Social Security number. Ceri didn't have one, and I knew without asking Keasley wouldn't want to put his down. I had a suspicion by the lack of government checks that he was playing dead.

"Could you excuse me?" I murmured as Ivy's shadow behind the glass was eclipsed by a swirl of mist from the hot water she was running into the sink. Kisten's hold loosened. Takata's blue eyes met mine before I turned away, an unknown emotion in them.

I paused to put the cedar wreath back on its hook before I went in. The warmth of the church hit me, and I took my hat off and tossed it to the black hearth. I entered the kitchen to find Ivy leaning against the counter, her head down and her hands gripping her elbows.

"Hi," I said, hesitating in the threshold.

"Let me see the contract," she said, extending her hand and her head coming up.

My lips parted. "How did . . ." I stammered.

A faint, sour smile crossed her and was gone. "Sound carries well over flame."

Embarrassed, I pulled it out of my pocket, feeling it both cold from the night and warm from my body. She took it, her brow furrowed. Turning her back on me, she unfolded it. I fidgeted. "Um, I need three witnesses," I said. "I'd like you to be one of them."

"Why?"

She didn't turn around and her shoulders were tense. "David doesn't have a pack," I said. "It's harder to fire him if he does. He gets to keep his job working solo, and I can get my insurance through him. It's only two hundred a month, Ivy. He's not looking for anything more than that or he would have asked a Were woman."

"I know. My question is why do you want *my* signature?" Paper in hand, she turned, the empty look on her face making me uncomfortable. "Why is it important to you that *I* sign it?"

I opened my mouth, then shut it. My thoughts touched on what Newt had said. Home hadn't been a strong enough pull, but Ivy was. "Because you're my partner," I said, warming. "Because what I do affects you."

Ivy silently plucked a pen from her pencil cup and clicked it open. I suddenly felt awkward, realizing that David's little paper granted him something she wanted: a recognizable connection with me.

"I did a background check on him when you were in the hospital," she said. "He's not hooking up with you to help him out with a preexisting problem."

My eyebrows rose. I hadn't thought about that. "He said this was a no-strings-attached affair." I hesitated. "Ivy, I live with you," I said, trying to reassure her that our friendship didn't need a paper or signature to be real, and both our names were above the door. Both of them.

She was silent, her face empty of emotion, her brown eyes still. "You trust him?"

I nodded. I had to go with my gut feeling here.

The barest smile appeared on her. "Me too." Pushing a plate of cookies aside, she wrote her name on the first line in a careful but almost illegible signature.

"Thanks," I said, and she handed it back. My gaze went past her as the back door opened. Ivy looked up, and I recognized a softening in her gaze when Kisten's familiar footsteps thumped on the rug beside the door, knocking off the snow. He came into the kitchen, David on his heels.

"Are we signing the paper or not?" Kisten said, the tension in his voice telling me he was ready to argue with Ivy if she was balking.

Ivy clicked her pen open and shut so fast that it hummed. "I already did. Your turn."

He squared his shoulders, grinning as he took the pen when she extended it, adding his masculine signature under hers. His Social Security number was next, and he handed the pen to David.

David edged between them, looking small beside their tall grace. I could see his relief as he wrote his full name. My pulse increased and I took the pen, pulling the paper closer.

"So," Kisten said when I signed it. "Who are you going to ask to be the third witness?"

"Jenks," Ivy and I said together, and I looked up. Our eyes met and I clicked the pen closed.

"Will you ask him for me?" I said to David.

The Were picked up the paper, carefully folding it and tucking it away in an inner coat pocket. "You don't want to ask someone else? He might not."

I glanced at Ivy and straightened, tucking a curl of hair behind my ear. "He's a member of this firm," I said. "If he wants to spend the winter sulking in a Were's basement, that's fine with me, but he had better get his little pixy butt back here when the weather breaks or I'm going to be royally pissed." I took a deep breath, adding, "And maybe this will convince him he's a valued member of the team and that I'm sorry."

Kisten took a shuffling step back.

"I'll ask him," David said.

The back door opened and Erica tumbled in, her cheeks red and her eyes snapping. "Hey! Come on! He's ready to play! God save you, he's warmed up and ready to play, and you're inside eating? Get your asses out here!"

Ivy's attention went from the snow she had tracked in to my eyes. David lurched into motion, pushing the flighty goth vamp out before him. Kisten followed, the noise of their conversation heady with the sound of companionship. Takata's music rose, and my eyes widened when Ceri's ethereal voice was set to a carol older than even she. She indeed sang in Latin. My eyebrows rose and I looked at Ivy.

Ivy zipped her coat up and got her mittens from the counter. "You really okay with this?" I asked her.

She nodded. "Asking Jenks to sign that paper might be the only way to hammer it into his thick skull that we need him."

I made a face and went before her as I tried to come up with a way to convey to Jenks how wrong I had been to not trust him. I had slipped Algaliarept's snare, managing to not only get rid of one of my demon marks but also break my familiar bond with Nick, too—not that it mattered now. I had gone out on a date with the city's most powerful bachelor and had breakfast with him. I had rescued a thousand-year-old elf, learned how to be my own familiar, and discovered I could throw a mean craps game. Not to mention I found you could have sex with a vampire and not get bitten. Why did I have the feeling that getting Jenks to talk to me was going to be harder than all that put together?

"We'll get him back," Ivy murmured behind me. "We *will* get him back."

Thumping down the snow-covered stairs and going into the music and star-filled night, I swore we would.